HOMEWORLDS

Volume Three of The Travelers' Tales

SALLY MALCOLM (EDITOR)

FANDEMONIUM BOOKS

An original publication of Fandemonium Ltd, produced under license from MGM Consumer Products.

Fandemonium Books, PO Box 795A, Surbiton, Surrey KT5 8YB, United Kingdom

Visit our website: www.stargatenovels.com

STARGÅTE
SG·1·ATLÅNTIS™

WWW.MGM.COM

ISBN: 978-1-905586-79-0

CONTENTS

EDITOR'S FOREWORD

ON JULY 27th 1997 *Children of the Gods*, the first-ever episode of STARGATE SG-1, premiered. It's testament to the incredible talent of the show's creators and cast that, twenty years later, our love for it remains undimmed. And it's testament to the enduring loyalty of Stargate fans that there's a continuing appetite for more STARGATE SG-1 and STARGATE ATLANTIS adventures.

So it's apt that in this twentieth year of STARGATE SG-1, we offered the opportunity for two Stargate fans to contribute to this third anthology of short stories.

Last September Stargate authors Sabine Bauer and Laura Harper joined me in judging a short story competition at the GateCon fan convention in Vancouver. I'm delighted to be including the winning entries in this collection: STARGATE SG-1: *Blinded by the Light* by Barbara Ellisor and STARGATE ATLANTIS: *Second Time Sateda* by Ron Francis. My enormous thanks go to both winners, as well as to everyone who entered the competition, and to the amazing people at GateCon who ran the event. I hope you'll enjoy reading Barbara and Ron's stories as much as we did.

And finally, I'd like to thank you — for reading, for supporting Stargate Novels, and for helping us keep the gate open.

Here's to another twenty years of Stargate adventures...

Sally Malcolm
Commissioning Editor
June 2017

STARGATE ATLANTIS
The Mysteries of Emege

Jo Graham

This story takes place after book eight of the Stargate Atlantis Legacy series.

"*Once when Arda ruled in Emege, it was a very great city indeed. It was beautiful and prosperous, and under his wise rule it became even more so, adorned like a great lady dressed in jewels. Yet its jewels were parks that ran with flowing streams and white towers that reached to the dawn, gardens beside the lake filled with fruit and blossoms, theaters and workshops, and its streets were filled with music. In Emege, all good things were possible. Arda ruled, and all was well. Indeed, so peaceful and prosperous had Emege become that the Ancestors gave to Arda three great gifts, scroll and sword and shield, that the city might ever be so.*"

"Why are you telling us this?" Dr. Rodney McKay demanded, leaning forward over his breakfast tray of half-eaten scrambled eggs. "I mean, it's a very nice fairy tale and all that, but what does that have to do with anything?"

Teyla clasped her hands around her mug of tea patiently. "Because it is important, as you will hear if you listen."

Beside her, John Sheppard stirred. "This is about the city, isn't it? The one you showed me the pictures of in the cave that first day on Athos."

Across the table beside Rodney, the fourth member of their party frowned. "The one the Wraith had culled?" Ronon said. He had not been there then, but he had heard about it often enough since.

"Yes," Teyla said. "But this was long before. Thousands of years."

"Go ahead and tell the story," John said. "We'll save our questions until you finish."

Teyla took a breath and continued. *"Under the wise rule of Arda and the favor of the Ancestors, Emege fruited, but as always happens the harvest-tide came, and in the day of Arda's great grandson there came the Reapers. Death came, and our world shuddered beneath the fury of her guns. But because of the blessings placed upon Emege, the city stood alone for a year and a day, and each beautiful street was filled with throngs of people who sought safety and mercy. But at last, when a year and a day had passed, the bright blessings that had protected Emege faded, and then Death drank deeply of the Children of Emege."*

"Like Sateda," Ronon said quietly. "It's a story about that happening to your people a long time ago."

"Yes," Teyla said. "But the reason I am telling you this is not because of what happened, but how."

"The shield," John said, putting down his mug. "The Ancestors gave him sword and shield. And the city stood for a year and a day. Literally a shield. Like the one on Atlantis. Like our shield."

"Until the ZPM ran out," Rodney said, sitting up straight, that idea-crackling expression on his face. "The city fell because they ran the shield until the ZPM failed. Not because it was destroyed. But just because they ran out of power. Which means...."

"That the shield generator might still be there," John said. "That the equipment might be salvageable."

"It's always handy to have another shield generator," Rodney said quickly. "We already have one, but a spare would be useful."

"It is not your shield generator," Teyla said. "It is our shield generator. If it is there. Which I think it is. The ruins of the city have been forbidden for many generations and left undisturbed since the last culling two hundred years ago. But clearly we were not able to get it functional then."

"You didn't have a ZPM," John said.

"Or we had not yet regained enough knowledge to make it work," Teyla said. "These things move in cycles."

"The Wraith knock down whoever gets too tall," Ronon said. "They weren't going to let you get to the point where you could use the technology."

Teyla inclined her head. "Yes. But I do not think we would have destroyed technology we didn't understand. We would have studied it, or at worst simply let it be. Without a ZPM, as you say, the shield could not have been activated. But it is quite possible that the installation is intact."

John nodded thoughtfully. "The Athosians didn't want us to go poking around in the ruins of the city before."

"You were strangers to us then," Teyla said. "Much has happened in six years. You are strangers no longer. And much has happened to us." Which was a great understatement, Teyla thought as she took a sip of her cooling tea. They had fled Athos for Atlantis and its planet only to be forcibly removed by the returning Ancients two years later. The Ancients had resettled them on a world they called New Athos, and many of them had died there at the hands of the abomination Michael. He had held many of them, including Teyla, prisoner for many months before they were at last freed. They had returned to New Athos then, a year and a half ago, but all was not well there. Their new world was inhospitable and their numbers had been culled to the bone. It was likely, Teyla thought, that hers was the last generation of Athosians who could properly be called that unless something changed. Peoples came and went, but it made her heartsick to think that the way of life she had loved would die, even if she no longer lived among the Athosians herself.

Rodney seemed to have followed part of that thought. "If the Athosians aren't on Athos," he said, "they won't know if we look around the city or not. We can go, have a look, and just not tell them."

John winced. "That's not how we treat our allies, Rodney.

We ask their permission before we go through their stuff."

"It's thousands of years old! They'll never know."

"It's theirs," John said. "How would you feel if some random people went digging through the ruins of Vancouver?"

"I'll tell you how we feel on Sateda," Ronon said. "We feel pissed. That's why we're not buying an alliance with the Genii. They went scavenging on our world without our permission."

"We must discuss it with the Council," Teyla said. "It is quite possible that everyone would agree to it."

"There's a lot of water under this bridge," John said. He was too polite, Teyla thought, to mention that pretty much everyone on the Council owed him personally for a rescue from Michael's twisted experiments. It would be awkward in the extreme to refuse the Lanteans' request, provided it was made courteously.

"As you say," Teyla said. She looked at Rodney. "And provided that it is understood that if we find a shield generator, it belongs to the Athosians."

"If we find a shield generator, it would mean a lot to your people," John said thoughtfully, and she knew he was thinking about Torren. It worried him each time Torren left Atlantis to stay with his father, Kanaan, on New Athos. There was no shield there, no protection except the word of the Wraith queen Alabaster, and that was a fragile thing to trust with the life of a child he loved as a second father.

"It would," Teyla said. "There are those among us, like Halling, who wish for the Athosians to return to our proper home. If there were a shield generator and it could be made operative, it would make doing so much safer."

Rodney leaned forward. "But isn't Athos, Old Athos I mean, in Waterlight's sector rather than Alabaster's? Do you think Waterlight wouldn't honor the treaty?"

Teyla sighed. "I think she will, at least for the forseeable future. But that is because I know Waterlight, queen to queen. I trust that she will not break her word to me. But I cannot tell the others the reason for this, and asking them to trust a Wraith blindly is too much."

"And you can't tell them about… everything." Rodney gestured at Teyla, and possibly at his hair, which was very short. It seemed that it might be growing back in brown, so Rodney had asked one of the Marines to cut it closely, hoping that he would trim out the white and leave only the brown roots. Instead Rodney was practically bald. But, as John said, it would grow.

"No, I cannot tell them about everything," Teyla said.

Ronon made a noise that Teyla chose to ignore.

"They'd freak," Rodney said.

"They would no longer trust me," Teyla said. "Even as much as they still do." Her eyes stung unexpectedly at the last, and John jumped in.

"But having a shield generator would mean that they weren't relying only on Waterlight keeping the treaty," he said. "They'd have a way of defending themselves if they went back." He leaned back in his chair. "I think it's worth a try. If we don't find anything, we're right where we are now. So let's ask the Athosians if we can take a look around. We could go over today, or tomorrow or whenever you're ready."

"Except for one little thing," Rodney said, waggling a finger at John. "You're still in charge in Atlantis. Elizabeth is back, but she's not cleared for duty yet. And the IOA hasn't decided if she's staying. You're still the guy behind the desk."

John looked annoyed. "Fine," he said. "Then I can authorize the mission. Teyla, ask the Athosians if they'll let us look around the city. We'll take it from there if they say yes."

"I will do so," Teyla said.

Teyla considered at length who to take with her to Athos while she warmed up that afternoon in the gym, long stretches that were meant to quiet the mind but did not when a question like this weighed on her. John would be ideal. The Athosians knew him and trusted him, and he was more than capable of being diplomatic. Despite his insistence that he was no diplomat, he was actually quite adept at getting along with people. Teyla sunk into a low lunge, then rolled neatly out of it. John listened, and that was more unusual than he thought.

Unfortunately, it was true that he could not leave Atlantis unless it was necessary. The IOA was very insistent on that since the time the plastic eating virus had gotten loose in his absence. True, Major Lorne had handled it well, but the IOA had been furious that Colonel Sheppard had been outside the quarantine zone. This trip to Athos was not actually necessary.

Teyla sighed, coming gracefully to her feet. She could ask Ronon to accompany her, of course. Ronon had been to New Athos on many occasions. But Ronon had made it known in no uncertain terms that he disapproved of the treaty between Atlantis and the Wraith queens who had allied against Queen Death. Given that one of the points of debate was certain to be whether or not they could be trusted, Teyla would rather that Ronon didn't muddy those waters. Which left Rodney.

Teyla leaned forward, balancing on one foot and her fingertips. Taking Rodney was perhaps the best choice. Though his hair had begun to return to its normal color, his Wraith telepathy that allowed him to speak with her showed no signs of fading. Among the Athosians, the Gift was a lifelong ability, and she doubted at this point that Rodney's Gift would be any different. It did grant them the unexpected advantage of being able to speak privately and silently, which could only help in a diplomatic situation. And if the Council did permit them to search the city which had been Emege for a shield generator, Rodney was the logical person to lead the search. He could certainly assure the Council that he would not harm or destroy any buildings or artifacts they discovered. Rodney, then. She would take Rodney with her to New Athos.

So it was that Teyla Emmagen and Dr. Rodney McKay stepped through the Stargate on New Athos on a glorious day in early summer. The meadow the Stargate stood in was abloom with small yellow and pink flowers, while the woods beyond were cast deep in shadow by the green leaves of forest giants. Teyla stopped for a moment as the gate deactivated, breathing.

"What are you doing?" Rodney asked.

"Reminding myself where I am and what season it is," Teyla said. "I have come from autumn on a much colder world. It is worthwhile to take a moment when one can and remind one-self where one is and when."

"It's hot," Rodney said.

"That is because it is summer." Teyla put her hand on his arm. "Rodney, there is no great hurry. Just close your eyes and be here for a moment."

"This is one of those zen things, isn't it?" he said, but he did close his eyes, taking a deep breath through his nose. "I can feel my allergies kicking in already. What are those things?"

"Flowers," Teyla said firmly. "And I do not know their name because this is not my world."

Rodney opened his eyes and looked at her all too keenly. "And that's the problem, isn't it? This isn't your world. Any of you."

"That is one of the problems," Teyla said. "Another is that we are too few after all that has happened."

"You've dropped below genetic viability."

"To put it bluntly, yes." Teyla looked toward the path that led among the trees, winding its way toward the settlement. "And so we have done what we have always done when pressed — we have taken in those dispossessed by Queen Death's wars. Some are Manarians, who have always been our friends, and there are others from scattered worlds who have suffered and look only for a place that will be safe. But they were not of Athos, and they do not know our stories."

"The old problem of assimilation and change," Rodney said. "Yeah, we've got that. Pretty much everywhere on Earth."

"So I have seen, and your solutions are no better than ours."

Teyla shrugged. "Our governance depends on trust. We do not have kings anymore, as we did in Arda's day. We do not have dictators. We have a Council, but its power rests on the trust given to it. If people simply refuse to recognize its decisions as binding on them, we have no governance at all."

"You mean, if the Council says, 'don't put a well there' and someone does it, there's nothing you can do about it?"

"We can fill it in. But if the man who dug it resists, what are we to do? We can, at a full vote of the Council, tell him that he is no longer welcome to live among us, but that is a terrible punishment and the result of many offenses. It does not happen quickly or until the peace has been disturbed many times. And then there are the Manarians."

"What about them?" Rodney fell into step beside her as they began to walk to the settlement.

She glanced at him. "Have you ever had a roommate who bothered you because the things that were their own preferences were no trouble to you at all when you were only friends but became enormous problems when you shared an apartment?"

Rodney snorted. "You mean like being a neat freak? I had this roommate in grad school who steam mopped the entire house every night. Every single night."

"Like that, yes." Teyla smiled. "The Manarians follow an elaborate code of taboos regarding food — what can be prepared when and how, what can be hunted or slaughtered when and how, and who can eat what. Some foods cannot be prepared by women and other foods cannot be eaten except by certain people or on certain days. It did not matter to us at all when they were on Manaria, and we simply observed their customs when we came to trade. But now that we live together, it is a point of constant contention that we do not observe these customs. The wrong person is always preparing the wrong food at the wrong time and offending everyone. They are upset and words are spoken and many of them are growing impatient at being told what we can do in their home."

"Their home." Rodney's thought was as clear as if he'd spoken aloud. *Not your home.*

Teyla stopped, looking up to the branches of lowering trees. "This world is not my home, no. I have never lived here."

"And you're planning to stay in Atlantis."

"Yes." She had not said so before, not simply and without qualification. But it was easier to be honest with Rodney than most, her dear friend who was not so tangled in his own choices.

"Good," Rodney said. "Me too. Not that I can go back to Earth right now because the IOA is saying that I might still be Wraithy or something, but I don't want to anyway so it doesn't matter. I chose to come to Pegasus and there's still lots to do here. Atlantis is…." Words failed as to what Atlantis was.

"And that perhaps is the difference," Teyla said. "You chose. These people did not choose. They were driven out by Queen Death in fear for their lives, as we were driven from Athos by the Wraith and then from Atlantis by the Ancients. None of us chose this place. None of us wanted this. We have made the best of it, to survive as we always do. But it satisfies no one."

"Maybe it's time to do some choosing," Rodney said. "I mean, if nobody's trying to kill anybody right now. Maybe people can figure out what they want. I totally get that beggars can't be choosers, but maybe you're not beggars anymore."

Teyla felt an enormous wave of affection for him. Sometimes Rodney saw through to the truth of something like no one else. "I think you are exactly right," she said. "We are not beggars. We are partners in this treaty. And we must decide our future for ourselves."

"So what we're doing is making it possible to move back to Athos."

"I hope that is what we are doing," Teyla said. "Rodney, I do not know if there is a shield generator there, or if there is whether we can make it function, but if it could be so, we would have a different choice. I should like to give my people that choice, even if I do not intend to go with them."

"So this isn't about making it safe for you to go home?"

"I am staying in Atlantis," Teyla said. "For the foreseeable future." It felt good to say that firmly. She had not said it to anyone else.

Rodney shrugged, his usual cocky expression returning. "If there's a generator there, I can make it work."

"Then let us see if we can find one for you to work on," Teyla said.

"The Council does not meet at your pleasure, Teyla." Kanaan frowned, his hands on his hips in the brew house where great barrels of liquor sat in their cradles, waiting to be turned. He wiped his hands on his apron. "We are busy and Lattia is not here but on Tryphen on a trade expedition. We cannot meet today."

Teyla took a deep breath. It was certainly true that Lattia was not there, and she was definitely on the Council, but it was also true that Kanaan was not being as helpful as he might be.

"We have our own work to do," Kanaan said, gesturing around the brew house. "I have two apprentices at this craft, and we have mash that is half-cooked. It would be my suggestion that you return tomorrow when you were expected to pick up Torren and talk with people then, rather than arriving a day early and expecting others to accommodate you. Unless you intended to pick up Torren earlier than the schedule we had agreed upon."

Teyla gritted her teeth. It came back to that, of course. "I did not intend to change the schedule we had agreed upon," she said evenly. "I had hoped to talk with the Council. That is all."

"Then perhaps you should go before Torren sees you. You know it confuses him at his age when he has been led to believe that the schedule is one thing and it is another. I do not come to Atlantis unexpectedly and disturb his routine there."

"Hey, you know," Rodney began, and Teyla gave him a quelling glance.

"You are quite correct," Teyla said. "You do not." She refrained from any further comments about how Kanaan made himself scarce from Atlantis even when expected. There was no need for those old discussions to weigh upon Torren. "I shall do that. But first I will look in on Halling and ask if he will request a meeting tomorrow evening, when Lattia has returned."

"As you wish, of course," Kanaan said.

Rodney followed her out of the brew house. "Joint custody's a pain, isn't it?"

Teyla couldn't help but smile. "Is that what you make of this?"

He shrugged. "Not everything is politics."

"That is very true."

"I think you guys do a good job of not fighting," Rodney said. His eyes were serious. "Nothing sucks for a little kid more than parents who fight all the time."

She stopped. "Was that what your parents did?"

"Mine? Nah." Rodney looked across the square between houses. "Just saying. So we're going to find Halling?"

"Yes. And we will ask him if the Council can meet tomorrow night."

Halling was in the haybarn, his red hair now long enough to tie back at the collar again. He was handing enormous bales up to the rafters above, lifting them over his head as if they weighed nothing, and Teyla waited until he finished before she called. His smile when he saw her was gratifying. "Teyla! I did not think to see you today! What has brought you here?"

"I cannot stay," Teyla said, "But I thought that I would stop in and ask if I might address the Council tomorrow night if it is convenient."

"Of course." Halling's eyes flicked from her to Rodney and back, and he drew her away from the others who were moving bales. "What is the matter? Is it the Wraith?"

"Nothing is wrong," Teyla said. "I simply had an idea that I wanted the Council to consider." Quickly, she sketched out the request — that they be able to search the ruins of the city of Emege in hopes of finding a shield generator.

Halling heard her out soundlessly. Then he sat down on one of the bales and mopped his brow where the sweat ran down in the heat. "It's an interesting interpretation of the story," he said.

"And that may be all it is," Teyla said. "It may be that there has never been a shield generator there. But I think it is quite possible that our ancestors have handed down to us a story containing truths they did not understand, but that were true all the same. It is possible that Emege was once a powerful ally of the Ancients, and that they gave to our world a shield generator as they did to a few others. If so, we could have held long against the Wraith."

"And the city fell only when the generator failed," Halling said.

"No," Rodney said. "When the ZPM ran out. When they ran out of power. It could be that there is absolutely nothing wrong with the generator itself."

"Or it could have been destroyed when the Wraith breached the city," Halling said.

"That is so," Teyla agreed. "They may have blown it into a million pieces. Or they may not have. What I would like to ask is that Dr. McKay and I have permission to go and see."

"Not an entire expedition of Lanteans? A lot of people are going to be reluctant to let a bunch of Marines tramp around Emege, where so many of our people have lain unburied since the last attack." He looked at Rodney. "The city is a graveyard, a war grave. We leave it respectfully undisturbed."

"We do not need an entire expedition," Teyla said with a quelling glance at Rodney. "Not to merely see if there is a generator there. Rodney and I will not disturb the resting places of my kindred."

Halling nodded. "I know that you will do nothing disrespectful. Nor you, Dr. McKay. You are an honest and honorable man."

"Thank you?" Rodney said doubtfully.

"Tomorrow night we will meet and you may present your

request to everyone," Halling said. "But I think most will agree that it is worthwhile to look. What we will do if you find one…." His voice trailed off.

"If we find one and the ZPM is out of power, we still can't get it going," Rodney said. "At least not until we locate another ZPM, which is possible. We've found several over the years. So…."

"At the very least, it will fill in a piece of our history," Halling said. "Even if it does not solve problems in our present." He glanced over at three women Teyla did not know who were tying bales with string.

"Manarians," she said quietly.

"And many others." Halling sighed. "We have opened our doors to many others, as we needed to. But never so many at a time. We are changing."

"We have always changed," Teyla said. "We lived in Emege and we were a great kingdom."

"That is so." Halling put his hands on his thighs and made to stand up. "But I do not want us to lose our great strengths. Nor to become…quaint."

Teyla did not know what to reply, and so she said nothing.

"Well, we'll see if we can find a shield generator," Rodney said. "And you can take it from there."

"Thank you, my friend," Halling said, clasping hands with Rodney. "I will look forward to seeing you again tomorrow night. And Jinto can go back to Atlantis with you. He's supposed to bring the milk from this morning's milking according to our trade agreement. Jinto!"

Jinto popped his head out of the other end of the barn, the end where the goats were kept. "I'm coming," he said. "Just loading the wheelbarrow."

"We will help," Teyla said. It was not right for a child to work while adults stood about, she thought, but as she went into the goat barn, Jinto hoisted the barrow up on its wheel though it was full of big plastic jugs of goat's milk. He was now taller than she, with dark hair held back in a low ponytail, and strong arms that did not strain to hold the barrow at all.

"You grew," Rodney said. He had not seen Jinto in many months.

"I'm sixteen," Jinto said. "I'm supposed to grow."

"You are indeed," Teyla said. "You will be as tall as your father soon." It was rather alarming how fast he had grown.

"Ok," Jinto said, his satchel slung on his back. "Let's go." He pushed the wheelbarrow easily with what must be seventy pounds of milk in it.

"Sure you don't want me to carry some of that?" Rodney asked unconvincingly.

"I've got it." The satchel slung forward, nearly catching Teyla in the chest with what must be another twenty pounds of something.

"I will get your bag," she said.

"No, that's ok. Really...." The bag flipped, the flap opening and two big hardback books spilling out onto Rodney's feet.

He bent and picked them up, looking at them curiously. "Engineering textbooks?"

Jinto winced. He let go of the barrow handles and snatched the books, putting them safely back in the satchel. "Shhhh!"

"Why are they secret?" Rodney whispered back in a stage whisper.

"Let's walk and I'll tell you." Jinto looked nervous.

"That might be best." Teyla took Rodney's arm and led him out, Jinto following with the satchel and the wheelbarrow. She waited until they were up the path to the Stargate and out of earshot of the settlement before she let go.

"Where did you get those?" Rodney asked.

"They belong to Dr. Zelenka," Jinto said. "He loaned them to me. I didn't take them. He said I could use them."

"Of course you didn't take them," Teyla said. "Neither of us thought that."

"Why do you want them?" Rodney asked. "Who wants engineering textbooks?"

"I do," Jinto said, and there was a stubborn light in his eye. "When I take things to Atlantis, I often wait to take other things back in trade. I usually have a while to wait. Dr. Zelenka has been tutoring me."

"In what?" Rodney asked.

"Science, mathematics, even English. And engineering." Jinto's voice had a touch of pride. "He says I am a very good student. And that he understands what it is to want to learn things you are not supposed to."

"Why aren't you supposed to?"

"We don't need those things, my father says. He says Athosians don't build cities and bridges and weapons. We don't do those things because they call the Wraith down and because they aren't who we are. We're peaceful. We're agrarian. We are proud that we live without depending on technology. But...."

"But you want to know these things," Teyla said gently.

Jinto stopped, his eyes passionate. "We built cities once! I know we did. It was us, not the Ancestors. We could do so many things that we've forgotten or that the Wraith took from us because they were afraid of us. They were afraid we'd fight them too well. They were afraid that we'd build too much. Because we can. We don't have to be children living in the ruins of things the Ancestors built, or turned off our lands because the Ancestors say, 'we are the parents and we know what's best for you' like they did on Atlantis. We're not children. We can learn anything that you Lanteans can!"

"At the cost of not being Athosian," Teyla said. As she had. The cost of Atlantis was being no longer of her people.

"Maybe we need to change what being Athosian means," Jinto said. He folded the satchel across him. "I'm going to be an engineer. And I'll get the knowledge wherever I need to."

"Even if your father disapproves?" Teyla asked. And that was the crux of it — not that he hid the books from them, but from Halling.

"I'm nearly a man," Jinto said. "My father can't tell me what books to read."

"No," Teyla said. "I see that he cannot."

The next evening Teyla and Rodney returned and waited while the Council assembled in the four-sided meeting room the Athosians had built of raw logs. There was a central hearth, but on this summer night no fire was lit. It was still hot from the heat of the day. On one side of the hearth the Council members sat on the front bench, while other curious people who wanted to hear sat around the other three walls. Teyla was not surprised to see how many there were. The Lanteans had often brought important news.

Rodney, however, was surprised. He nudged her. "Big audience," he said. "Is that good or bad?"

"I do not know," Teyla said quietly. "Any Athosian is welcome to hear and take part in the debate. This seems to be a matter that concerns many."

"Halling's been stacking the deck?"

"I do not know." Mentally she added, *Rodney, it is not tactful to talk of that so openly.*

Sorry.

Let our words to the Council speak for themselves. And let me speak first.

I was going to. His mental voice sounded a little hurt.

I know. And I trust that you will explain the shield generator well when the time comes. Only these are my people, and they will take the proposal better from me.

Are they your people? Rodney looked around the room doubtfully.

Most of them. It was true that there were many new faces, far more than Teyla had expected. Even in her childhood on Athos, when they had lived in many family groups that moved with the seasons, she had known almost everyone who came to an assembly, at least by sight if not by name, but perhaps half of the people who filled the benches tonight were complete strangers to her. Manarians, as Halling had said. Some of them looked Manarian from their dress. Others.... It was impossible to tell what their original homeworld had been. The Athosians had welcomed any who came fleeing Queen Death. She could not place perhaps fifteen of the newcomers or guess where they had come from.

However, many of the people who came in were old friends. Many were people she had known from childhood, friends as old as Kanaan who had been their agemates. They invariably came over to greet her, several being pointedly friendly to Rodney as though expecting to be introduced to him as her new partner, and Teyla remembered the awkwardness a few months ago when it had been rumored that Rodney had replaced Kanaan in her affections. Teyla was very quick to say that Rodney was simply visiting with her because of the proposal they intended to put before the Council, but she wasn't sure how many people believed her. There were a few knowing glances and "I'm always glad to see your friend," comments, enough that even Rodney noticed.

Hey, they'll get over it, he said mentally. *I mean, not that it's an insult or anything. At least not to me. I mean, you're not my type, but there's nothing wrong with you.*

There is nothing wrong with you either, Teyla replied gravely, refraining from rolling her eyes. If this was how Rodney generally complimented women, it was no wonder his last relationship had ended so abruptly. Jennifer would not have appreciated being told there was nothing wrong with her, as though that were all the good that could be said.

The crowd quieted suddenly as Halling stepped out to the center, raising his arms above his head. "We are gathered in Council," he said formally. "We are gathered at the request of Teyla Emmagen, who has brought a proposal for us to consider. Will we grant her leave to speak?"

There was the expected chorus of assent, and Teyla got to

her feet, giving Halling a warm smile as she stepped out to stand beside him. "I give you good evening, my friends, and good rest after," she began. "Many of you already know Dr. McKay. He has come with me so that we might put before you a matter of importance." She gestured for Rodney to come and stand beside her. "As most of you know, near the Ring of the Ancestors on Athos is a ruined city which stories tell us was once called Emege...."

After Teyla and Rodney had spoken, and entertained questions at length, they were asked to leave the Council and wait in the cooking tent. It was almost deserted. The night meal was done and the dishes cleared away. Only two of the cooks remained, cleaning up the last of the cooking utensils and setting a big pot of dried peas out to soak overnight. There was tea in the urn, stewed to hair-raising strength and sweetness, but Teyla sipped it out of a small cup anyway.

"Why don't they want us in there?" Rodney said, pacing.

"It is normal to ask those who have proposed to leave the debate after they have answered questions," Teyla said. She settled down on one of the benches, her tea in her hand. "It is so offense will not be given if the debate turns on the trustworthiness or competence of the people proposing."

"But they'll still know," Rodney said.

"They will not have to hear people speak against them," Teyla said. "And if they do not have to hear, they do not have to treat anyone differently." She smiled up at him. "We are a small town, Rodney. We have to preserve relationships and civility between people because we know we have to live with them. We are not like your great cities on Earth where people can offend each other as they wish, knowing that they will never see this person again. We are more like Atlantis."

"Where every grudge and fight lasts forever. I see that." Rodney sat down too. "We're not good at that. At managing conflicts."

"You have never had to be," Teyla said. "For most of your people, this is the first time in their lives they have not been free to insult people with no consequences."

"You make us sound awful."

"You are not awful. You are used to telling a stranger to stuff it and walking away. If there were no strangers, if everyone you knew was someone you had grown up with, or the spouse of your co-worker, or the mother of your client, you would be careful what you said." Teyla shrugged. "People adapt. But I do not know if I could adapt to living in a place where I did not matter to almost everyone I saw."

The flap of the tent opened and Jinto came in, his satchel under his arm. "Teyla, Dr. McKay."

"Hello, Jinto," Teyla said. She had seen him in the back of the Council meeting, but he had not spoken, young as he was. "How is the discussion going?"

Jinto shrugged, his lanky frame awkward as he sat down on the bench beside Rodney. "Pretty well. The Manarians don't really care whether you look for a shield generator or not, so they're not going to vote against it. I mean, Athos was never their world, so why would they care if there was a generator there or not?"

"That is true," Teyla said.

Jinto shrugged again. "But there are a bunch of us who do care. You know. People who feel like the old city is a shrine. It's a war grave and it shouldn't be disturbed. That it would be disrespectful. So that's what the debate is about right now. Is it disrespectful for you to poke around looking?"

"We're not going to go toss somebody's grandma's bones out in the street," Rodney began.

"That is a valid question," Teyla said. "But I hope the answer is that they know me and they know Dr. McKay, and they trust that we will be respectful of our dead."

"That's what my dad says," Jinto said.

"What does Kanaan say?" Rodney asked.

Jinto opened his mouth and closed it again, and Teyla shot Rodney a look. "We do not need to know what each individual Athosian says." But she knew what that look meant, and it burned in her even as she told herself to be reasonable, that Kanaan was not speaking against this just to spite her. That was not like him. If he spoke on a different side, it would be out of sincere belief, and he was entitled to speak from his beliefs like any Athosian.

Jinto plopped his satchel on the table hurriedly. "Dr. McKay, I was wondering if you would help me with something."

"What?"

"Dr. Zelenka gave me some homework, and I don't actually understand it. I'm supposed to figure out which formulas I'd use to know how much stress different building materials can handle in terms of weight bearing, and then figure out which material would be best to build a column of a certain size."

Rodney snorted. "That's just the kind of stupid homework Radek would give. Like people go around building columns! Ok, show me the problem."

Jinto grinned, his eyes flicking to Teyla. "Thank you, Dr. McKay."

Teyla cupped her hands around her tea and sat back, letting Rodney explaining the mathematics wash over her like so much white noise. Here, in the cooking tent, it was possible to believe that little had changed since her girlhood thirty years before. The tables were much the same, the scents of cooking the same, the flavor of the tea in her mouth. And yet they were on a different world, and they were different people. She was not the same person at all as the girl she had been, or the young woman who walked through gates and refused to be bound to only one world, a trader always looking for something new. There were few now among the Athosians who even remembered that girl.

The tent flap lifted again, and this time it was Halling who ducked through. Teyla got to her feet to greet him, hearing the scramble behind her as Jinto dropped things back in his satchel. "Halling! What did the Council decide? I assume they must have reached a decision if you are here."

Halling went over to draw himself a cup of tea. "They've reached a decision on some points, and we've adjourned. There are other things that are going to be the subject of many discussions, and they cannot all happen tonight."

"Well?" Rodney asked. "What about the shield generator?"

"You may look for it."

"Fine, then…."

Halling held up one big hand. "Just you and Teyla. That was the compromise. Everyone is willing to agree that you and Teyla will be respectful of the remains of our ancestors and will do no harm to the city or its buildings, or our heritage. You are known to many, and you have our trust." He glanced at Teyla. "Teyla, of course, is one of us. But there are to be no Marine teams tramping around the city. There are to be no scientists newly come from Earth to photograph the bones of our relatives and write papers about them. You and Teyla may look for the shield generator, and you will tell the Council what you have found."

"But we need…." Rodney began.

"We do not," Teyla said. "Rodney, you and I can look for the generator. We do not need ten people to help us, or even John and Ronon. This is the City of Emege. There are no large predators or strange creatures. It is Athos. The two of us are more than adequate to see if there is a generator or not."

She thought that he would at least argue further about the need for more scientists, but to her surprise Rodney shrugged. "Ok. It will take us longer because more people could cover the ground faster, but sure."

Halling visibly relaxed. "I am glad this will do."

"It will do admirably," Teyla said. "After all, we do not know if such a thing exists there or not. Or if it once did, if it was so utterly destroyed by the Wraith that there is no way to make it operable again. It is best not to get people's hopes up too much."

He nodded. "I, for myself, would welcome the chance to go home. Athos is our home, Teyla! I miss it like a hole in my heart."

"I know." Teyla met his eyes. "This world is fine, but it isn't Athos. I hope we can at least give everyone a choice."

"And that choice is what is hotly debated, and will be much discussed in the coming days. But we have adjourned the Council for now since we have said that there is no point in debating to death a hypothetical. If there is no shield generator, there is no point in arguing."

"True," Teyla said. "Rodney and I will find out if there is one. And then a decision can be made, or there will be no need of one."

The pale morning light was slanting across the gate field when Teyla and Rodney stepped through the Stargate to Athos. The sky was a perfect autumn blue, high and clear and bright, while the tall grass had turned golden, heavy seedheads not even stirring in the still air. As the gate deactivated and the wormhole died, Teyla took a deep breath. This was home. This smell to the air, this slant of the light — this was home.

"Ok," Rodney said. "Let's go. How far is it?"

"It is several of your kilometers around the lake," Teyla said. "If we walk around the north end, that will be shortest."

Rodney snorted, slinging his weapon across his chest. "You'd think people would, just once in a while, build the city next to the Stargate."

"I suspect there was a town here too then, when the Ancestors put the gate here," Teyla replied. "The city was there, across the water, and there was once a wide road. I think there was a town around the gate, a traveler's pale, perhaps. When we dig down on these plains we often find ancient stones and pavement."

Rodney looked up as they walked, as if measuring the distance between lakeshore and any major stand of trees. Behind the ruins of Emege on the other side of the lake, the mountains reared up green and cool, already crowned with the first snows on the heights. They ringed the valley about, casting long shadows before the sun rose high. "The road was over there?"

"I think so. We are roughly following its course."

A water bird started from the reeds by the lake, spreading its white wings as it lifted in to the growing light — an osprey. For a moment Teyla felt the world shift, the landscape before her juxtaposed with ancient memory, the lineage memory of the Wraith queen, Osprey, who stood among her ancestors — another morning, this same lake, a white bird rising against shadowed water. Teyla shook her head to clear it. That was not the track of memory she was following today, not the ancestor she honored. She sought a later time, when Osprey's descendants made war upon the people of Emege.

Rodney had stopped and was looking at her, and she realized she had completely missed what he'd said. "I'm sorry, Rodney. What?"

"I said, have you seen a map of the city? Do you know where we're going?"

"I have not seen a map. I do not think one survives. I have seen pictures, and when I was a girl I was in the city once or twice. But there are many stories that tell us about Emege's form."

"Stories."

Teyla smiled. Once he would have scoffed. Now he knew the truth of too many stories. "The stories tell us that there was a great central tower, like the one in Atlantis, though there were many lesser spires around it. I would presume that the generator would be beneath it, if Emege was built like Atlantis and the other Ancient installations we have discovered. I think that is the best place to begin looking."

"Of course it's the best place to look," Rodney said. "The Ancients were rather boring really. If you think about it."

This time she laughed. "They were. But Emege was not an Ancient city. It was Athosian, belonging to human allies, not the Ancestors themselves. So it might not be the same in all

ways. However, there is a description of the city in the Tale of
Saite. Have you heard that story?"

"Er, no." And didn't sound like he particularly wanted to.
But while they were walking around the lake, Rodney was a
captive audience. He would have to learn something that was
not science whether he wanted to or not.

"It is the story of how the woman Arda loved was captured
by the demon Urtel, and how he rescued her even though she
was held in the bowels of the earth. Arda and his kinsman,
who was married to Saite, traveled into the underworld itself.
But in the first part there is a description of Arda's city, which
is Emege. Once, when Arda ruled in Emege...."

They stopped to rest halfway around the lake, Rodney taking sips from his water bottle and then offering it to Teyla, who
took it gravely. They sat for a moment.

"This story about Saite is all great and all," Rodney said,
"but how does it tell us about the city?" His words had no heat
in them, and he seemed in no hurry to actually get up and
get moving. Perhaps he was mellowing, Teyla thought. The
Rodney she had first met would have been too impatient to
wait even a little, too disinterested to hear her out. Perhaps
being in a tale himself had given him a greater appreciation
of them.

"I am just coming to that part," Teyla said. "Now when Saite
came to Emege, this is the form of the city. The city was built
in three parts. Oldest and prime was the Old City, which was
built on the hillside following the curve of the land, more or
less in the shape of a tava bean. It had been walled and made
of stone long ago, before the Ancestors walked among their
children. The second part of the city was the Outer City, which
had grown up outside the great walls and was made of wood
with roofs of pottery. Last and newest was the High Citadel,
which had been built in the very center, in the curve of the
Old City, by the Ancestors themselves. The highest tower sur-
passed all, and from its height the entire plain could be seen

as far as the southern mountain peaks on the other side. All the land that could be seen from the high tower, Arda ruled."

Rodney nodded. "So the human city predated the Ancients."

"That is what I take from it, yes. The Ancestors brought us here and then left us for some considerable amount of time, long enough for us to build cities of our own, before they returned."

"That makes sense. Lots of the Ancient installations we've found were built not long before the war."

"Yes." Teyla got to her feet, clipping Rodney's water bottle back to the back of his pack. "I wish I understood what changed among them. Why did they begin to bring these peoples under their rule, no matter how benign it might have been, when they had been content to watch from afar? Why did they..." Her voice trailed off.

"Why did they start experimenting on people?" Rodney asked. He had his familiar quirky smile. "You want to know what I think?"

And time was she would have brushed off his opinion as irrelevant, based on Earth prejudices that had nothing to do with the situation, but she had learned better than that. "Yes, Rodney. I do."

"I think that the more stuff you have, the more you want." Rodney shrugged his pack back on. "I mean, look at them. They had all this stuff and more besides. They could blow up suns and they understood time and space like nobody else, maybe even more than the Asgard! They could do anything they wanted. Except live forever."

"The Asgard wanted that too," Teyla observed, falling into step beside him.

"Yeah, and look how they screwed up! They got their individual immortality at the expense of the future of their species."

"The Ancestors wanted to Ascend. But only a few were good enough to do so on their own."

"I don't know about good," Rodney said. "But most people couldn't do it. And their devices don't really work. So they tried to figure out how to genetically engineer bodies that wouldn't age."

"And created the Wraith," Teyla said grimly. Now that she had opened them, Osprey's memories were always there just beneath the surface, as close as her own. Sometimes they were horrific and sometimes searingly sad, but often they were happy, a thing astonishing and appalling in its own right. Surely someone so destroyed, so altered and twisted and doomed, would be pitiable. Yet Osprey was not. The more of her memories Teyla recalled, the more she found indomitable joy. She had loved her people and her children and her Consort and had lived a long life full of love despite all sorrow and pain. Surely that was not what one should expect of the legacy of tainted Wraith blood. It would be easier to pity. It would be easier to reconcile with all she had been taught.

She and Rodney walked in silence for a while. The path turned away from the lake, beginning to ascend between curved low hills.

After a while Rodney gestured to the mounds. "Is this what's left of the Outer City?"

"I think so," Teyla said. "I am sure Dr. Jackson and Dr. Lynn would be very excited about digging into them. But they are not going to do so."

"Hey, not saying they should," Rodney said. His mental voice added a thought perhaps not meant for her. *There wouldn't be anything good here anyway.*

"This is where we are going," Teyla said. Ahead, twisted beams of metal rose into the air, remains of framed buildings that had once had facings of glass or brick. They were all shapes and sizes, and the rough path they had been following became more recognizably a broad street. Here and there along the curve of the hill, the remains of a cyclopean wall could be seen, though the later buildings eclipsed it in places.

Rodney frowned. "Those buildings can't all be from before the war with the Wraith."

"They are not," Teyla said. "The most recent ones are less than three hundred years old, from the last time we rebuilt before the Great Culling."

"So this is what Sateda will look like in three hundred years."

"No," she said. "Because we chose not to build back on the same site, as the Satedans are doing. We had done that many times before, and all it had done was allow the Wraith to find us easily. That is why we adopted a different policy. We would not gather in great cities with large populations in one place. We would not build things that would be easy to identify and destroy. We would not trust in weapons, because our weapons could not defeat the Wraith. Instead, we would disperse and deliberately reduce our energy and technology footprint. It would be much harder to find widely dispersed bands, and if the Wraith found one band they would kill a hundred people, not a hundred thousand."

To her surprise, Rodney nodded. "Makes sense. You guys aren't Luddites who think technology is bad. But if you can't win by fighting, hiding makes a lot of sense."

"The Genii chose the same course," Teyla said.

"And the Hoffans and Satedans…."

"Let us not speak of the Hoffans," Teyla said. "And look! We must consider where we shall go next. See how the streets divide just past that building there? We should decide how best to reach the city center."

Rodney stopped, frowning. "Wait. That." He pointed at a stubby concrete dome half buried beneath the twisted steel beams fallen from a newer building that had been far taller. "That looks like a drone installation."

"Does it?" Teyla shaded her eyes from the bright morning sun. "It does not look like the ones in Atlantis."

"That's because they're beneath the surface. They're built into the superstructure. This looks like the one in Antarctica." Rodney started toward it, clambering over a pile of broken concrete.

"We are not here to look for drone installations," Teyla called after him. "We are here to look only for the shield generator, remember?"

Rodney stopped. "We can always use more drones."

"The drones would have been expended before the city fell," Teyla said. "The siege was a year and a day. They must have fired every weapon they had." Her voice choked, trying not to imagine the despair the defenders must have felt, their last drones used, hoping that the Ancients would come to their aid. They had not. Perhaps they had no longer been able to even defend themselves.

"Yeah." Rodney looked across at the dome longingly. "There probably aren't any left."

"Probably not," Teyla said. "And you have seen drone installations before. We need to find the shield generator."

He scrambled back down the pile of concrete. "As galling as it is to say it, you're right."

Teyla grinned. "Thank you, Rodney."

At that he laughed. "Had you going."

"You did."

"You thought you were going to have to pull this 'I am in charge here' thing."

"I hoped not."

"You know, it did occur to me that the drones had all been used."

"I am glad it did." Together, they walked on.

The closer to the city center they got, the harder their journey became. The streets were choked with rubble sometimes as high as the second story windows, fallen masonry, steel, bricks, concrete, and whatever had been on the streets beneath them. Twisted metal here and there protruded, the wreckage of some sort of caterpillar-treaded transports, here and there a little green or blue metallic paint remaining. There were other things too, plastic bottles and plastic shoes, scraps of deteriorating cloth. Some of them were wrapped around bones, and

Teyla looked away. This was not decent. The dead should not lie in the open air, their arm bones scattered near the things they had carried when they fell, for the curious to stare at.

Rodney seemed subdued as well. He said nothing. They did not speak except to discuss their direction among the confusing ruins.

"There's a tunnel," he said, pointing to the shored up entrance of something beneath a building, steps going down. "It might take us to the center."

"I do not think we want to go that way unless we must," Teyla said. Rodney looked around, and she said, "They sheltered in the tunnels, at the last."

He opened his mouth and then closed it again. "Right. We'll find a different way."

The sun was past its zenith when they finally stopped. They were near the center, certainly, the rubble indicating a concentric set of circles — buildings that once ringed a park from which the central tower had risen. Now the area was choked with debris now overgrown with young trees and many hanging vines. Athos was a water rich world. There had been plants here, and good soil beneath. Even as time claimed the city, life was finding a way. Moss masked fallen stones, the weathered glitter of pulverized glass gleaming between the roots of trees whose branches spread over Teyla's head. There were no remains here. The green had already claimed them.

Rodney took a deep breath.

"It is better so, is it not?" Teyla asked. "Better than if we rebuilt? Let these trees be their grave markers."

He shrugged. "It's not my decision."

"Then perhaps we should have some lunch." Teyla sat down on one of the tilted stones, pulling off her pack and opening an MRE. John would have thoughts on this — good thoughts and worth hearing. Something about time as a healer, and other things she could not guess. She would tell him of this and ask him.

Rodney chewed on an energy bar thoughtfully. "You wouldn't have to build right on top of this. Atlantis' energy shield is seven kilometers in diameter when it's extended. That's all the way out beyond the mounds at the Outer City and well up onto the mountain behind Emege. There's plenty of room to live under the shield and leave this undisturbed if that's what you want to do."

"Is it that large?"

"Yeah. It's just harder to see on the ground here than it is from the tower in Atlantis. It looks bigger here, but it's actually not."

Teyla nodded slowly. "That does give us a choice then. I think we would want to leave this as a shrine."

There was a skitter behind them, like small stones falling on a larger one, and Teyla spun around.

Nothing was there. She saw nothing except a tiny puff of dust where a scattering of gravel had fallen against a great, sloped slab of concrete taller than her head.

Rodney had his weapon in hand, though he was still chewing. "What was that?"

"I do not see anything," Teyla said. She stood still, listening.

There was a call, and a gray bird slightly larger than her hand landed on the top of the slab, regarding her out of one beady black eye.

Teyla relaxed, lowering her P90. "It's a Housedove, Rodney. They're harmless." She looked at the bird and it looked back at her curiously. "They live in eaves and ruins, and sometimes they even roost in our tents."

"It looks like a big fat pigeon," Rodney said. "I suppose if you blew up New York or Vancouver, the pigeons would still be there."

There was a flurry of wings, and four more birds dove down to perch beside the first. "I expect so," Teyla said.

"Are we going to be mobbed by those birds? Because if we are, I think we need to go. I was mobbed by pigeons once when I was five. I was eating popcorn and they swarmed me."

Teyla turned and stared at him. "Really, Rodney?"

"It was very traumatic."

"I do not think the birds are going to attack you," Teyla said. She sat back down, shaking her head. "And I am going to finish my lunch."

"You never know," Rodney said darkly.

"There are no large predators in Emege!" Teyla said. "Truly! There are large animals in the mountains, but there is absolutely nothing here that could possibly attack a human being. This has never happened in my lifetime."

"Well, if people don't go in the city, how do you know there aren't large predators here?"

"Rodney...."

He raised both hands. "Ok! Ok! You say there aren't any large predators. Fine. We'll just carry on like it's all perfectly safe."

"It is perfectly safe," Teyla said between gritted teeth. She stood up and neatly stowed the trash from her lunch in her pack. "But we have rested long enough. We should go on while the light is good."

"Suits me," Rodney said, giving the birds a dark look. "Before some flock of evil demon pigeons attacks us. Weirder stuff has happened."

That was inarguable. Teyla didn't even try. She just shouldered her pack and considered their best direction. Rodney was looking at the ruined buildings too. "What is it?" she asked.

He pointed to a particularly large heap of tumbled stone. "You see that? No, not the rubble. The bit behind it. The way that big piece has that curve? And then next to it, do you see that slab with metal attached? Doesn't that look like the top of the tower in Atlantis? Like the curve of the jumper bay window and the vane above?"

Teyla shaded her eyes, and then nodded slowly. "It does indeed."

"I think that's part of the top story of the central tower. Which means the bottom of the central tower would be just behind it."

Teyla's heart sank. "Underneath that enormous pile. Rodney, it would take heavy equipment for us to get through there."

"Above ground." Rodney gave her a cocky grin. "But we know that the Ancient installations are always accessible on multiple levels. If they had mass transit, they had entrances from the tunnels. It only makes sense."

"That is true." Teyla steeled herself. "We must use the tunnels now. Surely there was an entrance somewhere around this main square."

"There," Rodney said, pointing. "That looks like it might be."

They descended through a roofless atrium, crumbled stairs littered with the debris of the fallen ceiling, some shards of glass still as long as Teyla's arm. There were no bones until they reached the bottom. Then there were many.

"Ok, I'm just not going to think about this too hard," Rodney said, tiptoeing along the edge of the stairs holding onto the railing.

Teyla didn't reply. She turned her flashlight on and shone it ahead. The vaulted roof of the tunnel seemed intact. It was best to look at the roof only. So many had sheltered here in the end and had died here.

And then there were the blank spaces, the areas of tunnel where seemingly inexplicably there were no bones at all. "Culling," Teyla said. The people who had been there had been swept up. The further they went, the more it was like that. Perhaps landing parties had been through this area, rounding up survivors for Wraith feeding pens. It was a grim thought. Whatever Rodney was thinking, he kept it to himself.

"Ah ha!" he said suddenly, playing his light over the walls ahead. "Look at that. See those doors? I bet that's the way up." He hurried over to a pair of metal doors, their azure paint peeling, stuck open just enough for a person to slip through.

"Be careful," Teyla said. "This may not be the bottom of the shaft."

"It's not," Rodney said. "I think the elevator car is one floor below."

She slipped in beside him and looked down. It looked very much like one of the elevators in Atlantis, stopped in a crunch of metal a few feet below the doors.

Rodney winced. "Nobody survived when that thing fell."

"I think it fell long after there was anyone to survive," Teyla said, shining her light around. "See how the cable is rusted through? It was probably stopped far above and only fell generations later when the cable gave way."

"Yeah." Rodney shone his light up. It failed to illuminate more than a story or two above, the shaft disappearing into distance. "I don't think we're getting up that. But there must be access stairs. And I'd bet that the installation we want isn't far above this. They liked putting the shield generator way underground."

Teyla nodded. "It does not seem that the destruction was so great down here."

"Probably wasn't," Rodney replied. "Most of this is decay. I don't see a lot of structural damage down here. The Ancients built solid." He rapped on the concrete wall with his hand. "So let's find the stairs. Off to the right? Gotcha!" Rodney ducked around the corner. "Do I know Ancient installations or do I know Ancient installations?"

"You know them very well," Teyla agreed.

However, before they were halfway up the first flight, Teyla considered that perhaps Rodney had been premature in saying there was little structural damage. She stopped, shining her light at the stairs ahead. Or rather, at the gap two meters wide where there should be stairs and weren't.

"That's a problem," Rodney said.

It appeared that a chunk of rubble had fallen from far above, plunging through the stairwell and knocking a hole in the stairs themselves. Along the edges the concrete was crumbly, suggesting that smaller pieces might fall at any time.

"If we had Ronon," Rodney began.

"We don't," Teyla said. "And unless we want to go home today and try to persuade the Council to let us come back with him, we must find another way."

"I don't think we can jump that," Rodney said, eyeing the gap.

"Not from the low step to the high one," Teyla said. "We might make it coming down, but not going up."

"Ok, there's got to be another way up." Rodney headed back down a few steps, a thoughtful expression on his face. "What are the various ways to get up the tower in Atlantis, besides the elevator and the stairs?"

"The transport chamber," Teyla said. "But surely any of those here have been without power for a long time."

"Yeah. And there's the ventilation system, which I'd hate to do given the state of the stairs. If we get in there, we might get trapped."

"There are some exterior stairs on the lower levels with the balconies, but surely the exterior of the tower isn't intact. We saw the ruins of the upper levels."

"We did," Rodney said. "But the lower levels might be intact. And they might be incorporated into some of these later buildings that grew up around it. Let's see if we can find balcony doors. We might find some outside stairs intact."

They went back down and turned left at the bottom, toward what would be a terrace in Atlantis. It wasn't. A solid wall greeted them.

"Around the other side of the tower?" Teyla said.

"It's worth a try."

They made their way around, and as they turned the corner stopped and gaped. "Oh wow," Rodney said.

The glass doors to the terrace were long gone, opening instead into a vast underground atrium. Light poured in from several stories above, dappling through the leaves of shade loving trees that had grown up around the natural depression that now held a pool of water. Birds flew in and out. Across the atrium, a building in an entirely different style from that of the Ancients closed off the space, intricate stonework with elaborate balustrades carved with leaves scrolling around spiraling staircases that wound their way upward. Each level had terraces. Once, this must have been a courtyard that melded old and new, the Emege of the Ancestors and that of Teyla's own folk a few generation ago. It was still startlingly beautiful.

Teyla blinked hard. "We must keep this unchanged," she said.

"Yeah."

Together they made their way across the atrium, birds startling up from the trees. After all, they had seen no people walking here in a long time. They paused on the other side.

"See?" Rodney said. "Where it joins the tower up there?"

"I do." Three stories up, the terraces on the other side met the central tower at a balcony there. "We go in there and then go down a floor or two."

"Yep."

The tower rooms were surprisingly intact at this level on this side, only broken glass making them unlivable. These rooms had either been swept by the Wraith or evacuated. There were even signs in the corridors. Rodney squinted at them. "That's not Ancient."

"That is Athosian," Teyla said. "Our people made these signs when they rebuilt a few hundred years ago. This one says 'The Hall of Deep Remembrance.'"

"A museum?"

"Or something of the Ancestors they did not understand," Teyla said, with mounting excitement in her voice. "Rodney, I think this may be what we are looking for."

The door was shut, but they pried it open with some difficulty, shining their flashlights around the space beyond before squeezing in.

"This is it!" Rodney said, bustling over to the familiar Ancient consoles, these neatly marked with signs in Athosian saying 'do not touch the displays.' "These are power control boards. Hmm, I don't see the ZPM slot, but there may be a ZPM room in a different place. That would be a pain in the neck. Ok, let me get these up and running and see what the story is."

"But if there's no power…."

"Let's find out." Rodney held one finger in the air. "Don't assume!"

"I shall not."

Rodney's hands flew over the boards, and Teyla let him work, instead wandering the perimeter of the room. It was not so long ago that her people had preserved this space. Had they known what it was? Or was it simply a mystery of Emege, a place of the Ancestors that was precious because of its antiquity? Had they understood that it might protect them? She turned, glancing back at Rodney. "Is it a shield generator?"

"I think so." He didn't look up from the cold instruments he was staring at. "But it's not like the one on Atlantis. It's a different design. Give me a minute here. I think I've seen something like it before."

"Of course."

There was a sudden whir, and the consoles blinked fitfully to life, lights flashing as the power stabilized.

"What?" Teyla said. "I thought you said the ZPM was depleted."

"Obviously it's not." Rodney didn't look up from the screens he was perusing. "Now. Let's have a look at you. Ok. The system's booting and it's going to take a minute. But it looks like the process is orderly. I'm not seeing much in the way of fluctuation. I can't get the power consumption menu up until it's finished booting. Then we'll see how much is left in the ZPM."

"If the ZPM isn't empty, why did they shut the shield down?"

Rodney glanced up. "The amount of power it takes to run this room is insignificant. You could run this room on .00001% of the ZPM. It would take lots more than that to run the shield. If they drained the ZPM almost all the way, they'd have enough power to run the control room but not keep the shield up. They could shut it down in an orderly fashion. This wasn't blown out or knocked down. It's doing a normal system boot like it was closed down the way Atlantis was."

"So there could be some power left in the ZPM?"

"A little bit." Rodney shrugged. "Not enough to do much more than this, but probably enough for some system diagnostics and so on. We can get a naquadah generator plugged in and do more. But I think the system is basically intact, and that's good news for you guys. But no, there won't be enough power to run the shield. As soon as this finishes, I'll pull up the power menu and see what's left."

Teyla nodded. "That is good news." And yet it pulled at her, the picture of those distant ancestors closing down the control room in an orderly way while the Wraith moved in, shutting down power systems neatly while Darts deposited landing teams in a city full of refugees. That was stranger and sadder than imagining the installation simply blown up.

"Ok, that's weird." Rodney's voice was suddenly concerned. "Really weird."

"What is weird, Rodney?"

"I'm reading full power. That can't be right."

"Full power?" Teyla came around the console, looking over his shoulder at the cascade of Ancient words on the screen, though she could read few of them.

"100%. That's impossible. That would mean the ZPM is brand new. What in the hell?"

"That doesn't make any sense," Teyla said. "Where is it? Maybe there is a malfunction in the reading or in the socket for it or something."

"Probably." Rodney's hands danced over the screen. "I don't see the ZPM socket in this room. Let me pull up a schematic of the power system and see where the actual ZPM room is. It's probably in the substructure, like it is in Atlantis."

"So we will have to find it and get there." Teyla was not looking forward to another search.

"Yeah, I…." Rodney stopped. "Oh you're kidding!"

"What?"

"There is no ZPM. There never has been. I knew I'd seen something like this installation before."

"Rodney, what are you talking about?" This was the point where John would start shaking answers out of him.

"Taranis." Rodney glanced up, an expression of triumph on his face. "Remember Taranis? We were there about five years ago? The people who found the shield generator and the Ancient warship? That we had to help evacuate?"

"I recall it vividly," Teyla said. She certainly remembered nearly being choked by toxic fumes. "The people who had the enormous erupting volcano."

"Their Ancient installation was running on geothermal power," Rodney said. "They didn't have a ZPM. It was tied into the geothermal power of the dormant supervolcano they were living on top of. They could pull plenty of power from it, enough to power their shield for more than a year before…." Rodney stopped again. "Oh crap."

"I thought you said this room drew almost no power?"

"It does. That's not an issue." Rodney glanced around as though he could see through the walls to the outside, to the valley and the lake and the encircling mountains. "This is too."

"A volcano? We have never had a volcano here. Not in our oldest lore."

"Your lore doesn't go back a few million years. This whole valley is the caldera of an enormous dormant volcano. It's probably been dormant for literally millions of years and will be for millions more. But the geothermal activity is there. It's deep underground, and it's an enormous amount of power, just like on Taranis. The problem on Taranis was that they used it to power the shield on full for a long time and they desta-bilized the volcano. If they'd used less power, or if they'd lis-tened when the warnings came that they were pushing it too much, they'd have been ok. It's like I told them then — the shield isn't meant to be run 24 hours a day, 7 days a week for months and months on end. It's supposed to be used at full power for brief periods only because it's a real power hog. If they'd just cooled it a bit, they wouldn't have had a problem."

Suddenly, terribly, all the pieces fit. "My people, the Athosians who lived in the time of the Wraith armada, had a shield. They ran it for a year and a day. And then…."

Rodney took a deep breath, looking around the control room. When he spoke again his voice was oddly gentle. "And then they shut it down. Neatly, tidily and completely. They did a full systems shutdown. Because they were getting the warnings and they knew what they meant. The people on Taranis didn't understand what they were. But the Athosians did."

Teyla pressed her hands to her mouth. "They knew."

Rodney nodded. "They knew that they were risking geological instability. That if they kept running the shield, they risked causing an eruption like the people on Taranis did, an explosion that would render their planet completely uninhabitable."

"What an awful decision." They had stood here, looking at these control panels and knowing that if they kept running the shield they would doom their world, doom every person and every animal and every plant on Athos that could not survive the eruption of a supervolcano. And that if they shut the field down, the Wraith would take this city — this beautiful city packed with refugees. "They knew," Teyla whispered.

"They shut it down," Rodney said quietly. "Your ancestors."

"No," Teyla said, blinking back tears. "Not my ancestors. Everyone who was here died. All the people of Emege, all the scientists who made this decision, all the rulers who agreed, all their families and all their children. They were food for the Wraith. But some people survived, people who lived in outlying areas and who had deep mines or remote farms. Some of the people of Athos survived. Just not the people of Emege."

Rodney didn't say anything.

"They preserved our world. They preserved the lives of people who weren't their kin, who weren't with them in the city, in hopes that some of them would survive the Great Culling. Instead of holding onto the shield and dooming everyone, they sacrificed themselves to save this world for people they would never know."

"I don't know I've ever heard anything that sad," Rodney said.

"It's not sad!" Teyla brushed her tears away. "It's a victory. Don't you see? Life won. Queen Death didn't win. Death itself didn't win. Those people died, and our world endured and this city was rebuilt and reinhabited and rose again. We rise again. Every time we fall, we rise!"

She touched the control panels reverently. "And this is their gift to us, another gift. We have a working shield generator, and we can use it as it was intended to be used, occasionally in emergencies to protect us."

"And you have a boatload of power the rest of the time," Rodney said. "This thing could power an entire city without breaking a sweat. If you were just using it for ordinary things like lights and computers, you'd never have to worry about it. You've got all the power you want."

"Enough power to let us decide our future." Teyla closed her eyes for a moment, her hand against the smooth metal. A story. A new story about how Emege had fallen. A hero story about the sacrifice its last defenders had made for Athosians to come — for them. A bridge from the past to the present. What does it mean to be Athosian? It is to be the heirs of those who died in Emege.

She opened her eyes. Rodney was looking at her worriedly.

"We will go back to the Council," Teyla said. "I have a new story to tell them. And then we have much to discuss."

"Does that mean the Athosians will be coming back here?" Rodney asked.

Teyla nodded. "I think you may count on that." Perhaps Torren would live here one day. Perhaps Jinto would rebuild the atrium and these other buildings. Perhaps Kanaan would open a brewery here, and Halling would plant fields of beans to feed them all. Perhaps, in time, these empty windows would shine with light pulled from beneath the ground, safely and warmly heating each room against winter's cold. She would visit here, walking through the gate from Atlantis. And in that day, the Children of Emege would prosper.

STARGATE SG-1
In Passing

Susannah Parker Sinard

This story takes place between seasons eight and nine of Stargate SG-1.

"UH…JACK?"

In his peripheral vision, Jack could see Daniel hovering in the open doorway. Half-silhouetted and backlit from the briefing room, he had an aura about him reminiscent of the first time he'd been ascended. It made Jack do a double-take. But no, this Daniel was flesh and blood — again — and wearing what Jack had mentally dubbed his funeral suit. Jack had seen it too many times these past couple of years, including Catherine Langford's memorial service last week. And, not unexpectedly, here it was again.

"Everyone else is ready." Daniel nodded in the general vicinity of the gate room. "We should probably go. We don't want to be late."

Jack bit back the well-conditioned first response that came to his mind. Keeping the Tok'ra cooling their heels was a bit of gamesmanship he would have had no problem with, under normal circumstances. But not today. He wouldn't do that to Sam, or the memory of Jacob Carter — although he was pretty sure Jacob might have appreciated the sentiment. Selmak too, for that matter. But, hey, they both were beyond the petty squabbles of this mortal coil now, and self-indulgently dragging his heels would only reflect poorly on Carter and the SGC, which was something he would not let happen. Not on his watch. And it was still his watch — for a while longer anyway.

"Tell Walter to dial —" The vibration under his feet told Jack they were well ahead of him. Daniel's eyebrows arched innocently. "Right." He swiftly slid the papers he'd been reading back into their folder and added it to the pile. The stack of folders on his desk would have to wait. Of course, by the time he got back, it would have doubled in size. Maybe tripled. The reproductive proclivities of SGC paperwork made rabbits look like amateurs. He didn't even want to think about the quantity of paper he'd have to push at the Pentagon.

Snatching his starched and pressed service dress jacket off the back of his chair and his equally uncomfortable hat off the desk, Jack followed Daniel across the briefing room. Through the wide window he could see Teal'c and Carter already at the foot of the ramp. T stood placidly, hands clasped behind his back, gazing at the spinning Stargate. Carter, on the other hand… He could sense her subdued tension from two levels up. She was fiddling restlessly with something in her hands, and Jack recognized the box the Tok'ra had provided — the one that now contained Jacob's and Selmak's ashes. Sam was giving it the once over for what he was sure must be the hundredth time. Two-hundredth, probably.

Jack hadn't realized he'd stopped walking until Daniel came back and stood beside him.

"I guess it hadn't really hit me that this is our last mission together — if you want to call it a mission," Daniel said, looking down into the gate room too. "It was lucky that the Prometheus' departure was delayed so Sam could be here."

Hammond was responsible for that. And for a few other things as well — like those orders on his desk. George always did have their six.

"Yeah. Well. Last I checked, deep space wasn't going anywhere." Jack turned away from the window and headed toward the stairs.

The fifth chevron was already locking by the time he and Daniel joined the others in the gate room.

"Did you ever anticipate, O'Neill, that the day would arrive when we would feel free to journey to the Tok'ra without our weapons at our sides?" Like Daniel, Teal'c was also wearing his civilian funeral clothes. Jack tried to picture him brandishing a staff weapon while wearing his turtleneck. It didn't work.

"I don't like it." Going off-world without so much as even a pocket knife was just wrong. He felt vulnerable. Exposed. Like he was about to walk through the gate naked.

"Considering it's a funeral, I hardly think a P90 would go with what you're wearing. Besides." Daniel patted at his own suit coat, to emphasize his point. "It's not like we even have a place to put them."

Jack glowered. "I'm just sayin'— it doesn't feel right, is all."

"I agree — it feels a bit strange." Carter spoke at last. Jack gestured toward her with both hands.

"*Thank you!*"

"But Daniel's right. Under the circumstances, it wouldn't be appropriate. I'm sure we'll be fine."

"*Et tu*, Carter?" Jack replied, archly. Fine. He knew when he was outnumbered. It didn't mean he had to like it.

Overhead Walter's voice announced the sixth chevron locking.

"Do you not feel safe amongst the Tok'ra, O'Neill, now that our common enemy has been defeated?" Teal'c asked.

"What I *would* feel a whole lot *safer* about, is knowing exactly where the hell it is we're actually going." This was the part about today's plans that made him edgy. According to the instructions they'd received, the address they were dialing was just a rendezvous point from which they would be 'escorted' to their final destination. Proof the Tok'ra were still as paranoid as ever.

"If you think about it, Jack, this has to be one of the most secure places in the galaxy." Daniel's attention was on the spinning gate as he spoke. "I mean, we're still the closest thing to an ally the Tok'ra have, and they're not even telling *us* where it is."

"And doesn't that strike you as just a little bit — odd?" Jack asked. "I mean, the bad guys are gone. It's safe to come out now. 'Ole-Ole-Olsen's Free'."

Daniel shrugged. "You can hardly blame them. Even with the System Lords nearly wiped out, I'm sure there are still some Goa'uld — Ba'al, for example — who'd be more than happy to make the Tok'ra pay for their role in bringing them down. And now that the Free Jaffa Nation is establishing itself as a key player in the new galactic order, it's understandable why the Tok'ra might want to continue to lay low."

"It *was* the Tok'ra who developed the symbiote poison which led to the death of many million Jaffa," Teal'c interjected, with an edge in his voice.

"The Trust did that, so technically not the Tok'ra's fault," Daniel pointed out. "Although I'm not sure the Jaffa are ready to make that distinction just yet."

"Indeed."

Jack fidgeted as the Stargate finally blossomed to life. Some other time he'd take a moment to wax nostalgic about this final trip through the gate. Right now, though, he just wanted this whole event over with as swiftly as possible.

Beside him, Carter took a deep breath.

"You sure you're gonna be okay?" he asked her as Teal'c and Daniel started up the ramp.

"Yeah. I'll be fine." She indicated the box in her hands. "I know Dad wanted this, for Selmak, so it's the least I can do."

Hardly the least, as far as he was concerned, considering they'd been through this once already when they'd spread some of the ashes at her mother's grave. But then, underestimating Sam Carter was something he'd learned a long time ago not to do. And because there really wasn't anything more he could say at the moment, Jack gestured toward the gate. "Then, shall we?"

Out the corner of his eye he saw her shoulders straighten with brutal determination as they moved forward.

Oh yeah. The sooner this day was over with, the better.

"Hold on, are those actually…buildings?" Daniel Jackson was shielding his eyes against the setting sun to get a better

look at the vast plain stretching in front of them. In the forefront was an immense pyramid, the hallmark of almost every
Goa'uld home world Teal'c had been to. But behind it rose several dozen structures — if one could call them that — which
were anything but Goa'uld in design. From this distance they
more aptly resembled a collection of stunted crystals which
a child might have haphazardly placed in the sand. But using
the pyramid as a frame of reference, Teal'c could gauge their
height, and there was nothing child-sized about them.

"They are only in their early stages of growth. It will be some
time before the structures are fully formed and habitable."
Their Tok'ra escort, Ker'ai, paused to allow them a moment to
appreciate the sight. A tall man with evidence of some prior
trauma marking his face, he had been awaiting them at the
designated rendezvous planet. Although pleasant in disposi-
tion, he had nonetheless refused to reveal their final destination, dialing the Stargate out of their line of sight to further
conceal the gate address. The frustration on O'Neill's face had
been most apparent.

"Wait — you're saying you actually grow buildings? From
crystals?" There was no missing the hint of excitement in
Colonel Carter's voice. "I didn't know you could do that."

"It is a much slower process than excavating tunnels," Ker'ai
explained. "And it is only feasible on certain planets, as massive quantities of a certain mineral in the soil are required."

"Silica," offered Colonel Carter.

The Tok'ra nodded. "In time, this will become a great city."

"A city," Daniel Jackson repeated, sounding surprised.

Teal'c understood why. "That would suggest that the Tok'ra
have no intentions of leaving this place." To the best of his
knowledge, the Tok'ra had always been a nomadic people — a
necessity of their resistance against the Goa'uld.

A disconcerted look passed briefly over Ker'ai's scarred
face. "So it would."

"You do not approve?"

"The defense provided by the tunnels are all we have ever known. It will be an adjustment to live a life so — exposed."

"But that's good, right?" Daniel Jackson's enthusiasm was undiminished. "That the Tok'ra finally feel secure enough to build a stable, permanent society?"

"It is my experience, Dr. Jackson, that what can be built up, can also be torn down," the Tok'ra replied, but then, forcing a smile, added, "But yes. Soon, perhaps, the Tok'ra will no longer live life in the shadows." He glanced at the box Colonel Carter carried and then at the fading light. "Please come now. The Rite of *Hak'tyl* must begin at sundown."

Teal'c contemplated the distant buildings a moment longer, allowing the others to walk ahead. In many ways, the Tok'ra were not unlike the Jaffa now: two societies faced with the task of having to redefine themselves in the wake of their ultimate success. These structure were as symbolic as they were practical, in much the same way as choosing Dakara was symbolic for the Free Jaffa Nation. Neither was a small undertaking, as Ker'ai's reticence demonstrated, but without a vision on which to anchor the future, how could either expect to move forward?

It was a conversation he and Bra'tac had had many times these past few months, as his old mentor continued to press him to help the Jaffa shape that vision. Teal'c had, in his own way, been as reticent as Ker'ai, but for different reasons. Abandoning his friends was not a decision he had taken lightly, and when he had, at last, chosen, it was not without a sense of great loss. But, as he had read in one of the books Daniel Jackson had given him, there was a season to everything, and he knew his season with the Tau'ri was at its end. Oddly, seeing how the Tok'ra were embracing their new role gave him comfort with his decision. It was time for him to move forward as well.

The others were already well ahead of him, although it would not take him long to catch up. Teal'c was certain of their destination. The great pyramid loomed before them, its dense stone in sharp contrast to the translucent crystalline structures growing around it. Weathered by wind and sand, a remnant of some Goa'uld long forgotten, it seemed an apt symbol of the past.

And, perhaps, a reminder of how unyielding that past could be.

"The Rite of *Hak'tyl*." Daniel Jackson was saying, as Teal'c rejoined them. "*Hak'tyl* means 'liberation', doesn't it?"

"It does, Daniel Jackson." Teal'c replied, falling into step with him. "Which is why it was the name chosen by Ishta for her warriors. But I have also heard it used when speaking of death. It refers to the releasing of the spirit into the universe so that it might continue on its journey."

"Teal'c is correct," Ker'ai said over his shoulder as they walked. "For the Tok'ra, the traditional Rite of *Hak'tyl* begins with a funeral pyre, into which the body is placed. Afterwards, the ashes are gathered into a *so'ros* and set in a place of reverence for all to see. Then, beginning at sundown, songs are sung of the deceased's accomplishments until sunrise the following day, at which time the *so'ros* is either consumed by the vortex of an activating *chaapa'ai* or, for those such as Selmak, placed in the *Arc'tus*." He glanced again at the box in Colonel Carter's hands. "Obviously, under the circumstances, the first part of the rite will be unnecessary."

"So, basically, it's a wake," remarked O'Neill. He had been remarkably silent thus far.

"A wake is an Earth custom in many cultures," Daniel Jackson quickly explained when Ker'ai appeared perplexed. "It's a sort of social gathering among family and friends of the deceased, meant to honor their memory and celebrate their life."

The Tok'ra nodded. "A close approximation."

"What exactly is the *Arc'tus*?" asked Colonel Carter. It was not a term Teal'c was familiar with either.

"The *Arc'tus* is our most treasured relic — made even more so now that it holds the ashes of our beloved queen, Egeria. It has traveled with us wherever we have gone, and only those Tok'ra who have been our most venerated leaders are given a place of honor within it. There is no greater symbol of the Tok'ra's esteem than to be chosen for this."

"Oh *really*?" Teal'c could detect a high degree of skepticism in O'Neill's tone. "Esteem, you say?"

"I'm sure Selmak would have appreciated the honor," Colonel Carter interjected before O'Neill could speak further. "As would my father."

If O'Neill had intended to say more, the pointed look which Colonel Carter directed his way appeared to make him reconsider. Daniel Jackson cast a relieved glance over his shoulder at Teal'c, who concurred. Considering O'Neill's unrelenting distrust of the Tok'ra, it would, perhaps, be for the best if his opinions, at least for today, remained unspoken.

Two Tok'ra stood guard at the entrance to the pyramid, neither of them acknowledging Ker'ai or the visitors as they entered. Teal'c did note that they were armed, which was to be expected, and for a moment he too felt the sense of vulnerability that O'Neill had expressed upon their departure. It swiftly passed, however, once the door had closed and Ker'ai was leading them down a well-lit corridor.

The pyramid was unusually plain. The walls were of unadorned stone — no sign of the ornate gold-encrusted décor so coveted by the Goa'uld — and there was a clean, simple feel to the place. Either the former occupant had been one of the less affluent Goa'uld, or the Tok'ra had seen fit to strip it of its excesses.

Ker'ai brought them to a modest-sized chamber from which several more corridors led in various directions, like spokes of a wheel. No others were in sight, but Teal'c could hear muffled activity coming from elsewhere.

"Please wait here. I will tell them you have arrived so that the rite may begin." The Tok'ra disappeared down one of the passageways.

O'Neill let out a sigh, as if he had been holding his breath the whole time.

"Jack?"

"Daniel?"

The two faced each other.

"It's probably best if we don't insult our hosts to their face."

"Did I say *anything*?"

"Technically — no. But sometimes it's the way you don't say anything."

O'Neill screwed up his face in irritation. "See — if I even *knew* what that meant, I'm sure I'd have a pithy response."

"I won't deny, it is a bit hypocritical that they're honoring Selmak this much, considering how they mostly shunned him these last months," Colonel Carter remarked, bluntly. "Especially considering they wouldn't even be here if he and my Dad hadn't smuggled us some of their technology."

"There!" replied O'Neill. "You see? I'm glad someone else noticed. But that's the Tok'ra for you — always talking out of their —"

"*Please — do not underestimate the true affection we feel toward Selmak, or Jacob Carter. I assure you, our esteem for them both is most sincere.*"

A tall, dignified woman, accompanied by Ker'ai and a small entourage, had quietly come up behind them from one of the corridors. Teal'c recognized the woman.

"Garshaw." Colonel Carter's face reddened at the realization that their conversation had most likely been overheard.

The woman smiled and bowed her head in greeting. She was little changed from the first time they had met her, which was to be expected. Her host, Yosuuf, seemed not to have aged a day.

"*It is good to see you again, Colonel Carter. General O'Neill. Dr. Jackson. Teal'c. The years and the losses have been far too many since last we met.*"

"It's good to see you too." Daniel Jackson's smile was sincere. "We didn't know…I mean, no one ever mentioned —" They had not interacted with Garshaw since their initial encounter with the Tok'ra. But then, comprehending the ever-changing leadership of the Tok'ra had been its own challenge. In the midst of so much secrecy, her fate had been, until now, unknown.

"Yes, I am still very much alive, and grateful to be able to regret my doubts about the Tau'ri which I expressed at our first encounter."

"Well, far be it from us to say we toldcha so —" O'Neill began, edgily.

"Indeed you did, General. But please — let us save such fond reminiscing for another time." There was a sarcastic edge to her tone that none of them missed, including O'Neill, who oddly seemed to appreciate it. Garshaw smiled and continued, *"Today we come together for a far more noble purpose: to pay tribute to Selmak of Indaara and Jacob Carter of Earth."*

Garshaw moved aside and another woman stepped forward. Teal'c could not begin to guess her age. She was certainly not young, but neither did she appear old. There was, however, a wariness in her eyes with which he was familiar, one which suggested that experience, as much as time, had taken as much as it had given.

"And of course, here is Ser'náme, who will be joining you, Colonel Carter, in the place of honor tonight."

Ser'náme barely acknowledged the introduction, saying nothing. Her deliberate gaze, however, assessed each of them in turn, her attention lingering longest on Colonel Carter.

"Were you a close friend of Selmak?" Colonel Carter finally broke the uncomfortable silence.

The wariness in Ser'náme's eyes intensified. "I would not exactly call us friends. I had not seen him in many, many years."

Yet another awkward silence was interrupted by Yosuuf, who appeared slightly flustered and apologetic.

"I'm sorry, Colonel. But, I thought surely — are you not aware of who Ser'náme is?"

"Actually, I'd have been more surprised if she *did* know."

Ser'náme's tone was cool and indifferent. "Or if Selmak had ever mentioned me at all, considering we have been estranged most of my life. You see," she clarified, in response to Colonel Carter's obvious bewilderment. "I am Selmak's daughter."

Daniel was brimming with questions, but Garshaw hustled them off down one of the corridors, allowing no time to process the bombshell Ser'náme had dropped.

"Carter?" Jack's voice was low enough for only SG-1 to hear.

Sam shook her head, her eyes wide with surprise. "I had no idea."

Jack growled something unintelligible, but his meaning was fairly clear. There seemed to be no end to the Tok'ra's secrets. And as far as secrets went, this one had the potential to be enormous. Daniel wasn't sure Jack fully comprehended what the implications of it were just yet. He wasn't even sure he did.

They were ushered into a dim, low-ceilinged hall into which several dozen Tok'ra had already gathered. At Garshaw's direction, escorted by Ker'ai, Sam and Ser'náme placed the box — the *so'ros* — upon a cloth-draped pedestal in the center of the room. Without speaking, Ker'ai motioned all five of them to take their place behind, where two rows of cushioned stools awaited. Apparently no one else was expected to sit, as they were the only seats Daniel could see.

Still standing — because no one had indicated they do otherwise yet — Daniel took in the rest of the hall. The Tok'ra were attired in coarse robes of various shades of brown and gray, and as they pulled the cowls up over their heads, their faces descended further into shadow. The room itself was lit only with torches and candles. The erratic light thrown across the dark, hooded figures put Daniel in mind of a medieval monastery — even more so when a low chanting began.

"What the hell?" muttered Jack, under his breath.

"It is a recounting of the life of Selmak," explained Teal'c, after listening for a few moments. "Beginning with his spawning by Egeria."

"Wait — wasn't Selmak, like, 2000 years old?" hissed Jack, realizing the implications.

"Indeed."

Jack groaned.

"We are not required to stand the entire time," Ser'náme whispered. She and Sam were in front of them. "Although it is expected until the recitation of the names of Selmak's hosts is complete. When they begin to tell of his many and wondrous deeds, we may sit." There was a trace of contempt in her voice. Whether it was for Selmak, the ritual, or both, Daniel wasn't sure.

Personally, he found the rite itself enthralling. He had never really viewed the Tok'ra this way before. They had their traditions and their culture, of course, but as far as Daniel knew, this was the first time anyone from Earth had been included in something so intimate. It made sense that, with the establishment of a permanent home world, the Tok'ra would begin to embrace their cultural identity more deeply. Having to flee at a moment's notice from attacking Goa'uld would have made maintaining formal ceremonies difficult at best. With that threat now removed, it would be fascinating, from an anthropological perspective, to observe Tok'ra society evolve. The opportunities for discoveries like this across the galaxy — across many galaxies — now that Earth was relatively safe, were limitless.

The thought of it made his heart beat faster.

Daniel didn't realize that they'd come to the end of the names of Selmak's hosts until he saw the others settle into their seats. He quickly joined them.

"So this goes on all night?" Sam asked Ser'náme, quietly.

"Tedious, is it not?" She grimaced. "But then, what do you expect? The Tok'ra never have been able to let go of the past. It is our worst failing."

"Then, you yourself are Tok'ra?" Daniel leaned forward, so as not to speak too loudly himself. All the questions he'd put on hold when the chanting had begun came rushing back now.

"That depends upon your definition, Dr. Jackson. Physiologically, I am human. Just like all of you. Well — except for you." She indicated Teal'c.

"You don't have a symbiote," Sam said. Of course, she would have picked up on that.

"No, I do not."

The hairs on the back of Daniel's neck prickled. If she didn't have a symbiote —

"So, if Selmak was your dad — how does that work, exactly?" Jack leaned in to join the whispered conversation. Daniel's stomach tightened. Leave it to Jack to ask the six million dollar question without realizing it.

Ser'náme sighed heavily, as if this were a question she had grown weary of answering. "A human by the name of Kadon was my biological father. He was blended with Selmak when I was conceived and born. My biological mother was a woman name Pria. She was host to Selmak's mate, Ja'nok. I had, in essence, two sets of parents."

"I guess it never occurred to me that the Tok'ra actually had children," Sam reflected.

"They do not," Ser'náme replied. "At least, they are not supposed to."

A chill passed through Daniel. That was it, then, just as he'd feared. "Then you are *harsesis*," he concluded. "Or, at least the Tok'ra version of one."

"No!" Ser'náme's response was swift and vehement. It earned them all a sharp glance from Ker'ai, who was standing nearby. "I am not *harsesis*."

"But if both your parents were hosts — how is it any different than with the Goa'uld?" Daniel tried to keep his voice low, yet loud enough to be heard over the chanting which had now progressed to a sort of antiphon between the primary chanters and the rest of the assembly.

"There is no difference. And had nature been allowed to take its course, I *would* have been *harsesis*." She turned to face him and Daniel could see a flash of anger in her eyes. "But unlike the Goa'uld, who merely kill any child born to host parents, the Tok'ra have devised a far worse fate for theirs."

She had the rest of SG-1's interest now too, their attention to the rite forgotten.

"I don't understand," Daniel replied.

Ser'náme's face hardened. "The Tok'ra, in their infinite ingenuity, discovered a way to deactivate the *harsesis* gene before a child is born. If Tok'ra hosts insist a child be carried to term, it is required that the fetus undergo such a procedure. It is difficult to do, and very dangerous, for both the mother and the child, and not something undertaken lightly."

"Was not Saroosh host to Selmak prior to Jacob Carter?" asked Teal'c. "And had they not been together for nearly 200 years?"

"One hundred and eighty-three," clarified Ser'náme. "Kadon was Selmak's host prior to Saroosh."

"So that would make you —" Jack was trying to do the mental math.

"A great deal older than I look," she supplied, curtly. "The one benefit of being Tok'ra-born which they could not take from me."

Daniel's thoughts raced. If only he'd known about this procedure before — but no. He had found Sha're too late. It would have changed nothing.

"When was the last time you saw Selmak?" Sam's question brought Daniel back to the present.

Ser'náme shrugged with seemingly forced exaggeration. "Our paths last crossed many years ago. The encounter was brief and not particularly amicable."

"What about your mother — *mothers*?" Daniel wished they were somewhere less public where he could more easily ask all the questions that were popping into his mind. This was too much like whispering in church.

"Killed. Both of them. Some undercover operation, trying to undermine Bastet, I believe. I was fairly young and no one ever told me all of the details."

"I'm sorry," Daniel offered, but Ser'náme merely shrugged again. He wondered if it was a practiced indifference.

"You cannot miss what you do not have, Dr. Jackson. I rarely saw my parents anyway. Duty is the first order, when you are Tok'ra."

"But you've stayed with them all these years?" This was yet one more side to the Tok'ra Daniel had never seen before today. He realized just how little they truly knew about their allies, even after all this time.

"Hardly." Ser'náme gave a small, bitter laugh. "I had no intention of wasting my life fighting the Goa'uld. I left as soon as I was old enough to fly a tel'tak, and I have been on my own ever since."

"No offense," Jack interjected. "But it's pretty clear you're not especially fond of the Tok'ra — or Selmak, for that matter. So I've gotta ask — why are you even here?"

"Jack —" Daniel's attempt at admonishment was waved away by Ser'náme.

"It's all right, Dr. Jackson." She leveled a steady look at Jack. "As I said, General. We are a duty-bound people. It is our tradition, and I had no choice but to come."

"Even after all these years?" Teal'c asked, picking up a bit on Jack's incredulity.

"Strange, isn't it?" Her smile was not exactly warm.

Over their shoulder, Ker'ai cleared his throat. Daniel looked up and saw Garshaw giving them a reprimanding stare from across the hall. Their private conversation had become a little too obvious.

Duly chastised, Daniel and the others lapsed back into silence, but he could not concentrate on the chant. The ramifications of a Tok'ra *harsesis* were something he'd never before considered. If it worked the same way as with the Goa'uld — and there was no reason to believe otherwise — would such an offspring have the genetic memory of only the Tok'ra, or of the Goa'uld who predated them as well? Egeria, he knew, had instilled in her children the ethos that made them reject the ways of Ra and the System Lords. Would that be passed on to a Tok'ra *harsesis* or would it have to vie for control with the darker knowledge from the millennia of Goa'uld who preceded her? Would Egeria's legacy, diluted by a generation and placed within a human mind, be strong enough to prevail? Or would it lose the battle, as he himself had, when Shifu had shown him what it was like to be tempted with such vast power?

Daniel wasn't sure the others fully grasped the implications of what Ser'náme had told them. They had obligingly turned their attention back to the antiphony, Ser'náme's story probably little more than a curious footnote. And he supposed they were right. He was the one who was over-reacting. Any questions about a Tok'ra *harsesis* were, after all, merely academic at this point. Ser'náme wasn't one, and that was the end of it. He needed to drop the matter and focus on the ritual before him, as the others were doing.

Once he actually listened, Daniel found he could follow the chant fairly easily. Some of Selmak's early efforts against a pre-ascended Anubis were being recounted. It was fascinating, really — so much of the Tok'ra history being retold. He knew Selmak had been a leader and much respected in his time, but Daniel hadn't understood until now the extent to which Selmak had personally been responsible for so many of the Tok'ra's accomplishments. The past 2000 years of galactic history was unfolding like an epic poem. Daniel felt like he should be writing it all down.

He hoped, now that the conflict with the Goa'uld was behind them, he could get back to things like this. It was why he'd become an archeologist in the first place, and there was so much out there still to learn and discover. With Sam temporarily assigned to the Prometheus and Teal'c returning to the Free Jaffa Nation, there really wasn't much point in his staying at the SGC any longer. Now that Atlantis was back on the grid, Daniel was determined to step up his pressure on Jack to be allowed to go. He'd already pored over most of the reports Elizabeth Weir had sent back, but nothing could substitute for actually being there.

Right now, though, he had an excellent opportunity to learn more about Tok'ra history, if only he could pay attention. Apparently he wasn't the only one having difficulty. Jack had already given up and was dozing. Teal'c's gaze had a distant, glazed look to it, leaving Daniel to wonder if he hadn't entered into a state of pseudo-Kel'no'reem. Only Ser'náme and Sam still gave the appearance of listening, although in Sam's case Daniel was sure it was more out of courtesy than comprehension. Then there was Ker'ai, standing off to their right, whose focus seemed to be more on Ser'náme than anything else. Daniel wondered if maybe he hadn't been told to keep an extra careful eye on her, given her less than filial feelings toward Selmak.

After another hour or so, even Daniel began to feel restless. Sam started absently checking her watch every few minutes and Jack, periodically waking up, would clear his throat and shift position before nodding off again. It reached the point where Daniel thought he couldn't endure another moment of sitting, when, to his relief, a chime echoed throughout the chamber. In response, the chanting momentarily swelled in crescendo and then stopped.

Ser'náme stood and the rest of SG-1 followed suit, once Teal'c had nudged Jack awake. The chime sounded again, and Garshaw and the others began to slowly and silently file out of the room. As Ser'náme and SG-1 followed them, Daniel noticed Ker'ai remained behind, having stepped in front of the *so'ros* to serve as guard.

The solemn procession brought them to yet another chamber. However, this one was well-lit and laid out with food and drink. The atmosphere here was relaxed. People stood in groups, their heads uncovered, talking and eating. It had all the earmarks of a party.

"And this would be — ?" asked Jack looking around.

"At the half-way mark, the Rite pauses so that we might refresh ourselves with nourishment and rest," explained Garshaw, coming up to them. *"Please, help yourself to the food and drink, and if you have need, we have prepared quarters where you might sleep a while, if you so require."*

Ser'náme bowed slightly. "If you all will excuse me, I believe I will take advantage of this opportunity to rest."

Garshaw's eyes narrowed slightly, but she eventually returned the bow. *"Of course. The chimes will alert you when the ceremony is to resume."*

Without bothering to acknowledge the others, Selmak's daughter left the room. Daniel was disappointed. There were so many things he had wanted to ask her. Perhaps later he would have a chance.

"So. Tok'ra food —" Jack was eyeing the buffet table skeptically, after Garshaw too had walked away.

"I do not think you will find it objectionable, O'Neill," Teal'c assured him.

"I guess this is the 'wake' part of the wake," Sam said. "For some of us, anyway," she tossed Jack a disparaging look. Apparently Daniel wasn't the only one who'd caught him napping.

The food was surprisingly appealing and Daniel tried a little of everything. Teal'c, likewise, filled his plate, although his selection seemed confined to mostly fruit.

"Is that *guango*?" Daniel thought he recognized the morsel Teal'c had just popped in his mouth as the fruit Harry Mayborne had named.

"I believe you are correct, Daniel Jackson." He took another bite. "I highly recommend it."

Jack and Sam joined them, although going by the token servings on both their plates, neither was particularly tempted by the Tok'ra cuisine. There was no place to sit — apparently the Tok'ra were averse to chairs — so they stood, balancing their food and drink.

As they ate, Daniel voiced his concerns about the significance of a Tok'ra *harsesis*. As he suspected, the others hadn't realized the possible implications.

"So you're saying it could have been bad," said Jack, frowning as he fished his finger around in his drink for what Daniel was sure was nothing.

"Very bad."

"As bad as that Shifu kid might have been?" Jack looked up, shaking liquid off his finger.

Sam nodded. "If, what Daniel says is true, then yes, at least as bad — possibly much worse."

"Well, chalk one up for Tok'ra science, then," quipped Jack with a slight fist pump.

"Are not these concerns unwarranted, Daniel Jackson?" asked Teal'c, finishing the last piece of fruit on his plate. "I fail to see what threat Ser'náme herself poses. She is, after all, not *harsesis*."

Teal'c was right, of course. Daniel didn't know why he was still dwelling on it — aside from the fact that it brought up a slew of memories he'd tucked away a long time ago. The Tok'ra undoubtedly knew what they were doing, and, at least on this matter, second-guessing them was completely counter-productive.

Garshaw eventually rejoined them and explained what would happen next. Apparently the rite would continue as before with more chanting, after which they would carry the *so'ros* outdoors so that, at the moment of sunrise, it could be placed in the *Arc'tum*. Once the *Arc'tum* was returned to its sanctuary, the ceremony would be concluded.

"*The Tok'ra are grateful to you, Colonel Carter, for allowing us this opportunity to honor Selmak in this way,*" Garshaw told her. *"I know he and the High Council did not always see eye to eye in later years, but we would like to believe that our bonds remained strong, in spite of our disagreements."*

"My father assured me that Selmak had no objection to being returned to the Tok'ra should such an invitation be extended." The coolness in Sam's voice was evident to everyone, including Garshaw. According to Sam, the Tok'ra had tried to mend fences when her father was on his deathbed, and while Jacob had been accommodating, he'd made Sam promise not to completely let them off the hook. Daniel thought she managed to do that quite well. Even Garshaw had the sense to look abashed.

The chimes announced that it was time to resume the ceremony. As his eyes adjusted to the lack of light, Daniel saw that Ker'ai still stood vigil in front of the *so'ros*. If he had to guess, he'd say the man hadn't twitched so much as a finger the entire time they'd been gone.

As they took their places, there was no sign of Selmak's daughter. Daniel shot Sam a questioning look, but she just shrugged. Across the way, whispered concerns began amongst Garshaw and the others.

"Can't they begin without Ser'náme?" Sam asked Ker'ai, who had relocated to his former spot beside them.

"It is up to Garshaw."

Looking displeased, Garshaw nevertheless seemed inclined to proceed, as she nodded toward the cantor who raised his cowl. The others did likewise and the recitation of Selmak's life began again.

"I will look for her," Ker'ai whispered, but to Daniel's surprise, Sam shook her head.

"No — I think I should go. They won't mind, will they?"

Ker'ai's hesitation suggested that they might, in fact, mind very much, but Sam didn't give him a chance to object. "Which way?" she asked, and Ker'ai tilted his head toward the nearest arched exit.

Nodding her thanks, and ignoring Jack's whispered

"Carter?", Sam slipped out. Daniel wondered if someone ought to go with her, but realized it probably would look bad if any more of them left. He had a feeling Sam wanted to do this alone. She would be fine. After all, he was the one who'd argued about how safe they were here.

One glance at Jack, though, and Daniel realized how ineffectual that argument had been. And if he were being honest, deep down in his gut, Daniel wasn't sure he completely bought it either.

Sam usually didn't give much credence to hunches, but when she arrived at the quarters one of the Tok'ra had identified for her as having been assigned to Ser'náme, she wasn't a bit surprised to find them empty. And not just devoid of Ser'náme herself, but of all signs that anyone had ever been there or intended to return.

Somehow she'd just had a feeling.

She was having another one now. Ser'náme had mentioned flying a tel'tak. Sam needed to find where the ships were kept.

Another helpful Tok'ra gave her directions. The air outside was cool and fresh, and Sam realized just how many hours they'd been cooped up inside the pyramid. She supposed she'd better get used to it again. The prep work over the past few weeks had afforded her the opportunity to spend a fair amount of time topside, but with that done, the Prometheus' orders were to push the boundaries of known space in their galaxy. It might be a month or more before she had a chance to breathe anything but recycled air again.

Not that she wasn't excited to go — it had been a while since she'd been able to devote so much time just to pure science. But it was one more change amidst so many other recent changes in her life — in all their lives, really. It was going to take some getting used to.

With twin moons overhead to light the way, Sam had no problem finding the Tok'ra's equivalent of an airfield, although trudging through the sand in her regulation pumps had her longing for her combat boots. Several dozen ships of various shapes and sizes were lined up in neat rows, their hulls reflecting the moonlight. Scanning them, Sam spotted one with its interior lit. It was a tel'tak — and someone was on board.

In a way, Sam could empathize with Ser'náme. Had things not worked out as they had, she herself might have been in the same situation, left with only bitter words spoken in anger and regrets enough for the rest of her life. There was a certain irony that she had Selmak to thank for the very things which he seemed incapable of giving his own daughter. Sam doubted that anything she might say to Ser'náme would make a difference, but she felt she had to try.

It must not have occurred to Selmak's daughter that anyone would follow her, because the exterior door was not secured. It had barely shut behind Sam when the door in the bulkhead opened and Ser'náme appeared. She pulled up sharply and gaped.

"What are *you* doing here?" Her tone suggested that she had been expecting someone, Sam realized. Just not her.

"I thought you'd want to know." Sam gestured vaguely in the direction of the pyramid. "They've resumed the Rite of *Hak'tyl*."

Ser'náme glanced uneasily over her shoulder into the bridge before stepping fully into the cargo bay and slapping the panel, shutting the door behind her. But not before Sam glimpsed a familiar box on the floor of the bridge.

"Is that Selmak's *so'ros*?" So much for trying to be sympathetic. But how could it be the *so'ros*? When she'd left the hall, it had still been on the pedestal, exactly where she and Ser'náme had placed it. Not to mention that Ker'ai had been guarding it the whole time.

Or had he?

Ser'náme eyed Sam appraisingly and finally countered, "And if it is?"

Sam's eyes narrowed. "Then I guess I'd want to know why you took it — and why you replaced it with what I presume is an empty one."

Ser'náme sniffed. "Maybe, like you, Colonel Carter, I would prefer to keep my father's remains close to me, rather than entrust them to the Tok'ra."

Sam shook her head. "I highly doubt that. Why would you care now, when you couldn't be bothered when he was alive?"

Ser'náme's response came in the shape of the zat she withdrew from behind her and aimed at Sam. "I don't. At least, not in the way you mean it."

Sam sighed. She should have seen this coming. "Ker'ai helped you, didn't he?" It was the only way she could have stolen the box. The pieces were falling into place now. "That's who you were expecting — not me." Maybe they'd been going to run away together, although, relatively speaking, Ker'ai seemed awfully young.

"It isn't what you think." Ser'náme's voice shook slightly. "When he was a boy, I saved his life by bringing him to the Tok'ra. He's like —"

"A son?" Sam supplied. Ser'náme didn't answer, but her silence did. "They're going to realize you switched the boxes, you know. When they go to put it in the *Arc'tus*. Ker'ai will be the first one they suspect."

She knew she'd found a soft spot by the flash of remorse in Ser'náme's eyes. But just as swiftly, it was gone. Her voice turned hard.

"We were supposed to have been gone by then. But he's clever. He'll figure something out. And he'll understand why I had to leave him behind."

So much for appealing to her maternal sense, although it had been worth a try. Without a weapon herself, Sam didn't have much leverage. She could almost hear Jack muttering "I told you so —"

Still. A little authoritative insistence couldn't hurt. "I can't allow you to take the *so'ros*." She gave it her best Lieutenant Colonel voice.

Ser'náme merely shrugged. "I really don't think you have much of a choice, Colonel." Keeping the zat pointed at Sam, she keyed the door to the bridge and reopened it, motioning Sam to go through. Sam took a final look around the cargo bay, hoping to spot something useful, but the space was mostly empty and nothing remotely helpful presented itself. She had no choice but to comply.

Once they were on the bridge, Ser'náme locked the door behind them.

"Why *are* you doing this?" Sam still couldn't figure out Ser'náme's motives. "To get back at Selmak, somehow?"

"It is not my intention to harm you, Colonel." Ser'náme ignored the question again, stepping up to the helm. Sam felt the vibration of the engines as the ship fired up. "Once I am safely away from here, I will drop you at a planet with a Stargate. You can find your way back from there."

"Is it to get back at the Tok'ra for what they did to you?" Sam persisted. "Is that what this is about?"

Ser'náme stiffened with rage. "You cannot *begin* to comprehend what they did to me — what they took from me." Her voice was ice as she engaged the downward thrusters. The ship slowly rose.

"I know what a *harsesis* is," Sam replied, cautiously. There was a new and dangerous tenor in the tone of Ser'náme's voice which worried her more than the zat, which was still pointed her way. "I also know there are inherent dangers of having that much knowledge. Did you ever consider that maybe you were better off, in the long run, without that burden?"

They were high above the Tok'ra city now, the luminous glow of the crystal buildings fading swiftly as they climbed.

"Don't talk to me about burdens, Colonel," Ser'náme retorted. "You have no idea."

Flashes of Jolinar's life sprang into Sam's thoughts. Memories. Emotions. She pushed them aside.

"Then tell me."

Ser'náme kept her eyes fixed on the viewport. "There is a stigma, being a Tok'ra child. Even when they've taken everything away from you, it's still not enough for them. They're watching — always watching — worried that they might have gotten it wrong." She paused, adjusting their heading. Sam kept silent, waiting for her to continue. "They tried to couch it in meaningless terms like 'an abundance of caution', but when I grew old enough, I understood. It was fear. Their fear. Of me. So do not speak to me of 'burdens.'" Her voice rose. "Do you know what it's like, for over two hundred years to be seen only as a potential threat — to see the people who might otherwise have loved you, look upon you as if somewhere, inside of you, lurks a monster — to have those *you* loved turned against you — not because of what you were but because of what they feared you had the potential to be?" She turned and faced Sam, her eyes fierce. "Have you ever looked into the eyes of those you held most dear and seen only fear look back at you, Colonel?"

Sam took a deep breath as her own memories came: the horror on the face of her team, watching her through the bars of a cell when Jolinar had blended with her; the disdain in their eyes as they confronted the Entity who had hijacked her body. She swallowed. "Actually — yes."

Ser'náme was taken aback, some of the heat fading from her complexion. Her eyes narrowed, as if weighing the truth of Sam's response. "Then perhaps you can understand. If only a little."

Through the thinning atmosphere Sam could see the ochre colored land mass receding. They were coming up through the planet's thermosphere.

"And how does what you're doing now help?"

Ser'náme gave a mirthless laugh. "Because now I can finally

become the monster they always feared."

It took Sam a moment to grasp what she meant. "Wait — you think you can make yourself a *harsesis*? How?" There was only one way to be a *harsesis*, as far as Sam knew. Her eyes lit on the *so'ros* again and Ser'náme's meaning became chillingly clear. "You want to rewrite your own genetic code?"

"Not rewrite. Switch back on," Ser'náme replied, matter-of-factly. "It's taken me the better part of two lifetimes, but I now know it can be done. And how to do it."

"With Selmak's DNA."

"Precisely."

The scientific ramifications of what Ser'náme was proposing were tremendous. Research like that —

Sam reined herself in. The science would have to wait. If Daniel's concerns about a Tok'ra *harsesis* were valid, then stopping Ser'náme was all that mattered right now.

There was one thing that might work in her favor.

"You do realize that all you have there are ashes." Sam nodded toward the *so'ros*. "The comingled ashes of Selmak *and* my dad. Good luck getting Selmak's DNA out of those."

"Fortunately, I only need a small sample of a single bone fragment, Colonel." Ser'náme was undeterred. "And because of the naquadah in their system, symbiotes have incredibly durable bones. I have seen them survive even the worst inferno."

Sam frowned. Ser'náme seemed to have covered all the bases. She was going to need a different strategy.

They were coming through the planet's upper atmosphere now. The field of stars broke into view as the reflected light from below began to diminish. It wouldn't be long before Ser'náme could engage the hyperdrive.

"So, you become a *harsesis* — then what?" Talking Ser'náme out of this seemed like Sam's only option for now. "Destroy the Tok'ra? Take over the galaxy? Reboot the universe, like Anubis tried to do?"

Ser'náme's dismissive silence gave Sam hope. If this really

wasn't about galactic domination, then maybe she could be reasoned with.

"Look — I may not know what it was like for you, but I do understand what it's like to have other people try to define who you are." The bitter exchange with her dad over joining NASA still pained her, despite their having forgiven each other for it long ago. "Even people who love you and have the best of intentions for you can make you feel trapped and resentful. And sometimes we get so wrapped up in what others expect us to be, that we end up defining ourselves in the same limited terms." How many years had she seen herself only within the narrow scope of soldier and scientist? Ironic that her dad had, in a way, been the one who'd helped her move beyond that.

"The point is," Sam continued when Ser'náme still hadn't spoken, "if you do this, you're giving in to the Tok'ra — you're allowing them the final say in who you are. They're the ones who'll win in the end, because you'll prove them right. If you want power — real power — then defy their expectations. Whoever you are or think you want to be, make it your choice. Not Selmak's. Not the Tok'ra's. Yours."

Ser'náme cursed heatedly. At first, Sam thought it was directed at her, but then the ship shuddered violently. They were under fire.

"So much for Tok'ra hospitality," growled Ser'náme. "They must have had my ship under surveillance." She turned her attention to the helm and the ship jinked, avoiding another shot. Overhead, Sam saw two Tok'ra gliders circling around for another pass.

A hit from behind nearly knocked them both to the floor.

"We have lost the hyperdrive." Ser'náme's hand flew over the control panel when she'd righted herself.

Sam joined her at the console, checking the other readings. She didn't like what she saw. "The shields aren't going to hold much longer." One more hit and they'd be down. Sensors showed the three ships regrouping, and another three rising from the planet's surface to join them. Sam hoped they were only trying to disable the tel'tak, not destroy it. Unfortunately outcomes didn't always match intentions.

"It's not too late, Ser'náme — just go back."

"No — no!" Selmak's daughter pounded the console with such fury that Sam backed away. "I can't!" Beneath the arrogance, Sam detected a true note of despair in her voice. "I…I can't. Even if I wanted to — it's too late."

"I'm sure if you explain —"

"You do not understand — if I go back now, they will never allow me to leave. They will lock me away forever in those tunnels, just as they tried to do when I was a child." Sam saw desperation in her eyes. "I could never live like that again. I won't." She took the ship into a hard dive. "I'd rather die first."

Sam had to grip the console to keep her balance. "Well, I wouldn't," she shot back. Great. Now it was a race between who would destroy them first — Ser'náme or the Tok'ra. She needed another option — quickly.

Something slid against Sam's leg. It was the *so'ros*. She picked it up.

Maybe —

"If there was a way out of this, would you take it?" she asked.

"I'm not going back down there, if that's what you mean." The ship was weaving back and forth. Sam couldn't tell if Ser'náme was trying to avoid the Tok'ra's shots or fly into them. In either case, the inertial dampeners were having a hard time keeping up. Sam was glad she'd gone light on the refreshments.

"That's not what I mean. Look. I can fix the hyperdrive and you can leave. Here." Sam held out the *so'ros*. "You have as much right to this as I do. What you do with it is up to you." It was a calculated risk, but she had to take it.

Ser'náme looked at the box as if she'd never seen it before. Then she looked at Sam.

"I never wanted the knowledge — or the power, you know," she said finally. "Not really."

"Then move on," Sam told her. Simple to say, much harder to do. Leaving behind what was safe and familiar was never easy, as she was learning only too well these days. "Surprise yourself — be someone new."

Ser'náme almost laughed. "At my age." She eyed the box again. "I'm not sure I know how. Still." She sighed and turned back toward the console. "I suppose it *is* better than dying. Very well, then, Colonel. You seem to have all the answers. Tell me what you want me to do."

"The timing of your escape was most fortuitous, Colonel Carter," remarked Garshaw, smoothly. *"We have just received word that Ser'náme was able to activate her hyperdrive and flee before our ships could escort her back to the surface."*

For someone who'd ringed back to the planet supposedly just in the nick of time, Jack couldn't help but think Sam looked particularly composed. The side glance she shot him confirmed that there was more going on here than met the eye — and also that this was neither the time nor the place for specifics.

At least his blood pressure could go back to normal now. Yelling at Garshaw for the past ten minutes hadn't exactly helped either.

The two women were regarding each other appraisingly. "I think the important thing is that no harm was done," Sam finally replied, unperturbed. "And that Selmak's and my Dad's wishes can be carried out." She held the other woman's gaze another moment before Garshaw finally dropped her eyes and nodded.

"Just so, Colonel. And we have you to thank for that," she conceded. *"Now, if you will kindly return the so'ros, we can conclude…"*

Sam interrupted her.

"Actually, I don't think so."

Garshaw's chin raised in irritation. *"I beg your pardon?"*

"Um…Sam?" Daniel stepped forward, prepared to mediate.

Jack looked at Teal'c who merely raised an eyebrow. He hadn't a clue either, apparently.

Sam ignored Daniel — and the Tok'ra who had stepped forward to take the box. Jack recognized the tight Don't-Mess-with-Sam-Carter smile she was giving Garshaw.

"I'm afraid there needs to be a slight change of plans."

The blue glow of the active wormhole shimmered across what remained of the tall table that had stood there moments before. Slowly the now unsupported legs collapsed upon themselves and fell, just as the Stargate deactivated itself, plunging everything back into the pale light of early dawn. There was a lingering moment of collective silence and then, just like that, it was over. The soft rustling of robes and quiet murmur of voices signaled the end of the ceremony.

Jack breathed a sigh of relief.

"You are all, of course, welcome to remain here a while to rest and refresh, General." The hospitality of Garshaw's invitation wasn't quite matched by her tone. *"But should you prefer to return home, I can certainly accommodate that as soon as you wish."* She smiled sparingly and walked away.

"Here's your hat, what's your hurry," muttered Jack after her. Not that he had any intention of sticking around one minute longer than they had to.

Sam was staring at the spot where, only a few moments before, the box with her dad's and Selmak's ashes had been. Jack went to stand beside her.

"For what it's worth, I think it was the right call."

She nodded. "Me too. I'm pretty sure I got through to Ser'náme, but even so — as long as the *so'ros* remained intact, it might always have been a temptation. Sometimes you just have to help people get rid of the things that keep them from moving forward."

"That you do."

There must have been something in the tone of his voice,

because she was looking at him questioningly.

Not exactly how he'd wanted to do it, but he supposed there was no time like the present.

"The transfers came through. I just got them this morning."

"DC and Nevada?" There was a hint of excitement in her voice.

"Yup. Hammond's doing." Jack didn't even want to know how. "You'll still be able to go out with Prometheus, though. Pendergast insisted."

She nodded, thoughtfully. "Do Daniel and Teal'c know?"

"Not yet. Teal'c's all wrapped up with the Jaffa stuff. And Daniel —"

"You know, you're going to have to let him go to Atlantis eventually."

Jack merely shrugged. "No rush." He might just leave that little privilege up to his successor — whoever that turned out to be. He did have a few ideas.

Daniel and Teal'c joined them in front of the Stargate. Over Sam's shoulder Jack had seen them talking to Garshaw. Whatever it was they'd been discussing had Daniel flush with excitement.

"The Tok'ra have agreed to give us this gate address." The enthusiasm in Daniel's voice was palpable. "And although they request that we keep it confidential, Garshaw did say they would be open to establishing communication with the Free Jaffa Nation, in order to share information about the remaining Goa'uld at large."

"A proposal I will be happy to bring before the Jaffa High Council," Teal'c replied, inclining his head.

"Oh the times, they are a-changin'," quipped Jack. There was more truth to that than he really wanted to think about right now.

"Yes. Yes, they are," Daniel reflected, gazing out over the Tok'ra's shiny new city. Jack figured he had a day, at most, before he was being dogged with another Atlantis request.

Teal'c made no reply, lost in his own thoughts as he too

seemed to contemplate the landscape. Jack knew that look. He'd seen it in short-timers before. The big guy had already moved on.

Only Carter was looking his way. In the midst of everything, Jack had nearly forgotten the whole purpose of this trip. She looked tired, but managed a half-smile, nonetheless.

"Time to go back?" she asked. Jack found himself shaking his head.

"Time to go forward," he replied. She gave a small nod of understanding.

"Dial it up, Daniel," Jack said, still holding her gaze. "Let's go home."

STARGATE ATLANTIS
Worshipper

Melissa Scott

This story takes place after book eight of the Stargate Atlantis Legacy series.

GEMMION Saer woke before the dream's dreadful end, as she had taught herself to do over the centuries, and lay gasping in the hive's embrace until her heartbeat slowed and the dream-images faded. At the back of her mind, she could feel the hive's concern — well, perhaps that was too strong a word; *Sanctuary* was no more sentient than any other hiveship, but it was aware of her fear, and troubled by it — and sent a cautious thread of mingled concern and reassurance to calm the air. She took a deep breath, marshaling her strength — she did not want to draw the attention of the Hivemaster — and let the light rise around her, driving back the last of the nightmare. Familiar shapes surrounded her: the curved cup piled high with pillows and soft wool that was her bed, the vines that wound around the support pillars, blooming with warm light, the fountain that trickled down one wall, and she unfolded herself from the nest, the air soft on her skin. It was still early in the day-watch, and a tendril of mist crept under her door, a last gift from *Sanctuary* itself. She sighed — humans, even worshippers who had served the Wraith as long as she, found the mists more chilling than soothing — but allowed a flash of thanks to reach the ship. She felt its satisfaction, and perhaps relief, and then its attention was withdrawn.

And that was good, a space of privacy that would allow her to rid herself of the last of the dream. She shrugged on a robe and turned toward the door, intending to call for tea and food,

but before she could signal, the door slid open to reveal her
senior assistant.

"Oh. You're awake."

Gemmion lifted an eyebrow at that, and Sytia let out her
breath in an exasperated sigh.

"You know what I meant. Anyway, the Queen wants you."

"Officially? As Chatelaine?" Gemmion frowned, trying to
remember anything that had happened among the hive's human
servants that might have warranted the Queen's attention, but
Sytia shook her head.

"As an advisor."

Better, Gemmion thought. If this was a matter of advice, it
was unlikely there was any problem with the small colony of
human worshippers who lived outside the hive's holding cells,
no longer considered food except in extreme emergency. Still,
it was important to honor the Queen, and she turned to the
section of wall that concealed her storage space. "Help me
dress, then."

With Sytia's help, it didn't take long to don the blood-
black gown that was her second-best, and the weight of jewelry that had been the Queen's gifts over the last centuries,
the coronet with the strands of fire-opals and the great bib
necklace that hid the feeding scar on her breastbone, brace-
lets and anklets as wide as armor. They were all rough gold,
embossed with flowers and stars and the heads of animals
real and imagined: the Wraith of *Sanctuary* preferred silver
for their own adornment, and decked their human follow-
ers in gold instead. She worked her shoulders, settling the
familiar weight more comfortably, and waved her hand to
open the door to her own quarters.

As always, the worshippers' section was brightly lit, and
drier than the rest of the hive. The central meeting space
was nearly empty now at the start of the day, the individual
living cells around its edges mostly closed, their residents
still sleeping. Only Tyan was awake, busy with the bread for

first-meal; he straightened, seeing her gown, but she did not give him time to question.

There were drones on guard at the single entrance to their quarters, and a young blade in charge of them. He dipped his head in respect, long silver hair whispering across the leather of his coat, and spoke mind-to-mind, his mental presence like water swirling over mountain stones. *Chatelaine. The Queen bade me escort you. Will Sytia accompany us?*

Gemmion paused. "No, she will not."

Sytia looked annoyed at that, but she had not arrayed herself, was not properly dressed to meet the Queen. That was a mistake Gemmion had never made, when she was first assistant to the old chatelaine, and Sytia needed to learn not to make that error again.

"You'll wait here," Gemmion said, and Sytia bowed her head. Of course, if they had miscalculated — if they had misunderstood, and this was punishment or demotion, then Sytia would be in charge until the Queen chose a new chatelaine. She looked back at the blade. "Thank you. I appreciate your company."

Torrent bowed unspeaking, and she followed him through the maze of corridors. The worshippers were housed in the outer edges of the hive, in a segment that in other hives would house a secondary feeding cell; the Queen's quarters were at the heart of the hive, shielded by the greater part of the ship's mass, fantastic, filigreed chambers grown from bone and the hive's willing flesh. It was a long walk, and she was regretting her missed meal by the time they entered the last spiral.

The antechamber was tenanted only by drones and the older blade in charge of them. He passed them through to the queen's private chamber with a bow and a nod, and Gemmion made her deepest obeisance to the figure that lounged in the central throne. The Queen inclined her head in acknowledgement, and spared a smile for Torrent.

Thank you. You may leave us now.

Torrent backed away, and Gemmion straightened cautiously. This was, it seemed, as informal as Sytia had promised: the Queen herself was clearly at ease, a loose black coat over her narrow gown, and only two of the members of her zenana — the favored blades and clevermen who held authority from her — were present as well. There was even a game abandoned on a side table, a spiral of opalescent pieces covering most of the board. The Consort Jewel leaned against the back of the Queen's throne, a tall, powerful blade of the lineage of Night. His first queen had been killed in the wars with Queen Death, and the Queen had found him commanding a damaged cruiser, struggling to keep himself and what remained of his crew alive. He was new to the role of Consort, but none of the other blades seemed to grudge him the promotion, and that alone was enough to impress. By contrast, the Master of Sciences Biological was the Queen's own brother, Flame to her Ice, who had chosen to stay with her rather than to seek a queen elsewhere. They both looked concerned, Gemmion thought, and perhaps Flame was curious, as befitted a cleverman, but neither seemed actually angry.

Chatelaine, the Queen said, and Gemmion curtsied again. "Lady."

I expect you've heard of this new arrangement with the Lanteans, Ice said. *That we will agree on borders and sort out our feeding grounds among ourselves, leaving their chosen systems alone.*

Gemmion waited, and when it became clear that the Queen would not continue, she cleared her throat. "I had heard that, yes."

And had you heard about the retrovirus? That was Flame, cocking his head to one side.

"There have been rumors of such a thing," Gemmion said. "That there might be something that would allow us to serve the Wraith without dying in the process. But no more than rumors."

Oh, it's true enough, Flame said. *The Lanteans have worked with the clevermen of Alabaster's hive to develop a retrovirus that allows us to feed on humans without killing them. Or at least without killing them immediately, no one knows all the parameters — *

Which are not really important here, Jewel said.

Well, but they might be, Flame answered. *Probably will be.*

The Queen lifted a hand, and he subsided into silence. *The intent, apparently, is that we should distribute this retrovirus among the humans of our feeding grounds, rendering it unnecessary for us to hunt in Lantean space. I'm not opposed to this — we've always preferred to cultivate our humans, to receive tribute rather than hunt them down like animals, and it seems an excellent exchange for both our peoples.*

"So it would seem," Gemmion answered. So much so, in fact, that it hardly needed her input, and she controlled thought and expression to hide her sudden wariness.

One would think, Jewel said, with a flash of the sardonic humor that seemed to have helped elevate him in the Queen's favor.

Ice allowed herself a smile, her off hand briefly closing on his wrist. *Which is why I find it so hard to believe that any humans refused the offer.*

"Refused it?" Gemmion bent her head in apology. "Forgive me, Lady. I don't understand."

Neither do we, the Queen said. *I hoped you could help us comprehend it.*

"I'll do what I can, of course," Gemmion answered, and Jewel pushed himself away from the Queen's throne.

I think you're from Tanator yourself?

Gemmion froze, the nightmare rising again in the back of her brain. "Yes, I — you'd chosen Tanator for the test, Lady?"

In spite of herself, she could hear the shock in her voice, and the Queen's brow ridges drew together in question. *You think that unwise?*

"I think —" Gemmion made herself stop, mastered her emotions before they could betray her. "I think that if you wished to test this Lantean retrovirus, you would do best to test it on those of us already aboard. You know we would be glad to serve you."

The Queen blinked, and Gemmion felt a wave of affection sweep over her, palpable as a caress. *I would not so misuse you.*

Flame looked equally indignant. *And if it didn't work, or caused harm? It would be a waste and a cruelty to test it on our own humans.*

Gemmion looked from one to the other. She could feel their sincerity — and indeed, she had served them both long enough to believe that they felt genuine fondness for the community of humans they sheltered in *Sanctuary*. No more had Tanator's scientists experimented on the vel-cats they kept as pets. But that did not explain why the people of Tanator would refuse something that would save the lives of every single person taken by the Wraith — except, of course, that Tanator chose its tribute from among the dregs of society, glad to be free of the tainted and the criminal; the sick, too, when they could get away with it, though the Wraith generally refused them as unwholesome. They wanted the tribute, the taken, to die, and to suffer doing so. She could still remember the smell of fear and hate that had filled the hall when the Wraith had appeared and the tribute had been herded forward, could remember the look of disgust when Edoric — She shoved that memory back into the nightmare where it belonged, drew what she knew was a ragged breath, and saw the Queen still watching her with compassion.

I had not meant to cause you grief.

Gemmion took another breath, steadying herself with the strength honed over more than two centuries of service. She was no longer the scared girl she had been when they were herded aboard the hive — that had been the Old Queen's hive, Ice's mother's, and it had been the Old Queen who had separated her from the rest, her and the handful of the tainted, born with the ability to hear the Wraith's mind speech, and set her feet on the path that had led her here. There was nothing in that past, nothing at all, that she would wish to change. "I am well, Lady. It was — I had not thought of Tanator in years."

But now that you have, Jewel said, *have you any idea why they would refuse us?*

His brisk tone was steadying, and Gemmion made herself consider the question. "I don't — it's been centuries since I've been there, since I was taken aboard by the Lady's mother. At that time, they would have liked to see us punished further. What do they say themselves — is it still the Twelve who rule?"

It is, Jewel answered. "The Elders. The Eldest Coyt speaks for them." He returned to mind speech, the name given. *He says only that it dishonors their ways and breaks our bargain, and if we cannot agree to the change, they wish to join the Lanteans, perhaps in trade for some other world.*

And that's not such a bad idea, Flame said. *There are other worlds where we could test the retrovirus, ones that would be just as grateful, and make no demands on us. In fifty years, who knows what they'll decide?*

Too late for that, Jewel said, *and that's my fault. It never occurred to me that they wouldn't seize the chance.*

I doubt it would have occurred to any of us, the Queen said. *And now they have chosen to stand against us openly. We cannot allow that to continue.*

There have been suggestions, Flame said, and beneath the words, Gemmion caught ghostly images, a world culled and broken, none left alive in the wreckage of a great city.

We do not break our word, Ice said. *Regardless of their choices.* She rose from her throne and began to pace, the coat swirling like a lashing tail. *And we have to assume that they have already contacted the Lanteans. No, I think they have chosen the board and set the pieces, and we must play out the game. Which brings us back to you, Chatelaine. Will you come to Tanator with us, help us find a way out of this tangle?*

Gemmion bowed her head, hiding her feelings behind her

strongest walls. There could be only one answer to such an appeal. "Yes, Lady. Of course I will."

Good. The Queen returned to her throne, settling her robes about her, and Flame gave her a brisk nod.

If that's the way of it, shall I have the Hivemaster set our course for Tanator?

Tell him to prepare it, the Queen answered, *but first I wish to speak to Alabaster. And the Lantean cleverman —*

"Jennifer Keller," Jewel said aloud, pronouncing the name with care. *If the Lanteans involve themselves —*

Do you truly think they won't? The Queen showed teeth in a fighting smile. *I would, if I were they. If Tanator joins them, it moves our borders — to their advantage. No, we should expect them to take part in this.*

As you say, Jewel answered, bowing, and he and Flame turned toward the door.

Gemmion started to follow, but the Queen's mental touch stopped her in her tracks.

Chatelaine. Stay.

Gemmion turned back, offering another curtsey as the door slid shut behind the departing men. "Lady?"

Little River. It was the name the Queen had bestowed on her soon after Gemmion had joined her household, the flavor, so Ice had said, of Gemmion's thought, a narrow, bright-flashing stream between green banks. *I am sorry to have hurt you. Can you do this?*

At the Queen's gesture, Gemmion settled herself at the throne's foot, leaning against the sleekly curved bone. "I can. If there were another way, I would prefer not to — but I don't see one. I don't think there's anyone else from Tanator currently of the household."

Certainly no one I would trust as well as you.

"Thank you for that."

There was a silence between them, calm and ordinary, only the distant respiration of the hive itself to mar the quiet, and

then the Queen sighed in turn. *You came to my mother's hive
first, I chose you only after you were settled there — and I have
never regretted that choice, I assure you! But now — with all
that's at stake here, I need to know why Tanator has refused me.
You said you thought they wanted to see their tribute suffer?*

Gemmion managed a nod, feeling her muscles tighten
involuntarily.

*Tell me why. Ah, Little River, I would not ask if I didn't
truly need to know.*

Gemmion nodded again. She could understand the politics of the problem as well as anyone: if Tanator managed to
weasel out of the deal, it would weaken every other aspect of
the treaty that Alabaster had fought so hard to obtain. The
Lanteans would not refuse to help their own kind, and there
were enough dissatisfied hives on the one side and unhappy
humans on the other that it wouldn't take much to break the
fragile peace.

"I know — I do, believe me. And it was a very long time ago."
She rested her forehead on her drawn-up knees, marshaling
her thoughts. "I was — not quite turned twenty-two, twice
eleven, which is the year we come of age. I was a student at the
University in the Gate City, Channos; I had a scholarship that
would keep me another year and the promise of work when it
ended, I had good friends, and most of all I had a man I was
to marry. Edoric, his name was, Edoric Almoragen, and I was
very much in love with him. I was so in love that I applied for
a dispensation to marry before I was fully of age — it was only
a few months until my birthday, you see, and if we were wed,
I could accompany him on a research trip into the southern
archipelago. But to marry before majority, you must be certified fit, and my best friend Elya went with me to the appoint-
ment, because that's what friends do."

Fit? The Queen's mental voice brushed at the surface of her
mind, barely disturbing the images. *Fit to breed?*

"Free of genetic taint," Gemmion answered. The words were

bitter on her tongue, and she could see again the sterile cubicle, the technician, bored and not particularly careful as he pricked her thumb to draw her blood. He had fed it into the machines — Wraith-derived technology, she knew now, even more bitter irony — and folded his arms to wait, one more routine test on a dull and pointless day. Then his face had changed, first disbelieving, and then accusing: the test showed the Wraith taint, enough to send her instantly to the tribute pool, and what did she plan to do about that?

She had frozen for a second, but then from somewhere she had dredged up the same desperate strength that had served her on the hives: surely these tests were not always completely accurate; perhaps if run again, the result would be different? As she had spoken, she had stretched her arms to show the bangles she wore on both wrists, good weighty gold, and in the end he had given her the clear certificate in exchange for every scrap of jewelry she wore — her dower price, proof that she could keep herself and provide for her household — and the credits in her purse.

She had staggered away white-faced and shaking, swearing to Elya that she had eaten bad clams at lunch. Elya had insisted on taking her home and tucking her into bed, and in the process had seen that she no longer wore the necklace Edoric had given her for their betrothal. So Gemmion had confessed, sick and terrified, and felt Elya shrink away from her in fear.

"If I had thought — if I'd known more, I would have fled as soon as Elya left me alone." Gemmion tightened her muscles to keep from shaking, and felt the Queen's hand on her hair, gently soothing. "But I was confused and upset and frankly terrified, and when Elya brought Edoric back to me, I thought he'd come to save me." She closed her eyes as though that could erase the memory of how she'd thrown herself into his arms, weeping, begging him to help her. He had held her close while she stammered out her truth — even now, even with the full benefit of hindsight, she couldn't remember feeling anything but safe, as safe as she had felt every other time he had held her. She could still remember the musk of his aftershave, the first touch of afternoon stubble on his cheek and the green-flecked tweed of his coat. "Instead, when I'd told him what had happened, what I'd done, he called the Guard, and I was arrested. There was no question about the result of the second test, and I was sent to the Tribute Hall to wait for the next ship to arrive." She paused, striving for humor. "The one thing I can say is that the technician was sent for tribute, too." And long dead, fed upon two centuries ago: not quite so amusing after all, though she could not find it in herself to regret it.

Ah, Little River. The Queen's touch was barely a whisper. *I didn't know.*

Gemmion's cheeks were wet, and she drew in a sharp breath, angry at her own weakness. "It was a very long time ago, and they are all dead." Some in the feeding cells, some of ripe old age, and she — she had prospered in service to the Wraith, had been granted life and power among her own kind, and the favor of two different queens. She turned her sleeve carefully inside out, dabbed at the tears with the lining. "But that, I think, is why they would refuse the offer of the retrovirus. To be given to the Wraith has always been the fate of the tainted and the criminal, not something that happens to ordinary, decent folk."

The Queen's answer was colder than ever. *That shall change.*

It took nearly two weeks to arrange the visit to Tanator, two weeks of constant work, and Gemmion was grateful to be kept busy. The harder she worked, the less time she had to waste in dreams, though the ghosts of friends-turned-accusers still stalked her nights. They are long dead, she told herself fiercely, waking, and drove herself harder still. At last, *Sanctuary* leaped out of hyperspace to take up orbit around Tanator, and a few hours later Alabaster's hive joined them. Gemmion braided the Queen's hair while the lords of the zenana made their last preparations, and Jewel shook his head from the doorway.

I still don't understand why you've involved her.

Because her clevermen are the ones who made this thing, and she has the Lantean woman as well, the Queen answered. Gemmion fastened the last thin braid, and reached for the pins that would hold them in graceful loops. It was, if she said so herself, an exceptionally becoming look for Ice, and also kept her hair out of her face if it came to fighting — unlikely, she thought, but the possibility could never entirely be dismissed. The longest of the pins could double as weapons, just in case. *It's just possible that reassurance from the Lanteans might change people's minds.*

I'm not convinced, Jewel said. *And haven't we enough to worry about with the Lanteans coming themselves?*

It's only a small delegation, Flame said, appearing behind him. *And besides, the Tanatori insisted. Ice, it you don't leave now, we're going to be late.*

The Queen bared teeth at him, and Gemmion deftly inserted the last pin.

"Done, Lady." She stood back, shaking her own gown into place, and Ice gave her a quick glance.

And are you ready, Chatelaine?

Gemmion bowed her head. "I am."

Then let us begin. The Queen rose to her feet, blue-black gown falling in elegant folds, and swept from the chamber.

They met on the old Muster Field beyond the Stargate, the city buildings stark on the horizon. In the old days, this had been where the tribute was gathered, lined up for inspection under the guns of the militia and the eyes of the Wraith, a flat, barren plain where the grass had never been permitted to grow above ankle height for fear it might conceal some fugitive. Now the grass reached almost to Gemmion's knee, and pale blue flowers were scattered among the stalks. Lad's-love, Gemmion remembered, with a pang. She had picked them for Edoric, a great crown of them to celebrate his majority, and he had kept them through the tavern crawl that followed the official dinner. She could almost see him pushing it back into place, lamplight gleaming on his dark curls. She shook the thought away, focusing on the approaching Wraith.

The stranger queen, Alabaster, was very pale, her hair streaming scarlet nearly to her waist. Her gown was just as pale, a milky sheath that shimmered like the inside of a shell, slit in front to show boots of the same nacreous color. Her retinue was all in black for contrast, even the human woman who stood warily to one side, hair the color of dried grass pulled up and back in an untidy fall. The Lantean cleverman, Gemmion assumed, and took her place behind her queen.

Alabaster. It was Ice's place, as the ruler of fewer men, to make the first approach, and she made it with dignity, ceding nothing more than numbers.

Well met, Ice. Alabaster inclined her head, a gracious greeting. "Perhaps we should speak aloud, for the benefit of our — human colleagues?"

"If you wish it," Ice answered, though Gemmion felt the ripple of confusion. Why would a human decide to live among the Wraith, if she could not feel the mind speech? "Let me present, then, my household — my Consort, my Hivemaster, my Master of Sciences Biological. And also my Chatelaine."

Gemmion curtsied at that, head lowered, feeling the attention of Alabaster's Wraith sweep over her. One pair of eyes lingered, thoughtful — the blade with the star circling one eye, who Alabaster introduced as her old queen's consort, Guide; the Lanteans, she remembered, had called him Todd, though she had never known the meaning behind that name — but then he, too, had turned his attention to the problem at hand.

"It is not in our interest to distress our human kine," Ice was saying, "and indeed we felt it was to their advantage to accept this new invention. We were as shocked as anyone that they refused."

"And just as shocked that they wished Atlantis to interfere," the old queen's consort said, with a smile that meant no particular good, and Alabaster laid a hand on his wrist without looking back at him.

"Guide speaks truly," she said. "We had thought the matter settled. I do not like that Atlantis has been invited to change our agreement so soon after it was made."

"No more do we," Ice said. "And that is part of why we have invited you to be present — after all, you have such excellent relations with the Lanteans."

Both Guide and Alabaster's Hivemaster showed teeth at that, and Gemmion dropped her eyes again, not wanting anyone to read her satisfaction. They could keep on at this for hours — and very likely would, until one of the queens gave in and offered to help the other, or the Lanteans arrived — and instead she glanced at the Lantean woman. She was skin and bone, tired circles under her eyes, though her hair, at least, was sleek enough that Gemmion didn't think she was actively malnourished. But Alabaster's hive had never been one to keep humans, and she took a step sideways, trying to catch the woman's eye.

To her surprise, the Lantean — Keller, she reminded herself, Jennifer Keller — moved toward her, frowning slightly. Gemmion maneuvered herself to the end of Ice's entourage, and Keller took a quick step to close the distance between them.

"Hello. You're — she said 'Chatelaine'?"

Gemmion blinked. "That's right."

"Are you all right?"

Gemmion lifted her head at that, stung by what she thought was a note of pity. "Of course. Our hive at least knows how to feed humans. Have they found anything for you but children's food — fruit and pap?"

To her surprise, Keller gave a quick smile. "And I was worrying about you. Yes, I'm properly fed — I brought supplies with me, and Guide has been... conscientious about seeing that I'm supplied from the worlds we have visited." She paused. "Chatelaine — on Earth that means something like 'keeper of the castle'?"

"I'm the leader of our queen's human household," Gemmion

said, and didn't try to hide the pride in her voice. "I'm here because our queen thought I might be able to persuade the Tanatori that your retrovirus was a good idea."

"I think it is," Keller said. She lowered her voice slightly. "I don't think anyone likes it very much, but something has to change."

Before Gemmion could think how to answer that, a symbol lit on the Stargate. They all stopped to watch as the connection was established, and the wormhole whooshed outward, then stabilized. The familiar boxy shape of a Lantean shuttlecraft emerged from the pool, and circled to land a cautious distance from the Wraith ships. Gemmion heard Keller's breath catch, saw her strain to see the figures that emerged, and then sag back again as she recognized them.

"The one you were expecting isn't here?" Gemmion asked. It was impossible not to be curious about the Lanteans, who had appeared out of nowhere to upset the balance of power in the galaxy, and especially not to be curious about Keller, who had gone against every Lantean instinct to travel with the Wraith, even to help them develop this miracle sure, and apparently done it without even the consolation of the taint to let her hear their thoughts.

Keller looked startled, and then color rose in her cheeks. "No — well, I wasn't expecting him, he wouldn't have come, I —" She stopped, shaking her head. "Colonel Sheppard and Teyla. And Major Lorne and Marines. I knew Ronon wouldn't come, but Rodney — well, it's not really his sort of job."

A husband, a lover? Gemmion wondered. A friend, certainly, and a close one, but there was no time to question further. The man in the lead — Colonel Sheppard — raised one hand from the stock of his P90 as they came within earshot.

"Guide! Alabaster! And you must be Ice. We've heard a lot about you."

This time, it was Jewel and Flame who showed teeth, but Ice's voice was tranquil. "I am Ice. And you?"

"Lieutenant Colonel John Sheppard, USAF. This is Teyla Emmagen and Major Lorne. And Sergeant Peters and Corporal Ramos."

Those were the Marines, who followed closely, weapons not quite at the ready. Probably there were more of them in the jumper, just in case.

"It's good to see you again, Colonel," Alabaster said. "And you, Teyla."

The dark women in Lantean dress inclined her head in polite answer. For all that she was not Lantean by birth, Gemmion realized abruptly, she held very nearly as much power as the man Sheppard.

"We are glad to be here," she said. "We hope that all of us can come to an easy and peaceful resolution of the problem."

"But for that," Sheppard said, with a crooked smile, "we'll need to have the Tanatori here, too."

There was something in his voice that made Gemmion look toward the city. Sure enough, a party of humans was marching toward them, the city's blood-red flag unfurled above them, and it was all she could do to suppress a snarl of her own. The last time she had seen that flag had been on this very field, with a Wraith cruiser filling half the ground, its hatches gaping wide to take in the tribute... She saw Keller looking curiously at her, and controlled herself sharply. This was not the time for those memories, or any other; she was here to serve her queen.

She straightened her back at the Tanatori approached. The Elders' ceremonial robes hadn't changed at all in the centuries since she had been taken, knee-length dove-gray coats buttoned with the enormous pearls from the Southward Sea. They wore great ropes of those pearls as well, and the Eldest Coyt carried a staff topped with a golden tower. They stopped at what was clearly a careful distance, well out of reach of the Wraith but close enough to be easily heard, and the Eldest lifted his free hand in greeting.

"On behalf of the Council, I welcome all of you to Tanator. I hope we will be able to achieve a satisfactory resolution."

"We would like nothing better," Ice answered, "though I am disappointed that you found it necessary to involve the Lanteans so soon. But since they are here, they are welcome to observe our discussions."

"We are grateful for your forbearance," Coyt answered. "Though we are confused about the need for a second hive here in orbit. We have always given our allegiance to you."

"They are here at my request," Ice said. "It is their clevermen, with the help of the Lantean physician, who developed the retrovirus. I hoped that they might answer any questions you had, and quell any doubts as to its safety."

"Its safety is not the question." That was one of the other Elders, a younger man with a curly black beard, and Coyt held up his hand.

"Peace, Devor, we can discuss the details at a later date."

"They cannot call us cowards," Devor answered. "We have given them their tribute since time immemorial — and yes, they have kept their bargain as we have kept ours —"

"We see no need to change," a third man said, with an apologetic smile. "It would be... destabilizing."

At his side, an older man stiffened. "With respect, there are other choices —"

"Peace," Coyt said again, more sharply this time. "We are here to welcome you — all of you — and to escort you back to the city. We have prepared a feast, as we always do when the Lady graces us with her presence, and we hope that everyone can be made comfortable before we settle to work."

Gemmion saw the looks of discomfort that passed over the Marine's faces at the mention of a feast, and kept her own face expressionless. Ice's people, and her mother's before her, had always fed well before coming to take the tribute: it was too easy to miss someone who might be of use to the household in the confusion of the tribute pens, there was no point in making things worse by adding hunger.

"That is kind of you," Ice began, and to Gemmion's surprise, Keller took a step forward.

"Perhaps you'll let me have a word with your own medical people? I am sure I can show them that the retrovirus is both harmless and effective."

"That's irrelevant," Devor said, and Coyt broke protocol to turn and glare at him.

"Enough, I said. This can be discussed later. If you will follow us, Lady, good people, we will see you well bestowed."

Channos had changed. Gemmion knew she should not have been so surprised, but it was still startling to see the new buildings rising four and five stories above smoothly paved streets. In her day, the tallest building had been the Commandary, three stories with the observatory dome on top, and the streets had been cobbled, except for the center rails where the ox-drawn trolleys had run. The Commandary was still there, red-brick walls even more weathered, the carvings above the main entrance blurred and rain-streaked, but the observatory's dome was sealed, its view obstructed by the newer buildings that had sprung up around it. They were mostly stone, not brick, as pale as new bread and polished to a shine, and the trolleys moved along new rails, drawing power from wires that followed the line of the streets. The people lining the streets and peering from the housetops looked different, too, women in narrow, calf-high dresses and men without hat or hood. It was as though she'd come to any other world in Ice's hunting grounds, not her original home, and she was glad when the Elders led them down a street that had not existed in her day, turning away from what had been the city's center.

It led to another new stone building, this one easily seven stories high, set back from the road in a lawn planted with a single neat row of trees. They, at least, were familiar: in another month, or maybe two, they would burst into a riot of blooms in every shade of yellow.

"One tree for each of the states," an Elder said, to Teyla, who nodded as though it interested her, and Gemmion counted. Seven trees: there had been only six states when she was taken.

As the doors swung back, trumpets sounded, and young men and women in white tunic and trousers came forward to set wreaths on the guests' heads. Gemmion knew these flowers, too, twists of scarlet piper and tiny white starfire; she had not forgotten the symbolism, either, pipers for hope, starfires for perseverance, and the heady fragrance caught in her chest, so that she ducked her head and coughed. Ice accepted hers with gracious patience — she had been through similar ceremonies before — but the Lanteans looked startled and uneasy, the Marines in particular eying each other until the younger officer, Lorne, said something to them in a low voice. Teyla accepted hers as gracefully as Ice had done, though Gemmion thought she and Sheppard exchanged wry glances.

A banquet had been set up in the inner hall, an enormous room lit by narrow windows that ran the full length of the wall, and a waterfall of iridescent silk fell from the ceiling's central height to pool like water in the center of the room. Tables had been set around it in a single large square, and servers were already bustling to fill carafes and tidbit platters. Music sounded from the narrow mezzanine that surrounded the room, bisecting the windows, and Coyt clapped his hands for attention.

"Good people, it is the custom of our folk to postpone business until such time as we have eaten together, as we believe those that share a meal share much goodwill. And as we know that certain of our guests require different sustenance, we offer them a more suitable option."

He waved a hand, and the hurrying servers moved aside to allow a line of people to move forward. They, too, were dressed in white, and wore wreaths of bell-flowers, in every shade of purple — funeral flowers, Gemmion remembered, the kind you spread on the grave at the end of a long and well-lived life. There was one of them for each of the Wraith, except for the drones. She felt Ice's shocked surprise, echoed by Jewel and Flame, and saw a flash of pure horror cross Teyla's face before the Lantean woman had mastered herself. Sheppard took a step forward, and was stopped by Teyla's hand on his arm.

Ice spoke almost in the same moment, her voice firm. "That is a — gracious — offer, but it is not required. Not on my account, nor on my sister queen's."

"No, indeed," Alabaster said, and Gemmion felt the same shocked surprise give way to relief.

"This seems — unnecessary," Teyla said, her voice tightly controlled. Behind her, one of the Marines muttered something unfriendly, but Gemmion couldn't quite make out the words. "We are here to discuss whether you need to continue to render such… services, not to witness them."

"That is not entirely so," Coyt said. Behind him, the tribute waited silent, though two of the women held hands tightly.

"If that's what you want," Sheppard said, with a sudden flash of anger, "we'll just turn around and walk. We didn't come here to see people fed on —"

"The Colonel is right," Teyla said. "You do not need us for that. Perhaps there is some better way to make your point."

Coyt gave her a level stare. "We are merely fulfilling our current obligations —"

"Yes, we're making a point," Devor interrupted. "It's not us who want to change the terms, it's the Wraith. We are content with things as they are."

"But why?" That was Keller, the words sharp as through ripped from her throat. "We've made it so nobody has to die —"

"And does that erase all the deaths that have gone before?" Devor glared at her, and Coyt stepped forward, putting himself deliberately between them.

"Enough. This is a matter to be discussed after we have eaten."

"And we thank you," Ice said, "but your kindness is unnecessary."

Alabaster nodded with her. Someone in the crowd gave a

gasp of relief, and Gemmion saw the women's hands tighten for just an instant. Even Coyt looked momentarily grateful, though he controlled himself instantly. "Then will you join us at the tables? We've brought wines that you have liked before."

"Thank you." Ice bent her head in agreement.

Teyla said, "Indeed. Let us... eat."

The crowd thawed into motion, servers deftly guiding the off-worlders to their seats, the Elders retreating toward their own section of the tables. Gemmion looked back as she followed Ice's household, but the tribute had disappeared, vanished into the crowd. Only a single bell-flower was left, lost from a wreath and trampled into the stones of the floor.

She found herself at the edge of Ice's group, with Keller on her right hand and Teyla and Sheppard beyond her. Surely Keller should have been seated with Alabaster's party, she thought, and in the same moment one of the servers said the same thing, bowing apologetically.

Keller blinked innocently. "I was told I could sit with the other Lanteans."

Not likely, Gemmion thought, as the server backed away. It would be more like Alabaster to keep her human cleverman close at hand, not quite a hostage, but a reminder. Although now that it was done, it would be hard for Alabaster to reclaim her without losing face. And perhaps she was merely homesick after all. "I think you were expected elsewhere."

"And if she was, are you going to tell?" That was Sheppard, leaning forward to glare at her around the other women.

Gemmion felt herself flush. She had not really meant to speak aloud, but the appearance of the tribute had unsettled her. She managed to shrug. "Why should I care where she sits?"

"Because your queen might?" Sheppard's smile was oddly feral.

"Colonel," Teyla said.

In the same moment, Keller said, "I told Guide I was going to sit with you. Besides, I wanted to talk to her." She nodded toward Gemmion. "I thought she might have some idea why the Tanatori are acting like this."

Gemmion shook her head. "I do not. Though they have always hated the tribute —" She stopped abruptly, not wanting to betray herself, but Teyla tipped her head to one side.

"You know this planet. You are from here?"

"I was. But that was long ago." Gemmion leaned back to allow a server to fill her glass, grateful for the soft smell of fruit instead of flowers.

Teyla went on as though they were old friends. "I do not understand why, if they asked us for help leaving the Wraith sphere, that they would be willing to provide humans for your queen to feed upon."

"And if they're going to do that," Sheppard said, "why would we want them?"

Beside him, Lorne grunted in agreement, but Teyla pointedly ignored them both.

"No more do we," Gemmion answered. "My queen chose them for the test because we have always had good relations with them." It was not exactly a lie, but the words were ashes on her tongue. "They have always provided a tribute without complaint — it's a symbiotic relationship, almost."

"But that's no reason not to take the retrovirus." Keller sounded frustrated, her ponytail lashing like the tail of some angry animal. "It's more of a reason to want it! I don't get it —"

"Neither do I —" Gemmion broke off as a server stumbled on the far side of the table. A mere misstep, she thought, but then the man leaned forward, his platter spilling an avalanche of little cakes and then shattering on the stones. He sagged to his knees, one hand dragging blindly at the tablecloth, and then collapsed into the wreckage of cakes and pottery. Someone shouted something, perhaps a call for help, but another server was falling, and then a third, and among the Tanatori one of the Elders' escorts rose to her feet and then pitched forward among the dishes. A pitcher fell and broke, splashing the stones with wine like watered blood.

"Don't touch anything!" Keller called. "Did anybody eat — drink?"

Gemion could hear the same call spreading among the Wraith, the queens already on their feet, snarling, the blades of their escort pressing close. Sheppard was on his feet, too, the Marines and Lorne copying him, and Gemmion heard the heavy snap of their weapons arming.

"What is this?" Teyla called. "Elder Coyt!"

"I don't understand!" Coyt was on his feet at last, staring bewildered at the chaos around him.

Keller ducked under the table, evading Sheppard's one-handed attempt to grab her, and dropped to her knees beside the nearest server. She felt at his neck, grimacing, then rolled him onto his side as he began to heave, retching uncontrollably.

"Anybody eat anything?" Lorne demanded, and Gemmion saw the Marines shake their heads.

"I had maybe a swallow of the wine," the older one said. "But I feel fine."

"Colonel? Teyla?"

"We are both unscathed, Major," Teyla answered. "Quickly, Colonel." She ducked under the table, following Keller, and Sheppard followed without grace. For an instant, Gemmion considering following them, but knew her place was with her queen. She turned to find Ice braced between blades, Flame himself in front of her to shield her from attack, Jewel at her off hand, both with teeth bared and weapons drawn. Beyond them Alabaster was equally surrounded, though from the look she was giving Guide she did not entirely appreciate the protection.

"Elder Coyt." Ice laid her off hand on Flame's shoulder and the cleverman moved reluctantly aside. "If this is how you bargain, I don't think much of it."

"Lady, I swear, I don't understand!" Coyt was sweating and afraid, looking over his shoulders as though he expected someone to come at him with a knife. "This is not our doing —"

"This is your feast," Ice said, and Teyla pushed her way through the crowd. There were at least a dozen bodies sprawled across the floor, and at least as many more doubled over clutching their bellies. Most were servers, Gemmion saw — probably they had seized the chance to taste one of the treats before they carried them to the tables.

"The queen has a point," Teyla said. "You arranged all of this."

"But why would we poison you?" Coyt wailed.

"Teyla." That was Sheppard, shouldering up to stand at her side. "Looks like it was the wine. Ramos is starting to feel queasy, though he says he's ok for action."

"Of course it would be the wine," Gemmion began, and Ice nodded.

"If it was intended for us, you mean?"

"Yes, Lady."

Teyla nodded in agreement. "That is the only item that all of us would have consumed."

"But why —" Coyt began again, and stopped abruptly.

Jewel lifted his feeding hand, ready to seize him, to drag answers from him, but Ice stopped him with a look. "Well, Eldest? Have you an answer after all?"

"To end these negotiations," Devor said. "To be sure no one will force us to betray our people." He stepped past the other Elders, spreading his hands to the Lanteans. "No one will die, or be harmed permanently. This is an emetic, a sickener, nothing more. But. Now we have defied the Wraith — worse, we've made them look foolish before their greatest rival — and they will never forget it. You have to take us in, have to protect us, or one day they will come back and cull us so deeply that we will never be a people again."

Coyt glared at him. "Fool. You've doomed us all."

Sheppard had both hands folded on the butt of his P90, his mouth twisting as though he'd like to use it. "Is that right, Ice?"

"We came in good faith to offer a favor to a people who have served us well," Ice countered. "So well that we saw no need for them to die in our service." She bared teeth at Devor. "Our offer was made in honor: we offered you the chance to ally yourselves more closely with us, and instead you have tried to poison us. I admit it's tempting to cull here and walk away!"

Coyt drew himself up, squaring his shoulders under the gray silk coat. "Lady, this renegade does not speak for anyone but himself—"

Devor spoke over him. "The offer dishonors those who had been taken, those whose lives have already been consumed in service to the Wraith. How can we take the easy path, and call ourselves worthy of our ancestors' sacrifices?"

Ice lifted her head, her feeding hand flexing involuntarily. "And yet — the tribute you bring us, it's drawn from those you already wish to be rid of. Criminals, vagrants, those whose blood you call tainted, who can hear our mind speech: they make up your tribute, not your honored kin."

"That's not true!" Devor glared as though he would strike her.

"I have heard it from the lips of one taken here," Ice answered implacably.

"That was true once," Coyt said. "To our shame. But we changed those laws. It took rebellion, revolution, but now everyone's name is placed into the great lottery, and the tribute is drawn from there. Those with the taint are permitted to volunteer, and often do, but everyone shares in the danger." He paused. "Devor's own daughter was taken in the last tribute, and we honor her memory."

Gemmion stood frozen, trying to make sense of what she was hearing. "How?" she said, and saw both Ice and Teyla slant glances in her direction. "How did it happen?"

Ice repeated the question without hesitation. "How did this happen? Tell us the tale, so that we can understand you."

"I don't see—" Coyt began, and Devor interrupted again.

"Of course it matters, and I will gladly tell it. Though it is a long story—"

"I'd say we've got time," Sheppard said, still with that crooked smile, and Teyla inclined her head.

"We are also curious, if it has driven you to these extremes."

"It's a matter of pride," Devor said. "For all of us, for all Tanator."

"Enough," Coyt said. "I am Eldest, it's my place to speak. We all know the story, after all." He paused, frowning, and Gemmion felt a shiver almost of anticipation ripple through the room, as though the Tanatori who were not tending the sick had all stopped to listen, to remember.

"Long ago, we on Tanator made a bargain with the Wraith," Coyt said. "They would refrain from culling us at random, and in turn we would pay a tribute of lives, of bodies, gathered and held waiting for their arrival. Their deaths bought life for the rest of us. In the past, as the Lady has said, the tribute was chosen from criminals and those who carry the Wraith taint, but over time, more and more crimes were exempted from the tribute. After all, should a starving man be sentenced to certain death for stealing bread for his children? Some argued that such a man bought his family's freedom with his own life, and that was tried, but there were few who'd volunteer even to save others, and the number of the tribute remained the same. Next we tried seeking out those with the taint, testing for it at every opportunity, and that was generally held to be fair, though the numbers of the tainted waned as a result, and there were always ways for the powerful and the wealthy to avoid being tested."

A dry voice — another of the Elders? Gemmion wondered — interjected. "There was… considerable discontent."

"Just so." Coyt drew a careful breath. "And then at last, in the middle of this unstable situation, three young people fell into the most ordinary of troubles: a girl loved a boy who loved a different girl. The couple sought to marry, and both parties had to be tested for the taint. The boy passed, but the girl did not. Terrified, she tried to bribe the testing technician, but her friend — who also loved the boy — told the boy what she had done, and the boy turned her over to the authorities. She was taken for tribute, and disappeared. The two who were left could not find peace, knowing what they had done. They quarreled and argued and finally decided that they could not live with each other or with themselves if they did not act to make sure that this could never happen again. They gathered supporters — there were many who agreed with them, given the chance — and on Midwinter Day they stormed the Old Hall here in the capital and demanded a change to the tribute. There was a battle, short and sharp, and the girl was killed, but the boy went on to be elected an Elder and then Eldest. And so the world changed. There is now a lottery, impartial, unavoidable; all take the same chances."

There was more, but Gemmion was no longer listening. Surely that couldn't be her story, couldn't be Edoric and Elya — Elya had never been in love with Edoric, except that those words, once spoke, explained so much that she herself had never understood. If Elya had been in love with him, too — there had been a shadow over her, those last months, as Gemmion babbled about plans and travel. She had taken it for simple regret, the knowledge that Elya had another year of study, perhaps even two, before she could seek her own future. She saw Ice glance in her direction, frowning as though she was wondering the same thing, and fought to keep face and mind without expression. This was nothing to do with her, couldn't possibly have anything to do with her...

"And it is because of those deaths — the death that was the tipping point, all the ones that came before, and most especially the ones that came after, that were chosen at random and yet gladly gave their lives for others — it's because of them that we can't accept this retrovirus." Devor shook his head violently. "It makes a mockery of everything they've given."

Gemmion could feel Ice's eyes on her, could feel, too, the Lantean Teyla looking at her, her attention drawn by Ice's sidelong stare and startled expression. Was it possible? After what they had done, after that betrayal, could Edoric have changed his mind? She ran her hands through her hair, heedless of the arrangement she had so carefully made. She would have said it was more like him than the betrayal, except that she had had two centuries to accept what he had done.

"Are you all right?" Keller asked, and she forced a smile and a nod.

"You know something," Teyla said, soft and fierce.

Little River? Ice's mental touch was gentle, worried.

Gemmion shook her head, felt a pin fly loose, her hair coming down in frizzy strands. "Names." She stepped forward, shouldering through the line of people between her and the milling Elders. "What were their names, these heroes?"

Most of them looked at her in shock, a few shifting to disapproval as they realized who and what she was, but to her surprise, it was Devor who answered. "Edoric Almoragen. Elya Tyil. And the girl who died was Gemmion Saer."

Gemmion laughed aloud at that — it was that or cry, weep for a past she had thought long dead — and she felt Teyla move next to her, Sheppard at her shoulder, felt Ice's shock and pity roll past her. "Gemmion Saer never died. She was given to the Wraith, yes, but she was — tainted. And so she was valued — I was valued. And I live still, servant to my queen."

"You can't be." Devor's voice broke in horror, but he rallied. "Even if she wasn't killed outright — fed upon, let's say the words — she'd have died of old age long ago."

"I have been given many gifts for my long service," Gemmion answered. "Long life is one of them."

She could feel at least half the hall recoil, shock, disbelief, and then horrified acceptance.

"How is this possible?" someone shouted. "It has to be a trick."

"I have made her my chatelaine," Ice answered, baring teeth. "There is no trick in it."

"And here I am," Gemmion said, and caught her breath in a

strangled sound between laughter and a sob. "Edoric — Elya. Oh, my dears."

Teyla lifted a hand. "And indeed, is this not a sign that things have changed already? Perhaps, instead of dishonoring the sacrifices of those who have gone before, this is truly a chance to take another step away from death."

Coyt took a step forward, his hands outstretched as though he would embrace her, and then at the last minute he let them fall again. "Is this true?"

Gemmion nodded, suddenly utterly weary. "It is. Make of it what you will."

"And you have served the Wraith all these years."

"I have."

"And what do you say to this offer?"

Gemmion sighed. "I say you'd be a fool to refuse it. No one taken in tribute would have refused it. Let the world change." She felt, from a distance, Ice's approval, a warmth along her spine, and saw Teyla nod.

"That is indeed wisdom. Everything changes in the end."

Gemmion took a step backward, her knees suddenly weak. The blade Torrent steadied her with his off hand, and, at Ice's nod, shifted to take some of her weight.

"I'm all right," she said, and heard her voice waver as though with tears. *I wish I had not come.* She couldn't say the words aloud, not without undoing the good she had done — and it was better, surely, to accept the retrovirus, to let everyone live rather than leave survival to the accidents of genetics and the interest of the Wraith. Ice and Coyt were deep in conversation, Coyt nodding as though in agreement, then Ice cocking her head to listen to some request. And yet she would still rather be anywhere else, where the memories could reach only her dreams — Edoric, smiling across the table on the day of their engagement, heedless of the elegance surrounding them, the most expensive restaurant in town; Elya dragging her from her books to see a traveling puppet-show, sharing laughter and soft new cider beneath the brilliant autumn sky. And still and always the betrayal, the look on Elya's face when Gemmion sobbed out her story, the pity in Edoric's words that did not match his eyes.

"Chatelaine? Are you ok?" That was Dr. Keller, wiping her hands on a strip of tablecloth, and Gemmion straightened.

"I'm well. Surely you're needed?" Needed elsewhere, she meant, though she managed not to say it. Ice would not thank her if she were openly ungracious to Alabaster's protégé.

"No, it looks like everyone's going to be all right." Keller glanced over her shoulder anyway, and shook her head. "That guy, Devor, he's just lucky some of the servers decided to taste things ahead of time. I don't think your queen would have been happy if any of her people had gotten sick."

"She would not have been pleased," Gemmion said. And probably Devor had counted on just that, to force Coyt's hand without actually injuring any of the Wraith. The Elders had always been a twisty group, and she doubted that had changed any over the years. To her relief, someone called Keller's name, and the doctor turned away, leaning over the Marine who had tasted the wine.

"You have not forgiven them."

For an instant, she thought it was Ice's voice, and then realized that it was Teyla.

"I have not. Why should I? What they did after — they sent me to die, and just because they felt guilty afterward doesn't change anything. I thought — I loved them both, they were my dearest friends, and I thought they loved me." Gemmion drew a shuddering breath — this was nothing the Lanteans needed to know — but to her horror, she couldn't seem to stop. "I hope they felt guilty all the rest of their lives, I hope thinking about me made their dreams hideous, I hope —" She stopped then, the anger draining out of her. "And they are dead, long dead, and I live. It doesn't matter what I feel."

"No," Teyla said, but her voice was gentle.

"And we've saved the treaty."

"We have," Teyla said. "That is no small thing."

It was not. Gemmion took a deep breath, feeling herself steady at last. There would be other tests, other dangers, but this time, peace had held. She bent her head in answer, as though to a queen, and turned back to her people.

STARGATE SG-1
Blinded by the Light

Barbara Ellisor

This story takes place in season three of Stargate SG-1.

THE UAV burst through the gate and immediately banked hard right. Following its pre-programmed search pattern, it climbed to a safe cruising altitude and soared through the morning sky, sweeping the ground below with cameras and transmitting the results back through the gate.

Back at Stargate Command, the monitors showed a single sun shining down on an expansive plain. Bounded to the south and west by a large lake, it was separated into two roughly equal halves by a line of tree-covered hills running east to west. A single cliff-lined pass joined the two halves and a range of snow-topped mountains was visible to the far north.

Several thousand large animals roamed the flatland, feeding on the waist-high grass or resting under the occasional shade tree. Similar in size to American bison, their most striking attribute were pairs of long tusks that jutted from their snouts and curved backwards over their heads. Flocks of small, feathered creatures darted through the air in search of insects and the temperature was warm and balmy. A veritable paradise.

Twenty minutes later, its mission complete, the UAV guided itself to a soft landing near the gate and waited to be retrieved.

"I have a funny feeling about this place."

Major Sam Carter scanned the immediate area, her senses shifting to high alert. She knew better than to discount the colonel when he had a 'funny feeling'. "I don't see anything, sir."

"Nor do I," said Teal'c from his position guarding their six. "The area appears quiet."

"That's what worries me." Colonel O'Neill surveyed the forest, its gloom broken only by intermittent shafts of sunlight forcing their way through the dense canopy. The quiet was absolute. In fact, other than a few distant hoots, they'd neither seen nor heard any signs of life since they'd entered the woods. "It's creepy."

"It's just trees, Jack. Trees aren't creepy." Daniel took advantage of the pause to kneel down and brush away the leaves and twigs littering the surface of the road. "Just look at these cobblestones! See how the stones are cut to fit together precisely? The Romans themselves couldn't have built a better road."

"Bet the Romans wouldn't have left that lying around." With a jerk of his chin, O'Neill indicated a tree limb blocking half the road. He turned to Sam. "Are you sure the UAV didn't see any sign of civilization? Lights? Cars? Smoke signals?"

"No, sir." She could tell he was uneasy. Though he stood at ease, his shoulders were tense and his eyes never stopped moving, constantly searching the underbrush for danger. "But in all fairness, the UAV can't see through trees. There could be buildings hidden in here and we'd never know."

"But no radio waves, nothing like that, right?"

Sam shook her head. "No, sir."

"What about the totem?" Daniel said. "That's clearly the work of civilization."

The 'totem' Daniel referred to was a tall pole mounted at the top of the cliffs overlooking the Stargate. Other than the road and the gate itself, it was the only artificial artifact detected by the UAV. Obviously old, it had weathered to a dark greenish-black color and was covered in angular writing that reminded Sam of a toddler's scribblings. Daniel had gone into raptures at the sight of it, claiming that the writings were similar to ancient Babylonian or Mesopotamian or something equally obscure, but Sam knew the colonel wouldn't care. The planet appeared deserted and he'd be ready to leave the surveying to a follow-up team.

After three years, Daniel knew the colonel, too. "C'mon Jack, we can't turn back already. This road was made by someone."

"But that 'someone' doesn't seem to be here." The colonel made a pointed show of checking his watch. "We've been tromping through these woods for exactly fifty-three minutes and haven't found a thing."

"This place can't have been abandoned for long." Daniel patted the exposed cobblestones gently, almost reverently. "I'd guess no more than five, ten years. The road is still in good repair. The people must have gone somewhere and we can't find out what happened unless we keep going. This has to lead to *something*."

O'Neill couldn't deny Daniel's logic but solving the mystery of where the people had gone wasn't his concern. "I still don't like it. Teal'c, any thoughts?"

"I sense no danger but it is impossible to see for any distance. The grasslands around the gate are more defensible."

"Carter?"

Sam shrugged, unwilling to be caught in the middle. "Whatever you say, sir."

The colonel came to a decision. "Okay Daniel, fifteen minutes, not a second more. We don't find anything by then, we head back and let one of the survey teams take over."

According to his watch, they'd been on P23-796 for less than an hour but O'Neill couldn't shake his sense of unease. The feeling wasn't rational. The trip through the gate had been uneventful and the area as peaceful as the UAV had reported. The buffalo creatures had continued to graze quietly, seemingly undisturbed by either the whoosh of the gate activation or their presence. But he did see something the UAV had missed — a group of predators haunting the edge of one of the herds. Heavy in the forefront and sloping down to weak hindquarters, they looked like under-sized hyenas from the neck down. From the neck up was another story: a thick, two-foot long, hairless neck topped by a narrow head that reminded O'Neill of a snake. And he *hated* snakes. Daniel had nicknamed them 'hy-afs' — a combination of 'hyena' and 'giraffe' — but O'Neill simply called them butt-ugly.

Maybe it was just the closeness of the trees through which they walked as they circled around and up to reach the bluff where the totem stood — like Teal'c, he preferred being able to see what was coming. Long experience had taught him that something was *always* coming and he wanted as much advance notice as possible. He surveyed the area again, paying special attention to the interplay of light and shadow, alert to any movement. Still nothing. "Carter, you and Teal'c drop back a bit."

Daniel glanced around, but everything looked peaceful. "Jack?"

He wiped the sweat off his face with his sleeve. He couldn't explain his unease but experience had taught him to pay attention to it. "Remember our bounty hunter friend on… on…?"

"Aris Boch? On PJ6-877?"

How does he remember those planets like that? "Yeah, him. Things seemed peaceful there until he showed up."

Daniel raised his eyebrows. "That was two hundred light years from here."

"And your point is…?" He jerked his head and Carter and Teal'c obediently dropped back twenty feet. "If we walk into something unexpected, I'd rather we weren't all bunched together." He sneaked another look at his watch. Just another five minutes.

"O'Neill."

The colonel froze. "Teal'c?"

"There." Teal'c pointed into the forest. "I saw a flash from that tree."

Daniel immediately started forward, only to have Jack block his way. "Wait." He edged forward, MP-5 at the ready, his gaze sweeping in all directions. "Where was it, Teal'c?"

"Left side, chest-height."

Jack approached the tree and carefully peered around the trunk. After a few seconds, he relaxed and waved Daniel forward. "Congratulations, Teal'c," he called out. "You found a gerbil."

Daniel joined him at the tree. Approximately the size of a chipmunk, the creature was pressed flat against the tree bark, obviously hoping that its fur, irregularly splotched in shades of brown and black, would serve as camouflage. It had erect, bat-like ears, over-sized eyes, and a long tail that curled up and forward over its body. The tip of it flashed at irregular intervals with a yellowish-white light. "Aw, isn't it cute?" he said. "I bet it eats insects and uses the light on its tail as a lure. There's a fish on earth that does the same thing."

"A fish?" Apparently interested despite himself, Jack leaned in for a closer look. "An Earth fish? Where?"

"It lives in the deep—"

"Gaahh!" Jack stumbled backwards, one hand still holding his gun, the other rubbing furiously at his face. His boot caught on a tree root and he stumbled. Daniel grabbed for him but was pulled off-balance by Jack's momentum. They both crashed to the ground.

Sam rushed forward while Teal'c snapped to attention but remained in place, guarding their rear from any danger. "Colonel? Daniel?"

Daniel rolled to his knees and waved her toward Jack. "I'm fine. Check on Jack. The gerbil thing spat at us. I think it got in his eyes."

"Colonel?" He had pushed himself upright but remained sitting on the ground, his hands covering his eyes.

"Are you all right?"

"Give me a minute." Jack blew out a breath and slowly lowered his hands, keeping his eyes closed. The skin around them looked a bit reddened but there were no obvious signs of damage. "I can't see anything."

If he's joking around, Daniel thought, *I'm going to kill him.* "It would help if you opened your eyes."

"They're closed?" Jack let out a quick breath of relief. "I thought I was blind." Then a note of tension re-entered his voice. "Are they still closed?" He pressed several fingers carefully against his eyelids. "I can't feel anything."

Damn. He's not joking. Everything Daniel knew about eye injuries flashed through his mind. It didn't take long. About all you could do in the field was rinse and cover — anything more needed a doctor. Sam apparently concurred.

"Colonel, we have to wash out your eyes. Daniel, give me your canteen."

Uncharacteristically cooperative, Jack let Daniel tilt his head back. Though he flinched when Sam pulled his eyelids apart, he didn't move as she carefully poured water over his eyes, then released them and blotted the area dry with a clean handkerchief. "Any better?"

He gently touched his eyelids. "I still can't open them."

"Do they hurt?"

"Not anymore. They did for a second but now I don't feel anything." He waggled his fingers for emphasis. "I don't even feel my fingers touching them."

"Ok, Colonel, I'm going to lift the eyelid and you tell me what you can see. Just relax." Sam braced the side of her hand against his face and used her thumb and forefinger to gently raise his left eyelid. His pupil was hugely dilated, turning his dark-brown eye almost black. "Look to your right, then to your left." Whatever she saw made her smile, giving Daniel a small thrill of relief. "What do you see, sir?"

"Just a blur." Jack pulled away and his eyelid drooped shut. "A very bright blur. It's almost painful."

Sam nodded to herself in confirmation. "Your pupils are enlarged. That's why it seems so blurry and bright to you. In the human eye, pupils enlarge and constrict depending on the amount —"

"Carter!" Clearly, Jack wasn't interested in how or why, he just wanted answers. "Ten words or fewer."

"I think your eye muscles are paralyzed." When he didn't immediately respond, she continued, "I think the liquid from the—"

"It's spit, Carter. Gerbil spit. Go on, you can say it."

"Yes sir. I'm guessing that the, uh, gerbil spit contains a neuromuscular toxin that was absorbed through the mucous membranes of your eye and eyelid. That's why you can't keep your eyelids open and the pupil won't constrict properly." Before he could interrupt her with questions, she hurriedly continued. "On the bright side, it just seems to be affecting what it actually touched. The muscles further back, the ones that control the eye's movements, seem fine and the fact that you see light indicates that the optic nerve is working normally."

Jack had only one concern. "Can you fix it?"

"Sorry, sir. We need to get you back home." She glanced at Daniel, her expression at odds with the confidence in her voice. "Janet will get you all fixed up."

Jack's bullshit detector was probably working overtime; they all knew that Sam had no idea whether the doctors could help or not, she was just trying to keep his spirits up. But whatever Jack thought about it, he just nodded and turned his head toward Teal'c. "Everything all right, Teal'c?"

"Everything appears normal, O'Neill. But I am detecting an odor that was not apparent previously."

Daniel took an exploratory sniff. "I smell it too. Smells sort of like apples." He leaned forward and sniffed Jack's shoulder. "It's coming from your jacket."

"It must be from the gerbil," Sam said, more concerned with the immediate problem. "Sir, we need to get back to the gate. And"—she hesitated—"we need to bandage your eyes."

He reacted just as Daniel expected. "I don't need a bandage."

"Colonel, a bandage will keep your eyes from drying out and causing permanent damage."

"So you don't think the current problem is permanent?"

She chewed her lip. "Sir, I honestly don't know. There's a good possibility it might just wear off in a few hours."

"Or...what?"

Daniel caught her look. "We'll worry about that later," he said. "Jack, we need to protect your eyes and get you back to Dr. Frasier. Sam, why don't you and Teal'c work out the details while I wrap up Jack's eyes?"

Sam flashed him a brief, grateful smile, patted Jack on the shoulder and left to explain the situation to Teal'c.

While Daniel wrapped O'Neill's eyes in several layers of gauze bandages, he kept up a steady stream of light conversation. "If it makes you feel any better, I don't think the gerbil meant to hurt you," he said, tying off the last knot. "Judging by its teeth and size, its primary food source is insects. I think you just scared it. In fact, I'd bet a lot —"

"Daniel, you're not helping."

"I just thought you'd feel better knowing —"

"Daniel!" He knew Daniel was trying to help, but right now he needed to remain focused. "I feel like a lamb being led to the slaughter," he grumbled, hoping Daniel would accept his statement as the apology it was. He hated feeling helpless. He didn't even have someone to blame for the situation, other than the gerbil who, if Daniel was correct, was probably just trying to defend its nest.

Of all the stupid —

"O'Neill?" Teal'c's voice came from slightly to his left.

Grateful for the interruption, O'Neill responded, deliberately keeping his voice matter-of-fact, as if being blind and helpless on an alien planet was an everyday occurrence. "What is it, Teal'c?"

"Major Carter feels we should take the most direct route back to the gate. If we guide you, are you capable of running?"

"Lead on."

It was terrifying, running blind with only Daniel to guide him, but thirty minutes later, O'Neill felt the sunlight on his face as they emerged onto the windswept bluff overlooking the grassland. He could feel the bare rock beneath his boots and could imagine the totem pole still standing watch over the Stargate below. Or maybe it was a warning. *'Watch out for spitting gerbils.'*

Daniel pulled him to a halt. "Hold up a second." He took a couple of deep breaths, then O'Neill heard him swing his pack off his back.

"What's the matter, Daniel? That little jog tire you out?"

"That 'little jog' was a good four miles," Daniel retorted. "Besides, something in my pack is digging into my kidneys. Let me fix it."

"Ok everyone, take five." O'Neill heard two sets of footsteps — Sam and Teal'c — head in different directions. He gave them a minute to reconnoiter, then called out, "See anything?"

Teal'c responded first. "Major Carter, I believe there —"

"Hey!" Though he couldn't see anything — a temporary condition, he assured himself — he was still in command of the expedition. "Who's in charge around here, Teal'c?"

Teal'c sounded faintly abashed. "My apologies, Colonel. You are in charge."

"That's right. So what were you saying?"

"I believe there is something here you need to see."

Walked right into that one. "Carter, check out what Teal'c found." He squatted next to Daniel who, by the sounds of it, was busy sorting through his pack. "If I didn't know better, I'd swear Teal'c did that on purpose."

"Huh?" Occupied with his backpack, Daniel had missed the byplay. "What did you say?"

"I said —"

A fist-sized rock whizzed by Daniel's head. Startled, he looked up, then lunged at Jack, barely managing to knock him out of the path of another incoming missile. "Sam! Teal'c!" He swept his gaze through the trees and caught a flicker of motion to one side. "Incoming! Two o'clock!"

"I see it." For a big man, Teal'c was surprisingly fast. Crouching, he ran to the base of the tree Daniel had indicated and fired his zat upward. Something screeched. Branches swayed and leaves fluttered down as whatever it was fled.

"Get off me!" Jack pushed at Daniel who was lying across his legs. "What the hell is going on? Teal'c?"

"I believe it was one of the creatures we heard earlier. They seem to correspond to what you call 'monkeys'." As if in response to Teal'c's voice, they heard several more screeches, then a chorus of answering hoots from deeper in the forest.

"Uh oh," Daniel said.

"Uh oh?" Jack rolled to his feet and instinctively reached for his gun, then lowered it with a grimace. "Uh oh, what?"

Daniel knew he sounded worried. "I think our little monkey friend is calling for reinforcements."

"Reinforcements for what?"

"I think they're going to attack."

Jack's jaw clenched. "Why? Do we look like bananas?"

Three years ago, such a question would have thrown Daniel for a loop but now he could follow it without losing a beat. "Monkeys eat meat whenever they can. It's good protein. In fact, chimpanzees have been known to attack —"

Sam cut him off. "Colonel, I'm afraid we have another problem. The hy-afs have left the lake area and are heading in this direction. And they're closer to the gate than we are."

"They're probably just heading for the pass. We'll give them a few minutes to go through."

"I don't think so, Colonel. They're heading for the road leading up here, not the pass."

"Today just keeps getting better and better." Jack patted his MP-5. "But this will take care of them."

"That is unlikely," Teal'c said as he rejoined the group. "They are small and very fast."

"And there's more of them," Sam added. "Some must have been hidden in the grass. There's thirty, thirty-five, of them heading this way." Two more tennis-ball-sized rocks came hurtling at them — Sam blocked one with her pack and Teal'c stepped backwards and let the other sail harmlessly over the cliff. "But we can't stay here." A chorus of angry chattering answered her and she responded by firing her zat at the nearest tree.

"C'mon." Daniel grabbed the colonel and hustled him toward the alien totem pole. "Stay here."

"Daniel, I'm not cowering behind some old pole while my team fights off deranged monkeys." He pulled his arm free. "Blind or not, I give the orders around here. Carter, Teal'c — take them out."

Dutifully, they opened fire. But it was hopeless. "Sir, we can't *see* them."

Sam's anxiety was obvious. Firing blindly was worse than useless and the clamor of hoots was coming closer. It sounded like a whole tribe of monkey-creatures. "Jack, we can't stay here," Daniel said. "They're going to brain one of us eventually and then we'll really be in trouble."

Jack rubbed at his blind eyes in obvious frustration. "Teal'c, if we meet the hy-afs on the road, they'll be bunched together. Can we take them then?"

"Given their numbers, it is possible but unlikely." Teal'c kept a wary eye on the trees, alert for signs of movement. "The odds would be against us."

"The odds would be a lot better if I wasn't —"

"Colonel?" Sam said as Daniel dodged another rock and both she and Teal'c opened fire again. "We might have another problem."

"Could you be more specific?"

"I think the hy-afs might be poisonous."

Jack cursed, flinching as a rock thumped against the totem pole just above his head.

"Sir, get down!"

He hit the ground, Daniel following suit as several more rocks struck the dirt around them. They'd crack a head as easily as a soft-boiled egg, he thought grimly.

"Carter, why do you think they're poisonous?" Jack called. "And keep it short."

"Their size. Teal'c noticed the same thing — they seem too small to take down the buffalo, even as a pack. And the horns — the buffalo's horns — seem defensive, not offensive."

Daniel caught her train of thought. "Designed to protect the face." He turned to Jack. "So they might be like the gerbils. If they blind the buffalo first, they can kill it easily."

He left unsaid what he knew Jack would already be thinking — that predators go after the weakest target. And that, right now, was him.

"Okay," Jack said, "let's say they're poisonous. What are our options?"

In the end, they had only one.

They went over the cliff.

It wasn't a bad plan. It should have worked. But it didn't.

O'Neill was deeply unhappy. His shoulder ached from where he'd banged it against a protruding rock and he'd wrenched his knee — *my good knee, dammit!* — when Teal'c had pushed him onto the ledge. On the other hand, he supposed he should be grateful — if the ledge hadn't been within reach, they'd be in trouble. More trouble, anyways. "Carter. Report."

She took a deep breath. "We're about fifteen feet up from the base of the cliff. The ledge we're on is roughly three feet deep and ten feet long. It falls off about two feet to your left."

"So don't step sideways," Daniel murmured.

Carter continued, "The gate's about three hundred meters below and to our right, but there's a pack of hy-afs waiting at the bottom of the cliff."

"I thought you said they were coming up the road?"

"I did. This is a different pack. They must have come from the other end of the pass. I'm sorry, I should have seen them coming."

"It is not your fault," Teal'c said. "I should have been watching—"

"Actually," Daniel interrupted, "I'm the one who—"

"Ok, stop it." O'Neill already knew what his team refused to admit — that if they hadn't been so focused on getting him down the cliff safely, they would have seen the new hy-afs sooner. Not that it would have done much good. "It's no one's fault so forget about it. What's our situation now?"

Between a rock and a hard place. The devil, and the deep blue sea. Fire and frying—

"As I said, we're about fifteen feet up from flat ground," Carter said. "The cliff slopes forward a bit below us, we could almost slide down."

Teal'c's low rumble came from his right. "But it is too steep for the hy-afs to climb up. And the rock bulges out a few inches above us. Enough to deflect any rocks from the monkeys," he added, anticipating O'Neill's next question.

"So we're safe here, at least for the next few minutes."

"It appears so."

Jack called a brief rest while they reassessed their situation, and handed his canteen to Daniel. "Drink up."

"Thanks." Even though the water was tepid and metallic-tasting, at least it was wet. Daniel took several deep swallows, then capped the canteen and handed it back.

"On our next day off," Jack said, "what say we all go to the zoo and throw rocks at the monkeys?"

Daniel grinned. "Sounds good to me. I never liked the monkeys anyway. I usually just ignore their section."

"I wish these monkeys had ignored us."

Ignored us.... Of course!

Daniel mentally slapped himself on the forehead. *Idiot!* "Jack, take off your clothes." It was only when he saw Teal'c's eyebrow shoot skyward that he realized what he'd said. "Your jacket anyway. Take off your shirt and jacket. That's why they're after us."

"You are referring to the odor from the liquid on Colonel O'Neill's clothes?" Teal'c said after a second's pause, the inflection in his voice changing the statement into a question.

Daniel nodded. "The monkeys ignored us earlier. So did the hy-afs. The only thing that's changed is Jack getting sprayed."

"They have learned that the odor will lead them to something helpless," Teal'c said. "Easy prey."

Sam came to join them. "I think Daniel's right. Maybe we can distract them using your clothes as bait."

"If we tie them to a rock, I can throw them some distance from us," Teal'c offered.

"And that should lure them away," Daniel concluded triumphantly.

"But wait a minute," Sam said, a thoughtful look on her face. "Let's think about this."

Jack paused, his jacket part-way off. "What is it, Carter? You think I need to take *all* my clothes off?"

She didn't dignify his quip with a response. "Colonel, I didn't want to say anything earlier —"

"I hate it when you say that."

" — but we need to get you back as fast as possible." Daniel suspected she'd purposefully avoided talking about his medical situation in any detail, but he guessed now she didn't have a choice. "The way I see it, the venom will do one of three things. One, it can gradually wear off by itself after a few hours or days. Two, it —"

"Days! I can't wait that —"

"Colonel, that's the *best* option." Though he was her commanding officer, Sam had never had a problem standing her ground when necessary. Confident she had his undivided attention, she continued. "Two, it could destroy or permanently affect the muscles, leaving you effectively blind. Three" — she paused — "it could spread."

"Well, that sounds bad."

"Yes, sir. You might end up dead. Or paralyzed." She was being deliberately blunt, and Daniel admired that. They both knew that the possibility of living blind and helpless, forever trapped in his own thoughts, was something the colonel wouldn't wish on his worst enemy. But he deserved to know the truth. More importantly, he needed to realize the importance of getting back as quickly as possible. "Janet might be able to come up with an anti-toxin," Sam went on, "but she'll need a sample to use as a starting point. Like the liquid on your clothes."

The deep rumble of Teal'c's voice broke the silence. "Then we must get the colonel to Dr. Frasier as quickly as possible, along with his clothes."

"Agreed."

Jack was silent, but beneath the bandages covering his eyes, shielding his expression from the others, Daniel saw him hide a flinch. After a moment Jack said, "So no strip show today. Any suggestions for Plan B?" The insouciance in his voice only sounded a little forced.

Daniel carefully leaned forward and looked down the cliff face. "We could just slide down. Go in fast, surprise the hy-afs. Maybe we could get through."

Teal'c shook his head. "It would be extremely risky and the odds would not favor all of us getting through. On the other hand, a single person has a better chance." He straightened to attention. "Colonel, I am the fastest runner. I could lure the hy-afs northward while the three of you proceed to the gate."

"Absolutely not." O'Neill's tone brooked no argument. "We stay together."

"But, sir," Sam said, "I think Teal'c might —"

O'Neill held up his hand to cut her off. "Can you see the UAV from here, Carter? Does it look undamaged?"

Sam squinted down at the gate. "Yes, sir. It looks fine."

"And didn't you once say something about the UAVs having a secondary power source?"

"Sargent Siler and I were talking about replacing it with infrared sensors. I didn't think you were listening."

"Major, I listen to everything you say." Which was true — Jack might feign indifference but Daniel knew he *listened*. Most of the time, anyway. "Is there enough power to get it flying again?"

"Not for long. Maybe ten minutes or so. Why?"

"And it has a couple of missiles, right?"

"Small ones, yes."

"Perfect."

While Carter fiddled with the UAV's remote controls, the rest of them double-checked their equipment — laces tied, packs secure, safeties on. Daniel helped O'Neill perch on the edge of the ledge, and then sat down next to him. "Nothing to worry about, Jack. We'll just slide down like kids at a playground."

"Kids on a slide, huh?"

"A steep slide," Teal'c added as he took his position to his right. "With rocks."

"We'll be fine." Daniel patted O'Neill on the shoulder. "No need to worry. We'll get you to the gate."

He wasn't worried. He'd long ago learned not to worry about circumstances he couldn't change. He was concerned, maybe — concerned that his team would risk themselves trying to keep him safe. But he knew better than to say anything to Daniel; he was too idealistic, too determined to only see the best in any situation. It drove him crazy sometimes, but he wouldn't change it. "Just try not to hold us up," he said. "My *legs* are fine; it's my *eyes* that are the problem."

"But it's different if you can't see where you're going," Daniel said. "Teal'c is a better shot so he's taking your right side. I'll take the left."

The colonel reached out to pat Daniel's shoulder but hit his neck instead. "Give yourself some credit. You've become a much better shot since we first met."

"I'm not sure that's a good thing," Daniel muttered. "Anyway, once the hy-afs are gone, we'll slide down, then run for the gate. Teal'c and I will guide you while Sam watches our back."

O'Neill nodded his understanding, and then leaned toward Teal'c. "If anything happens," he whispered, "make sure the others get back." He didn't need to say more — Teal'c was a warrior and would accept the order in the spirit it was meant.

Teal'c's voice was low and reassuring. "Many years ago, Master Bratac taught me there are times a warrior must accept help so that he may rise and fight another day. We will not fail you."

O'Neill was saved from answering by Carter's announcement. "Ready," she said. "Everyone set?"

"Let's do it."

O'Neill couldn't hear anything from this distance, but suddenly Daniel let out a breath. "It's away! Out of the tall grass, sailing upward."

"Okay," Carter said. "Banking left, heading toward the lake and the buffalo."

"Don't spook them," O'Neill warned. "Just gather them up slowly. Work from one side to the other. Don't worry if one or two get away. Bunch them together. Tell me when they're ready."

Daniel leaned toward him, pressing against his shoulder. "So where did you learn so much about herding animals?"

"Didn't you ever watch old westerns on TV?"

Daniel sounded vaguely affronted. "Uh, no."

"See what you missed? But," O'Neill raised a cautionary finger, "don't try herding goats. They'll knock you flat on your ass."

"Personal experience?"

"Several. I wasn't always such a quick study."

"Colonel?" Carter's voice was tense. "I think we're as ready as we're going to be. They're getting a bit uneasy."

"Good." O'Neill faced the lake, wishing he could see through the bandages covering his eyes. "Shoot the first missile directly behind them. We want them to head this way, along the base of the cliff. Let them take care of the hy-afs."

Much to Daniel's surprise, Jack's plan worked. The missile exploded and the herd spooked, running as one, an unstoppable mass of flesh and blood and horn. When they reached the bluff, they swerved and ran along the base, mowing down bushes and small trees as if they didn't exist. Sam launched the second missile to encourage them to keep moving, and then shoved the UAV controls into her pack.

The hy-afs held their ground until the last second, snarling and snapping, then scattered like a bevy of quail, racing to avoid the buffalo's pounding hooves. The front of the herd reached them a few seconds later, the backs of the animals passing just beneath their feet.

Sam had to shout over the thunder of hooves. "On the count of three. One. Two. Three!"

As one, the team slid to the bottom, setting off small avalanches of gravel and soil. Handicapped by his lack of sight, Jack landed awkwardly, his right leg twisting under him. Disregarding dignity, Teal'c and Daniel grabbed Jack's arms and pulled him forward.

The four of them ran for the gate.

The buffalo's hooves had left the surface a churned-up mess of loose dirt and scattered rocks. O'Neill stumbled repeatedly but Daniel and Teal'c kept him moving forward. They tried to pick up speed when they reached the undisturbed ground but the thick grass conspired to slow them down. It felt like running through thigh-high water. O'Neill concentrated on keeping his balance as he counted steps...1017...1018...1019. "How much further?"

"We're almost there," Daniel panted. "Another hundred yards."

"First thing, you get the DHD," O'Neill ordered. Then he

heard the *bzzzt* of a zat to their rear. "Teal'c, what's going on? Where's Carter?"

"Hy-afs." Teal'c shoved the colonel toward Daniel. "Go ahead. I will assist her."

O'Neill resisted as Daniel tried to haul him forward. "We've got to help." Even as he spoke, he knew how ridiculous he sounded. He couldn't help anyone in his current state. *Helpless as a baby*, he thought bitterly. But he wasn't going to leave her behind. That was simply not going to happen. He heard two more *bzzzt's* and felt Daniel pulling on his arm. "Jack, it's all right. Teal'c's got her. Now come on, we've got to get the gate open."

"They're okay?"

"They're fine. Now c'mon!"

Reluctantly, O'Neill let himself be pulled forward. They stumbled through the thick grass — 58, 59 — then Daniel released his arm and started dialing home. He heard the chevrons slam into place with reassuring *thumps*, then the *whoosh* of gate activation. "Where are they?" he demanded as Daniel urged him up the ramp.

"Right behind us."

O'Neill jerked his arm free. "We'll wait for them."

Daniel knew better than to argue. Instead, he fired off a long burst to the left, then another, shorter burst to the right. O'Neill heard a yelp, then a chorus of snarls and yips. Twenty seconds later, he heard two sets of footsteps pounding up the ramp. "We're here, Colonel," Carter panted. "We made it."

O'Neill resisted the urge to touch her, to make sure she was really in one piece. "Then let's go home."

Teal'c straightened as Dr. Frasier came through the door. "Good news," she said, stripping off her gloves. Though Teal'c's expression remained impassive, Janet could detect a minute lessening of muscle tension around his eyes. Sam and Daniel were more demonstrative — they wore matching grins. Even General Hammond permitted himself a grin. "As you suspected," she nodded toward Sam, "both the gerbil's and hy-af's saliva contained neurotoxins. We're still working on antitoxins for future visits but the gerbil version seems to be wearing off on its own. I expect the colonel should be back to his old self in another day or two."

"His eyesight...?" General Hammond asked.

"Will be fine. The pupils are still dilated and he can't control his eyelids but the muscles are starting to twitch. Luckily the optic nerve is unaffected." Janet focused on Sam. "You're sure the hy-af didn't bite or scratch you at all?"

Sam held up three fingers. "Scout's honor," she said. "They jumped me from behind. Teal'c shot them before they figured out what a backpack was."

Janet shifted her focus to Teal'c. "Bringing one of the bodies back with you was good thinking. The toxin in its saliva is very different from the gerbil's. We won't know without further testing but I suspect it's more potent."

"Because it is intended for bigger animals," Teal'c said.

"I suspect so." Now that their immediate worry was over, she could feel the team's impatience to see the colonel. She really should order them to get some rest, but she knew that none of them would relax until they had assured themselves their leader was all right. "Before you ask — yes, you can go see him but keep it short. He needs rest. As do you all."

"Just a couple of minutes," Sam promised. Teal'c and Daniel nodded.

She held up her hand. "One more thing. I'm letting him sleep in his own room only because he promised he would leave the bandages alone. So don't let him talk you into taking them off for him." Janet gave all three of them a stern look. "That's an order. Don't make me do something you'll regret."

General Hammond added his authority to hers. "I second the order. Understood?"

There was a chorus of "Yes, general" and then the room emptied.

"We brought pie," Sam said.

"And coffee," Teal'c added. "Decaf as per Dr. Fraiser's orders."

"As long as it's hot and black," the colonel said. "Bless you both, I'm starving. Where's Daniel?"

"He'll be here in a minute," Sam said. "There's something in his room he wanted to get."

Colonel O'Neill held out one hand for coffee and gestured toward the back of his head with the other. "Teal'c, can you help me with this knot? It's a bugger."

"Dr. Frasier told us you would request our help to remove your bandages."

"She did?" The colonel replied, his voice pure innocence.

"She also warned us not to assist you in any way."

He straightened to attention, a difficult feat to manage while sitting in bed and holding a cup of coffee. "Are you going to listen to her or to your commanding officer?"

"General Hammond seconded the order."

"Damn." The colonel muttered something under his breath — Sam thought she heard the words 'Napoleon' and 'mini-me' — but then his expression brightened. "Did you say 'pie'?"

It took about a minute for him to wolf his slice down. "And what kind of pie did you get Daniel?" he asked as he used his fingers to swipe up the last crumbs from his plate.

Sam exchanged an amused look with Teal'c. "Blueberry," he said.

"His loss." The colonel waggled his fingers in Teal'c's direction. "He's not here, so hand it over."

As the colonel enjoyed Daniel's pie, Sam brought him up to date. "Janet analyzed the samples from your jacket and my backpack. Similar but different. She's working on antitoxins and General Hammond will make sure that follow-up survey teams have proper protection. Daniel has already said he wants to return — he thinks the writing on the totem might explain what happened to the people."

"I can tell him what it says." The colonel used his left hand to sketch imaginary words onto an imaginary blackboard. "It says 'Beware of spitting gerbils'."

"About the gerbils," Sam said. "I might have been wrong about them."

The colonel feigned disbelief. "Carter, I'm shocked. You? *Wrong* about something?"

She swallowed a smile, even though he couldn't see it. "I agreed with Daniel initially — I thought it was just defending itself. But now I think it was actively attacking."

"I do not understand, Major Carter," Teal'c said. "The animal is small and eats insects. Why would it deliberately attack something as large as the colonel?"

Glad to be asked — she loved explaining the answers to puzzles she'd figured out — Sam said, "They and the hy-afs, and the monkeys, have an opportunistic relationship. When the gerbil spits at something, the hy-afs or monkeys smell the venom —"

"The apple smell?"

"Yes, the apple smell. Odors can travel for miles. They smell it and come to take advantage of the situation. It doesn't help the gerbil directly but insects would be attracted to the, uh, decomposing parts left over."

"Thereby providing the gerbils with food," Teal'c observed, his voice as impassive as ever. "A relationship beneficial to all."

The colonel forked up the last piece of Daniel's pie. "Hey guys, that's all well and good but it's *my* rotting parts you're talking about. I'm trying to eat here."

Sam blinked. "Of course, sir. I'm sorry, I just —"

"Besides, I figured it was personal. I never liked gerbils."

Not long after, Daniel knocked on the door. "Come on in," the colonel called. "Did you bring a piñata? I'm all ready."

"Sorry, no piñata." Daniel pulled up a chair and accepted a

piece of pie from Sam but waved off Teal'c's offer of coffee. "We can't stay much longer. Janet caught me outside and threatened us with bodily harm if we weren't out of here in two minutes."

The colonel must have heard the unmistakable sound of fork on plate because he reacted with mock outrage. "Hey! Where did that pie come from?"

"I brought two pieces for Daniel," Sam replied, unperturbed by his outburst. "I knew you'd take one."

Oblivious to the colonel's chagrin, Daniel carried on. "Anyway, Janet sounded serious about us not staying much longer. She said something about a 'low-fat, low-salt, low-cholesterol diet' and I don't want to chance it." He held up a bag. "On the bright side, I brought you my portable CD player. I thought a little music might help you relax." Knowing the colonel couldn't see him, Daniel winked broadly at Sam and Teal'c and jerked his head toward the door. "Janet thought it was a good idea too."

"It's not one of those 'natural sounds' CDs, is it?" the colonel asked. "You know — the ones with waterfalls and crickets and stuff. Because I'm really not in the mood. And no Buddhist monks. Or artesian folk songs."

"That was *Armenian* folk songs and it's not my fault you don't appreciate good music." Daniel gave the other two a significant glance and jerked his head toward the door a second time. "Anyway, we'd better get going. Janet was pretty insistent."

When they stood outside the colonel's door, Sam whispered, "What was that all about?"

Daniel put his finger to his lips in the universal *keep quiet* signal. "Just listen."

After the rest of SG-1 had left for their well-earned rest, O'Neill lay back in the darkness and listened to the silence. Things could have been worse. A lot worse. But his team hadn't given up. They'd stuck together, worked together, and made it home together. All of them. Together. Carter, Teal'c and —

Speaking of Daniel... He leaned over and, after a bit of fumbling, found and pressed the play button. Maybe some music *would* help him sleep. He pummeled his pillow into submission and tried to relax as the music started but jerked upright as he recognized the insistent beat.

"Daniel!"

He grabbed for the player but couldn't turn it off before the beginning of Manfred Mann's best known song burst into the room.

"Blinded by the Light..."

STARGATE ATLANTIS
Second Time Sateda

Ron Francis

This story takes place in season five of Stargate Atlantis.

SHEPPARD tapped his watch when Rodney shuffled into Atlantis' conference room and fumbled for the steaming cup on the table in front of him.

"Welcome to the party, sleepyhead." He smiled as Rodney lifted the cup to his lips. "You take your tea with lemon, right?"

Rodney's hands stopped just before the cup touched his lips. "You *are* joking, right?" He cast a suspicious glance into the cup, tentatively inhaling the aroma confirming it was in fact lemon-free coffee. "Hilarious. Are you *trying* to give me a heart attack?"

"Just trying to wake you up. Mission accomplished."

"Oh, ha-ha."

"People," Woolsey said in his usual even tone. "May we move on to the reason you're all here so early this morning?"

"Please," Teyla said, sharing an exasperated look with Ronon.

As Woolsey was about to speak, Major Lorne arrived and took his seat without a word. Sheppard shot a querying look at Woolsey, which he ignored as he stood to begin the briefing.

"We've just received a report from the Genii that people are returning to Sateda," Woolsey said, and Ronon sat up straighter at the mention of his homeworld. "Early indications are that the settlers are Satedan, and that their aim is to rebuild their civilization. Best estimates put the number of people at close to six hundred, with more arriving every day."

"So many?" Sheppard sent a careful glance in Ronon's

direction. If the big guy was excited about the news, he was hiding it well.

"Yes, Colonel, six hundred."

"And these people, they are all Satedan?" Teyla said.

"That's what the Genii have indicated. And what I would like you to confirm."

"Wait," Rodney said, "how did they get there? The Wraith bombed the gate from orbit when they brought Ronon there to hunt him."

"According to the Genii, the gate wasn't destroyed, just toppled. Some of the settlers were able to convince someone with a ship, possibly the Travelers, to give them a ride back. Once they had the Stargate online, the rest of the people began to arrive."

Rodney glanced at Lorne. "And the major's here because?"

"Due to the extreme prejudice with which the Wraith destroyed Sateda, Major Lorne has been asked to accompany you. Just in case." Woolsey's face remained impassive, but Sheppard knew the unspoken reason was in case they ran into any more of Ronon's old friends — and he suspected Ronon knew it, too.

"So, we count some Satedans and then what?" Rodney said around a mouthful of coffee.

Ronon looked at him. "Then we make them leave."

Woolsey's eyebrow rose, and in a neutral tone he said, "Why would we do that?"

"Because they're not Satedan. My people wouldn't be that stupid." Ronon leaned forward and held Woolsey's gaze. "And these people have no right to be there."

Woolsey didn't back down. "Do we have any reason to believe that the Genii are mistaken?"

Before Ronon could reply, Teyla said, "The Wraith have been known to return to planets as advanced as Sateda to make sure the survivors do not rebuild. Every Pegasus culture knows this to be the case, which is why this news comes as a surprise. If the settlers are Satedan, it would be an unprecedented event."

Sheppard swiveled in his seat to face Teyla and Ronon. "And if they aren't Satedan?"

"Then they are trespassing on my planet and need to leave."

"Right," Sheppard said slowly.

"Looks like there might be a little more to this situation than we first thought," Woolsey said. "You leave in twenty. And remember — this is a diplomatic mission." He fixed his eyes on Ronon. "Will that be a problem?"

"No problem," Sheppard said with a smile. "Diplomacy is his specialty."

Twenty minutes later, they stood in front of the gate. Waiting. McKay huffed. "What's the holdup, Chuck?"

"We're not getting a lock on Sateda."

"Maybe the gate is currently in use?" Teyla offered.

"Maybe the Wraith are already culling them." Ronon's expression suggested he believed that to be the most likely scenario.

McKay dropped his pack with a grumble and stomped up the stairs to the control room. Without a word he interposed himself between Chuck and the terminal. "I'm running a diagnostic on the gate." A moment later, he said, "Huh, that's interesting."

"What's interesting?" Sheppard called up to him.

"Hmm? Oh, nothing. Just something unusual to note."

"Well, note it later."

Rodney shot him a glare before rechecking the status of the gate. "Looks like it was just a hiccup. We're good to go."

This time, the seventh chevron engaged and the satisfying whoosh of the Stargate flaring to life filled the room.

"Report in six hours," Woolsey said from the top of the stairs. "And good luck."

Sheppard stepped out of the Stargate and into a battle. "Cover!"

He threw himself behind a damaged wall and surveyed the scene. Darts zigzagged above the city, an aerial bombardment pounding the buildings and sending its people fleeing.

"The Wraith are already here!" Lorne yelled as he hunkered down next to Sheppard, bringing his P90 to bear.

"How? We only just learned there are people here." Sheppard edged up alongside Ronon, who was staring intently at the destruction. The intensity emanating from the man was unusually high, even for him, and a sinking feeling took root in Sheppard's gut. Something was wrong here.

"I thought you said the city was destroyed years ago?" Lorne said as he took cover.

Teyla joined them, keeping low. "How have they rebuilt so quickly?"

"What?" Rodney yelled over the din of battle as he crawled towards Sheppard's position. Looking back, he said, "Why hasn't the gate shut down?"

Sheppard just stared at the city. Many of the buildings were still undamaged, and a full scale battle was under way. Looking back to his team, he said, "This isn't right." Raising an eyebrow. "Rodney?"

"What did *I* do?"

Before Sheppard could respond, Ronon cursed, vaulted over the wall, and took off toward the city center.

"Ronon!" Sheppard yelled. "Damn it!"

There was nothing to do but go after him.

Sheppard approached what looked like a warehouse district, soot and grit buffeting his skin as he ran. Many people lay dead from the orbital bombardment, while even more had been fed upon. The lone constant was that they were all dead. With a grim shake of his head, he ran past the skeletal corpse of a Satedan soldier. Clearly, the Wraith had already taken this part of the city. But several of the buildings still stood, relatively undamaged — had he missed this neighborhood the last time he was here?

Catching a glimpse of Ronon disappearing around the corner at the far end of the street, he continued after him. They were behind enemy lines, so he couldn't shout. Lorne and Teyla would keep Rodney's voice down, too.

Passing the remnants of an obliterated depot, he heard the distinctive sound of Ronon's gun firing. He hurried through the smoke-filled rubble of a street that looked more like the Sateda he remembered and saw several Wraith drones, and a few warriors in black leather dusters, advancing on Ronon's position. Sprinting the remaining fifty meters, he raised his weapon and readied himself for battle.

Ronon was already locked in combat. Sword in one hand, gun in the other, he shot the first two Wraith, spun away from a stun beam and slashed through the throat of a third, nearly severing its head. Sheppard joined in, firing short bursts from his P90 into three more attackers. Ronon seemed intent on fighting through them; he clearly had somewhere he thought he needed to be.

Teyla caught up with them and joined the fray, shooting a Wraith that had slipped behind Sheppard. "Ronon!" she shouted. "We must withdraw and regroup."

He didn't seem to hear her.

"Ronon!" Sheppard tried. "Are you trying to get us all killed? What are you doing?"

He spun, plunged his sword into the abdomen of another Wraith. "Look around! They're destroying my planet."

Sheppard cast a puzzled glance at Teyla; Sateda had been destroyed years ago. A half dozen Wraith charged their position, blue energy flaring past him. As he returned fire, Teyla dove out of the path of a dart's culling beam and came up firing. The dart swung around for another pass but was hit by ground-based Satedan artillery.

Ronon was a blur of motion, slashing and shooting his way through the hapless drones. Another squad of Wraith slowed his advance, and Teyla hurried to help dispatch them. Aerial fire continued to pummel the city, sending showers of debris raining down. Sheppard dodged another stunner blast before stopping to reload.

Smoke billowed from the battered buildings surrounding them, shrouding Teyla who was fighting in close quarters with one of the warriors. Ronon slashed through another Wraith with a loud yell while Teyla finished off her foe. And then, for a moment, there were no more.

"Ronon!" Sheppard yelled, watching the streets for more trouble. "Fall back to the gate. We need reinforcements. Woolsey will send the *Daedalus*."

Ronon stalked back toward Sheppard, thrusting his finger into his chest. "You don't have a *Daedalus* yet."

"We don't have a... What are you talking about?"

"He's right, Sheppard." Rodney was bent over with his hands on his knees, trying to catch his breath.

"What the hell are you talking about, McKay?"

"Not what, *when*." He looked pale. "Sheppard, I think this is the original attack on Sateda."

"Thirteen years in the past?" Lorne said. "That's not possible."

"Solar flares, a glitchy Satedan gate — of course it's possible. Colonel Sheppard's already been to the future. Same thing happened to SG-1 when they were accidentally sent back to 1969."

"Rodney," Sheppard said with a flare of annoyance, "what were those readings you found so interesting in the gate-room?"

He looked uncomfortable. "Solar flares."

"Rodney!"

"What? We gate out during solar flares all the time. It's like a trillion to one chance that this could happen."

"Well, it did happen, didn't it?" He huffed out a breath. "Fine. How do we get back?"

"A good question," Teyla said. "But maybe we should find a safer place to discuss it?"

They took cover in the remains of a mechanic's shop. Ronon paced back and forth like a caged predator, his mouth fixed in a thin impatient line. "I need to get out of here."

Rodney threw his hands up in warning. "Whoa — hold on. Whatever you're thinking of doing it's a bad idea." Blanching from Ronon's withering glare, he turned to Sheppard. "Look, we may have already altered the timeline just by setting Conan here on those Wraith."

"Killing Wraith is always a good idea," Ronon said.

"Normally, I'd agree with you. But what if one of those Wraith were destined to kill someone that would have betrayed humanity? Except now that guy gets to live and screw up the future because these Wraith weren't alive to kill him before he could betray us all."

Sheppard shook his head. "We don't know that's gonna happen, Rodney."

"Exactly, we don't *know*. We don't know what will happen if Ronon runs into his younger self. Will one of them cease to exist? We don't know what will happen if he saves some of his people, or if one of us dies here. All we know is that one wrong move could be the difference between us having an Atlantis to get back to or us screwing up the space time continuum."

"So, you want us to be bystanders while the Wraith destroy an entire planet?" Sheppard said. "I don't think we can do that."

"Too bad, we have to. We could be mortgaging our future by meddling here."

"Look," Ronon growled, "I don't know how we got here, and I don't care about the space time... whatever. I have someone I need to save. Now get out of my way!"

Arms crossed, Rodney stuck out his chin. "No."

But Ronon just shoved him aside and started running.

Ronon raced through the city with abandon. All he could think about was saving Melena. More orbital fire shook the ground as he crouched behind a wall, waiting for two approaching Wraith to get close enough for a quiet kill. A full swing severed the head of the first, while the second paused in surprise. His shock was quick to wear off as he ducked Ronon's next swing and landed a blow to his chest, slowing him.

Ronon flashed a feral smile as he whirled his sword in his hand and settled into a battle stance. Sheppard caught up to him and raised his weapon, but Ronon said, "No guns."

The Wraith used the opportunity to pounce, but Ronon was ready for him. Rolling through the Wraith's attack, he thrust his sword behind him into the warrior's midsection. Pulling the sword out, he spun and decapitated his injured foe.

Teyla had come after him too. "Ronon, I know it is difficult, but we must not interfere here."

"I told you, I have someone to save."

"Melena?" Sheppard's question drew a raised eyebrow from Teyla.

"You can't stop me," Ronon said and adjusted his grip on his pistol.

"No, I can't." Sheppard gestured for Ronon to lead the way. "So let's go."

"John," Teyla said, "I do not think this is wise."

"She was his *fiancée*."

"But Rodney is right: the potential damage to our own future —"

"Look, the way I see it, if we take her from here right to Atlantis in the future, there's no way we can mess up the timeline. She won't be alive and unsupervised, fiddling around for thirteen years, she'll go straight from here to our future." He looked at Ronon. "Maybe it's the one thing we *can* do."

"I doubt it works that way," Teyla said. "But I hope you are right."

Ronon was surprised. Not that he would have turned around if Sheppard had refused to help him, but he was glad to avoid a confrontation. And he was glad of Sheppard's support — his friendship. With a nod of thanks, he turned down a deserted alley, stopping to make sure there were no Wraith in sight. The avenue had taken very little damage and served as a poignant reminder of what his life had once been. When he first enlisted in the military, he had lived in a red-brick building much like the ones that lined these streets. Pushing thoughts of the past from his mind, he turned and said, "This way."

They followed him through the city until their path was blocked by a cluster of Wraith. Ducking behind a building, he motioned for Sheppard and Teyla to be still. Sweat trickled down his neck as he cast a covert glance around the corner. "That's the Council Hall," he said. "I think they're using it for a base of operations. We need to find another way around."

Leading them back down the alley, they passed two intersections before he ushered them into a vacant building.

"Where are we going?" Sheppard asked.

"There's an access tunnel under this warehouse. It's a straight run past the Council Hall."

Teyla followed them into the expansive structure. Exposed steel girders held corrugated sheet metal walls while scattered crates and pallets littered the cement floor, but it was clear that no one had occupied this space for quite some time. "What about the Wraith? Do they know of this tunnel? I do not relish the idea of being trapped underground by the Wraith."

"I think they are still a couple days away from discovering our tunnel system." Ronon threw a pallet aside and opened a hatch.

"You *think*?" Sheppard eyed the hatch dubiously.

"It'll be fine."

Ronon dropped down the ladder into the tunnel and, after a hesitation, Sheppard followed. They waited for Teyla to close the hatch behind her before they took off at a run, the flashlight on Sheppard's weapon lighting the way.

After a few minutes, Ronon heard Satedan voices coming from an intersection in the tunnel several meters away. He dropped flat. Teyla followed suit while Sheppard extinguished his light and hunkered down next to them.

"All I am saying is Kell had the right idea, leaving before the Wraith showed up." Two soldiers, carrying a large crate, appeared at the intersection and turned left without noticing their uninvited guests.

"Maybe," the second man said, "but he's one of our best and we could use him right now."

"We could use a miracle right now," said the first. "Let's just get this ammo to the front line."

They picked up the pace and hurried down the passageway.

"That was close," Sheppard murmured once they'd gone, pushing back to his feet. "Which way now?"

"Up," Ronon said, chancing a look around the intersection to make sure no one else was approaching. "Third ladder along will bring us out in a warehouse close to the hospital."

He led the way, Teyla keeping pace as they jogged down the empty tunnel. When they reached the ladder she put a hand on Ronon's arm, stopping him before he could climb. "Ronon," she said, "are you certain Melena is still alive?"

"I remember this day like it was yesterday." Every second was etched into his memory. "I still have a few hours to save her."

Sheppard looked as if he wanted to say something but didn't know how to broach the topic. Ronon let go of the ladder and said, "What?"

"I was just thinking, if you couldn't get her to leave with you last time, how are you going to do it this time?"

Brandishing his weapon, he said, "I didn't have a stun setting last time." He didn't wait for a reply, climbing the ladder and stealing out into another dark warehouse.

"The fighting sounds heavy outside," Teyla whispered from behind him.

It did. Through a broken window he could see a pitched battle underway, dozens of Wraith overwhelming a troop of Satedan forces.

Ronon unsheathed his weapons. "I'm not asking you to come," he said, and strode into battle without a backward glance.

Rodney followed Lorne through several blocks of destruction. He heard shouting and gunfire, but it was always in the distance, like a dream where he was continuously running towards something but never quite got there.

All around, the city was in ruins. Bodies, turned to husks by the Wraith, littered the ground and the stink of death hung heavy in the air. Lorne stopped and dropped into a crouch behind the remains of a wall, motioning Rodney to do the same.

"What? What's happening?"

Lorne pressed his finger to his lips and crouched lower. Rodney was about to speak again but was met with a glare. The reason became obvious as three Wraith warriors sauntered by. Lorne had his P90 ready as Rodney prayed they remained unseen.

Stopping in the middle of the pockmarked street, the Wraith searched the area. Lorne hefted his weapon a little higher behind their meager cover as the Wraith turned in their direction. Gripping his own weapon tighter, Rodney tried to take a steadying breath; battle seemed inevitable. Then a burst of heavy artillery fire in the distance drew the Wraith's attention.

A tense moment passed until the Wraith turned and headed toward the explosions. Once they were gone, Lorne stood. With a flash of annoyance he said, "How many years have you been in the field?"

The question struck Rodney as odd in light of the circumstances. "Almost six, why?"

"Six years," he repeated with a scowl. "How is it that in six years a genius like you hasn't figured out that when you're in a warzone and the man in front of you stops short, you should probably be quiet?"

"Well excuse me for not being captain commando. I don't see you wading through the Ancient database for anything that might be useful to Atlantis."

"It's not about intelligence, McKay, it's about common sense." He turned and continued through the rubble.

"You know what *is* about intelligence? Figuring out how we're going to get home," he replied, nursing his bruised ego.

"So can we just find somewhere safe to hide so that I can, you know, *do* that?"

"Working on it."

"Work faster, Major."

They continued on through the devastation. Building after building had been reduced to charred foundations and twisted girders. Plumes of smoke rose from everywhere, making breathing a chore. But Lorne led him into a small structure. The walls had taken significant damage, part of the roof had caved in, and a few tools scattered amid the rubble suggested it had once been a hardware store.

"Look for a hatch or a stairwell," Lorne said.

"Why?"

"The foundation feels sturdy. If there's a basement, we should be safe for a little while."

"Right. Good thinking." Searching the other side of the store, he took care as he moved larger items and fallen shelves out of his way. Finally, he reached a door and shoved it open. "Major," he called in a loud whisper. "I've got a stairwell here."

Lorne took point, switching on his weapon's flashlight as they descended the gloomy stairs. The basement was packed with crates full of tools and building supplies. Lorne navigated the narrow aisles between stacks of crates until he arrived at a small area that had been cleared out. Two chairs and a table sat next to a sink, opposite a brown couch. "Looks like a breakroom of some sort," he said as he slung his backpack onto the table, raising a small cloud of dust. "You can work on what went wrong with the gate while I scout the area."

"You're leaving? I think that's a bad idea."

"I just need to make sure we're not stuck in the middle of a thousand Wraith. I also want to leave some bread crumbs for Colonel Sheppard."

"Ooh, breadcrumbs. That reminds me, I've only got two protein bars with me. Did you bring extra?"

"Looks like you'll be starving 'til you get us home. I'll be back in twenty."

"Fine, just don't lead any Wraith back here."

"I *have* done this before," Lorne replied as he disappeared behind the crates.

Opening a protein bar, McKay said to himself, "Now, let's figure out how we get home."

He'd been working for some time, absorbed in the problem, when voices in the store above caused him to stop cold. He stared at the ceiling. "Don't come down here. Don't come down here. Don't come down here."

Gunfire.

He flinched, ducking involuntarily. Had someone decided to make his haven their last stand? The deep boom of Satedan weapons mixed with the higher pitched stunners while McKay looked for a place to hide. Somehow he didn't think under the table would cut it.

Soon, he heard screaming mixed with Wraith growling, and he grimaced at the thought of what was happening above. The gunfire grew more sporadic until he heard the familiar tat-tat-tat of a P90 firing controlled bursts. Lorne.

Crap. He couldn't hide down here while Lorne was fighting. Could he? No. No, he couldn't.

Taking a deep breath, he trudged up the stairs to back Lorne up. Taking the last bite of his protein bar — he tried not to think of it as his last meal — he burst through the door with a yell. Then dove for cover as a triple-barrel shotgun swung his way.

"It's okay. He's with me!" Lorne shouted. "Nice entrance, McKay."

"You're welcome." Rodney picked himself up out of the rubble, eyeing the Satedan soldier whose weapon was still trained on him. "Who are our new friends?"

A tall man wearing a tan duster replied, "Name's Devin and this is Steed. We're all that remain of the western defenses. Who are you?"

"That's a long story." He threw a look at Lorne — long, and impossible to answer. "You didn't happen to see a couple other people dressed like us and a big Satedan guy with crazy hair, did you?"

"That almost sounds as if he is speaking of Ronon," Steed said.

"As if Ronon would ever fight with the likes of him."

"What? Why wouldn't he?" He hated feeling defensive, but he should have expected it. All the Satedans he had met were brutes and had little use for the type of intellect it would take to actually defeat the Wraith.

As Devin and Steed took off towards a distant tree line, visible now through the ruined city, Rodney felt his bag being pushed into his hands.

"Come on," Lorne said. "Let's go. There'll be more Wraith on the way."

Teyla fired from cover as the rout continued.

This was a bad idea: they would either end up dead, or with no future to which to return. A dart screamed overhead, its high-pitched whine assaulting her ears as it beamed more drones into the battle. Several Satedan soldiers remained, but they had to know it was a lost cause by now.

Satedan artillery hit a dart, sending it into a red brick building. The dart's death knell was deafening, ending with a fiery explosion. Three soldiers were thrown by the blast and one stayed down, scorched beyond recognition, the acrid smell of burnt flesh filling the air.

"We need to withdraw!" she shouted, but Ronon was too focused on saving the woman he loved to hear her.

Breaking cover, she considered what she would do if she had the chance to save her father. A great deal, no doubt.

She raced toward Ronon and Sheppard, flinging herself out of the path of another culling beam. But it caught two soldiers and she watched with a sickening lurch as they were swept away.

"We cannot remain here," she yelled as she reached Sheppard

and Ronon. "They will overwhelm us."

"Agreed," Sheppard said. "Ronon, we have to find another way."

A second dart was hit and spiraled into a dozen Wraith, engulfing them in the detonation — and opening a path through the enemy forces.

"This way is fine," Ronon grunted as he took off, slaloming around the dart's flaming debris and sprinting through the hole in the Wraith line. Sheppard cursed, but followed, and Teyla brought up the rear.

Ronon was several steps ahead of them as he raced towards the hospital. But a blast from the orbiting hive hit the building and hurled him across the street.

Teyla dropped to the ground, arms over her head as debris rained down. When she looked up, Ronon was trying to stand, blood streaming down his face. But he stumbled, fell back to the ground, and didn't move.

"Cover me!" Sheppard was on his feet, running towards Ronon.

Teyla followed, weapon raised, surveying their surroundings.

Sheppard crouched next to Ronon. "He's out cold. We need to get him out of here. Help me get him on his feet."

Teyla resisted the urge to point out that she had been saying that all along. "We are exposed," she said. "We must find shelter immediately."

"We need one of those tunnels," Sheppard said. "And a wheelbarrow would be nice."

Taking some of Ronon's weight from Sheppard, she feared how Ronon would react when he woke to discover he had failed to save Melena again. She could not imagine the horror of watching her people annihilated for a second time.

Three close encounters later, they found their way back into the tunnels. Safe from the battle raging overhead, they began to move a lot faster. Ronon was still unconscious, but she and John had fallen into a rhythm that allowed them to make good speed. Their luck held and they didn't run into anyone else. Perhaps there was no one left in this part of the city to run into?

When they reached the end of the tunnel, Sheppard said, "You stay with him. I'm going to recon the area and look for Lorne and Rodney."

It was a long fifteen minutes before he returned.

"I didn't find them," he said as he dropped back into the tunnel, "but I did find this." It was a wrapper from one of the Lantean food bars. "I guess Rodney got hungry."

Teyla smiled. "Do you think they're close?"

"If I know Lorne, he headed north. He'd want to find a safe place for McKay to work, but he wouldn't want to go too far from the gate." He crouched next to Ronon. "C'mon, let's get him out of these tunnels."

They crept on through the remains of the city, staying in the shadows wherever possible. Not that there was much left to cast a shadow in this part of the city. Judging by the numbers of bodies — Wraith and Satedan — the fighting had been fierce. She prayed that Rodney and Lorne had survived.

In the distance, the sound of battle continued, but nothing moved here except them. Thick smoke hung over charred buildings and the ruins extended all the way to a distant tree line.

That's where Sheppard was taking them, stopping every so often to study marks and scratches in the rubble. "Trail of breadcrumbs," he said with a smile when Teyla asked.

When they reached the forest, he laid Ronon against the trunk of a large tree and began to scan the area for another marker. Peering at something carved into the bark, he smiled. "They're close."

"Are you sure?"

He indicated the carving. "McKay says they're half a klick away."

"Then let us go." With a weary sigh, she helped John lift Ronon one more time.

Five minutes later, Lorne came running out to meet them with Rodney in tow.

"What do you mean you have to go back, Colonel?" Lorne knew his tone bordered on insubordination, but didn't much mind.

"There's still a chance to save Melena. I have to try."

"You already tried," McKay said. "And Ronon almost got himself killed. Anyway, there's no way you can get there in time now."

"I think I can."

"But there's no reason to risk yourself, we should —"

"Yes there is!" Sheppard gestured at Ronon who lay unconscious on the ground. "He would do the same for any one of us, without question. We have to try."

"No. We have to get home," McKay said. "That's our priority."

"This is not a debate, Rodney. Just figure out the problem with the damn gate." The colonel looked at his team. "Teyla, stay here. And Lorne, keep them out of trouble. I'll be back as soon as I can."

Before they could reply, Sheppard was heading back to the dying city.

Into the silence he left behind, Lorne said, "Okay, let's get Ronon a little more comfortable."

As much as Lorne considered the team his friends, he sometimes felt like an outsider among them. Sheppard's unit contained no other member of the military and, as a result, their style was unorthodox to say the least. He preferred things by the book, but he was willing to adapt for this team.

Maybe that's why they're so successful, he mused as he helped Teyla lift Ronon.

"How's the gate problem coming, Dr. McKay?" he asked with a grunt as they carried Ronon deeper into the woods. "Any chance we're getting home?"

"The *gate problem*, as you so eloquently describe it, is an incredibly complex set of calculations requiring a massive power source and a perfectly timed solar flare, neither of which we have at the moment. So our chances of getting home are slim. Unless I perform another miracle."

Lorne couldn't help himself. "So, half an hour?"

"Ha-ha, Major." McKay's scowl deepened.

"How massive a power source are we talking here, doc?"

"A ZPM would be nice, but in lieu of that, a Wraith blast from orbit should do the trick. The timing would have to be perfect, but it may be our only option."

"So we would need to lure the Wraith into firing on the gate at the precise moment we need them to?" Teyla stopped for a moment to adjust her grip on Ronon.

But Lorne decided they were far enough into the woods to take a break. "Let's put him down here, we're deep enough to be hidden."

Rodney started, snapping his fingers. "What if we use a — No, that won't work." Furrowing his brow, he pulled out his tablet and sat down.

"Perhaps I should go after Colonel Sheppard," Teyla said as she propped Ronon's head on one of the backpacks.

"That would be a bad idea," Rodney replied without looking up.

Teyla opened her mouth to object, but Lorne said, "He's right, we should stay together." The last thing he needed was to be looking for scattered teammates in a warzone. Sheppard had ordered him to keep them out of trouble and that's what he planned to do.

Ronon began to stir, muttering a few unintelligible words. Teyla exchanged a look with Lorne. Neither of them wanted to tell him what had happened.

"What...?" he asked, his hoarse voice little more than a whisper.

Teyla helped him lift his head, offered her canteen. "You were caught in an explosion and injured." She let him take a sip of water. "You've been unconscious some time."

"Where are we?" He blinked up at the trees with unfocused eyes.

"Colonel Sheppard and I brought you to the forest north of the city."

"What about...?" Gulping hard, he found it difficult to finish the question.

Lorne could see the pain set in as Ronon became more alert. He couldn't imagine what the Satedan was going through. "Colonel Sheppard returned to the hospital to try and save Melena."

"He what?" The confusion in his eyes stemmed from more than just the head injury. "Why?"

"He's hell-bent on getting himself killed, that's why," McKay said.

Teyla shot Rodney a glare. "What Rodney meant was that Colonel Sheppard believed you would do the same for him, and returned without hesitation."

"No." Ronon tried to sit up, but Teyla held him in place with one hand and he slumped back to the ground. "No, he shouldn't have done that."

"He was quite adamant that he should." Lorne could see the emotion playing across Ronon's usually stoic face. To say this had been a difficult day for the man would be an understatement, and it was far from over. Taking a deep breath, he said, "In the meantime, what sort of power sources do you have here on Sateda?"

Ronon looked at him with a blank stare and McKay said, "I know where you're going with that, Major, but it won't work. It has to be orbital bombardment."

Teyla lifted an eyebrow. "Why?"

"Do you really want me to waste time answering that incredibly complex question? Or are you going to trust me when I say we need an orbital bombardment to coincide with a solar flare?"

"Whatever, McKay," Lorne said. "Since we have no way of

knowing when, or if, there will be a solar flare that will match the previous activity —"

"Future activity."

"Whatever!" Lorne threw his hands in the air.

"We must also entice the Wraith to strike at the correct moment," Teyla added.

Ronon said, "That's the easy part."

"Oh really?" McKay peered at him skeptically. "And how exactly is that the easy part?'"

Wincing as he sat up, Ronon said, "By tomorrow morning, the Wraith will stop dialing in to our gate. But they'll remain in orbit for three days. That's our window."

McKay was interested. "Window for what? The proper solar activity?"

"All we have to do is set off an explosion large enough for the Wraith to register from orbit, then we dial Atlantis."

Rodney's eyes lit up. "Once we have their attention, they'll want to make sure we don't get away and they'll try and take out the gate." He looked back at his tablet. "Now all I need to do is figure out the solar activity around the planet…"

Lorne smiled at the thought of Ronon figuring out a problem Rodney had yet to solve.

As the sun marched towards the horizon and dusk settled in around them he looked at his watch, wondering when — or if — Colonel Sheppard would return.

Sheppard exited the tunnel in the same warehouse Ronon had led them to earlier. This time, however, there was no warehouse, only twisted steel. Plodding through the rubble, he saw the hospital still standing and prayed he wasn't too late. The fighting was over in this part of the city, and dusk had given the area an eerie feel. The battle ending didn't bode well for the successful completion of his mission. Darting across the street, using piles of debris for cover, he approached the medical center. Windows were blown out, the walls were scorched and black, but the building remained standing.

His gut clenched, however, when he got inside and realized there was nobody left alive. The building had been bursting at the seams earlier. Now there was nothing here but death. Wiping sweat from his brow, he paced through corridor after corridor of skeletal remains and charred bodies. He was too late.

"Damn it!" he yelled, kicking an empty gurney. How the hell was he going to tell Ronon? Aside from the wayward mission with his three Satedan friends, saving Melena was the first thing Sheppard could ever recall his friend *wanting*. Ronon always had his back, but Sheppard had failed him when he needed him the most.

As he left the facility, he saw three shadows drop into the tunnel he'd used to traverse the city. The passageway was compromised; there was no going back that way. Plumes of smoke, rising from hundreds of buildings, obscured the darkening sky and without the use of the tunnels it would be difficult and dangerous to navigate the ruined city. But he had no choice. With a heavy sigh, he headed north towards his team.

Two hours later, he could make out the tree line in the hazy moonlight. *Half a klick through the city, a few hundred meters to the trees, a kilometer through the forest.*

But as he prepared to round the next corner, he heard a noise so subtle he almost ignored it. Glancing around, he yelped as two pale hands reached out and picked him up, hurling him several meters.

He landed awkwardly on a pile of rubble, a searing pain stabbing through his shoulder. A piece of rebar, gored with blood, stuck out through his uniform. With a pained cry, he pried himself off of the metal rod and staggered to his feet, facing the half a dozen Wraith sauntering towards him.

"Today you die, human!"

The Wraith's arrogant gaze ended with the first burst from Sheppard's P90. Three more went down before the other Wraith were on him. A blow to his face staggered him, opening a gash above his eye. The Wraith ripped open his vest and reared back with a growl, thrusting its hand towards Sheppard's chest.

He blocked it, plunging his field knife through the creature's feeding hand.

The Wraith snarled, cradling its hand, and Sheppard followed by emptying his Beretta into its chest. It fell back, dead, but was immediately replaced by another. Squinting hard in concentration, Sheppard focused through the pain. He released the empty magazine but fumbled his sidearm, blood in his eyes, his wounded shoulder making his arm useless.

A blow to his stomach sent the gun and the magazine flying from his hands and two rough hands hoisted him against the remains of an office building. Each movement sent agony through his shoulder, but worse was the realization that he had not only failed Ronon, he had failed his entire team.

"I will kill you slowly for what you have done here, human," the Wraith said, so close he could smell its fetid breath on his face.

Sheppard grunted his defiance as the Wraith hissed, pulling back to feed. Sheppard closed his eyes, refusing to give the Wraith the satisfaction of seeing his fear as he waited for the end to come.

The sound of a Satedan triple barrel shotgun jolted his eyes open in time to see the second shot launch the Wraith into a wall. He looked over to see a young Satedan soldier with dreadlocks standing with a frightened little girl. Wiping the blood from his eye, he realized it was a younger Ronon. He wanted to hug him but remembered this Ronon had no idea who he was and would probably shoot him if he tried.

"You need to get out of here. If you still have family, go be with them," Ronon said.

"Thanks." He turned to go but felt compelled to stop and say, "Hey, listen. Things are gonna get bad, but don't lose hope. You're gonna make it."

Ronon scowled. "What?"

"Never mind." He couldn't say more or he'd risk changing too much. "Just keep fighting."

Ronon shook his head and picked up the child, taking off toward the west of the city.

John watched him go, then grabbed his sidearm and limped on towards his team.

Rodney was not an optimistic man. In his experience, hope usually led to soul-crushing disappointment. A vast sampling of personal memories stood ready to refute anyone claiming otherwise, but still he hoped. As much as they teased each other and argued, John Sheppard was one of his very few true friends. Rodney wanted that to continue, but it would be difficult if Sheppard got himself killed on this fool's errand.

The first light of dawn was lightening the sky when, through the trees, he saw a backlit figure limping towards the camp.

Squinting to get a better look, he got to his feet. "Major Lorne? I think Sheppard's back and he's not moving well."

And he was alone.

Lorne and Teyla hurried over, but Sheppard dismissed their concerns. "I'm fine. Just a minor disagreement with some Wraith."

He winced as Teyla ducked under his arm to help carry his weight. "You do not seem fine, John."

Ronon looked up expectantly, but Sheppard shook his head. He looked pale, his face blood-streaked. "I'm sorry," he said. "I was too late."

Ronon nodded, like he'd expected it all along. He probably had. "You tried," he said. "That means something, Sheppard."

"It's what friends are for, buddy," Sheppard said, grimacing as Teyla helped him to the ground.

Ronon didn't reply, but the silence between them felt significant. Even Rodney could sense the emotion.

Retrieving a first aid kit from her backpack, Teyla quietly set about tending Sheppard's wounds. After a while, and around a grunt of pain, Sheppard said, "Where are we on a way home, Rodney?"

Nowhere, he wanted to say, given that predicting solar activity using a tablet computer was proving impossible. "I'd like to remind you that, the only other time this has been done before, SG-1 had a literal message from the future to tell them the exact time and date of the next flare."

"What if— Ow." He flinched when Teyla applied some anti-bacterial ointment to the laceration above his eye.

"What if what?"

Sheppared touched the gash over his eye and Teyla batted his hand away. "Remember that crystal with Teyla's location on it that I got from future-you a couple years ago?"

"Possible-future-me. Yeah, why?"

"Well, if possible-future-you is anything like present-annoy-ing-you he probably put a whole lot more than Teyla's location on that crystal. And if I know present-you, you downloaded it all." He raised an eyebrow. "Didn't you?"

Rodney squirmed as everyone looked at him. "Okay, maybe I did. Why?"

"You probably would have included information on places we would be likely to visit or care about—"

"Yes." He felt a pulse of hope. "And given what possible-fu-ture-me knew about SG-1's missions..." Was it possible? Could he have ever anticipated this scenario? The database he'd downloaded from the crystal was searchable—future-him wasn't an idiot—and it didn't take long to find what he was looking for. With a surge of triumph he punched the air. "Yes! It's here. I'm a genius! Now, let's just hope... Yes, yes, here it is." His heart stopped. "Oh crap."

"Oh crap?"

Rodney looked up. "We've got just under three hours to get to the gate, set up an explosion, and get the Wraith to notice us. Or we're stuck here forever."

With one kilometer to go, and just under half an hour remaining, they were hunkered down watching several Wraith comb the desolate area close to the gate.

"Do we wait for them to leave or engage?" Lorne hissed.

"We have twenty-eight minutes remaining to get to the gate and get everything set," Rodney said. "We can't wait."

On Sheppard's signal, they opened fire. It was bloody and brutal but all the Wraith went down. Almost all. "One was able to escape," Teyla said, rising from her cover. "He will most certainly alert others to our presence."

Sheppard shifted his weapon in his good hand, his injured arm immobilized against his chest. "Then let's get to the gate before they do."

Arriving at the Stargate with seven minutes to spare, Lorne set the charges around a damaged but intact brick building while Rodney took cover behind the DHD, ready to dial. The wreckage of a dart smoldered to the left of the gate and Teyla, Sheppard, and Ronon crouched behind it. Lorne joined them with three minutes to spare.

He flashed a grin. "We just might make it."

As if on cue, a couple dozen Wraith emerged from the ruined city. "Why would you jinx us like that?" Sheppard said as the Wraith opened fire. "When they're close to the wired building, light it up."

"Not yet!" Rodney yelled from the DHD. "It has to be timed perfectly."

"How much longer?" Lorne opened fire on the oncoming Wraith. "I'm almost out of ammo."

"As am I," Teyla added.

"Seventy-five seconds."

As the Wraith drew even with the wired building, Sheppard said, "Intensify your fire, see if we can hold them here until we need to go."

"Forty seconds," Rodney yelled. Three stun blasts impacted near the DHD and he hit the dirt. "Thirty seconds!"

It felt like forever.

"I'm out!" Lorne yelled, drawing his sidearm .

Rodney shouted. "Twenty seconds!"

The Wraith began advancing at a run. There was no more

time. "Blow it!" Sheppard yelled.

Lorne hit the switch and the building detonated, taking out most of the Wraith in the blast. "Rodney, dial the gate!"

One of the Wraith staggered to its feet and Teyla poured a burst of gunfire into its chest, sending it staggering. She dropped her weapon to her side. "I am out as well."

"Rodney!" Sheppard ducked into a crouch as the orbital bombardment began.

"Ten more seconds." The next blast was closer and Rodney began dialing, holding off on the last symbol.

"Rodney, now!" Another blast sent Sheppard to his knees. Teyla grabbed his arm, helping him up as Rodney pushed the last symbol.

The event horizon erupted and Rodney started running. "Go, go, go!" he shouted as the orbital bombardment intensified. Now they just had to hope the Wraith actually hit the gate while they were in transit.

As the others flung themselves into the wormhole, Rodney sent his IDC and dived after them as another blast half threw him into the wormhole.

Landing with a thud, Rodney looked up. "Oh, thank God." He was staring at the gate-room ceiling.

"Med team to the gate-room!" It was Lorne's voice, behind him.

He sat up as Woolsey ran down from the control room and looked at his ragged team in dismay. "Colonel Sheppard, you didn't report in. What happened?"

"Long story," he grunted through the pain. "But it's good to be back where we belong."

"Yeah," Ronon said, from where he sat on the floor. "I guess it is." He and Sheppard exchanged a look but said no more.

Woolsey broke the silence. "Very well," he said, sweeping a glance across them all, clearly aware he was missing something. "Debrief in twenty."

"Uh?" Rodney said as the med-team arrived. "Better make

that debrief in the infirmary."

"Yes," Woolsey said, finally noticing their injuries. "Of course. In the infirmary."

"And I'm going to need something to eat first. I haven't eaten in days."

"Days?" Woolsey frowned. "But you've only been gone a few hours."

Sheppard laughed, the sound snapping off as he grimaced in pain. "Like I said, it's a long story…"

STARGATE SG-1
Sun-Breaker

Keith R.A. DeCandido

This story takes place three years after season ten of STARGATE: SG-1.

"AM I DISTURBING you, Colonel Carter?"

Samantha Carter looked up from her tablet to see that Teal'c had entered the crew lounge on the *General George Hammond*, the 304 ship under her command. He wore a sleeveless vest and a much more relaxed smile than he'd ever have had back when she'd first met him on Chulak all those years ago.

She gave him a smile right back. "Not at all, Teal'c. I was just stargazing. What can I do for you?"

"We have received a communiqué from Rak'nor. He should be in the system within the hour."

"Good."

Teal'c walked around the couch where Carter was sitting to stand in front of her. "Stargazing?" he asked with his trademark head tilt.

Carter held the tablet display out toward the Jaffa. "Just looking at the view from the *Hammond*'s port camera."

"To what end?"

She hesitated. "When I was a kid, the stars were my one constant. We moved around all the time, whenever Dad was transferred somewhere else, and there wasn't much I could hang onto as being consistent in my life — especially after Mom died. But the night sky was always the same. I could look in my telescope, and no matter if we were living in Lincoln or Dover or D.C. or Colorado Springs, the stars were right where I left them."

"Yet now, they are different."

Carter chuckled. "Yeah, now what I enjoy is how everywhere I take the *Hammond*, the stars are different. Every time we come out of hyperspace, it's a new set of stars. The constant is that it's never the same. Does that make sense?"

"Indeed it does. The progress of life is such that one's perspectives change. My own views have altered considerably over the decades I have lived."

Before Carter could respond to that, the voice of the watch officer came over the intercom. "Bridge to Colonel Carter."

"Go ahead," she said.

"Colonel, a cargo ship identifying itself as belonging to the Free Jaffa Nation has decloaked, and we're being hailed by its sole occupant, who calls himself Councilor Rak'nor."

Nodding, Carter said, "Pipe it to my tablet, please." She looked at Teal'c and patted the couch. "Teal'c?"

Inclining his head, Teal'c sat next to her.

The tablet altered from a view of the stars to that of a Jaffa with scarring on his forehead. His Goa'uld sigil had been burned off by his father, a rebel whose life Teal'c had saved. Rak'nor himself eventually became a valued member of the Jaffa Rebellion, and now served on the Free Jaffa Council.

"*Tek'ma'te*, Teal'c. Greetings, Colonel Carter."

Carter was somehow not surprised that Rak'nor greeted his fellow Jaffa first, even though protocol dictated he greet the commander of the ship before anyone else. She was almost not offended. "It's good to see you again, Councillor Rak'nor."

"Thank you, Colonel. We've both come a long way since you defeated me on Cal Mah."

In fact, Carter had forgotten about that until Rak'nor mentioned it. She didn't really think of it as a victory for her, more a demonstration of how much more useful a P90 was than a staff weapon. Although she had to admit that utterly destroying the target with her P90 that Rak'nor had only been able to hit two out of three times with his staff weapon was very gratifying — especially given the Jaffa's tendency in general to dismiss her because of her gender.

It hadn't been the first or last time Samantha Carter had been so dismissed. It also hadn't been the first or last time she had made those dismissals look incredibly foolish.

Rak'nor continued: "I have discovered that the Lucian Alliance has taken over the planet Armak."

"I don't know that world." Carter turned to look at Teal'c.

"I believe that the Tau'ri refer to the planet as P7X-942."

"Still doesn't ring a bell." Looking back at Rak'nor's image on her tablet, she said, "Not that any of us here are big fans of the Alliance, but why does its activity on this planet matter so much?"

"Once, Armak had significant naquadah deposits. It was one of Heru'ur's slave worlds. I was posted there for a time when I joined Heru'ur's service. When the mines were stripped dry, Heru'ur abandoned the world."

Teal'c added, "After Apophis defeated Heru'ur, the world remained abandoned, and it became a supply station for the Jaffa Resistance. We stored many weapons there."

"For a time," Rak'nor said. "Then the sun's flare activity increased to the point where it was no longer safe. We had to abandon Armak, and also leave the weapons cache behind."

Carter frowned. "If it's too dangerous for the Jaffa, wouldn't it also be too dangerous for the Alliance?"

"That was what I believed as well, which is why we must discover what they are doing there. Perhaps the flares have lessened, perhaps the Alliance has technology that protects them. Or perhaps it is just as dangerous, but the Alliance has either discovered the Jaffa weapons or a new vein of naquadah."

"Okay." Carter regarded Rak'nor. "I'm confused, though. The Jaffa Council obviously wants our help in this investigation of Alliance incursion onto P7X-942."

"What is the source of your confusion?" Rak'nor's tone was almost belligerent.

"Why that request is coming through you in a cloaked cargo ship instead of through official channels to Earth."

Rak'nor hesitated.

"The Jaffa Council rejected your request to investigate because it's too dangerous."

"Even if they did," Rak'nor said in a tone that indicated that there was no 'if' about it, "we would still require your help, Colonel Carter."

"The Jaffa have plenty of ships that are more advanced than the *Hammond*."

"I mean *your* help, Colonel. The Jaffa have ships, but we do not have scientific minds of your caliber."

Teal'c gave Rak'nor a dubious look. "There is a saying among the Tau'ri, Rak'nor: flattery will get you nowhere."

"Then you will not help us."

"Help you, you mean." Carter sighed. "Here's the thing — we've been having our own issues with the Alliance. I've had more than one run-in with them since we took the *Hammond* out, and I'm not thrilled with the notion of them getting their hands on naquadah or a stash of Jaffa weapons."

"Then you *will* help?"

"I can't promise that, yet. What I will do is speak to my superiors. Why don't you bring your ship on board? We'll clear a 302 bay for you to dock in, and Teal'c can give you the grand tour while I call Earth."

Rak'nor nodded. "Very well. Thank you, Colonel."

"Don't thank me, Councillor — just be a little more straightforward the next time you ask a favor. Stand by for a signal from the bridge."

After another nod from Rak'nor, the connection was cut, the screen reverting to the image of the stars.

First Carter contacted the bridge and instructed the watch officer to clear space in the 302 bay for Rak'nor's ship, and also to put a call through to the Pentagon on Earth.

Once that was done, she turned to Teal'c. "What's your take on Rak'nor?"

"He has always been both impulsive and passionate."

"Shoots first and asks questions later?"

Teal'c nodded. "I believe that Tau'ri saying does indeed apply."

"All right. I'm going to head to my cabin and wait for General O'Neill. Why don't you meet Rak'nor in the 302 bay?"

"Of course." Teal'c got to his feet, and Carter did likewise a second later.

"Look, Carter, I'm the last person to deny you a chance to get back at the Alliance for Icarus, but this sounds pretty thin. Besides, Rak'nor isn't exactly what I'd call a reliable source of intel. I mean, this is the same guy who turned Teal'c over to Heru'ur's pet sadist, right?"

Carter nodded at the image of Jack O'Neill that looked back at her on the computer monitor on the desk of her office. "Yes, sir, but that doesn't make the concern any less legitimate. There's something else — while I was waiting for you to respond —"

"I was meeting with the Joint Chiefs. They won't let my adjutants interrupt those meetings, no matter *how* many times I beg."

Chuckling, Carter said, "Regardless, it gave me time to look up P7X-942 and cross check the data Stargate Command has on that world with NASA and also with what Rak'nor provided. Rak'nor's data indicates that the sun surrounding P7X-942 is a flare star, in a constant state of flux. But that doesn't match what we have at the SGC or what NASA has observed with their telescopes — it should be a regular G-type star like ours that only flares occasionally. Of course, NASA's data is by nature several thousand years old."

O'Neill nodded. "Yeah, stars don't just change like that overnight." He smiled. "I know that from looking in *my* telescope." The smile fell, and he spoke in as formal a tone as he ever did.

"Colonel Carter, your request to have the *Hammond* investigate the peculiar characteristics of the sun that P7X-942 orbits is hereby granted. And if the Lucian Alliance has a problem with you being there, you can tell them that's why. If you happen to find out anything else along the way, fine and dandy. Tell Teal'c I said hi, and I'm still waiting for him to get his ass back to Earth so we can see the new *Star Trek* movie together."

Carter grinned. "Yes, sir. *Hammond* out."

Teal'c led Rak'nor into the largest of the *Hammond*'s labs, which contained a number of workstations.

"This is quite impressive, Teal'c," Rak'nor said. "It was not long ago that the Tau'ri were unable to even leave their own planet without the *chappa'ai*. Now they have ships that rival a *ha'tak* in terms of raw power."

"Indeed."

Rak'nor noticed something on one of the workstations. "That is Goa'uld technology!"

Teal'c nodded. "The *Hammond* was constructed following the fall of the Goa'uld. The technology now in the Jaffa's possession has been made available to the Tau'ri."

Rak'nor nodded appreciatively. "So this vessel combines Tau'ri, Asgard, *and* Goa'uld technology. Impressive."

A voice from one of the workstations said, "Goa'uld tech was always part of the design process, actually. But it was stuff we salvaged, not that we acquired legitimately like we can now."

Teal'c turned to see a short human with red hair. She wore a major's clusters, and after a moment, Teal'c recognized her.

"Major Hailey," Teal'c said. "It is good to see you again."

She stood up and gave both Jaffa a quick nod. "Likewise. You must be Rak'nor. I'm Jennifer Hailey, the new chief science officer."

"Once again," Teal'c said, "Colonel Carter has brought you under her command."

Hailey allowed herself a small smile. "I owe my career to

the colonel. Always happy to serve under her." At Rak'nor's querying look, Hailey added, "Colonel Carter mentored me in the Academy, and helped me through a rough patch. She sponsored my entry into the SGC. I was on SG-9 for a while, then I served under the colonel when she ran Area 51 a few years back. Her last act before she left to rejoin SG-1 was to approve my transfer to the 304 project. I helped build the *Apollo* and the *Sun-Tzu*, and the *Hammond*."

Nodding, Rak'nor said, "So you are her apprentice."

"I guess?" Hailey tilted her head.

Colonel Carter's voice came from the entry to the lab. "More like protégée, really. And after all this time on Earth building ships, and after spending some time in Atlantis, I thought it was time she got back out in the field."

Rak'nor turned to eagerly face the colonel. "Were you able to obtain permission?"

"Yes. Ostensibly, we're there to investigate the flare star. Once we arrive in the system, Teal'c, you and Rak'nor will take the cargo ship and investigate the planet surface under cloak." She pointed a finger at Rak'nor. "Only investigate, though. Do *not* engage the Alliance until after you've made a thorough scan of P7X-942. Once we know what we're dealing with, then we can figure out our next move."

For a moment, Rak'nor tensed, and Teal'c sensed that his fellow Jaffa was bridling under Colonel Carter's restrictions.

Colonel Carter sensed it as well, it seemed, as she stared up at Rak'nor and said, "Those are the mission parameters, Rak'nor. If you want our help, this is how you're getting it. The alternative is to go there on your own without us as backup."

Rak'nor relaxed. "Of course, Colonel. My apologies. It is just—" He hesitated. "When the flares forced us to abandon Armak, keeping the weapons cache safe was my responsibility. If the weapons fall into Alliance hands, I will have failed in that responsibility."

"I understand. If you do find those weapons, best to ring

them up to your cargo ship. No sense in giving the Alliance a chance to grab them."

Bowing, Rak'nor said, "Thank you."

Colonel Carter then turned to Major Hailey. "Jennifer, you'll be in charge of investigating the star. I want to know why a star that NASA's telescopes still read as G-type has become a flare star."

"Yes, ma'am."

"Goa'uld mothership is on approach and hailing us."

Carter shook her head and smiled ruefully as she entered the bridge to those words from her executive officer. She had just left Teal'c and Rak'nor in the 302 bay, where they were preparing to take the cargo ship out. "That didn't take long."

"No, ma'am," the executive officer said as he vacated the center seat.

Taking her seat between the weapons and helm consoles, Carter said, "Raise shields. And let's see what they have to say."

"This is the Lucian Alliance. State your business."

Carter smiled. "Simple and to the point. Let's respond."

"Channel open," said the pilot, seated on Carter's left.

"This is Colonel Samantha Carter of the *George Hammond*. We're here to —"

"They're powering weapons!" the pilot cried out.

"What? Alliance, we're here on a mission of —"

The Alliance commander sounded like he was sneering. "Your mission is of no interest Samantha Carter. You are an enemy of the Lucian Alliance and I will be amply rewarded when it is learned that I ended your miserable life."

"Dammit," Carter muttered. Both as a member of SG-1 and as commander of the *Hammond*, she'd had plenty of run-ins with the Alliance. She should have realized that her presence — and Teal'c's, for that matter — might be provocative.

The mothership's weapons fire struck the *Hammond*.

"Shields are holding," the pilot said.

"Evasive maneuvers." Carter didn't want to have to get into a firefight. "Keep the channel open. Lucian Alliance, we are on a scientific mission and have no quarrel with you."

There was no response — but no new weapons fire, either.

For several seconds, there was tense silence on the *Hammond* bridge.

Then another voice came over the speakers. "Forgive my lieutenant, Colonel Carter. I am Kefflin. I command this vessel and all Alliance interests in this system."

Carter blinked. Kefflin was a very reclusive Alliance boss. Her SG-1 teammate Cameron Mitchell had gone undercover as Kefflin for an Alliance summit, which was only successful because very few had seen his face.

So it was rather a surprise when the pilot said, "They're requesting visual communication."

"O-o-okay. Bring it up."

The face of a craggy, blond-haired man appeared on the screen, standing in the *pel'tak* of a mothership. Next to him was a shorter man with darker hair and a *very* angry expression.

"Vashin has a particular animus for you, Colonel," said the blond-haired one, "as well as your erstwhile teammates. He used to be Netan's lieutenant before SG-1's actions led to his ousting. In fact, he was the one who put out the bounty on your team's head on Netan's behalf. He works for me, now."

"I would have expected some animus from you, too, Kefflin. And I'm surprised you're showing your face to an entire ship full of people."

Kefflin's lips curled up — Carter couldn't bring herself to call it a smile. "Your comrade Colonel Mitchell's impersonation forced me to take on a more public role — as did Netan's fall. And to the contrary, I have nothing but respect for you, Colonel. You played your hand supremely well, and exposed many weaknesses in the Alliance in general and Netan in particular. Thanks to you and your teammates, those weaknesses have been eliminated."

Carter didn't like the sound of that.

"You say your mission is scientific?"

Welcoming the chance to end this peacefully, Carter quickly said, "We've been sent here by Earth to investigate this system's sun."

"Very well. You may do so. But I would ask that you remain proximate to the sun only. If you come within the orbital path of the innermost planet of the system, it will be considered an incursion into Alliance space. Likewise if any of your subsidiary vessels do so, or attempt to land on Armak. That is *our* world, and we will not have you invading it."

"No plans in that regard, Kefflin. You have my word, neither I nor any of my crew will come anywhere near the planet."

"Good. I hope your scans of the sun bear fruit."

With that, he closed the connection. Carter let out a breath.

"That was weird," the XO muttered.

Doing her best impersonation of Teal'c, Carter smiled and said, "Indeed. Keep shields up — we'll need their protection from solar radiation this close, and besides, I don't trust Kefflin not to leave a cloaked ship or three to keep an eye on us."

"Yes, ma'am," the pilot said.

"And speaking of cloaked ships, tell Teal'c and Rak'nor to commence at their discretion under cloak."

The intercom sounded. "Hailey to Carter."

"Go ahead, Jennifer."

"Ma'am, the preliminary scans of the sun are confirming that it's a red giant. We're only a few thousand light-years from Earth, and there's no way it would advance this far in its life cycle in so short a time frame."

Smirking, Carter said, "I'm guessing you have a theory, Major?"

"Yes, ma'am." Hailey, as ever, was utterly serious. "I think someone — probably the Goa'uld, or the Alliance using Goa'uld tech — has been tampering with the sun."

Teal'c and Rak'nor moved swiftly through the caverns. They had left the cargo ship cloaked in orbit and used the rings to transport to a mine shaft that, according to Rak'nor, had suffered a cave-in. That cave-in had, in fact, been manufactured by Rak'nor himself to keep the Jaffa weapons hidden. His concern had been that the Alliance had dug the mine out.

But while the Alliance appeared to have taken up residence in the primary base on a large mountain, the mines themselves were untouched. Scans had revealed no traces of naquadah, so whatever the Alliance had planned, mining was not a part of it.

Teal'c carried a P90 with a flashlight attachment, enabling them to see where they were going, as the cavern was not illuminated. For his part, Rak'nor carried a *ma'tok*. Teal'c himself only eschewed a staff weapon due to the P90's ability to light their way.

Rak'nor approached a solid wall, then ran a hand over one particular stone.

The wall shimmered and vanished, revealing a chamber filled with boxes, as well as another ring transporter.

"The containers appear to be untouched," Teal'c said.

"Yes." Rak'nor let out a long sigh of relief. "Let us move them to the rings. The false wall also kept the rings deactivated. With the wall down, we may transport the weapons to the cargo vessel."

Teal'c nodded. When this mission was complete, the weapons would be brought to the Jaffa Council, who would decide what to do with them.

It did not take the two Jaffa long to maneuver the containers inside the ring assembly. Teal'c then programmed the rings to take them back to their cargo vessel on a delay, stepped onto the platform and waited.

A moment later, the circular hatch slid aside and the rings rose from beneath the cavern floor. The two Jaffa were engulfed in light.

But when the light dimmed, Teal'c saw that he and his comrade were not in Rak'nor's cargo vessel, but instead in a large chamber surrounded by men and women holding *zat'nik'tel*s.

The one person who wasn't armed stepped forward. "I was wondering why anyone would be poking around those dried-up mines. So we intercepted your matter stream, and look! You brought us gifts!"

A man standing next to the leader pointed at Teal'c. "That is the Jaffa named Teal'c — he is a member of SG-1."

"Even more gifts. Contact Colonel Carter and inform her that I've lost some of my respect for her."

Suddenly, an alarm blared out. Teal'c looked past the weapons pointed at him to see a workstation against one of the walls. A woman was seated at the controls and she whirled toward the leader showing a panicked expression. "Kefflin, the latest run didn't work. We've lost control of the device again!"

The leader — who was apparently the legendary Kefflin of the Lucian Alliance — said, "Very well, we —"

"There's a massive flare heading straight for the planet. It will be here in an hour!"

"Raise the shield," Kefflin said calmly.

"It may not survive another flare," she said somewhat less calmly.

"Raise it in any case. And why have I not been put through to the Tau'ri ship?"

"Colonel Carter is not responding."

Next to Teal'c, Rak'nor muttered, "Sun-breaker."

Kefflin apparently had excellent hearing. "You know of the weapon Heru'ur left here?"

Rak'nor said nothing.

Kefflin sneered. "Typical Jaffa defiance. It matters little what you say. We have re-created Sun-breaker. Heru'ur wished to create a method of rapidly aging a sun — no doubt to use against rival Goa'uld systems. According to the database, he was never able to make it work. But I'm willing to bet my scientists are smarter than those of a dead false god." He turned away and said, "Keep trying to raise Colonel Carter!"

Once he turned away, Teal'c whispered to Rak'nor, "Does he speak the truth?"

Rak'nor simply nodded.

"Transporter down, beam weapons down, shields at ten percent."

Carter gritted her teeth at the damage-control report from the flare. "Move us away from the sun."

"Hailey to bridge," said the major over the intercom.

Hesitating only for a second — Hailey wouldn't have called if it wasn't urgent — Carter said, "Go ahead."

"Ma'am, that flare that hit us happened immediately after a beam of some sort struck the sun. I traced its source, and it came directly from P7X-942. Wavelength and frequency consistent with Goa'uld technology. Also, the flare is on course for the planet, ma'am."

Everything Hailey told her made Carter more apprehensive. So did what the pilot said next: "We're still being hailed by the Alliance on P7X-942."

She checked to make sure that they were a safe enough distance from the sun that, should there be any other flares, they'd at least have more warning than they'd received from this first flare, which had already trashed her ship before they even knew it was there. Once she was assured of that, she finally replied to the Alliance's call.

The screen lit up with Kefflin, surrounded by several Goa'uld workstations and several more Lucian Alliance members — and also Teal'c and Rak'nor, who had zats pointed at them.

"I'm disappointed, Colonel. You gave me your word."

"Yes, I did," Carter said without hesitating. "I gave you my word that I and my crew wouldn't come near the planet. Neither Teal'c nor Rak'nor are on my crew."

"Such semantic trickery is unworthy of you, Colonel."

Someone at one of the Goa'uld control stations cried out, "Kefflin, I can't get the shield up! The incoming flare's going to reach us in fifty minutes."

"Having a little trouble?" Carter asked.

"We will tame Heru'ur's weapon, worry not."

"No you won't," Carter said. "Trust me, I've spent the last fifteen years of my life dealing with the technology used by the Goa'uld. And what you've got there is something that can only be operated *by* a Goa'uld."

"Colonel Carter is correct," Rak'nor said. "Heru'ur's scientists designed Sun-breaker in the same manner as the *kara kesh* — only one of the Goa'uld themselves can wield the weapon."

Carter said, "I can help you, Kefflin."

"Can you, now?"

Teal'c spoke up. "I believe you said that your scientists were the equal of those of the Goa'uld. That statement was likely hyperbole. However, Colonel Carter may make a similar claim without it being exaggeration."

"Thanks, Teal'c," Carter said. "But it's not just that — I was blended with a Tok'ra named Jolinar a while back. I still have enough naquadah in my blood that I can operate technology like that. Unless you've got a Goa'uld or a Tok'ra hiding on your base, I'm the only chance you've got of avoiding that flare."

"And in exchange for this, I return your Jaffa to you?"

Carter nodded. "Exactly."

The woman at the Sun-breaker console said, "It doesn't matter, their ship can't get here before the flare can."

"Yes we can. The *Hammond* will be in orbit of P7X-942 in five minutes. Once we're in orbit, I'll take a 302 down."

"What about your vaunted Asgard transporter?" Kefflin asked with a smile.

"The flare took it out. Which, by the way, is how I can guarantee that I won't just beam Teal'c and Rak'nor out and leave you to blow up."

"Very considerate. I await your arrival, Colonel."

The Sun-breaker operator crying out, "It's not possible for

her to get into orbit that fast!" was the last thing Carter heard before the communication cut off.

"Uh, ma'am?" the pilot said slowly. "How *is* it possible to get from here to orbit in five minutes?"

"Little trick I pulled a few years back with a cargo ship and a runaway asteroid. We open a hyperspace window just long enough to make a short jump."

"A cargo ship and an asteroid?" the pilot sounded understandably dubious.

Carter nodded as she relieved the pilot and sat at the helm controls. There wasn't time to explain this and it was easier for her to input the commands herself, especially since she had to rejigger her equations for the considerably larger mass of the *Hammond*, as well as the greater distance. That just needed to be a nine-thousand-mile jump. This was more like ninety million miles, but that worked in her favor, as it would be easier to jump the larger vessel across a greater distance.

It was still risky, though, especially with them this close to a flare star.

However, she suspected that the Alliance's attempts to futz with this Sun-breaker would be disastrous without her aid.

She wasn't entirely sure it would be so great *with* her aid, but at least she'd get Teal'c and Rak'nor free.

"Here goes," she muttered. She addressed intership. "All hands, prepare for a micro-hyperdrive jump. Secure all stations. Transition in ten seconds."

She counted down the remaining seconds, hoping her crew had indeed secured all stations, and then opened a hyperspace window, moved the *Hammond* into it, and immediately transitioned out of it.

Looking at the viewport, the stars were mostly the same. She was in the same system, but there was a planet and a mothership nearby instead of a flaring sun.

"Nice flying, ma'am," the pilot said with a smile. "That's almost as cool as the time you blew up a sun."

Shaking her head, Carter said, "Boy, you blow up one sun, and you just get a reputation." She rose, allowing the pilot to relieve her at the helm. "Major, the *Hammond* is yours. Keep her safe."

With that, she headed to the 302 bay.

"I'm unarmed."

Carter said that as soon as she stepped out of the cockpit of the 302 to find half a dozen zats pointed at her.

Kefflin stepped forward to greet her at the landing bay on a plateau of the mountain where the large base was located. Teal'c and Rak'nor were behind him, their hands bound behind their backs, zats pointed at their heads by two Alliance thugs.

"I'm sure you are," Kefflin said, "but you'll forgive me if I keep weapons pointing at your head for the duration of your stay." He turned to the two holding zats on the Jaffa. "Put them in the vessel. Once they're inside, remove the shackles."

Teal'c looked at Carter. Carter simply gave him a nod and said, "It's okay, Teal'c. They're expecting you back on the *Hammond*."

Whirling around to face Carter, Kefflin said, "'Back' on the *Hammond*, eh? So you admit your duplicity?"

Carter said nothing. She just hoped that Teal'c got the hint and would fly straight to the *Hammond* because she needed him to leave Rak'nor's cargo ship in orbit.

A few minutes later, the 302 took off with Teal'c in the pilot seat, while Carter was led into the base.

The woman who'd been at the workstation rose to her feet. "I hope you know what you're doing."

"I usually do. And when I don't, I keep at it until I figure it out." She sat down at the seat the woman had abandoned.

The first thing she did was activate the shield. That took all of a minute.

"Shield is active!" The woman turned to Carter. "I'm impressed, Colonel."

"Thank you, ah —"

"I'm Qirarra."

"Qirarra, I need you to keep an eye on the power output. The shield's at maximum, and I want to make sure it doesn't burn the systems out."

"Understood." Qirarra went to do that very thing.

Which was good, as Qirarra's task was wholly unnecessary. But Carter needed Qirarra to not see what Carter was doing.

She studied the device, and saw that it could indeed age a sun artificially, although from her quick look, Carter didn't see how it could be controlled. In fact, based on the readings, this sun would go nova inside a year. That time frame had been more like a decade before that last beam hit it.

Looking around, she saw that the rings were halfway across the chamber.

That was going to be the hard part.

Qirarra looked over at Carter. "I can't believe this. I've been struggling with this thing for months, and it won't respond to me at all."

"The Goa'uld don't like other people to play with their toys," Carter said. "It was their adaptation of the Ancients' technology that could only be used by someone with their genetic code. In this case, you have to have naquadah in your blood."

"Sounds disgusting."

Carter chuckled. "It has its moments."

While she spoke to Qirarra, she armed, but did not activate, the base self-destruct, and also preprogrammed the rings to send her up to Rak'nor's cargo ship, still cloaked in orbit

At least she hoped it was. If it wasn't, she'd wind up on the nearest ring transporter that could receive the signal — Kefflin's mothership — which would not be ideal.

Finally, she found the control for the lights in the chamber.

It took her the better part of half an hour to work her way through the base's systems, while ostensibly looking for ways to better control the Sun-breaker and strengthen the shields.

However, she was now ready to go.

The flare would hit in ten minutes.

After one final look to commit the direction and distance of the ring platform to memory, she set the rings to activate in fifteen seconds and then all at once she activated the self-destruct to go off in five minutes, lowered the shield, and turned out the lights in the chamber. Even if Qirarra or someone managed to deactivate the self-destruct, the flare would still do significant damage to the base.

With luck, one or the other would destroy this Sun-breaker technology once and for all.

Chaos reigned in the newly darkened chamber as Carter jogged in the direction of the rings, keeping her hands in front of her in an attempt not to bump into anything.

Briefly, the chamber was illuminated by a blast from a zat, and then another, and Carter also heard someone scream.

Ten seconds had passed, and she thought she was pretty close to the rings.

Then someone tackled her from behind and she and the tackler skidded across the chamber floor.

The rings activated and that illuminated the room, revealing that Carter was, in fact, on the ring platform.

And so was Qirarra.

After a blinding flash of light, Carter found herself in the hold of Rak'nor's ship, along with Qirarra—

—who was pointing a zat at her.

"Send us back, Colonel, right now."

"That would be a really bad idea. I set the self-destruct for five minutes. If Kefflin is smart, he's abandoning the base."

"You're trying to destroy Sun-breaker?" Qirarra asked.

Carter nodded.

"Good. I've been trying to wipe that thing out for months, but the controls wouldn't respond." Activating the zat from standby mode, she added, "Don't get any ideas, Colonel. I'm still loyal to the Alliance. But Sun-breaker doesn't work properly and it will only result in destruction. Now you're going to fly this cargo vessel to the mothership, and report to Vashin — or Kefflin, if he abandons the base like you think he might."

"Absolutely." Carter moved toward the door to the bridge and opened it. Then she hesitated.

Qirarra moved closer and put the zat at Carter's back with her right hand. "Move!"

Carter whirled around, grabbed Qirarra's right wrist with her left hand and twisted it. Qirarra cried out in pain and lost her grip on the zat, which Carter caught with her right hand and immediately fired at Qirarra.

The Alliance woman's stunned form fell to the deck. One of the first tricks they taught you in hand-to-hand training at the Academy was how to disarm someone holding a gun right at your back or at your head.

"Sorry, kiddo, but you get to be my prisoner, not the other way around," Carter said before entering the bridge and activating the flight controls. As she did so, she also activated the communications system, broadcasting on the frequency used by Earth's ships. "*Hammond*, this is Carter."

Teal'c replied. "It is good to hear your voice, Colonel Carter."

"Yours, too, Teal'c. Glad you and Rak'nor made it on board. I'm coming in hot in the cargo ship. I should dock in seventy-five seconds. Ready the hyperdrive and head back to Earth as soon as the cargo ship's secure."

Then her heart sank as she saw Kefflin's mothership fire on the *Hammond*.

Knowing her ship's shields were at ten percent and that the Asgard beam weapons weren't working, Carter feared for the safety of her command.

But then then weapons fire was dispersed by *Hammond*'s shields, which appeared to be at full power. A moment later, an Asgard beam weapon sliced through one of the mothership's outer struts.

"I'm impressed," Carter said, "I was only gone an hour."

"I believe you have Major Hailey to thank for the rapid repair of the shields."

Carter smiled. Leave it to her protégée to repair the tactical systems in record time. "Well let's get those shields down. I'm coming in."

The cargo ship entered the 302 bay, and Carter brought it to a smooth landing.

Moments later, the *Hammond* went into hyperspace.

Moments after that, there was a massive explosion on a mountain on P7X-942.

"I suppose you think you're clever."

Carter smiled at Qirarra's words, spoken from inside the *Hammond* brig. "I don't, honestly, but people whose judgment I trust keep insisting that I am."

"I'm not going to tell you anything. I told you, I'm loyal to the Alliance."

"I'm sure you are. You're lucky, Kefflin survived the destruction on P7X-942. The Sun-breaker is completely destroyed and based on what I found in the database, Heru'ur didn't re-create his research anywhere else. In fact, he viewed it as a failed experiment."

"He was right about that," Qirarra muttered.

"Maybe you'll be lucky and Kefflin will want to trade you for some considerations. Or maybe he'll view your inability to get the Sun-breaker to work properly as a failure and he'll cut you loose."

"I don't know about that," Qirarra said, "but the Tau'ri are still my enemy, and I won't do a thing to help you."

"Suit yourself." With that, Carter turned to leave the brig.

Teal'c was walking down the corridor when she exited. "Is your prisoner awake?"

Carter nodded. "And stubborn. She won't betray her people."

"Perhaps I may speak to her — tell her of the value of betraying an evil cause in service of a good one."

"I'm not sure she sees us as a good cause, but I won't stop you, either." She sighed. "I'd better call Earth and let General O'Neill know what happened — and that the night sky's going to look different in a few thousand years." Then she snapped her fingers. "Oh, and the general wants to remind you that he wants to see the new *Star Trek* with you when you're on Earth next."

"It will be my honor. Will you also be joining us?"

"Nah." Carter chuckled. "I prefer to leave the movie bonding to you two. Besides, I hear it involves time travel, and we get enough of that in real life…"

"Indeed."

STARGATE ATLANTIS
The Player on the Other Side

Amy Griswold

This story takes place in season three of Stargate Atlantis

"THAT'S strange," Rodney McKay said.

John Sheppard straightened up abruptly. He'd been sprawled in one of the lab chairs for an hour, despite probably having work to do of his own, but Rodney wasn't about to take responsibility for John's time management. "Weird as in interesting, or weird as in deadly? We've had a lot of deadly lately."

"Tell me about it," Rodney said. "I nearly died not that long ago, remember?"

"But you didn't."

Rodney was not about to debate how traumatic his near-death experience with the Ascension device had been. In his opinion, all near-death experiences were traumatic, and the extent to which John took brushes with death in stride was borderline pathological. "Do you want to hear what's strange or not?"

"I would like to hear what's strange," Elizabeth said, leaning in the doorway of the lab. Rodney straightened up in his own chair. He felt that he was skating on a certain amount of thin ice with Elizabeth since the other recent unfortunate incident involving what he had genuinely believed to be a computer game, but which had turned out to be an Ancient social experiment that controlled the lives of actual people. "Rodney?"

"Well," he began cautiously. "I've been checking to make sure that no one else was running the 'game' —"

"I think we agreed to stop calling it a game," Elizabeth said.

"Yes, right, the Ancient simulation that was controlling people on M4D-058. Which of course we would never have used if we'd known that it was provoking a real war."

"Or producing a society of Sam Carter lookalikes who plastered your face on their flag," John added, in Rodney's opinion, unnecessarily.

"I was inspirational to them. But it was still all very wrong, yes," Rodney said hurriedly. "So I've been trying to make sure that no one else was, for instance, inspiring a country's leaders to stomp around in black leather."

"That was practical," John said.

"I would like to think that if anyone else had been using the simulation, they would have spoken up as soon as we learned that actual lives were at stake," Elizabeth put in firmly, and Rodney frowned at John for distracting him from his point.

"Yes, I would like to think that too, but Sheppard and I started playing the — started interacting with the simulation program two years ago, and a lot of people have left Atlantis since then. So, just to be safe, I've been checking for any other files associated with the simulation in the Atlantis computer system."

"And?" John prompted.

"I just found another running simulation."

"Shut it down," Elizabeth said at once.

"Believe me, if it were that simple, I would have done it already," Rodney said. "Here's the thing that's actually strange. There are files being stored in the Atlantis computer system, but I'm pretty sure that the simulation isn't being controlled from Atlantis."

Elizabeth frowned. "How is that possible?"

"Presumably through subspace communication, like the way the console here communicated with the Oracle on M4D-058," Rodney said. "If there's another control console for the simulation, it could be located at another Ancient installation pretty much anywhere in the Pegasus Galaxy. The main Atlantis computer system isn't set up to decode the input or record its source."

"So what do we know?" Elizabeth asked, looking frustrated.

"Not much," Rodney had to admit. "What I'm getting is just a notification that PX7-MYB is involved in a game in progress. I can't tell you who's sending signals to their Oracle, or what the people there are being told to do, only that signals are still being sent."

"Do we know whether anybody's listening?" John put in.

"Good question, and, no, we don't. I can tell you that the Oracle still exists, because it's still sending back information to the other console. But it could be buried fifty feet underground, and we could be picking up what amounts to two computers playing a very pointless game of chess with each other. Without access to the equipment at either end, there's no way to know."

"PX7-MYB," Elizabeth mused. "Do we have anything on that world?"

Rodney switched to searching the city's database. "Not much there either. It looks like it was a farming world that supplied food to Atlantis when the Ancients still lived here. Apparently the locals called it Elista. That's what we have: a name, and a record of some vegetable purchases ten thousand years ago. It's on the list to be surveyed... looks like about eighteen months from now."

"Which could actually be a lot longer," John said. "Now that *Daedalus* is making regular supply runs, surveying farming settlements has moved down our list of priorities below checking out worlds that might have technology we can use against the Wraith."

"I'm not complaining, gentlemen," Elizabeth said. "But let's move this one up in our list of priorities. Colonel Sheppard, I'd like you and your team to check it out."

By the time the team was assembled, Rodney had reached the conclusion that he would like to have a word — actually, quite a few unprintable words — with the designers of the Ancient computer system. When he first came to Atlantis, he had felt what he had to privately admit was a sense of awe at being able to directly study the Atlantis computers and understand some fraction of the minds of their creators. After three years, he felt that he was beginning to understand their creators all too well.

Some of them might have been wise and enlightened, like the ones who had Ascended. He liked to think that his own recent experiments with Ascension had taken him some distance in the "wise and enlightened" direction, even if he'd mainly been trying to save his own life. But it had become clear to him that many of the programmers of the Atlantis computers had been just as prone to kludgy shortcuts and inadequate documentation as any team of programmers on Earth who'd were working with an impossible deadline and too little coffee.

That was the best explanation he could provide for dangerous devices like the one that had nearly forced him to Ascend being left unlabeled and unprotected from some idiot flipping a switch. In this case, he had been the idiot, but that was why things that could kill you needed to be idiot-proof, because under pressure, even certified geniuses flipped power switches before they thought through the consequences. And human beings — and probably even human-like beings — who found what looked like a game would try to play it.

If he had been one of the Ancients, he wouldn't have left Atlantis until he'd taped signs to everything attractive and lethal saying "don't touch this, even if it seems like a really good idea at the time" —

"McKay. You with us?" Sheppard prompted. Teyla was shouldering her pack, and Ronon was in the lead with Sheppard, looking eager to stride through the gate and into the middle of what was likely to be a war zone.

"Yes, let's find out what kind of mess someone's gotten these people into," he said.

Sheppard flicked on his radio. "We're ready. Dial the gate."

"I am not sure I see the appeal of video games as a pastime,"

Teyla said as the gate boiled blue.

Ronon shrugged. "It's fighting for people who can't fight."

"They're not only for people who can't fight," John said. "Come on, they must have had strategy games on Sateda, and I know you've watched me play chess."

"I don't see the point of chess," Ronon said.

"Strategy games are like that, only more realistic," John went on doggedly.

"This one's a lot more realistic," McKay said. "Watch out for falling bombs."

He ducked instinctively as he walked through the gate, half-expecting to walk out into a cratered ruin. Instead, they stepped out onto a dirt road lined with evergreen trees running toward the distant shapes of buildings on the horizon. It took a moment to realize what made the scene look oddly familiar, as if he'd stepped out onto a back road in Canada. It was the electric lights strung on light poles, their wiring looking amateurishly rigged but clearly effective.

"They have electricity," Ronon said. "You don't see that every day."

"No, you do not," Teyla said, sounding more cautious. "There are reasons for that."

"Well, town's that way," John said, straightening the straps of his pack. "Let's go make some friends."

The first locals they found were on the outskirts of town, checking on a large, clanking piece of machinery. As they approached, Rodney decided it might well be the steam-powered dynamo that was powering at least some of the electric lights. It occupied a shed that might recently have been a stable, given a strong smell of cow, and was driven by a steam engine that was probably an immense fire hazard given that the stable had wooden beams. Still, the white-haired woman checking levers and the much younger man tipping more coal into the steam engine looked cheerful, and the lights were staying on.

"Hi there," John said. "I'm John Sheppard. We're from Atlantis."

"We've heard about you." The woman came forward and clasped John's forearm with a dusty hand. "I'm Emille. This is Vasti." She nodded to the weedy man who put his bucket down with a clank and hurried over. "Welcome to Elista."

"The lights are impressive," John said.

"And unexpected," Teyla said. "We have visited few worlds that used electric power."

Emille looked immensely satisfied at that, and Vasti grinned. "Thanks to the Oracle," he said. "It's shown us so many things."

"Let me show you what we've done," Emille said.

They found themselves drawn into a whirlwind tour of the town. It was a small mill town, with wooden frame houses, a large textile mill built over a swiftly-rushing stream, and a few older stone buildings like the town hall. Emille ignored any possible historic sights, pointing out instead the town's newly-installed electric lights, the two looms in the textile mill that now ran on electric power, and half a dozen other gadgets and machines that had been converted from steam power or hand power to run on electricity.

"The ability to generate enough power is where we're still being held back," Emille said as they entered the town square. "We want to put food preserving devices like this in every home, but we can't power them yet." What Rodney had taken for a shed in one corner of the square turned out to be a hulking refrigerator that kept a bucket of milk more or less cold. It wasn't a bad effort, Rodney decided, although efficiency clearly wasn't their strong suit. "We don't mine coal here, we have to transport it, and trade for it. But Sigurd has made that a priority."

"Sigurd?" Teyla asked. Ronon was standing back and keeping his eye on the crowd, but no one here seemed hostile. Emille and Vasti nearly vibrated with enthusiasm, and the rest of the townspeople seemed mostly either politely interested or politely bored by the visitors.

"Our mayor," Vasti said, nodding at someone behind Rodney.

"I am Sigurd," a tall man said as Rodney turned. He was fair-haired and fair-skinned like both Emille and Vasti, but broad-shouldered and imposing enough that he looked like he could take on Ronon in a wrestling match. He offered his hand, and Rodney clasped his forearm gingerly while his own was squeezed hard enough to bruise. "I see that Emille is showing you the gifts of the Oracle."

"We are very interested in hearing more about your Oracle," Teyla said.

"This is a big sort of table with colored lights that talks to you?" John added. "We've seen something like that before."

"There is nothing like our Oracle," Sigurd said with a frown. "The Ancestors have chosen to speak to us through it, and only to us. This is a great honor for our people. It shows that they look upon us with favor and believe that we are worthy to receive their gifts."

"I was just showing the Lanteans how the coils of the food preservation device draw heat from the chamber without requiring ice," Emille said a little testily, tucking a flyaway strand of white hair behind her ear. "The Oracle provided the idea, but Vasti and I worked out the details of how it could be done. And with the ability to generate more power —"

"I am sure that the Oracle will share more secrets with us as we become worthy of them," Sigurd said in a voice that brooked no disagreement.

"I meant no disrespect to the Oracle," Emille said, clearly choosing her words with care. "It has changed our lives. Now that we have electric lights, the craftsmen can work longer at night, and we have more to trade. The weavers have their powered loom, and there is so much more that we have yet to even try, but that I am certain we can do." The excitement in her voice was contagious.

Rodney said, "You know, if you used a more efficient coolant for your refrigerator coils —"

"McKay." John cut him off.

"Has the Oracle always spoken to your people?" Teyla asked.

"Only in recent years," Emille said. "It was found before I was born, in ruins near the village."

"The only useful thing ever to be found there," Sigurd said. "Who needs to dig around in old runs when the Ancestors speak directly to us?"

"People used to leave offerings there," Vasti said. "There were legends that once the device had spoken, but it was silent. Then, one day, it began to speak again. Sigurd believes it is a sign that we have attracted the favor of the Ancestors through virtuous living."

"Is that what you think?" John asked.

Vasti looked at Emille, who in turn glanced at Sigurd before answering. "I believe that whatever the reason why we have gained the Ancestors' favor, we should be grateful for it."

"Excuse us, Emille, Sigurd," Teyla said. "We very much appreciate the tour, but we must talk for a few minutes about what goods we might have available to trade with your people."

"Of course," Sigurd said, his own eyes lighting at the sound of the word 'trade.' "Here, you folk, don't swarm the Lanteans. They need to talk business."

"Well, whoever's controlling the Oracle, they're sharing useful technology," Rodney said as they gathered at the other end of the square from the briskly-chugging refrigerator.

"Useful but dangerous," Teyla said. "This kind of rapid technological advancement will surely attract the attention of the Wraith."

Ronon looked grim. "Unless the Wraith already know. What if they're the ones talking to these people and giving them this technology?"

John narrowed his eyes. "Why would they do that?"

"To increase the population of this world before it is culled," Teyla said. "If that is the case, then I cannot imagine it will be more than a generation before the Wraith come to take their prey and destroy everything they have taught these people to build."

"Let's get back to the gate," John said. "We should see if Zelenka's come up with a source for those signals."

Teyla nodded. "And if we are posing as traders, we should bring back something to trade."

Radek Zelenka squinted over his glasses at his computer screen. "Yes, of course, it is terribly easy to determine who is using a video game designed by an alien civilization," he muttered under his breath. "I will just trace their IP address, and then we will be done. Only, strange enough, that does not work in subspace. So …" He continued working on the problem, while adding a muttered wish that Rodney would have to solve all mysteries he discovered rather than dumping them in Radek's lap.

"Anything?" Elizabeth said, coming into the lab. Radek bit his tongue to avoid saying that if he had solved the problem, he would have told her so, and took a moment to phrase a status report that didn't sound obviously frustrated.

"The system isn't designed to record the source of the input that it receives," he said. "It's backing up certain critical files on the Atlantis computer system, but the main — well, 'saved game' — for the simulation resides wherever the game controller is located. We can tell when signals are being sent, and thankfully we can tell where they're being sent to, but not where they're coming from."

"So we can't determine anything about who's controlling the simulation from this end," Elizabeth said. She was carrying a cup of tea that from its lack of steam had long since grown cold. Radek considered his own cold coffee and wondered, not for the first time, why he had chosen a job that along with constant deadly peril involved ridiculous working hours.

"I wouldn't say we can't determine anything," he said. "I believe I can add instructions to the programming of the simulation that will capture more information about its user the next time that instructions are sent. That is the good news."

"That suggests there's also bad news."

"The bad news is that the transmissions have been extremely sporadic. There may be six in a week, and then six months may pass before the next one."

"So we may be waiting a while," Elizabeth said. "Understood. But the sooner you get your setup in place, the less chance there is that we'll miss the next transmission."

"I am working on it now," Radek said, not mentioning vain hopes like dinner and sleep. "If we are able to capture any information, I will let you know."

"Well, that was supremely unhelpful," Rodney said as they hiked back to the village from the gate, this time with several sacks of tava beans and root vegetables on a wheeled cart.

"I am sure that Dr. Zelenka is doing his best," Teyla said.

Rodney waved a hand. "Yes, yes, I'm sure that he is, but he still hasn't gotten anywhere."

"Neither have we," Ronon said. "We need to ask them who's talking to them."

"I doubt these people know the source of the signals," Teyla said. "On M4D-058, the people of Geldar and Hallona believed that the Oracle was a divine entity that communicated with them." She shot Rodney a reproachful look, which he felt was unfair, as they'd been convinced that Sheppard was sending them divine messages, too. "Sigurd appears to believe that the instructions for how to build new technology are being sent by the Ancestors."

"He's wrong," Ronon said.

"Of course he is, but how do we prove it?" Rodney asked. "We can't bring them back to Atlantis and show them the game this time, because we can't access the game files."

"Besides, the problem isn't getting them to stop listening to the Oracle," John said. "They're doing fine right now. But we need to find out whether the Oracle is being controlled by the Wraith."

"Which is one thing they can't ask the Oracle and get an honest reply," Rodney said.

"No," John said slowly. "But I bet they could ask the Oracle whether to do something that we know the Wraith wouldn't like. Whether to create something like the Hoffan drug—"

Teyla shook her head. "None of their advancement so far has been in the field of medicine," she said. "It would be implausible for them to have taken even preliminary steps toward creating the drug the Hoffans used to make themselves inedible to the Wraith."

"So far they've mainly been experimenting with the uses of electricity. If the Wraith are letting them have technology at all, I don't think they'd have any particular reason to object to refrigeration, or to making cloth more efficiently—"

"Radio." Ronon paused as if he thought that should be sufficient, and then went on when it was obvious it wasn't. "The Wraith don't want anyone to have ways to communicate across long distances. It makes it easier for people to organize to fight them, or to escape from cullings. Most places on Sateda started using radio just a couple of decades before the Wraith attacked. I don't know how hard it would be for these people to figure out—"

"Not hard," Rodney said. "They may not have a Marconi or a Tesla, but Emille and Vasti are pretty competent engineers, and they'd just need a push in the right direction."

"So you could suggest that they make some suggestions in that direction to the Oracle, and see what kind of answer they get," John said. "If the Wraith are the ones controlling it, they're not going to like the idea."

"That is precisely why I have reservations about this plan," Teyla said. "If the Oracle is being controlled by the Wraith, even suggesting this kind of technological change could provoke them to cull this world prematurely."

"So what are you suggesting?" Ronon asked. "We don't tell them, and let them go on taking orders from the Wraith? If that's what's happening here, they need to know the truth."

"Both of you have a point," John said. "Let's make the suggestion and see what the people here want to do. If it's worth it to them to find out whether they're getting these messages from the Wraith, then McKay can figure out what questions the Wraith would really hate for them to ask. If they'd rather leave well enough alone, that's up to them."

"That would be a stupid choice," Ronon said.

"Nevertheless, it is their choice," Teyla said, equally firmly. "Colonel Sheppard will explain the situation to them."

"Oh, *I'll* explain," John grumbled. He waved at the first of the villagers they saw on the road. "Hey, there! Can you tell Sigurd and Emille that we need to talk to them? It's important."

Sigurd came out to greet them cheerfully in the town square, Emille following him with a tangle of wires trailing from the pocket of her apron. "Friends from Atlantis! Have you returned with your trade goods?"

"We have samples of food that we are willing to trade for some of your cloth," Teyla said.

Sigurd frowned, opening a sack and letting the tava beans run through his fingers. "I had thought you would want to trade for the secrets of our electric lights. The price would be high, true, but the advantages for your people would be great."

"We have all this already," Rodney said. "In fact, we have a lot more than this."

"To start with," John began, "we have these devices called radios that let us transmit sound across long distances —"

"The Lanteans come from the city of the Ancestors," Emille said. "Who knows what they have learned from living there?" There was a hunger in her face that Rodney entirely understood.

"A lot," he said, feeling it was time to get to the point. "For instance, we've learned that the device that you call an Oracle can be controlled by someone on a world far away."

Sigurd's frown deepened.

"Of course the Ancestors speak to us from far away," Emille said. "Our stories say that they have Ascended to a place we cannot hear or see, but they still guide us."

"Yes, but what if it's not actually the Ancestors guiding you?" John said.

"Only the Ancestors could understand the secrets of electricity," Sigurd said.

"Actually, a lot of worlds have electricity," John said. "Ronon's homeworld Sateda used to have it before they were destroyed by the Wraith. Our homeworld — not Atlantis, but the world we originally came from — had electric power. And we're not the only ones in the Pegasus Galaxy who understand how to use it."

"He means the Wraith," Rodney burst out when it didn't seem like Sigurd and Emille were taking the point. "The Wraith have electricity, they know how to do all the things you've done here, and much more. It's entirely possible that they're just helping you so that they can fatten up your world before they swoop in for the kill."

Sigurd's brow furrowed. His fists clenched, and Rodney was abruptly very aware that he looked like he could lift a cow under each arm. "You are talking about the voice of the Ancestors."

"Or not," John said. "That's the question we're suggesting you should really—"

Sigurd raised a fist, and Rodney took a step back instinctively, realizing too late that Sigurd had been signaling to someone standing behind Rodney. He felt himself grabbed and grappled backwards, hands wrestling his P90 away from him. Beside him, John was also being wrestled to a standstill by two large men. One of them drew a knife and held it to John's throat.

Ronon drew his pistol, and he heard the sound of Teyla's P90 being cocked. Sigurd reached out and took Rodney's weapon from his captor, holding it like a toy pistol in one hand. He pressed the muzzle to Rodney's chest with a look of interest. "How effective are these weapons? It would be interesting to find out."

"You don't want to do that," John said.

"This has all been a misunderstanding," Teyla said. "Put the weapon down, and we will discuss it."

"Yes, put the gun down," Rodney agreed rapidly.

"If you know what's good for you," Ronon said, and leveled his own pistol at Sigurd's head. Rodney felt that the situation was rapidly getting out of hand.

"I will not kill you now," Sigurd said, although he kept the gun pointed at Rodney's chest. "But you must be punished for your disrespect to the Ancestors." He jerked his head, and the men holding John and Rodney began dragging them across the square.

"I can take them," Ronon said, but although Rodney had every confidence that Ronon was a match for Sigurd, he didn't feel like staking his life on Ronon's ability to take Sigurd down before Sigurd could pull the trigger.

"Get out of here, get backup," John said. "Now!"

The villagers were slower to move toward Ronon and Teyla, seeming uncertain whether they were included in the charge of blasphemy. Teyla nodded in answer to John's order and turned on her heel, sprinting back toward the gate. Ronon hesitated, then followed Teyla at a run.

"Let's talk about this," John said as Rodney watched the only members of their team who weren't being held at gunpoint sprint away into the distance. "We weren't trying to insult the Ancestors, but we're really sorry if we did, so how about you just let us go, and we won't bother you anymore."

"Take them away," Sigurd said to his men. "They have offended the Ancestors, and we will let the Ancestors decide their fate."

"Let me guess," Rodney said. "You're going to ask the Oracle. Do you not understand that we've been trying to tell you —"

"You will hold your tongue!" Sigurd boomed, and one of the men put a none-too-clean hand over Rodney's mouth. He struggled, but wasn't sure it was worth trying to bite. "I will

tolerate no more blasphemy against the Ancestors. Vasti—"
He waved a hand for the young engineer, who after waiting for
a nod from Emille scuttled forward to Sigurd's side. "Ask the
Oracle whether the Lantean blasphemers should live or die."

They were hauled through the streets to a building on the
outskirts of town. It was clearly some sort of shrine; wreaths
of flowers and plates of food lay against the walls and under
the trees that shaded the old stone building. The interior was
a single room just big enough to house the familiar game-
board display panel of an Oracle and what was unmistakably
a barred jail cell against one wall.

Rodney was shoved forward ungently into the cell. John was
tossed in after him, and their captors slammed the door shut.

"All right, all right!" Rodney snapped. "You do know that
the Oracle doesn't actually need us to be in here in order to
decide what to do with us, right? It's a machine. Most of its
processing power isn't even here, it's at the other end in the
input device—"

"Please be quiet," Vasti said nervously, his hands moving
over the Oracle's screens. "I need to explain the situation in a
way that the Ancestors will understand."

"So do that," Sigurd said. He waited, none too patiently, as
Vasti tapped his way through screens on the device. It was clear
that Vasti read Ancient, although he seemed to have missed
several shortcuts that would have made it easier to use the
Oracle's interface. Rodney opened his mouth to say so, and
then closed it again. This probably wasn't the moment to provide an unasked-for tutorial.

"Wouldn't it be easier for us to just work this out without
involving the Ancients?" John said.

"You involved the Ancestors when you spoke against them
and compared them to the accursed Wraith," Sigurd said.

"I wasn't comparing them to the Wraith. I was trying to
explain—"

"Silence!" Sigurd said again, which put a real damper on their side of the conversation. He turned on Vasti. "Well?"

"Oracle of the Ancestors," Vasti said hurriedly. "What should the punishment for the Lanteans' blasphemy be?"

The Oracle spoke in the clear recorded tones of an Ancient who had probably been dead for tens of thousands of years. "For their crimes against the Ancestors, you must bring them before the village council in the morning to be tried for the crime of heresy."

"A crime of which you are certainly guilty," Sigurd said darkly.

"And what exactly is the penalty for heresy?" John asked.

Vasti swallowed hard before he spoke, but Rodney already had a sinking certainty of what he was going to say. "If you are found guilty, you will be put to death."

They were left in their cell with a plate of bread, a pitcher of water, and promises that their trial on the morning would be fair, whatever that meant by local standards. Through the bars, Rodney could see the Oracle still glowing, although it didn't appear to be receiving any more transmissions.

"This is just great," Rodney said. "Absolutely perfect. Why is it that every time someone believes that they have direct personal knowledge of the will of the Ancients, the will of the Ancients turns out to be that something bad ought to happen to us? Why aren't they ever convinced that the Ancients want them to throw us a party and bake us a cake?"

"Because these Ancients are being impersonated by the Wraith, and the Wraith never want us to have cake," John said.

"I don't see what the Wraith have against cake! If we're going to be eaten by the Wraith —"

"We're not going to be eaten by the Wraith."

"Only because we're going to be executed! We at least ought to have cake if we're executed!"

"If they made us a cake, you'd question whether their food handling practices were sanitary," John said.

"Only because I doubt they are. And you're changing the subject."

"No, now I'm changing the subject. Does anything strike you as screwed up about this?"

"Everything about this strikes me as screwed up," Rodney said. "We're going to die on an alien planet for an incredibly stupid reason, which is pretty much the scenario that I've spent a lot of time trying to persuade myself isn't going to happen every time we walk through the gate. Clearly the more paranoid parts of me were onto something."

"You're such an optimist, McKay," John said. "Look. Assume for a minute that the Wraith are controlling the Oracle. Vasti just told them that we're from Atlantis and that we've been snooping around here asking questions. Are the Wraith likely to tell these folks to put us on trial and execute us?"

"No," Rodney had to admit. "That's a lot more pleasant than what the Wraith would do."

"They'd tell them to keep us locked up until the Wraith could come and collect us for the whole 'kneel before me while I poke around in your head, puny human,' routine. If they're particularly smart Wraith, they might threaten our lives in order to draw Elizabeth and the back-up team into a trap."

"We're smarter than that."

"On a good day, but they don't know that. But the last thing they'd do is tell the people here that they can actually kill us outright. If we're dead, we're not even good for a midnight snack."

"You think it's not the Wraith?"

"I think something's screwy here, and I don't know what." John's radio crackled, and he thumbed it on immediately. "Teyla, Ronon, report."

"Colonel Sheppard," Teyla said, sounding relieved. "Are you well?"

"No, we are not well," Rodney said over John's shoulder. "We're in a jail cell that smells like the problematic end of a goat."

"We're fine for right now," John said. "Tomorrow may get dicier."

"I have Major Lorne here with a backup team," Teyla said. "He's prepared to extract you by force if that should prove necessary."

"I'd like to try to get out of here without Lorne coming in guns blazing," John said. "We're not exactly having fun right now, but a lot of innocent people are going to get hurt if we have a firefight in the middle of a crowded town square."

"What has Zelenka found out?" Rodney demanded. "And don't tell me 'he's working on it.' I expect him to be working on it, but I also expect him to finish working on it so that we can figure out what's going on."

"Dr. Zelenka said to tell you that he was able to trace the signal after the last transmission," Lorne's voice said. "Apparently someone used the Oracle less than an hour ago—"

"To determine our fate," John said. "Magic 8 Ball said 'ask again later.'"

"Here's the weird part," Lorne said over the radio. "Dr. Zelenka says that it looks like the signals are coming from somewhere here on PX7-MYB."

Rodney and John exchanged looks. "Was Zelenka able to pinpoint the source of the transmissions?" John asked.

"They look like they're coming from the village," Lorne said.

"Okay. Take your team and search the village. Pay particular attention to Sigurd—he seems really invested in the Ancestors being responsible, but that could just be to throw us off the trail. We need to find out who's sending these transmissions, and fast."

"Sheppard," Rodney said warningly. The door opened, and Vasti stepped inside. John cut the transmission at once, but Vasti came over to the bars, his face alight with interest.

"You're communicating with the other Lanteans," he said. "With a machine. A radio."

"That's right," Sheppard said.

"It uses radio waves to transmit sound," Rodney said. "It's a simple principle. It wouldn't require much more than you have here. You'd need a tower to get transmissions across any distance, but all you need to build a tower are trees, and you've got plenty of trees."

Vasti turned away from the bars. "I'm not interested in your advice. You're a blasphemer. But if the Ancestors gave their blessing to such a thing, it would be a great man who brought it to our people. Even Emille would have to see ..." He trailed off, and then said, as if to himself, "She is not the only one to whom the Ancestors speak."

Rodney turned to John, unsure whether he should be trying to discourage Vasti. John shrugged. After all, they'd intended to make this experiment in the first place, and there was only so far they could go to warn the locals of the consequences of their actions. Vasti had made it pretty clear that he wasn't interested in being warned.

Vasti poked at the computer screen, inputting data and frowning at the results and choosing from more menus. Finally he looked satisfied.

"Oracle of the Ancestors," Vasti said. "Can you tell us how to achieve the transmission of sound across long distances using 'radio waves'?"

There was a lengthy pause before the Ancient voice spoke. "Your own studies may yet achieve this end in time. Tell Sigurd that whatever materials you need for this study should be provided to you. We would be pleased if you developed a device for this purpose."

"I have to tell Sigurd," Vasti said excitedly, and burst out through the door, leaving it swinging for a moment before returning to lock it behind him.

"They said yes?" Rodney said, blinking.

John looked equally baffled. "They said yes."

"We should be looking for signs of the Wraith being here," Ronon said as he led Lorne in a wide circle around the outskirts of the village. He felt that was the most critical point, and that some of the others weren't keeping it firmly enough in mind.

"We have seen none," Teyla said.

"That doesn't mean there aren't any. It could just mean we're not looking hard enough."

"We don't know that the Wraith are responsible for any of this," Lorne said. "Let's just take a look around, scan for energy readings, and see what we can turn up."

"It's always the Wraith," Ronon said.

"It is not always the Wraith," Teyla said. "But it seems the most plausible explanation."

"Let's find the device," Lorne said. "Then we can look for explanations."

They skirted the back of Sigurd's house, a garden with a hanging electric lantern illuminating growing vegetables and a placidly munching goat. It was remarkably similar to the other back gardens they'd investigated, with no sign of an Ancient device. Lorne looked at his scanner and shook his head.

The houses were getting further apart as they approached the outskirts of town, and it was possible now to make out individual tracks on the muddy road, but they looked like normal signs of people and animals traveling around the village. Instead of the familiar tread of Wraith boots, all Ronon saw were blurred marks of leather-soled handmade shoes.

"Perhaps we should double back toward the center of the village," Teyla said in an undertone as they approached a wood-framed house half dug into the side of a hill. Beyond the house, the road petered out into a narrow trail winding up the hill through thick trees and underbrush. "I doubt there are many more houses to be found farther into the woods."

Ronon stepped over a low and crumbling wall, and then stopped to check it more closely. "Look at this."

Lorne crouched to examine the remains of the wall along with him. It was falling apart with age, but the stones were cut smoothly and fitted together neatly. All the stone walls they had seen in the village had been fieldstone. Ronon explored the stone with his hands, and found a metal seam, free of rust despite its obvious age.

"Old ruins," Lorne said.

"Emille did say they were close to the village."

"And there goes the scanner," Lorne said. "There's a power signature coming from inside that house that isn't from the local electrical power."

"Watch out for Wraith."

"When don't we?" They moved cautiously in on the house, Ronon and Lorne in the lead, Teyla and the two Marines who were the rest of the backup team following behind them. The house had a front door with an electric lantern hung from a hook to light its porch, but Lorne frowned at his scanner and then jerked his head to motion that they should circle around to the side of the house.

There, a door was set into the side of the hill at an angle, looking like it might lead down to a cold cellar or coal bin. Lorne opened it with care, and electric light blazed from within. He nodded to Ronon, and he moved in first, Teyla following him. The Marines were good fighters, but they weren't as good at moving quietly.

He descended a set of wooden stairs until he could see the cellar room. A table-sized control module that was clearly the work of the Ancestors stood in the middle of the room, its surface lit with colors and crawling with text. A tangle of wires ran from it, suggesting it had somehow been connected to the local power system.

Emille was bending over the device, her face lit by colored light, her fingers moving swiftly over the screen. Behind Ronon, the staircase creaked, and Emille looked up, and then flinched back, her face falling into stricken dismay. "I can explain," she said.

Ronon was already moving, his pistol out. "I'll bet you can. How long have you been working for the Wraith?"

"I'm not working with the Wraith."

"Liar. They've been feeding you all this information, haven't they? Did they promise you that they'd spare your life when they culled your world?" He backed her up against the wall, his pistol leveled at her chest. "They lie."

His radio abruptly crackled into life.

"Ronon, report," Sheppard said.

His finger itched to pull the trigger. Instead, he said, "We found the Wraith worshipper. It's Emille. She's been controlling the Oracle right from her house."

"I'm not a Wraith worshipper," Emille snapped.

"I don't think she's had any contact with the Wraith," Sheppard said. "But I do think I know what's going on here. Bring her back to the shrine. It's time we had a talk."

Rodney felt a surge of relief as the door of the shrine opened and Ronon came in, pushing Emille in front of him, followed by Teyla, Lorne, the back-up team. Emille stood stiff-backed, her chin high. "That took you long enough."

"We were busy," Ronon said. "Now. You. Talk."

"You have a right to be angry," Emille said. Her lips tightened. "But so do I. Do you understand how thoroughly you're about to ruin everything?"

"Why don't you explain," John said.

Emille ran one hand lovingly over the Oracle's console. "I've spent my whole life trying to understand the secrets of the Ancestors," she said. "Digging in the ruins when no one else would help. Reconstructing whole sciences when no one else cared. I figured out how to generate electrical power fifteen years ago. And Sigurd said that it was a waste of time and a waste of coal, and wouldn't give me a single bit of help."

"And then the Oracle spoke to you?" Teyla suggested.

"The Oracle never spoke to me," Emille snapped. "I worked for every single thing I learned, do you understand? No one taught me, no one helped me. Not for fifty years. I worked and

I experimented and I did everything the wrong way a thousand times before I did it the right way once, and finally I learned what our ancestors knew. But I couldn't go any farther without help. I'm old now. I needed young people with strong backs. I needed metal and coal."

"So you found a way to get Sigurd to give them to you," Rodney said.

He felt a surprising degree of sympathy. He could think of times when he would have lied without hesitation if it would have gotten him adequate research funding. All right, maybe he wouldn't have claimed that divine powers wanted him to study naquadah power generation, but on the other hand, if it would actually have done the trick …

"I found the control console. It was clear it had something to do with the Oracle. It took me years to figure out how to reactivate it. Once I did, I used it to tell everyone that the Ancestors were pleased with us, and wanted to give us the gift of new technology." She snorted. "Sigurd ate it up. He's always wanted to hear that he's wise and good, and this proved it."

"You also told the Oracle that we should be locked up and put on trial for our lives," Rodney pointed out, feeling his sympathy abate as he was reminded of that point.

"I didn't have any other choice," Emille said, with the first hint of remorse he'd seen in her expression. "Sigurd wouldn't have believed it if the Oracle had told him to ignore your disrespect. But I wouldn't have let them sentence you to death. The Oracle would have called for him to show you mercy by exiling you instead."

"You have taken a great many decisions into your own hands," Teyla said.

"Those were the only hands I had." Emille raised her chin. "And I'm not a bit sorry. Having electrical power has done so much for our people, and there's so much more that we're on the verge of being able to do next. Whatever you want to do to me — do it. But don't tell Sigurd that everything we've accomplished in the last few years is worthless because I lied."

"If I were you, I should be more concerned about the fate of my people than about my own reputation," Teyla said.

"That is what I am concerned about. I don't want them to stop making progress."

"This kind of progress is going to bring down the Wraith," Ronon said.

"Ronon is right," Teyla said. "His own homeworld was destroyed by the Wraith because they had made very similar technological advances. My own world has deliberately chosen not to embrace the technologies of our ancestors in hopes of preventing our complete destruction."

"Is this true?"

Ronon nodded shortly. "They bombed Sateda. Everybody died."

"But that wouldn't happen here," Emille said. "Surely it wouldn't." She looked at Rodney, and he hesitated, reluctant to give her the only answer he had.

"If you continue to develop electrical power, you're eventually going to attract the attention of the Wraith," he said heavily. "That's going to happen exponentially faster if you use radio, because you'll be sending signals that can travel into space. All those inventions you're thinking about right now — every one of them comes at the cost of making it more likely that your people are going to be attacked by the Wraith."

Emille was silent for a moment. When she spoke, her tone was bleak. "Then that's my choice?" she said. "Give up my life's work, or risk the lives of all my friends?"

"How about door number three," John said. "Tell them the danger, and let them decide. You've made your people's choices for them for long enough."

"Sigurd will not believe your warning," Emille said. "He truly believes the Ancestors speak through the Oracle, and he is immensely proud to have been chosen by the Ancestors to receive their favor. If you persuade him that I have lied, it will still not convince him that you are telling the truth about the Wraith. He will turn his anger and his shame at being tricked against you, and you will be lucky to leave this world alive."

"There's one way he'd believe it," John said. "If it comes from the Oracle."

Emille stared at him, and then breathed a laugh. "That's true."

"Warn your people through the Oracle that maintaining your current pace of technological advancement will attract the attention of the Wraith," Teyla said. "That will make the lack of any new revelations from the Oracle a sign of the Ancestors' care for your people, rather than their disfavor."

"That's still a lot of lying," Ronon said.

Teyla inclined her head to show that she accepted his point. "And yet it may be the most effective way to convey one very important truth."

"It would be a solution that would buy you some time," John said. "We're trying to fight the Wraith. We like to think we might be able to win, one of these days."

"But even if that is not possible, it would give your people time enough to make decisions," Teyla said. "They must agree upon some strategy for dealing with the Wraith: to limit technological growth in an attempt to escape their notice, or to plan to flee from them when they come, or to find some means of fighting back?"

Emille still looked bleak. "Do any of those things work?"

Ronon shrugged. "Better than not doing anything at all."

"I'm sorry to be inhospitable," Sigurd said, releasing John and Rodney from their cell. John shot Rodney a repressing look as Rodney opened his mouth to express his feelings about their captivity, and he settled for scowling instead. "I see now that the Ancestors sent you to warn us about the Wraith. It is not your fault that you did not fully understand their message."

"I am glad that you appreciate the threat of the Wraith to

your world," Teyla said. "We hope that they will stay far away from you for as long as possible."

"So do we," Vasti said. He looked dejected. "Which means that we have to stop work, at least for now. There's still a lot of maintenance to be done, of course. And maybe we could make some minor improvements ..." He trailed off at Sigurd's expression. "Maybe in time," he said, raising his chin.

"Let's hope so," John said.

Emille hadn't come out to say goodbye to them. Rodney tried to imagine his own feelings at being told to shut down all his research for the good of the expedition, and figured that she wasn't in the mood to face anyone at the moment. He wouldn't have known what to say to her, anyway. The choices the Wraith forced on worlds were nightmarish, and the worst part was knowing that even if these people played it safe, they might still wake up one morning to the whine of Wraith darts filling the air.

It was a quiet walk back to the Stargate. Lorne and the backup team had already left, and Ronon and Teyla had little to say, both of them probably absorbed in thinking about the Wraith and the way their own people had tried to deal with them.

"We're going to find some way to stop the Wraith," John said.

"Of course we will," Rodney said.

The silence drew out again.

"No, I mean we really will," John said.

Ahead of them, Ronon shrugged. "Or die trying."

"I'd like to win instead of die trying."

"So would I," Rodney said. "So we're going to figure this out, and we're going to find a way to stop the Wraith, and we're going to do it soon — because we'd better do it soon — so we will."

"That is a more than usually optimistic prediction, coming from you," Teyla said.

"Maybe my recent brush with enlightenment was enlightening, I don't know. Besides, I came on a one-way trip to another galaxy with no proof that we could even survive here, let alone get home," Rodney said. "You don't think I'm an optimist?"

"I think it would have killed you not to know what was here," John said.

"You're right. I had to find out what was here. Just like these people had to find out what they could do with electricity. Sooner or later, they're going to keep trying."

"So we'll find a way to make it safe for them," John said. "We'll keep trying."

"Until we win," Rodney said, and kept hiking toward the Stargate.

STARGATE SG-1
Sweet Herbs and Freedom

Suzanne Wood

This story takes place in season two of STARGATE: SG-1, after the episode Prisoners.

SHE STOOD beneath a sky dark with imminent rain. The air she breathed in, that first deep breath of freedom, was so moist she almost drank it. Static charges from the wormhole behind her prickled her skin and sent strands of hair frizzing in all directions. Exhale. Second breath, as good as the first. No people in sight. Flocks of avian creatures wheeled through the air, quick as thought they dove into the cover of thick forest surrounding the dais where she stood. Thunder cracked overhead. In the distance rain fell in sheets, rapidly working its way toward her.

The dull green garments she wore offered little protection from such a drenching. No need to walk into unattractive weather. The Tau'ri machines had revealed so many new worlds for her use; there were so many opportunities awaiting her. She walked down the steps, into the first hard drops of rain. The dialing device sat dumbly at the foot of the Great Circle, no, "Stargate" was what they had called it. A nice name. The symbols shone brightly golden in the gloom. Six for an address and one for the planet on which she stood — a simple matter of identifying the sole unique one — just as described in the Tau'ri's records.

A solid clunk and the Stargate connected to the galaxy with a sharp tang of ozone and steam. Linea smiled, and walked on to find her next world to conquer.

"We have to at least try!"

General George Hammond sent a quelling look down the

length of the briefing room table at Daniel Jackson. Internally he smiled, glad to have the passionate doctor, and the rest of SG-1, back from their incarceration on Hadante.

"Do we have any idea where Linea may have gone?" he asked, turning his gaze to Jack O'Neill.

Jack slouched in his chair, to all appearances at ease and unconcerned, but Hammond knew better. Just a couple of days ago SG-1 had been incarcerated for the term of their natural lives in an underground prison, for the crime of giving aid to a stranger. While Hammond and SG-9 were attempting to barter a release for their people, his premier team had engineered an escape with the help of a nice, older lady also 'unfairly' imprisoned. A nice, older lady who happened to be a homicidal maniac. A nice, older homicidal maniac who had stolen a number of planetary addresses from their own database and was now roaming free with who-knew-what intentions.

Jack twitched his gaze from Hammond to Captain Carter and nodded at her.

"Sir, we've analyzed the files that Linea accessed and it seems she was most interested in the addresses in the pending mission allocation." Carter slid a folder across the table to him. Inside sat a neatly typed list of ten planetary addresses and their Stargate glyphs. "Daniel found the notepad Linea must have used to copy these addresses." She held up a notepad with the impression of writing showing through pencil shadings.

"Makes sense, with so many addresses in our database, she went for the ones that we've already done a preliminary scan on," O'Neill said.

Carter squirmed in her seat. "Which I had shown her, sir. Sorry."

"Not your fault, Captain. No one was to know who she truly was until our unexpected traveler showed up."

Teal'c spoke up, his deep voice cutting through the gloomy thoughts in the room. "Daniel Jackson is correct, General

Hammond. We must endeavor to track Linea and ensure she is no threat to the people of those worlds."

Hammond took a careful look at his premier team. Their last mission had been trying but nobody had been injured and allowing them a chance to right this particular wrong would be a beneficial boost to morale. And despite what the Joint Chiefs might have to say, they did have a certain obligation to the unknown civilians out in the wider galaxy.

"Very well."

A relieved sigh came from Daniel and the captain. Teal'c nodded his pleasure, Jack grimaced and sat up straight.

"You have a go for a brief recon of each of these planets. This is not a full-out exploratory mission, just go in, check them out, question anyone near to the Stargate if they've seen Linea, and if not, move on to the next as soon as possible. Dismissed."

This was what she was looking for. This world would provide what she needed.

Five journeys through the Stargate. Worlds of such difference she had never imagined. Two inhabited, but by base, inarticulate people that would not serve her requirements. Beautiful worlds indeed; after living underground for so long the temptation was there to linger, lift her face to warm sun and fill her lungs with fresh air, but it was not her nature to walk through fields of flowers or dally when there was work to do.

Linea stepped down from the stone dais. The Stargate closed down with that strange sucking sound it made. The dais stood at the far end of a marketplace, which was surrounded by white painted stone houses with red roofs. Beyond the buildings towered high mountains, so steep-sided few trees clung to them. And on the far side of the town lay a lake of deep blue water: its still surface presented a perfect mirror image of the town and mountain above it.

In the market, men and women moved busily through stalls of food and goods. Small children darted around adults, intent in their play. Youths hauled bales and boxes, helping their parents in their daily work. Here and there pairs of males walked, wearing similar garb that could be a uniform. Few folk looked her way, but a pair of the uniformed ones approached.

"State your business, woman," one said, his tone neither friendly nor unfriendly.

"I am a travelling healer. I come to offer my knowledge to those who are in need." She smiled that smile that had opened doors in many places.

The man rested his long staff on the ground and looked her over carefully. "Healers are always required, that is true. What god do you serve?"

"I bear no allegiance to any god, nor do I bear animosity to any god. I simply heal the sick." *He must refer to the gods of which Daniel and Samantha spoke.*

"Very well, then." With a nod of agreement from his partner, the man moved aside. "You may go."

"My thanks. Please tell your people to seek me should they need my services." Her false smile pleased them and she walked off through the marketplace.

The people here were intelligent and industrious, not as advanced as her home world, but enough to support her plans. They wore robes and dresses with varying degrees of adornment. Some sported elaborate headdresses, the males in uniform all bore weapons on their belts and those long staffs that she suspected were also a weapon. She wove through the crowd, conscious that the drab green garments supplied by Samantha were out of place here. Her old garments were gone, discarded in the room they had given her. But in her pockets were a number of valuables, small precious things she had made sure to take with her in the escape from Hadante.

She stopped at a stall selling women's clothing. A deep red dress caught her eye and the seller was quick to accept a bright *vasus* gem in payment.

"My thanks, lady." She tucked the bundle of cloth under

her arm. "I seek a place to live and conduct my work — I am a healer. Do you know of any home that would be available?"

"A healer? What a fine thing. We've needed a healer since old Engles passed on many months ago, and not everyone is comfortable seeking the help of the priestesses in the temple." The woman indicated with a chuck of her head to a turreted building halfway up the mountain slope. "My friend's cousin's son has an empty house. His mother passed on a year ago now and he'd be grateful of the rent money, that's for sure, gambling all night in the garrison the way he does. Come along, I'll find him for you. Sanach is my name," she added as she swept her goods off the stall table and pocketed a clinking purse.

"I am Linea." She followed Sanach through the stalls, noting other goods that would be useful for her work: pots for mixing; beakers for pouring; plants that would offer useful properties; compounds and herbs...yes, all would be useful.

SG-1 shipped out at 1037 precisely. They travelled light for this mission: backpacks only and one MALP to scout ahead. Hammond had agreed that cost to the SGC would be lower if they moved directly from one planet to the next on the list that Linea had purloined, instead of gating back home and then out again. There was no guarantee that she would dial the first on the list but, Jack being the methodical man he was, decided to start at the top. Their first destination was P2K-589, which Technician Davis had cheerily assured them was a nice-looking forest area, before giving them the go-ahead.

Trees. Jack resisted the urge to voice his comment. "Okay, kids, quick recce for civili —"

Boom. The skies above crashed with thunder like the crack of doom, followed instantly by a spear of lightning that split in two a giant tree not twenty feet from them. Daniel started badly and bumped into Carter, both of them wildly looking around. Teal'c reached out a steadying hand, looking a little perturbed himself. As half the tree toppled in slow majesty, rain hit them like a million little sledge hammers, straight down on their heads with merciless weight. Jack was past his team like a shot, straight to the DHD. There was no discussion — not that any of them could be heard above the roar of the rain and the crash of timber. Carter saw his intent, grabbed the MALP control and turned the machine to face the Stargate.

Jack slapped the glyphs as fast as he could, shoulders hunched around his ears in trepidation of another lightning strike. Already, water was flooding across the clearing. The wormhole billowed out in a cloud of steam. The MALP rolled through and vanished. Jack bolted up the steps, hardly waiting for Carter to give the thumbs up before shoving his team into the event horizon and throwing himself after them.

Her new home was a little stone-walled cottage overlooking the glassy blue lake. Within days Linea had established herself as a healer and people began to arrive at her door seeking salves and bandages and tinctures, and even advice, though why they felt her opinion was of any more merit than their own was beyond her comprehension. She could deal with physical matters with ease, but to decide whether a woman she'd never met before should keep a secret from her male was something she neither knew the answer to nor cared about.

"I should tell him, yes?" the woman, barely out of her own childhood, blinked earnestly at her.

"That is not my business," Linea said tersely.

"But our god frowns upon those who hold secrets."

"What business is it of a 'god' whether you lie to your male or not?"

The girl gaped at her. "Apophis knows all and sees all. He will be angry with me if I lie, but if I tell Facher that I cannot bear a child he will seek another to wed."

"Apophis is your god?"

The girl, Mascha, nodded eagerly.

"I do not believe in mythical deities. Now, I have another seeking my help. You may go."

Mascha stayed planted on her stool. "Apophis is not a myth! He lives, he breathes. Why, he walked among us not two moons past."

Linea paused. Daniel had told her of the enemy the Tau'ri fought on distant worlds. Goa'uld — that was what he called them. People who bore a parasite in their heads, who walked amongst the naïve and pretended to be their gods. Interesting.

"Your god, is he of the Goa'uld?"

Mascha nodded happily. "Facher is one of his Jaffa. He hopes one day to gain Apophis' favor and maybe even become First Prime."

"Then you had best be honest with him, lest you draw the wrath of this god." Linea stood and shooed Mascha out the door.

Goa'uld. Human, yet gifted with strong healing abilities according to Daniel. What a challenge that would make…

"I think I lost my hearing with that last clap of thunder." Daniel shook himself like a very wet dog.

"What?" Sam bellowed in his ear. Her hair was plastered to her scalp and stuck in bedraggled rat-tails across her face.

"Oh, there it is. Never mind."

They were all drenched. Sunlight shone off Teal'c's wet head making him look like a burnished Buddha as he surveyed their new surroundings.

Jack struggled out of his soaked vest and jacket and dumped them on the stone dais. "Carter, make a note to cross that planet off the list of potential mission sites." He stuck a finger in one ear and gave it a good wiggle. "Or maybe Makepeace and his meatheads would like it. How's it look, Teal'c?"

"No intelligent beings are in sight, O'Neill."

"Present company excepted." Jack took a good look at their new surroundings. "Well, no trees at least."

"You have a thing against trees, sir?" Carter plucked ineffectively at her wet pants.

"No, I just like a bit of variety in my planets. Now this one, this is different."

The Stargate platform stood on a small plateau amid a tumble of grey granite rocks. Close by, the rocks were smaller, soccer ball sized, but quickly increased to small car boulders and away on the horizon to massive house-sized ones — if the house was a three storied Dallas oil mansion. The only plant life to be seen were thin stalks poking up from cracks in and between the rocks, with bright, tiny flowers angling their faces to the sun.

"I can't see Linea finding anything appealing here, Jack." Daniel draped his wet jacket over a warm rock.

"No, still, we'll go a short way, just to be sure." He stepped off the dais, balanced on a rock, then stepped across to the next. "Watch your footing kids, last thing we need is a sprained ankle or two."

Although he'd raised the issue himself, he'd been glad Daniel and then Carter had further pushed the general into allowing them this search for Linea. Jack was not one to wallow in guilt, but it had been his idea to take Linea with them in their escape from Hadante, not knowing what her crimes really were or that she would flee out into the wider network of Stargate-connected planets. Would she attempt harm on unsuspecting civilians? Who knew. He doubted they would find her, but at least they were making the effort to right their wrong. What they would do with her if they caught her was a problem for a higher pay grade. They didn't have the co-ordinates for Hadante, they couldn't really lock her up in Miramar or even Fort Leavenworth without a trial. Hand her over to the Goa'uld? Tempting. No, she'd end up working for them.

Wrapped in morose thoughts, Jack moved from rock to boulder, taking increasingly larger steps to get across the plateau. On his right, Teal'c moved with easy grace, placing his staff weapon in gaps between the rocks to aid his balance. Behind and to the left, Daniel and Carter hopped and jumped from one to the next.

"Boy, times like these I'm glad I'm on the tall side." Carter's voice carried clearly in the surrounding quiet.

They continued for ten minutes until they fetched up against a cluster of boulders the size of buses. Jack stopped and unhitched his pack.

"Okay, I'm calling this one. She'd never have made her way across this stuff, even if there are people living here." He took a long swig of water from his canteen. Across the valley, the MALP looked tiny against the Stargate, patiently waiting for their return. "We'll take a break and then head back."

SG-1 perched on the weather-worn boulders, their clothing quickly dried in the sun. Errant breezes wound through the rocks causing odd moans and whines to echo in this otherwise silent world.

Jack found Daniel regarding him thoughtfully. He raised an eyebrow in query. In response, Daniel turned to Teal'c.

"Teal'c, if Linea committed her crimes on a Goa'uld world, what would they have done with her?"

"Execution." Teal'c stared out at the empty valley. "Such aberrant people have been known on some Goa'uld worlds, but they are quickly caught and dispatched. Crimes such as Linea's are seen not only as crimes against the people involved, but crimes against the rule of the god. Apophis would never tolerate an individual maiming or killing one of his subjects — that is his purview, and his alone. Such a one would be seen to be challenging him. They are as much a traitor as I am seen to be."

Jack grunted. "Yeah, well, there's traitors and then there's traitors. I'll take our kind of traitor any day of the week."

Teal'c glanced over and inclined his head in thanks.

Within the first week of her stay in the village, Linea had identified fourteen samples from plant and mineral sources that would combine into a compound similar to the one she had come so close to perfecting on her former home. There, her experiments had progressed well; the sickness spread through the people with gratifying speed. The Taldor had called on her to assist with care of the sick, an opportunity which she had taken to further disseminate the plague. The death rate soared, the people bleated like the herd animals they were, rushing mindlessly from one place to another seeking any kind of cure, whether it was effective of not. Some had even found respite in the herb tansone, only to discover it accelerated the symptoms after a day of false-cure. That had been her downfall — she'd found the grower of the herb on Salos Island and bought all his stock to spread out amongst her test subjects. The grower had reported her interest to the Taldor.

Linea shoved her bowl away with force. The memories of that time rose fresh around her. The accusing faces of the soldiers who arrested her. The disbelief of the test subjects as they came to realize her assistance had in fact been killing them and their pathetic fellow weaklings. The hatred of the mob following her to the Tal'al. The cold, dispassionate voices of the Taldor delivering judgement and sentence upon her.

"Who are they to judge me?" She picked up the bowl and flung it against the wall. "Years in that stinking hole, playing petty politics with the likes of Vishnor just to stay alive." Well, she had survived, and now, now was the time to wreak her vengeance upon the Taldor.

And the first step was ready to implement. She picked up the gourd filled with the powder she had worked all through the night to refine. Pausing to wrap a shawl around her shoulders against a chill bite in the air, Linea ventured out into the marketplace.

The community wells sat in the heart of the bustle of stalls and shoppers. Four elaborately carved ponds surrounded the central well, where an ingenious self-perpetuating bucket and pulley system splashed water out into the ponds. Guards from the temple stopped here to drink from the cups ranged along the edge of one pool, women filled buckets for their homes and the temple while gossiping with their neighbors, animals drank from another pond while children played and soaked themselves in the fourth.

It was an easy thing to slip a measure of the compound into three of the ponds. She avoided engaging with any of the people, answered greetings with a non-committal bob of the head, then wandered away through the stalls. She brought out her notebook, helpfully provided by Samantha, and carefully recorded the time of dispersal. First symptoms should arise within four hours, allowing the majority of subjects to imbibe the water.

Linea smiled thinly. Anticipation ran a shiver along her skin. She had missed this feeling. Only a few opportunities had presented themselves during her incarceration on Hadante, and then she was limited to one or two subjects at a time. Once she had toyed with the idea of eliminating all the prisoners, but the thought of remaining there, surrounded by stinking corpses had deterred her. She needed space to move on once an experiment was complete. A deep sigh escaped her. She had space aplenty now. A whole universe to play with.

SG-1 emerged from the Stargate into stardust sprinkled darkness. Usually missions were timed so that teams arrived in daylight, but there was no point loitering on one planet until daylight rose on the next. The MALP showed no hostiles, so on they went.

"Oh, look at that." Sam almost tripped down the dais steps with her face turned upward to the magnificent celestial display overhead.

Billions of stars arced over their heads from one horizon to the other. Patches of dust shrouded parts of the galactic arm above them, which highlighted colorful clouds of gaseous nebulae and clumps of brilliant blue-white young stars

"Look, this planet has a ring," Sam breathed in a sigh of

wonder. The others followed her pointing finger to the sweep of thousands of tiny objects soaring through the ebony sky.

"Comet!" The colonel called, facing the other side of the Stargate. As they watched, a comet with a short tail of vapor rose into the sky and set a path straight for the ring. In no time it reached it and blew right through, creating a cascade of ice and shattered particles that followed along behind the comet to join its tail.

"Whoa, that's something you don't see every day." Sam belatedly grabbed for her camera and tried to capture some of the glory above.

"That stuff's not going to fall on us, is it?" asked Daniel.

"We won't be staying long enough to find out," the colonel replied. "Fifteen minutes, kids."

Despite there being no moon, the starlight's glow was adequate to see their way. Sam led the team across a barren landscape. There was no vegetation here, only stones and fine dust that pooled in hidden hollows and erupted into choking clouds when an unsuspecting foot went down. After a couple hundred yards, Jack sank knee deep into a dust hole. Daniel grabbed his arm and hauled him upright.

"Okay, Major, I think this is far enough. Linea wouldn't be interested in this place."

"She may not be, but I sure am. We have to come back here, sir. The celestial cartography we can do here could advance our understanding of space to unimaginable levels."

"Well, we can flag it for one of the geek teams. Maybe Hammond will let you tag along."

"It's not just of interest to Sam, Jack," Daniel said as he craned his neck to take in as much of the overhead wonders as possible. "I'm really curious why the gate builders put a Stargate here in the first place. There's no settlement in sight, but there is an obvious drawcard. Finding out what brought the Stargate here might tell us a lot about the builders."

"The heavenly bodies visible from this planet are most pleasing to the eye, O'Neill," Teal'c added in a rare show of astronomical appreciation that had Sam grinning.

The colonel sighed dramatically. "Fine. *We'll* come back. One day." He met Sam's hopeful look. "I'll get Hammond to put it on our schedule — alien attacks and unexpected end-of-the-world scenarios notwithstanding. Let's head back."

They turned back to the Stargate. It sat gilded in starlight, beckoning them back to continue their explorations.

First symptoms of the compound were visible in all subjects within three hours, earlier than expectations. Adolescents and children succumbed completely in the first twelve hours. Many of the women and townsfolk succumbed successfully by the fifteenth hour. Strangely, other adults resisted the symptoms for a further six hours. These were noted to be what they termed priests and priestesses from the temple above the town, and the guards who stalked the streets in service of their 'god'.

Linea looked up from her notebook. From where she sat on the edge of the well she could see many of her subjects scattered throughout the town, curled in the same knotted rictus. She rose and wandered a curving path through the bodies.

Subject Group B were incapacitated by the compound, but did not succumb immediately. Upon close examination a worm-like parasite extruded from the mouths of the priests and priestesses, and from the bellies of the guards. Once apart from their carriers, the humans expired quickly. The worms continued life for up to another hour. Some attempted to move toward me. I surmise these to be the Goa'uld that Daniel told me of.

For a brief moment she considered telling Daniel and Samantha of her success in eliminating the creatures that plagued the worlds in which they travelled. Surely they would welcome a method to end their war. But no. She stepped over a fallen man. The people of Earth were as enslaved to their consciences as the people under the Taldor had been. They would prefer to suffer their war rather than accept her assistance.

"Blind. Ignorant and blind. Why can they not see my way is the only way? *Fools.*"

Her voice echoed back to her. Blessed silence surrounded her and brought calm. Nothing moved apart from the animals she had set free from their pens. Birds flapped away from one group of carcasses and settled on another.

Something moved. Beyond the town, on the path to the temple. Someone came! Intrigued, she moved toward them. It was a woman, clad in an elaborate gold gown. She walked unsteadily, staggering now and again, hands clutching her belly. Her muttering reached Linea in a language she did not understand, then the moment the woman saw her she called out in the common language of the Tau'ri and the planets they travelled to.

"Help, help me please!"

Linea caught her as she sagged to her knees. "My dear, wherever did you come from? How did you survive this dread sickness that has claimed all these people?"

The woman looked up at her, pale and in pain, her dark hair plastered to her face in sweaty curls. "I was in the temple —" She cut herself off to search the empty road behind Linea. "Is everybody gone? How did this happen?"

"I know not, my dear. I am a traveler and only recently arrived." Linea regarded her carefully. The gold dress was stained with bodily fluids and torn at the hem. "You are the only one I have encountered, the only survivor." She tried to keep the excited curiosity out of her voice.

"My demon slept." The woman's voice was filled with bitterness. "When the guards fell and the priestesses became sick, it awoke from its slumber. It fought the illness in my body. Eventually it prevailed."

Cured by the worm inside her? How then was this parasite different from those who had succumbed? "Can you stand, my dear? You need rest and food." She helped the woman to her feet. "What is your name, child?"

Brown eyes looked up from a frame of dark curls, and she spoke with fierce pride. "Sha're. My name is Sha're."

Sha're walked with the woman, Linea, back to a little stone cottage. She was still weak after the bouts of purging the demon had initiated to cleanse the illness from her body. Gratefully, she accepted a clean dress and cool water. She settled on a bed and looked with interest at the woman who helped her.

"Why did you come here?"

"I travel between worlds seeking herbs and roots that will make medicines to heal the sick. Sadly, I arrived on this world far too late to be of use. Except to you, dear. At least I can help you." A smile creased the old woman's lined face.

"I do not understand how a sickness can affect so many people, so quickly."

"Nor can I, child. You must be well blessed by the gods to have survived."

"Blessed? By the gods?" Sha're spat her distaste at the thought. "There are no gods. Only demons."

"You said your demon awoke to heal you. What did you mean by that?"

Sha're closed her eyes for a moment, feigning weakness. Much as it was a delight to talk to another human being without the foul demon putting the words in her mouth, something did not feel right. Sour, like mastadge milk. A flicker of melancholy passed through her at the memory of Skaara's favorite saying.

"The worm that lives inside me, it pretends to be one of the gods that holds people like…those, in thrall." She glanced at the wall, seeing in her mind the dead littered beyond. "When I became with child—" Her voice faded. *Oh, Danyel, forgive me, my love.* "When that happened, the demon had to sleep, lest its presence cause the child to be born before its time. Apophis, the mate of my demon, hid me here to protect it and the child."

"And when the sickness came, it awoke?" Linea leaned forward eagerly.

"Yes. It purged the sickness. Healed me. Then slept again."

"I have seen creatures next to the bodies of some of the people. Is that what you mean, your demon is such a creature?"

Sha're nodded.

"How then did those creatures not heal the bodies they inhabited?"

"I believe my demon is of a higher order than the common ones who possess the Jaffa and priests. They live a very long time." She did not want to dwell on the Goa'uld. "Tell me about your travels. Have you been to many different worlds?"

"A few only," Linea shrugged. "Not very interesting places, but varied enough that I can make my way with my tonics and balms."

"You have not met any Goa'uld before?" If this woman only traveled between a few isolated worlds, would she have met Danyel or Jack? She knew in her heart that her husband would search for her, but it had been many seasons since her capture on Abydos.

"I have not met a Goa'uld, no." Linea did not elaborate on others she had met, though. "Why do they pretend to be gods? Do people like these really not know they are nothing more than a worm hiding inside them?"

"The demon Ra ruled my people for many thousands of seasons. It was the only way of life we knew. The Goa'uld give their hosts long life and protect them from sickness — from most sicknesses." She paused for a moment. "Many people consider it a blessing and an honor to host the children of the gods. Those who are chosen to host the adult Goa'uld, we do not consider it a blessing. The demon speaks through your mouth, moves your hand and foot. Its powers appear to be magic to those who do not know its true evil." Sha're looked away from Linea, picking at a thread of the mattress she sat on. "They cannot take your mind. They lie and convince others there is nothing left of the host once they take it, but..." Her voice faded to a furious whisper. "I am here, am I not? I live and think my own thoughts. I will continue, no matter what the demon does to my body. I know Skaara lives too."

"You are indeed yourself, my dear. Who is Skaara?"

"My brother. He was taken at the same time as I. He lives with his demon. Once, when it slept, he spoke to me." Tears trickled down her cheeks, bidden by the memory of that desperate, stolen moment. She glanced at Linea and flinched with shock at the expression on the woman's face. Not the compassion she expected, but a calculating hunger to know more of the evil of the Goa'uld. Suddenly anxious, Sha're held back the question she most wanted to ask: *Have you seen my husband?*

"Tell me of the worlds you visit," she asked instead.

"They are unremarkable. People grow food, live, die. Little of consequence is achieved."

"If they are free of the Goa'uld they must be good places to live."

"What is good to one is bad to another. Each world breeds its own kind of evil, I have found. One must find one's own way to work with that evil and turn it to an advantage."

"How can you work with evil? Evil must be fought. People should not live in ignorance of the power the evil ones have. They must fight it."

"To what end?" Linea seemed genuinely curious.

"So that they may live as free people, be able to decide their own path in life." It seemed so obvious now, but she had grown up under the rule of Ra, knowing her only destiny was to be married to one of his priests or Jaffa, to serve the god by serving his underling. Until fate brought Danyel and Jack to Nagada, and everything had changed.

Linea appeared unmoved. "Freedom brings many ties that bind a soul, my dear."

"Better a binding of your own choice," Sha're said. She found herself discomforted by this conversation. Linea did not appear in reality to be the person she had first presented herself.

"I am very tired. I will sleep now."

"Of course. Rest well." Linea pulled the blanket over her, then moved away to the far side of the cottage.

Sha're closed her eyes but sleep was far from her reach. After a time, she heard Linea leave. She sat up, hoping that the woman would not return for a long time.

"I do not wish to stay in this place." She stood abruptly. Realization flooded through her. "Nor shall I. I am free…" She clapped her hands over her mouth. Free! Yes, while the demon slept she had time. And she knew where she could go.

Sha're moved to the door. She stopped to pick up a shawl thrown on top of a pile of clothes in one corner. What lay beneath caught her breath. Drab green clothing: a shirt and leggings. Not the style of clothing worn here on Apophis' world. They were, however, very familiar to her. She held up the shirt and tears filled her eyes again. How could she not know this cloth? She had washed one just like it every day until it had worn so thin Danyel had given up wearing it. One of Skaara's boys had asked for it and born it with great pride, for it was the uniform of Colonel Jack and the soldiers who had set them all free.

"Danyel." She breathed his name. She could feel him so close to her. She held the shirt against her and realized it could not be his, it was too small. Small enough to fit a woman…

She glanced at the door, but it remained closed. Had Linea met Danyel? Or had she been to his world, his Earth? If she had met the Tau'ri how could she call them unremarkable, when they were clearly so very remarkable? Sha're had seen many worlds that lived under the rule of Apophis and none resembled the wonders that Danyel had described: wagons that moved under their own power, carrying ordinary people between towns with the speed of birds; drawings of people that moved and spoke, spreading stories well beyond the bounds of family or village; whole cities that lived in peace, surrounded by music, art and beauty; so many things no other world had achieved. She ran the tough fabric through her fingers. Yes, this could only come from Danyel's Earth. Linea had been there and she had not mentioned it.

Sha're dropped the shirt and replaced the shawl on top of it. She crept to the door, listened for a short while, then slipped out into the chill air.

The next planet on their checklist was at least brighter than the last. A lot brighter. Daniel shaded his eyes from an intense, hot sun and reached for his sunglasses. The sun reflected from pearly white sand that surrounded the Stargate and stretched away into the distance to dissolve into shimmering waves of rising heat.

"All clear, Colonel," Sam called.

Jack nodded and strode over to the DHD to check it. "Can't see Linea liking this one, either."

Eyes protected, Daniel managed to focus on a line of objects ranging away from the Stargate. Several lines. In fact, dozens of them. "Huh."

He walked over to the closest. Small, no more than ten feet high, they were neatly constructed of light-colored stone blocks. He circled around, looking for markings or some kind of identification, but there were none to be seen.

"What have we got, Daniel?" Jack ambled up, fingers drumming restlessly on the stock of his gun. Beyond him, Daniel could see Teal'c still standing on the edge of the dais.

"At a guess, I'd say these are burial pyramids. I've seen similar ones near the temple of Amun at Jebel Barkal, in what used to be Nubia. Sudan," he elaborated.

"Amun, eh?" Jack's face immediately soured at the mention of Egyptian gods. "Which one was he?"

"Uh, oh, well," Daniel indicated aimlessly with one hand. No, not going to get away with this one. "Ra."

"And we're outta here." Jack turned on his heel.

"Jack, it doesn't mean this place is one of Ra's planets. There's not even a temple here. This seems to just be a burial site, not an active place of worship or anything."

"Daniel Jackson is correct, O'Neill." Teal'c moved down to join them. He glanced at Jack then stared beyond him at the rows of pyramids. "I know this place."

"You do?"

"Really?" Daniel butted in. "Have you been here before?"

"I have not. I know of this place from stories my father told me when I was but a small child. It is the burial place of those who attained a high ranking in service to their lord. My grandfather is buried here."

"So," Daniel thought rapidly, trying piece together the few things Teal'c had previously told them about his family. "This planet belongs to Apophis, then?"

"It did. He barred all access to it when his first prime abandoned his place in Apophis's service and went to serve his enemy, Cronus." Teal'c stared at the neat rows of pointed structures.

Daniel traded a look with Jack, who was itching to pepper Teal'c with questions. Sam came up quietly to join them.

Finally, Teal'c directed his attention back on his friends. "That first prime was my father."

"Guess standing up for your principles runs in the family, eh, T?" Jack touched the bill of his cap in salute.

"I would request a short delay in our mission, O'Neill. I wish to locate the burial place of my ancestor."

"We can do that. Time for a meal break anyway. Daniel, why don't you see if you can help Teal'c. Carter, let's see if we can rustle up some food. Failing that, there's always MREs." He gave her an exaggerated grimace and she chuckled.

"Take an hour, kids, then we'll try one more planet. I think this search is not gonna pan out at all."

Sha're moved quietly as she could, keeping to the shadows of houses which were lengthening as the sun slipped down the sky. She did her best to avoid the bodies. She covered her nose with a fold of her dress: the stench of rot was all around her. Scurrying from one wall to another, the realization came that she did not know where the Chappa'ai was. Apophis had delivered her to the temple from his ship, through the ring transporter. Her demon had a dislike of clean air or exercise, so she had never walked further than the gardens at the rear of the temple. All she could remember was seeing farmers taking their goods into the town down the road that snaked along the lakeside.

She stopped. The street she was in was lined with little homes that all looked like the one next to them. Where would it be? Somewhere away from the houses? That seemed likely. A place where the Jaffa could move their equipment and themselves through from Chulak and other planets where Apophis kept his weapons and soldiers. Somewhere more open than here. She gazed up at the mountain, so close to the homes there was no real open space beyond the town.

There must be a marketplace, where the farmers go. Every town had a marketplace — Nagada's had been in the center of town where everyone could walk to it. She turned this way and that, then headed off down a narrow alley, crossed over a house-filled street and another just the same. Her steps wove through the dead town, the silence draped heavily over her. Once she thought she'd heard a child crying, but it was a goat held in a little pen beside a house. Sha're unfastened the bars and let it out; one more captive free.

Another alley ended in a dead end. She retraced her path and chose another small street. At the end, she peered cautiously out into yet another street. This one was wider than most, the houses larger with shop fronts in their windows. This looked more promising. She edged along the beaten dirt pathway, detouring around the fallen now and again. At the far end of the street she could see a more open area with brightly colored stalls — surely the marketplace!

Sha're moved as quickly as she could, her feet uncertain in

the shoes Linea had given her; they were just a bit too big, but certainly better than the flimsy slippers the demon favored. Ahead, the area opened into a marketplace as she'd hoped. It too held no living people, only the dead, many of whom were clustered around the drinking well. For a moment she was tempted to drink, but the contorted expressions of the bodies convinced her not to. She turned her back on them, and there, at the far end of the square stood the Chappa'ai.

Relief swamped her. A sob escaped her choked throat. Freedom. Danyel had called the Chappa'ai a gateway to the galaxy, a thing that would take you wherever you wanted to go, as long as you had an address to dial. And she had one. Just after she had been taken by the demon and Apophis had installed her as his consort on his home world, there had been a woman who had furtively crept into her chamber. The demon had called the guards and in the moments before the woman made her escape she had scrawled a gate address on the floor, whispering, "I am Jolinar of Malkshur! Host, if ever you seek to be free go to this world. Help will greet you." Then she was gone, but before the guards erased the symbols, Sha're had memorized them and ever since, in the quiet of deep night when the demon slept, she repeated them in her mind, over and over.

Now, with the demon asleep, she could use that address and seek her freedom.

"I am coming, my love. Wait for me."

Linea had completed her investigative tour of the town. The data she had collected would be analyzed and combined with the initial observations made during delivery of the toxin. She was confident that the optimum dosage was defined by her experiment. Once her notes were completed, she would make up a new batch of the toxin from the samples she had just collected. She might select another test site. Perhaps it was not necessary, though. She glanced around at the proof of her endeavor. These subjects were no different to those on her home world. They would succumb most efficiently.

Pleased with herself, Linea clutched her notebook to her chest and turned for home.

An unexpected rumble in the sky cut through her thoughts. Odd, the day had been cold but the skies were clear. Now, though, clouds suddenly boiled out of nowhere around the mountain peak.

Expecting rain, Linea hurried through the street and into the marketplace where there was one final ingredient to collect. To her surprise, there was one person standing amidst the fallen: the woman, Sha're. Not only had she awoken, but she had left the house and was walking toward the Stargate. Did she intend to leave? Linea frowned. She wished to know more about these Goa'uld the woman had spoken of. There were experiments to conduct. Once the Taldor were taken care of, she would have time to investigate what powers these creatures had and how they could be manipulated. She did not want her only source of information to leave.

"Sha're?"

The girl turned at hearing her name. Linea expected to see a welcome on her face, after all she had been nice to her, had she not? Instead, she saw an odd expression — apprehension, or was it suspicion?

"Where are you going? You should rest — for the child's sake." Linea thought that would have the woman concerned and returning to her side, but it achieved the opposite effect.

"I am leaving. Thank you for your care, but I must go — for the safety of the child."

"I do not wish you to leave." The words came out dull and flat, covering the surge of anger that swept through her. This Goa'uld was hers for the use of experimentation; she would not go searching for another.

Sha're shook her head with a toss of curls and resumed her course to the Stargate. "I do not care for your wishes."

Linea strode after her. "I cannot allow you to leave, you

need care." She had trouble forcing enough compassion into her voice, and by the stiffened back in front of her she knew the girl suspected her. "You must remain!"

"I will *not*." Sha're swung around, face furious. "You lied to me." A crack of thunder directly overhead emphasized her words.

Linea appraised her coolly. "How did I lie?"

"You did not say you had met the Tau'ri. You said you only saw planets of unremarkable people, but you know they are anything other than unremarkable."

"The Tau'ri?" She was surprised. This girl knew of the Earth people? How intriguing. "I met them in passing."

"You were with them long enough to take their clothing."

So that is how she knew… "How do you know the Tau'ri, child? You said you came from a planet ruled by the creatures."

"And the Tau'ri ended that rule. They set us free. Colonel Jack, Danyel…" Unconsciously, Sha're's hand went to her heart as her face crumpled in misery.

"Danyel — I met a young man called Daniel."

Sha're's eyes widened. "Daniel Jackson," she bit out the syllables carefully.

"That was he. A clever young man." Too clever. They all were. One reason she had not stayed on Earth too long.

"He lives? He is well?" Sha're surged forward to grasp her arm.

"He was very well, last I saw of him." She fingered the tiny weapon in her pocket that had killed Vishnor and very nearly taken Daniel with him. "Daniel came to your planet?"

Sha're nodded sharply. "He stayed, when the demon was gone, he stayed. He is my husband."

"Is he really? Well, the galaxy is a place of infinite surprises, is it not?" Linea casually shifted her arm so that she was holding Sha're. "You intend to go to Earth, to be with your husband?"

"I cannot. The Chappa'ai is barred. Apophis tried many times to breach their barrier, but he could not."

"Then you will go home?"

"No, that way too is blocked."

"Then stay with me, child. I will look after you." Thunder cracked overhead again, drowning out her words.

"I cannot." Sha're tried to shrug out of her grasp. "Let me go! I will not be a prisoner to you or anyone else, not ever again."

Linea dug her fingers into the girl's arm. "I do not wish you to go. I wish to…investigate the demon's power."

Alarm flickered in the girl's eyes. "No! Na'nay, na'nay, I will not —"

A high-pitched thrumming sounded close by. Sha're looked over Linea's shoulder and her face paled. "Let me go!" She pulled wildly but Linea was stronger than her implied age. She held tight and turned to see what new element had been added to their situation.

A series of rings emerged from a shaft of light that apparently descended from the heavens. With a whoosh, the rings vanished upward, leaving in their place a man dressed in flamboyant gold clothes, with two others behind him, dressed the same as the dead Jaffa in the marketplace. Sha're let out a despairing squeal and tugged furiously at her arm.

"Beloved!" The golden man stepped forward with a welcoming smile. He slowly became aware of the carnage around them and the smile slipped. "What has occurred here?"

The Jaffa behind him lowered their weapons, gold sparks spat from their ends to show they were charged.

Linea placed herself in front of the girl, still keeping a tight grip on her arm.

"A great illness has taken the lives of these villagers. This girl alone, survives." Linea repressed a laugh at the concern that crossed the man's face.

"Beloved, come to me," he demanded.

"She will not," Linea said softly.

For the first time, the man seemed to notice her. He studied her shrewdly. "You are not of this world. Unhand my consort." The glowing weapons behind supported his demand.

Linea returned his calculating gaze. So this was an adult Goa'uld, inhabiting the body of a human. How interesting. She could understand why the earthers were so determined to defeat them. She would very much like to study them.

The man glared at her non-compliance, then lifted his hand. Wide gold bands wrapped his arm and wrist, and a glowing red jewel nestled in his palm. He brandished it like a weapon. Perhaps it was. Linea pulled the girl close behind her. Quickly, she switched their positions so that the pregnant belly of the girl stood between the gold man and herself. He bared his teeth in rage and sent a blast of energy from his palm jewel sizzling past her ear.

"Release her!"

Linea pursed her lips. Disappointing, but she had priorities. Now was not the time to engage these creatures. There would be plenty of time, once her experiments were completed on the Taldor.

"I have no interest in you or your woman. I will leave now. You may do as you wish." To emphasize her point, she began to walk backward, angled toward the dialing device. She kept the struggling Sha're between them.

The Goa'uld waved his guards down and followed them, matching step for step. They had only reached the drinking fountain when another sound broke the silence of the town. This time, Linea recognized the deep clunking of the Stargate's chevrons engaging. The gate was coming alive.

Sha're continued to struggle against the older woman's grip. Blood dripped down her arm from the fingernails digging into her skin. She was furious with herself. She'd been so close to freedom. Had she moved quicker she would be gone, instead Apophis was here and her chances were shrinking with every second.

The sound of the Stargate gushing open drew all their attention. Incredibly, a contraption rumbled out of the wormhole. It stopped on the edge of the dais, one small piece on top turned from side to side as if it had eyes with which to see.

Behind them, she heard Apophis bark an order, and in seconds the ring transporter was whizzing down, depositing groups of Jaffa around their lord. Linea dragged her down behind the wall of the drinking well. The Jaffa scattered into cover as well, Apophis no doubt the first to hide.

A moment of silence. Then someone stepped through the Stargate. And another, then two more, and her heart seized as if some giant hand had reached into her chest and stolen her heart. Indeed, it had, for there on the platform stood her heart. Dressed in dull green, eye...*glasses* — that was the word — glinting in the fading sun, hair catching the evening breeze under the floppy hat — there stood Daniel Jackson. *How tall he stands, he looks like a soldier, not my happy husband in his robes.* Next to him was Colonel Jack, a little greyer than last she'd seen him. A woman stood with them, she looked familiar from the second time they'd come to Abydos. And sharing a friendly word with Danyel was Teal'c, the traitor. They looked to be friends. How curious.

Then it hit her. She was looking at Danyel. Sha're opened her mouth to scream out to him, a warning, a welcome, she didn't know what but nothing came out of her mouth. She gasped, tried again, but her voice was gone. She wrenched against her imprisonment, tried to throw herself around the concealing wall, but she could not move. Her muscles, her voice, they were no longer hers to control, and she knew — the demon was awakening. One last effort...she lurched forward and managed to unbalance Linea, who fell against the well and knocked a stone pot off the wall and into the water.

The small splash caused Danyel to look around. For a brief, stolen second she thought he looked right at her. His blue eyes seemed so close she could reach out and kiss them. Then the moment was gone. He ducked away and jumped off the dais as the Jaffa exploded out of cover and began to fire at the Tau'ri.

Sha're remained frozen behind the well as Colonel Jack fired his weapon over their heads at the Jaffa. She could see Teal'c at the dialing device. The Stargate belched open and they scrambled up and into the blue opening. Her last glimpse of Danyel was his lean body leaping into the wormhole. His boots disappeared and the gate shut down.

Gone. Her love was gone. Her chance at freedom was gone. Everything…was gone.

A shadow loomed over them. Apophis. He glared down at her, expression softening for a moment as he realized her demon was in control.

"We will leave now." He grabbed her arm and pulled her away.

Sha're felt a twinge in her belly. In the same moment she felt the demon's presence fade, and once again she was herself. *He is alive*, she thought fiercely. *He is alive. I am alive. We will meet again.*

Linea casually sat on the well wall. "That was interesting," she commented. She made no move to take possession of Sha're once more.

"Leave my planet," Apophis commanded. He touched a button on his arm-piece and the rings returned to sweep them away to his ship. He glanced at Sha're. "I will hide you away where no one will ever think to look for you."

Her final view of the planet was Linea, sitting on the wall, clutching her notebook to her bosom, her impassionate face watching them leave.

Left alone in silence, Linea sighed. The Goa'uld would wait for another time. She went to rifle through one of the market stalls for that last ingredient she needed. On one stall still laden with decaying vegetables she found it: potted in a gourd grew a little green herb with delicate purple flowers. She picked it up and inhaled the scent. So pretty. So deadly. She settled her bag across her shoulder and consulted the notebook for another world to visit. She picked one at random. The SGC notes said it was a world with an early development of technology. Good. These backwater undeveloped towns offered riches in the natural world, but a developing technology offered great opportunities for experimentation.

Linea walked toward the Stargate, looking forward to what the next day would bring.

STARGATE ATLANTIS
Going Home

Aaron Rosenberg

This story takes place in season four of STARGATE ATLANTIS, after the episode **Midway.**

"ARE YOU sure this is safe?" Teyla Emmagan stared with some concern at the dark, dank underground entrance. The steps leading down to it were chipped and cracked and in many places discolored, and at its base she saw a shadowy figure huddled either in distress or perhaps lying in wait for the unwary. She shuddered and looked away.

"Yes, it's safe," John Sheppard growled. "It's perfectly safe. It's a thousand times safer than flying around in a Jumper, that's for sure."

"I can clear any obstacles," Ronon offered, starting to draw his pistol.

Sheppard grabbed his wrist before he could completely free the long-barreled weapon from the confines of his coat. "How do you even have that?" he demanded, keeping his voice down and his body angled to block any passers-by from spotting the pistol. "We were supposed to leave any weapons behind."

Ronon stared down at him, the hint of a sneer showing through his short beard. "I told them I would kill them if they tried to take my weapon from me. They wisely chose not to insist."

Sheppard groaned and rubbed at his forehead. "Why did I think this would be a good idea?"

Behind him, he heard an all too familiar snort. "I'll confess, I have absolutely no idea," McKay replied. "But considering I don't have any personal stake in this, I'm finding it absolutely priceless." Rodney's smirk was significantly less subtle than Ronon's. "By all means, continue trying to tame the wild beast you thought it would be fun to take out on a walk through the city."

Ronon directed his glare at Rodney. "Call me a beast again and I will show you exactly what —"

"Calm down. He's just messing with you. Like usual." Though, much as Sheppard hated to admit it, Rodney did have a point. Bringing Ronon and Teyla here was starting to look like a truly disastrous plan.

Not that he'd really had much choice in the matter...

"Lieutenant Commander," called the gruff figure standing before the gate as Sheppard and his team emerged. "Welcome home."

Sheppard saluted. "Thank you, sir." Brigadier General Jack O'Neill was the man in charge of Homeworld Security — and the whole Stargate program. If it wasn't for him, none of this would exist. On top of which, he was a brilliant leader and a force to be reckoned with.

Which didn't change the fact that he had initially voted against Sheppard being part of the Atlantis Expedition — a fact that neither of them would ever forget. But they were both too professional to allow that little hiccup to interfere with their working relationship — or with the fact that they actually liked each other and saw eye to eye on a lot of things. In many ways Sheppard considered himself a younger version of O'Neill, and knew that there were far worse people to have as a role model.

"Ah, it's good to be back," Rodney declared, emerging from the gate and taking a deep, overly dramatic breath. He even made a point of pounding on his chest before turning to Sheppard with a grin. "Smell that? That's Earth. You don't get that scent anywhere else."

Ronon stalked down the ramp right behind them. "The smell of old machines, oil and grease and electricity, and human sweat?" He wrinkled his nose. "Same as on Atlantis. Or any other equipment room ever." He shouldered past Rodney to reach the floor and look around. His expression suggested that he was thus far unimpressed.

"Ronon Dex," O'Neill held out his hand. "Good to see you again, son."

For an instant nobody moved. Sheppard tensed, afraid there might be a problem — Ronon sometimes had a problem with people he felt were being overly familiar. And the big Satedan's way of dealing with that problem, like most, involved violence. Then Ronon accepted the handshake and Sheppard sagged a little with relief.

"Fewer Wraith this time," Ronon noted. "More politicians."

O'Neill made a face. "Sorry about that, but the IOA likes to flex its muscles and after you saved their collective butt from the Wraith, they want to debrief you in person." His gaze encompassed the whole team. "All of you. Don't worry, we'll get you out to D.C. straight away."

"We can hardly wait, sir," Sheppard managed with a straight face, earning him a disapproving look from Teyla.

But O'Neill only lifted an eyebrow, his eyes smiling. "On the plus side, Colonel, you'll have time for a little R&R in D.C. afterwards…"

Sheppard answered with a smile of his own. "There is that."

As it turned out, their appearance before the International Oversight Advisory proved less painful than Sheppard had feared: Ronon behaved, Teyla charmed, and Rodney managed to not insult anyone's intelligence. Not that they heard, at least.

The scheduled four hours stretched to six — and felt like twenty — but finally it was over and the team was allowed to clamber to their feet and walk, stiff and tired, out of the committee room.

To Sheppard's surprise, O'Neill was there to meet them. He carried a thick folder under his arm and a frown carved a deep line between his brows. Sheppard came to a wary attention. "Sir?"

O'Neill waved away the formality, scrubbing a hand through his grey hair. "'Fraid I'm gonna have to belay your furlough, soldier." His expression suggested he did feel at least a little bad about it. "We've got a situation, and unfortunately all my other teams are out of action." He made a face. "An off-world bug SG-3 picked up, and had the distinct discourtesy to pass around, has the SGC locked down. You and your team are the only ones I can put in the field fast enough. That's why I'm here — figured the least I could do was meet you halfway." He thrust the folder at Sheppard. "Read en route. There's a chopper standing by at Andrews Field."

"Sir?" Sheppard had taken the folder out of habit, and now glanced down at it. "Where are we going, exactly?"

For just a second, a smile touched O'Neill's face before his usual stony expression swallowed it whole. "New York City," he answered. "And you'd better hurry."

Normally, aircraft weren't allowed over the city, but clearly O'Neill had pulled strings because the chopper had set them down atop one of the tall buildings at the island's south end, in the Wall Street area. All of them had stared out the windows as the helicopter circled for a landing, transfixed by the sight of one of the Earth's greatest cities.

"It's so tall," Teyla had marveled. "And so . . . uplifting. I mean, Atlantis has buildings this height, too, but this feels more . . . elegant, maybe?" She waved a hand at two impressive spires arrowing up from midtown: the Empire State Building and the Chrysler Building.

"It is elegant," Rodney agreed. "New York City is one of the largest, most progressive, most significant cities in the world." He puffed out his chest. "And, as a former resident of the Big Apple, I feel I am uniquely qualified to give you a full appreciation of the city's finer points."

Ronon's brow furrowed. "You lived in an apple?" The big man was fearsome in combat, and a staunch friend, but subtleties in language sometimes escaped him.

"It's a nickname," Sheppard explained. "The Big Apple. The city that never sleeps. The city so good they named it twice. Gotham. Metropolis. It gets called all kinds of stuff." He glanced at Rodney. "When did you ever live here?"

Rodney glanced down at his shoes. "Well, perhaps not 'lived here,' per se," he admitted slowly. "But I have visited. Twice."

Sheppard shook his head, but let his irritation slide as he gazed happily down at the teeming urban center they were rapidly approaching. "Gotta say, I'm not thrilled about being sent on some wild goose chase, but if it means getting to walk Manhattan for a few hours, I'm game. I can practically taste the pastrami now."

Teyla was watching him closely. "What is pastrami?" she asked very seriously, and Sheppard laughed. But before he could answer the pilot came onto the comms they were all wearing.

"Setting you folks down now," she reported. "I'll be waiting here, fueled and ready — orders are to get you airborne and back to Andrews ASAP, where they'll have a jet to take you back to Colorado Springs. So no dawdling."

Sheppard felt that last part was directed at him.

They'd made their way off the helipad to the building's roof entrance, and from there to the elevators which had taken them to the ground-floor lobby. Fortunately, there was a subway entrance just a block away. Which was where they stood now, as Teyla wrinkled her nose and Ronon threatened to kill some poor old homeless guy. Sheppard sighed again.

Some R & R this was turning out to be.

"Who is this person we've been assigned to retrieve?" Teyla asked after they had successfully navigated the subway entrance.

Sheppard had worried that explaining Metrocards would prove difficult, but in the end that didn't wind up being a problem; Ronon hurdled the turnstile without even slowing his pace, and Teyla followed suit. Sheppard only hesitated a second before shrugging and vaulting the bars as well, leaving Rodney behind to curse and complain as he dug in his pockets for the Metrocards the helicopter pilot had handed them, and then struggled to make the card reader acknowledge him. Finally, he had gotten through and the four of them had descended the steps to the platform itself.

Sheppard frowned, raking his hair back out of his face as he recalled the information from the dossier he'd flipped through en route. "She's a scientist, name of Dr. Acuna…" He was distracted by Ronon, who was marching down to the platform's far end, darting behind each column as he passed it. "Ronon, what the heck are you doing?" Sheppard muttered. But he was pretty sure he already knew the answer.

Sure enough, when the Satedan returned he reported, "All clear on that end." He no doubt would have repeated the process in the opposite direction if Sheppard hadn't reached out to block him.

"Stand down," he ordered. "We're not in a combat zone here."

"Yeah," Rodney couldn't resist adding. "These commuters have enough troubles, they hardly need you shoving your ugly mug in their faces and scaring them half to death."

Ronon bared his teeth, much like a wolf would issue warning. The two men warred like this constantly. Although, to be fair, Rodney did this to almost everyone. Still, Ronon was a favorite target. "Drop it," Sheppard warned both of them, keeping his voice low so it wouldn't carry. "We're just gonna go fetch this lady and hotfoot it back to D.C. No need to make it complicated or messy. Right?" He glared at both men until they each grudgingly nodded. "Good."

"I hear something coming," Teyla warned, studying the empty tracks that stretched away in both directions. "Something big, and fast. This subway you mentioned?"

"Yeah." Sheppard could feel it now, that telltale crackle in the air, the hair standing up along his arms as the atmosphere changed, static coming off the track well in advance of the approaching car. He could hear it whistling along, the rushing sound growing louder by the second, and now he could just feel the brush of the breeze against his face. The whistling became a roaring, the breeze became a gale, and then with a powerful surge the subway shot into view, hurtling past them before screeching to a halt. One set of doors was almost directly in front of them, and as soon as it opened and people charged out Sheppard ushered his team inside. "Go!" he urged, hopping on after them just ahead of the warning to "Stand clear of the closing doors." The doors slid shut, and a second later the train lurched into motion again. Rodney stumbled and had to grab onto a pole for support. Teyla's hand tightened on the pole, but she kept her balance. Ronon stood rock steady with his back against the opposing door. And Sheppard himself had grabbed onto the pole out of old habit, and found his subway-riding instincts returning to him as they bounced and juddered and soared along. He'd spent a few weeks here with some college friends one summer and they had quickly become pros at navigating and riding the then-still-seedy subway lines. These clean, brightly lit new cars were a little strange to him, but the rhythm was the same, and the feel of the city racing beneath your feet even as you were the one racing under it.

"We're only going a few stops," he told the others, who all nodded. Sheppard couldn't help grinning. He would've liked to have more time to wander and explore and revisit and enjoy, but just being back in New York was a major rush.

Shame this mission seemed like such a cakewalk. They'd be back on the copter before he knew it.

"This is the place," Rodney announced with all the satisfaction of a master builder who had just completed his life's work.

Sheppard gave him a sideways look. "Yeah, thanks, Rodney. We can all read." Because, in large gilt letters, the awning in front proclaimed "312," the number of the building listed in their file.

"Are you sure about that?" Rodney tilted his head as he regarded Ronon. "Because I'm pretty sure I saw his lips moving just now."

Ronon's snarl was silent but eloquent. Not that it would shut Rodney down for long.

"We're looking for apartment 48," Sheppard said, hoping to prevent or at least stall yet another confrontation. He led the way under the awning. The building wasn't fancy enough to require a doorman, but it did have a double set of front doors that functioned like an airlock — and, of course, the outer one opened easily but the inner door was securely locked.

"Stand back," Ronon warned, but Sheppard stopped him before he could draw.

"Naw, we don't need to melt any locks just now," he said carefully. "And kicking it in would just draw the cops. We've gotta do this the old-fashioned way."

Teyla frowned. "You want us to remove the hinges or pick the lock? I did not bring the proper tools for either of those activities."

For a second, Sheppard considered asking what tools she preferred for each, and why she would normally carry them. But he decided against it. Instead, he just grinned. "Watch and learn." Beside the inner door there was a large panel that listed each apartment number, with the tenant's last name beside it. Next to that was a grid of buttons under a small circular speaker. He studied the list for a second, then picked a number at random and punched it in.

"Yeah?" a voice answered after a second. It was male, deep and gruff.

"Delivery!" Sheppard sang out in reply.

"What? I didn't order anything — buzz off!" And the line went dead.

Unfazed, Sheppard tried again. This time no one answered. The third time he got a woman, older by the sound of it, her voice high and quavery as she asked, "Who is this?"

"Delivery!" he repeated.

"Oh? All right." And a second later the door buzzed harshly. Sheppard didn't waste any time — he yanked it open and ushered the rest of the team through.

"That's how you get into a building?" Ronon asked as they marched across the lobby to the elevator bank. "I would never let you in."

"A lot of people don't," Sheppard agreed with a shrug. "But there's always somebody who does. Or someone coming back who'll hold the door open for you. The trick is to look anxious and unthreatening." He considered his tall, bulky warrior companion. "You'd probably need a hat. People like hats."

The elevator was the classic kind, small and cramped with large push buttons and an inner door that slid shut only once the outer door had clanged against the frame. It also moved at a snail's pace. And there wasn't even any music. But eventually it reached the fourth floor and the inner door creaked aside again. Sheppard pushed the outer door open and emerged onto a long, narrow, dimly lit hall, squinting to study the door numbers. "This way." His long strides carried him quickly to apartment 48, and he rapped on the door.

No one answered.

"Hello?" he tried again, knocking more loudly.

Still nothing.

"She might not be home, or she might not be answering," he said. "No way to be sure without getting inside."

Ronon gently but firmly moved him out of the way. Then, with a single powerful kick, he broke the door lock and sent the heavy metal door flying inward. It rebounded against the wall with a loud smack, but by that time Ronon was already through the opening, gun in hand.

"Yeah, that'll work," Sheppard agreed, following his friend inside. A quick glance showed a dark hallway with an opening on one side into a small kitchen and a rack on the other for coats and hats and umbrellas. The far end of the hallway led to what was probably a living room, and he guessed that the doors near it were to a bathroom and a bedroom. He didn't hear anyone scrambling to hide or calling for help, which suggested that this Acuna woman wasn't here right now. Still, they needed to check and be sure. "Spread out," he instructed. "She isn't dangerous, and she's not a threat, so be nice. But find her."

He checked the kitchen first, but it was cramped enough that he could tell at once that no one was in there. The sink was full of dirty dishes, but none of them looked recent, so they hadn't surprised her mid-meal or anything.

"Um, Sheppard?" Rodney called from somewhere further into the apartment. "You really need to see this."

Sheppard found him standing in the living room. Upon entering, he scanned the space, which looked like a small tornado had struck it — and froze.

Because taking up almost all of the far corner was a Stargate.

"What the hell?" Sheppard started warily toward the thing, his hand going to his side before he remembered that, unlike Ronon, he had surrendered his sidearm before leaving the SGC. How could there be another Stargate here on Earth?

He was checking the corners, worried that a Wraith or some other bad guy might suddenly pop up from behind the couch or under the coffee table, when Teyla laid a hand on his arm. "Breathe," she instructed, her voice calm and cool. Sheppard frowned but took her advice. He straightened up, closed his eyes, took a deep breath, and let it out slowly. Then he blinked and looked again.

The Stargate was still there.

Except that, he now realized, it wasn't.

"It's too small." The gate didn't even reach the ceiling. This was an older building, so the rooms had nice high ceilings, but they were still only ten feet up. A full Stargate was nearly fifteen feet tall.

Now that he looked more closely, Sheppard noticed something else. But Rodney beat him to naming it. "The chevrons are wrong," he said, gesturing at the symbols carved all around the ring. "A few of those are right, and some of the others look close, but about half are just dead wrong. That thing would never go anywhere — not anywhere real, anyway."

Real? Sheppard frowned and took a single careful step toward the diminutive Stargate. Then another. On his third, his foot caught on the rug and he stumbled, barely catching himself on his hands and forearms before cracking his head against the hardwood floor. Then a soft creak made him glance up to see the Stargate toppling toward him.

"Look out!" Ronon threw himself forward blocking the falling gate with his own body as he dragged Sheppard clear. One side of the circular gateway struck Ronon across the back and shoulder —

— and shattered, blocks and chevrons raining about him like some strange, stone-flecked snow.

"Well, that's something you don't see every day," Rodney remarked after a second, though even he couldn't mask his total surprise. "I knew you were hardheaded, Ronon, but hard-backed, too? You're like our own personal ninja turtle."

Sheppard doubted Ronon understood the reference, but he growled at Rodney anyway. For his part, Sheppard was too busy picking himself back up, catching his breath, and reorganizing the facts he now possessed.

"It's a fake," he declared, stepping over and stooping to pick up one of the broken segments. It weighed next to nothing. "Styrofoam painted to look like stone." He lobbed the piece at Rodney, who flinched away and then reddened at Ronon's laughter. "Whoever this Acuna is, she built herself a model Stargate." He rubbed at his jaw. "No wonder the SGC wants her."

"How does she know anything about it?" Rodney demanded. He looked like the model's very existence was a personal affront. "Everything about the Stargate is beyond Top Secret."

"These might have something to do with it," Teyla offered. While the rest of them had been staring at the model, she had been examining the papers strewn about on the floor beside an overturned coffee table. Now she held up a printout of a grainy photo — of a very real and very familiar Stargate.

"Let me see that." Rodney practically snatched the photo from her hand. "This is one of Catherine Langford's pictures from the original Giza dig. Look at the clothes."

Teyla was considering the broken model. "This Dr. Acuna obviously has some knowledge of the Stargates and their construction, and has been piecing together whatever information she could find on them. It is impressive."

Sheppard shrugged. "So she can do dioramas. Swell. I just want to find her and get her to D.C." The longer they wasted, the less time he would have to enjoy this trip.

Rodney had joined Teyla in studying the papers. "I recognize most of this," he said as he shuffled a few documents. "Early treatises, crackpot theories, and everything in between. Except for this." He held up a business card. "This looks new, and I haven't heard of them before."

Sheppard took the card from him. "Lightbridge Enterprises," he read aloud. "Taking you to the stars — and beyond." He shared a look with the rest of the team. "Gee, does that sound like anything else to the rest of you? Lightbridge? Stargate? Not exactly subtle."

"Subtle is overrated," Ronon said. "But if Acuna isn't here, and this card is, maybe they know where she went?"

"Or maybe they have her." Sheppard said. "If I were trying to get rich off a Stargate, it'd sure help to have someone who could build me one of my own." He eyed the mess all around them. "This place does look like it's been tossed — or like they came for her and she put up a fight." He sighed. "But even if this woman knows everything we do about the Stargate network, without access to Ancient technology she wouldn't be able to forge the naqahdah to build it. If she even had any naquadah.

And if the people at Lightbridge realized she's useless to them…"

He shook his head. So much for that R&R.

"All right, where are we now?" Teyla asked as they stepped off the train. "That was far less harrowing than the underground version we used previously. And far less . . . aromatic."

"Long Island Railroad versus New York subway," Sheppard explained. "Totally different beasts." He looked around. "We're out on Long Island, which is the island next to Manhattan."

"Ah." Teyla nodded. "So we have left New York City, which is the other island."

"Not exactly." Sheppard scratched his chin. "Queens is still part of the city, and it's on Long Island."

She frowned. "So we are in Queens?"

"No, we're on Long Island."

"But you just said that Queens was on Long Island."

"Yeah, it is, but we're past Queens. Queens is part of New York City. Long Island isn't."

"And yet Queens is on Long Island?" She shook her head. "That makes no sense."

Sheppard opened his mouth to try again, stopped, and shut it. "Yeah, okay, fair enough," he admitted. "To be honest, I could never figure that one out, either. But anyway, that's where we are. About an hour outside the city." He studied their surroundings. "Looks like a nice little town." There were only a few low buildings near the train station, but a block away was a cute little downtown area. The shops there would have looked right at home in the 1950s, with their colorful awnings and large plate-glass windows and somewhat worn-looking displays. It was like the Town That Time Forgot.

"Good place for a research facility," Rodney offered, making his way toward a set of stairs that led down from the train station. "You're not gonna get a lot of government interference out here." He sounded slightly wistful at the notion.

Sheppard was studying the map he'd bought at Penn Station

on their way to the train. "Looks like Lightbridge is just a few blocks from here." Folding the map back up, he shoved it into his back pocket and took the lead again.

He stopped a block later, when the building came into view — along with some of its more striking architectural elements.

"Impressive," Ronon said. "Well-fortified, well manned, and well-maintained. I can get us in but" — he shrugged — "it won't be easy. Or quiet."

Sheppard had ducked back out of view after also considering the building, which looked an awful lot like a fort. Now he shook his head. "What the hell does some start-up entrepreneur need with military-grade security?"

"They'd need it if they had their own Stargate," Rodney pointed out. Which was absolutely true.

Sheppard just hoped the company was only planning for the future. Because if they really had a fully functional Stargate in there already, not only were he and his team in trouble but the rest of the world was in trouble, too.

"Okay," he said, rubbing his hands together. "We need a plan to get inside. Suggestions?"

"This is the stupidest plan ever," Rodney hissed as he peered around the corner again.

"Duly noted," Sheppard said. "Now get moving."

Still muttering about abuse of power and endangering subordinates, Rodney nonetheless did as instructed and stepped out from behind the bushes. He stood there for a second, frozen, before squaring his shoulders and striding directly toward Lightbridge Enterprises, whistling loudly as he went.

"'ello!" he called out as he got close to the building. "I say, anyone in there, wot? Anyone home, eh?"

"What is he doing?" Sheppard whispered to Teyla and Ronon. The two of them just shrugged.

"Isn't that the way he always talks?" Ronon asked. As usual, he was so stone-faced it was impossible to tell if he was kidding or not. For the first few months of their acquaintance, Sheppard had been convinced Ronon didn't have a sense of humor. Since then he'd realize that he did, it was just very subtle. And often geared toward killing.

Shaking his head, Sheppard turned to watch Rodney's progress. The scientist had reached the building's front door and was banging on it with his fist, shouting something about looking for the queue to the lift, or some such. For a few minutes nothing happened, and Sheppard worried that this plan might be a total bust. Then the doors swung open, so suddenly and emphatically that Rodney was forced to take a quick step back to avoid being struck, and a small squad of men emerged. They were dressed in black combat gear and carried automatic rifles. They did not have masks or goggles, however, leaving their faces exposed.

"Sir, I'm going to have to ask you to leave immediately," the lead soldier barked at Rodney, stopping just far enough away to keep his weapon out of Rodney's reach. Definitely smart and definitely well-trained, Sheppard thought with an inward groan. Swell. Why couldn't they have been dumb and incompetent? That would have made this so much easier.

"Eh, wot?" Rodney was replying. "Sorry, laddie, I'm just a wee bit lost. Looking for the lorry, don't you know? Can you be a mate and help a bloke out?" His accent was not only atrocious but in constant flux, but at least it seemed to be baffling the security guard as much as it was annoying Sheppard.

Still, the man was unmoved by Rodney's apparent plight. "This is private property, sir, and you are trespassing. Leave or we will be forced to use deadly force." He and his men all raised their weapons — and aimed them directly at Rodney.

That was exactly what Sheppard had been waiting for. "Now!" he shouted, and launched into action. As did Ronon and Teyla, the three of them bursting from cover and leaping at the security team. The men and women jumped, surprised by the sudden onslaught, and struggled to bring their guns around to aim at these new threats. But it was too late. Sheppard and his team were already close enough to grapple and pummeled the men and women with blows to the jaw, chin, cheek, and forehead, knocking them down before they could step back or otherwise defend themselves.

Sheppard downed the last of the regular guards in time to see Rodney grab the leader's gun barrel and yank the man forward, then pop him in the jaw. The man staggered back but didn't let go of the weapon or fall down—until Ronon appeared behind him and slammed a heavy fist against the top of the man's helmet. Then the security guard's eyes rolled back and he crumpled.

"Not bad," Sheppard commented, straightening his jacket. "See, I told you the plan would work."

"That wasn't a plan, it was a comedy routine," Rodney said. "With me as the fall guy." He preened a little. "Still, I was awfully good, wasn't I?"

"If your goal was to portray a drunk whose accent wandered the globe, sure. Now let's get these guys inside before anyone sees them." He grabbed the nearest soldier under the arms and began hauling her toward the front door. All in all, that little fracas had gone quicker than he'd hoped, but now that he thought about it, it made sense. When you were used to facing the Wraith, handling a few human security guards was really no big deal.

He just hoped there weren't more of them waiting inside.

They caught a lucky break, though. Apparently that had been the bulk of Lightbridge's security force. A lone guard was manning the front desk but evidently she hadn't been paying close enough attention to her monitors and their using one of the downed guards' IDs to gain entrance took her by surprise. Ronon stunned her with a quick shot the second the doors opened. There were red lights flashing everywhere, so clearly she had hit the alarm at some point, most likely when the squad had first stepped outside, but Sheppard wasn't about to let something like that slow him down.

The guard's ID card got them past the inner doors. The building's long corridors were bare tile and bare walls with plain fluorescent lights set into the ceiling, making the place look and feel more like a research lab or a hospital than an office building. Doors were spaced along either side, each a heavy metal fire door with a small inset window at eye level, and a quick glance into the first few suggested that these were offices and personal labs. Sheppard didn't see anyone around, which was fine by him though it made him wonder. Where was everyone?

They rounded a corner and he got his answer as a bullet nearly grazed his temple.

"Put down your weapons and surrender!" someone shouted as Sheppard pulled back. "Do it now and no one gets hurt!"

"How can you say that when you're already shooting at us?" Rodney shouted. He was careful not to venture past the corner, however.

Ronon took no such precautions. Instead, he dropped into a crouch, raised his pistol, and rolled forward, firing as he came into view. Sheppard heard several shouts and groans, and then the clatter of weapons and the duller thump of bodies hitting the floor. "Clear," Ronon called.

Sure enough, he had stunned four guards.

"Nice work." Sheppard opened the nearest door and they dragged the guards into the small storage room. "That should keep them out of the way."

Next, they came to a set of heavy doors barring their path. The guard's ID was enough to unlock them and Sheppard led the way down another corridor much like the first. Except that there were people on this one, though not many of them. They were dressed more like researchers and scientists than guards, and they all looked terrified.

One man started to protest, demanding to know who they were and what they wanted. Ronon shot him. Someone else screamed, and Ronon shot him as well. That caused the rest to flee, but he carefully targeted and put down each one.

"That thing is still set on stun, right?" Rodney asked as they stepped over the bodies.

"What do you think?" Ronon growled back.

They reached another set of locked doors, and this time the guard's ID did nothing to help them. But Teyla grabbed one of the researchers' badges, and that did the trick.

When the doors opened, all four of them stopped and stared.

"Sonuva —" Rodney started.

Because, for the second time that day, they found themselves staring at an unfamiliar Stargate.

And this one was full-sized and very clearly not made of Styrofoam.

The strange Stargate dominated a large, open room cluttered with desks and workstations. Four people occupied the space — two guards, a man in a white lab coat, and a harried-looking woman he had by the arm. The guards reacted the second they saw Sheppard and his team, raising their rifles and advancing quickly, but two shots from Ronon and the pair were on the floor. The man and woman gaped.

"What is the meaning of this?" the man demanded, recovering his voice first. He was middle-aged and slightly portly, with thinning hair starting to go silver and an expensive but rumpled suit under the lab coat. He looked like a successful businessman playing at mad scientist. "This is private property and you are trespassing."

Interestingly, it was Teyla who got in his face. "Trespassing?" Her voice was calm but sharp. "How does that measure up against kidnapping?"

At that word, the woman seemed to wake out of her daze and tried pulling free of the man's grip. "He did kidnap me!"

she cried. "Please help!" She was young, Sheppard noted, perhaps late twenties, tall and slender, with long brown hair and a serious face. Sturdy glasses framed bright, intent blue eyes. The picture in the file had been a bit blurry, but it seemed to match.

Teyla smiled at her. "That's why we're here."

The man started to object again, but Teyla punched him full in the face and he collapsed like a broken puppet. As he fell, his grip loosened and the woman was left standing, staring down at her former captor.

"Dr. Acuna?" Sheppard approached her slowly with both hands out. She nodded. "I'm Colonel John Sheppard, United States Air Force. I was sent to bring you in for an interview, and we followed your trail here."

"An interview?" Her eyes narrowed, then widened. "You're with Stargate Command, aren't you?" When Sheppard nodded hesitantly, she broke into an enormous grin that transformed her from a frazzled scientist to a giddy teen. "I knew it!" she exclaimed. "I knew it was all real!" She gestured at the Stargate behind them. "Even before they brought me here to help them with this, I knew it had to be real!"

"If by 'it' you mean the Stargate Program, then yes," Rodney answered absently. He'd stepped past her to study the gate. "If you mean this particular Stargate, however, then no. It is not real." He rapped a knuckle against its surface. "A decent attempt by amateurs, granted, but this is like a cardboard cutout of a car — looks convincing from a distance, won't get you anywhere unless you pick it up and carry it."

"No interface," Ronon pointed out. "No dialing device."

"Exactly!" Rodney slapped him on the back, then quickly threw up his hands. "Sorry! But yes — clearly they were working off the same partial reports and conjectures as you, Doctor. They have the dimensions down, and a few of the elements right, but none of the internal workings, nor the necessary materials."

"Loose lips sink ships, Rodney," Sheppard warned. "She's a civilian, remember?" He nodded at her. "No offense."

"Yeah, yeah, okay." Rodney shrugged. "They are way off, though." He moved over to the nearest workstation and started tapping on the keyboard, frowning down at the monitor. "Still, best to be sure," he muttered, and typed in several quick commands. The computer beeped in response, and its screen flashed white, then blue, then went black. "Much better," he said with his usual self-satisfied smile. "Shall we?"

Sheppard knew better than to waste time asking. "Yeah, let's get out of here." He turned to Dr. Acuna. "Ma'am, the International Oversight Advisory would very much like to speak with you. May we escort you to D.C.?"

"That sounds like an offer I literally can't refuse."

He shrugged. "Not really, no."

She turned that brilliant smile on him. "In that case, Colonel, thank you. I'd appreciate the opportunity."

Given her recent treatment by Lightbridge, Sheppard supposed he shouldn't have been too surprised at her eagerness. His team must seem like regular knights in shining armor by comparison.

They headed for the door and made it back outside without any further incident. Once outside, they began the trek back toward the train. But on the way, Sheppard paused just long enough to make a quick phone call.

"Good work," O'Neill said as the team stepped into the gate room. "Dr. Acuna is already being debriefed. Assuming she doesn't raise any red flags, and can pass the security checks, I wouldn't be surprised if she winds up getting recruited into the program."

Sheppard nodded. "Considering she managed to figure out so much on her own, I bet she will." He rubbed the back of his neck. "We'll need to keep an eye on those Lightbridge guys, though."

Rodney grinned. "Well, they're going to have to recreate all of their data. I scrubbed their files before we left, then introduced a virus to make sure the drives would be irretrievable."

"I've already given the NID a heads-up on that one," O'Neill admitted. "They'll bring them in, people and hardware both, and shut that place down. Good thing you found them, though. There's no telling what kind of damage they could've done while trying to get that fake Stargate working." He clapped Sheppard on the shoulder. "But now it's time for you to head back."

Sheppard couldn't agree more. It was funny, but he found himself thinking about going home again — only this time, he knew that meant Atlantis. Maybe someday Earth would be home again, but not right now.

But as he stepped away, O'Neill's eyes went to the large paper bag at Sheppard's side. "What's that?" the general asked, his eyes narrowing a little.

Sheppard grinned and hefted the bag, the smells wafting up to him even through the heavy paper. "Four large pastramis on rye. Four cans of Dr. Brown's Cel-Ray Soda. Several pickles. And a full New York cheesecake. All from Carnegie Deli. I ordered it before we left Lightbridge, and they had it waiting for us when we got back to the chopper." He grinned, turning to the rest of his team. "When we get back, lunch is on me."

"What is pastrami?" Teyla asked as the four of them headed for the gate.

Sheppard smiled. He might be leaving Earth again, but at least he was taking a little piece of it home with him.

STARGATE SG-1
They Shoot Heroes, Don't They?

Geonn Cannon

This story takes place in season five of STARGATE: SG-1.

LONIO MOVED at a crouch with his head down so he couldn't be seen from inside the courtyard. He followed the long stone wall that surrounded the pavilion, moving silently through the wet grass. He could hear the hushed whispers of his foes within. If he could just make it to the entrance, he could cut off their retreat and victory would be assured. His hands were clammy around his weapon but he didn't risk letting go to wipe them on his trousers. He was wearing clothes that were a size too big for him, handed down from his older brother, but he didn't mind. He thought they made him look cool.

The weapon he carried was a chunk of stone with an edge big enough for him to hold onto. His schoolmates that made up the other contingent were armed with similar weaponry. He stopped and listened for them, dropping to one knee. He could hear them on the far end of the courtyard and risked peeking. Beyond the columns he could see Tessa and Claes kneeling on the ground to draw in the dirt. He smiled; this would be very easy.

Lonio broke cover and ran toward them. "Hands up, Goa'ulds!" he shouted. Tessa and Claes jumped and reached for their weapons, but he was already close enough to kick the oblong stones away. "Hah! Some System Lords *you* turned out to be!"

Tessa held out her hand, revealing a red stone held in place by a piece of twine wrapped around her wrist. "You're no match for my *kara kesh*, Colonel!"

Lonio stopped and glared at her. "You didn't have a *kara kesh* in your pack!"

She got to her feet. "I found it. When I was digging."

Claes rolled his eyes. "Lonio, you did the same thing two weeks ago when you found that tree branch and said it was a staff weapon."

"That was different, I..." His retort trailed off when he noticed Tessa and Claes were both looking past him with wide-eyed expressions of terror. He was also aware of the shade he now seemed to be standing in and turned slowly with the expectation of seeing their tutor looming behind him. What he saw was far more frightening.

The man had to be seven feet tall, and another three feet across at the shoulder. His eyes were black pools of oil that reflected Lonio's face so he could see just how scared he was. The monster was holding a black box against his chest. He bared his teeth and brought up one hand.

"Hey, kids."

Lonio, Claes, and Tessa replied with screams. They dropped their makeshift weapons and ran from the sanctuary as fast as their legs could carry them.

Jack O'Neill let his smile fall and dropped his hand, watching the three children race down the hill. Teal'c had approached in response to the screams and watched as well.

"Something I said?" Jack muttered.

"Perhaps they are merely... excitable."

"Right. I'm sure that's it." He pivoted to see what progress, if any, Daniel was making.

The team had arrived in a large pavilion enclosed on three sides by rows of Doric columns. The fourth wall was a stone fresco into which the Stargate was embedded. At first glance the Gate seemed to just be part of the artwork, but the space within it had been recessed to allow the event horizon to form. To his right, he saw Carter moving along the outer perimeter in search of potential non-child dangers.

"Daniel?" Jack prompted. "The locals have been made aware of us, so now might be a good time to declare your curiosity satisfied."

"Now? But..." He stepped back and gestured broadly to indicate all the artwork on the wall. "Look at this. If I had an entire week I'm not sure I would be able to document it all."

"So it won't matter if you stop now or five minutes from now."

"That's not exactly the point I was trying—"

Jack cut him off with a swipe of his hand. "The point is that we're about to have company. Hopefully they'll be friendly, but given the fact we just scared the crap out of their kids, I'm not very optimistic. So I'd like to have everyone on alert."

Daniel grimaced and looked longingly at the artwork, but began packing up his things.

"Good man. Carter?"

"All clear, sir. There's a city to the south at the base of this hill. If those kids are bringing anyone back, they'll be coming from there."

Jack walked back to where he had frightened off the children. He crouched next to one of the columns to watch for their return. It was only a matter of minutes before they saw the group coming up the winding dirt road. "Okay. Friendly faces, everyone."

Carter took a scope from her vest and peered through it. "I'm counting seven adults, sir. Plus three children."

Jack nodded. "Same."

The leader was a brunette woman wearing a simple purple-and-gold garment which was belted at the waist with a loose piece of braided rope. The children he'd frightened were walking to either side of her, and she was holding the girl's hand as they approached. Jack's optimism ticked up ever-so-slightly. He doubted any leader would allow a group of pre-teens to tag along on an assault.

The sight of the woman's outfit, straight out of a period

piece, reminded him of something he'd been wondering for a while. "Hey, Daniel... question for you. These civilizations we encounter, they're all transplanted from Earth throughout history, right?"

"Well, not all of them, but most."

"Still, we're talking centuries between when they were taken and now. So why do so many of them look like they were ripped right out of a history book?"

The answer came from Teal'c, not Daniel. "Life under Goa'uld oppression does not inspire great leaps forward in culture or society."

Daniel said, "He's right. These people are basically stuck in the Dark Ages. Any progress they might make is crippled by the Goa'uld and the Jaffa so they can't become a threat down the road. So the vast majority of people we meet are stuck right where they were when the Goa'uld first abducted them."

The group had nearly arrived. Jack adjusted the brim of his cap. "Okay, we're about to have our first conversation with these folks. Any idea which Goa'uld we're going to be debunking today?"

"If I'd had a chance to explore the artwork more completely I think I'd have a stronger —"

"Daniel!"

"Hades. Probably."

Jack raised an eyebrow and turned to look at him. "Hades?"

Daniel gestured at the columns. "Greek architecture, Greek god. There are multiple references —"

"All right, all right." He sighed. "Hades it is."

The woman led her group toward the entrance of the temple. Jack stepped out from behind his cover and tried for what he hoped was a friendlier smile than the one that sent the kids running.

"Hi, there," he said. "Sorry for scaring the kids."

She stopped a few paces away. She laced her fingers together in front of her and bowed her head slightly. "Apologies aren't required in this case. The children know they aren't allowed to play near the Kyklos."

Jack looked at Daniel who said, "Kyklos. Uh, circle." He pointed at the Stargate and Jack nodded.

The woman watched their exchange with curious eyes, but said nothing. "We're the ones who should be apologizing to you. We have no record that you were scheduled to arrive today so we were caught unprepared. Hopefully you can forgive us this inconvenience."

Jack glanced at Daniel again, hoping for insight, but this time he got nothing but a confused look in return. "Yes. It's... all right. We have a habit of dropping in unannounced."

The woman's focus shifted slightly and Jack realized she hadn't been looking at him, but rather over his shoulder. She'd been speaking to Carter. Carter realized it as well and raised an eyebrow, to which Jack replied with a slight incline of his head. If the leader was more comfortable talking to a woman, then so be it.

Carter said, "Even so, we hope the kids are okay."

"They're fine. Excitable as children always are. I am Tychia. Who are you with?"

"We're from Earth. The Tau'ri."

"SGC," Jack supplied.

Tychia looked confused for a moment before her smile returned. "Ah, I see. Your dedication is admirable. And what are your names?"

"I'm Major Samantha Carter. Colonel Jack O'Neill, Doctor Daniel Jackson, and Teal'c."

"Oh," one of the men behind Tychia said with a hint of boredom. "They're SG-1..."

Tychia tilted her head down and lowered her voice slightly. "Be kind, Colson. There's a reason they have the most *epikos*."

Daniel perked up. "*Epikos*... epic?"

"Yes. And I must say, your costumes are among the best we have seen. May I?" Carter nodded and Tychia approached her.

She lightly touched the edges of Carter's tactical vest, moving her hand to stroke the material of her jacket. She shook her head in amazement. "You truly paid attention to detail. These uniforms truly look battle-worn."

Jack was grateful he'd been spared the petting. "Well, we do what we can."

Tychia looked at Jack, then met Carter's eye with a knowing wink. "Your herald certainly has a long leash."

"My... herald. Yes. I've been trying to curb his impertinence."

Jack raised an eyebrow and mouthed 'impertinence?' Carter shrugged.

One of the men had approached Teal'c, craning his neck one way and then the other as he gazed up into his face. Teal'c attempted to remain stoic, but had to block the man's hand when he reached up to actually touch him.

"Do not."

The man held up both hands. "Apologies, sir. But I've never seen a First Prime marking that looked so authentic."

Jack scanned the crowd, as confused as ever. Daniel looked guilty, like he knew more than he was saying, but he didn't want to have everything spelled out in front of their new friends. "Yes, it's about as authentic as you can get. The people who applied it pride themselves on detail."

The local man said, "It shows!"

Carter said, "So... uh. If everything is okay with the kids, maybe we could..."

"Prepare?" Tychia offered.

"Prepare." Carter looked at Jack. "Yes. We would like to prepare."

Tychia nodded. "Of course. That's why we came to escort you to town. The people will be thrilled to hear we have an unscheduled *epikos*. Will you be ready by this evening?"

"It's hard to say," Carter said. "I think we'll have a better idea when we get to... the... preparation area."

"Okay. Follow us."

Tychia turned and took the hand of one child, leading the group out of the temple. SG-1 had little choice but to follow. Jack let Carter lead the way, seeing as she had been chosen as leader, and fell into step beside Daniel. Two of the locals lingered to bring up the rear. Jack didn't want to risk having a full conversation before he knew exactly what was going on, but his curiosity was eating at him. He leaned close to Daniel and lowered his voice.

"Do you have any idea what's going on here?"

"Uh... some." He looked back at the men following them. "But I have a feeling you're really not going to like it."

Samantha Carter tried not to look over her shoulder at the colonel as the team was escorted down the hill. Obviously the village was matriarchal and, therefore, their leader simply assumed she was in charge. She'd been in enough situations both on Earth and other planets where the inverse was true that she couldn't complain. Still, Colonel O'Neill was her commanding officer, so she had to be careful not to step on his toes. She noticed Tychia was watching her and tried to look non-threatening.

Tychia took it as an invitation to move closer. "Can you reveal which one you'll be doing?"

Sam thought for a moment. "I wish we could."

"Of course. I understand. All will be revealed in time."

"Right," Sam said. "So... you were expecting people like us to come through the Kyklos?"

Tychia nodded. "Certainly. I just enjoy knowing ahead of time. It gives me something to look forward to." She looked sideways at Sam as they continued to walk. "Your costumes really are remarkable. Do you make them yourselves?"

Sam furrowed her brow. "No, someone gave them to us."

"I see. Well, I know a good many people who would like to get their hands on something of this quality. A few years ago, some very high quality uniforms were going around."

Sam could only nod. The mention of imitation SGC uniforms made her think of the boot camp Apophis was running
to create infiltrators. She couldn't see any sign of barracks or
training areas, but the idea couldn't be ruled out. Daniel seemed
to have some clue of what was happening and he didn't seem
concerned about anything other than raising Jack's blood pressure. She tried not to put her guard up too high, but she did
keep an eye on the men who accompanied Tychia to greet them.
None of them were armed and she didn't read any aggression
from them, but things could turn in an instant.

The city stood on a cliff overlooking a steep drop to a calm
sea. The landward sides of the city were protected by an imposing wall manned by sentries at regular intervals. A small flo-
tilla of ships seemed to be following trade routes between the
city and a trio of small forested islands on the horizon. The
gates stood open but were flanked by armored men wearing
helmets she was ashamed to admit she mainly recognized
from Marvin the Martian. Each man carried a spear, the butt
of which was firmly planted against the ground. The guards
greeted Tychia as she approached, both men relaxing as they
examined the team's uniforms.

One of the men smiled behind the nose guard of his helmet.
"Is there to be a new *epikos*, Archontissa?"

Tychia smiled and held up a hand to calm his excitement.
"Patience, Agata. All will be revealed in time."

"Of course." He moved back into formation beside the gate.

"Forgive his eagerness," Tychia said once they were inside the
walls. The main road weaved through a maze of small white
buildings, tracing a line up the hill to a large Parthenon-type
building. Tychia led them into a town square. "It's always a
pleasure when an unknown group visits us. Repetition can
become dull."

Sam said, "So you get a lot of groups... like ours?"

"A few. Usually the same three or four groups who move
along the circuit."

"I see."

Sam started to say something else in the hopes of further enlightening the situation, but she saw something ahead that killed the words before they could form. She pushed up the brim of her cap with her middle knuckle as if a clearer view would make the sight more believable.

"Uh. Guys...?"

O'Neill pulled off his goggles. "Whoa."

"Oh boy," Daniel said just under his breath.

A statue stood in the center of the square. It depicted a man holding a P90 across his chest. The design of the weapon crude but unmistakable. He wore a cap and goggles and, though his chin was too square and his nose was a bit too flat, it bore an uncanny resemblance to Colonel O'Neill. Tychia smiled proudly as the team lined up shoulder-to-shoulder so they could get a clear view of the statue.

"Do you like it? No other city on our circuit has anything quite like this. One of our artisans made it a few seasons ago. We were hoping to entice more troupes to visit our world, and with your arrival, it seems as if it worked."

The man she'd called Colson said, "Are you certain it did? Look at them! They seem confounded. They weren't brought here because of the statue."

"You do seem a bit mystified." Tychia scanned the team, her expression of happiness fading as she registered their faces. "You heard about the statue and that is why you've come... isn't it?"

"No," Daniel said, "not quite."

Sam said, "What exactly is it you think we're here to do?"

Daniel sighed. "She thinks we're actors who are here to perform a play. From what she's said so far, a play about... us. SG teams, the Tau'ri, the fight against the Goa'uld."

Tychia's smile was completely gone now. She looked between Sam, O'Neill, and Teal'c. "You're not? Then... who are you?"

Jack stepped forward. "Well, ma'am, we'd be SG-1. The real ones. Pleasure to make your acquaintance."

Jack watched the doors to Tychia's office being pulled shut from outside, then heard the unmistakable click of a latch being thrown. He took off his cap and tossed it onto the nearest flat surface. "I suppose it's a better welcome than staff weapon fire."

They had been swiftly escorted into a building Daniel assumed to be their version of city hall, and now he guessed Tychia was in a meeting with her advisors. He'd started putting the pieces together as soon as he heard the word "*epikos*," but he wanted to believe he was wrong. The statue was the final confirmation. Sam and Teal'c stood by Tychia's desk while Jack began to pace restlessly near the windows. He tried to think of a way to defuse some of Jack's ire.

"This can't be much of a surprise, Jack. Word of SG teams has been spreading for years. The Goa'uld have bounties out on all of us. There were bound to be worlds where people like us are celebrated as folk heroes."

"Much like *Galaxy Quest*," Teal'c said.

"Well, yes, actually. It's the same misunderstanding, just in reverse. They think we're actors who travel from world to world recreating missions, when we're actually the real thing."

Jack turned away from the view. "Okay, so we tell these folks they made a mistake and head on back through the Gate."

Daniel stared at him. "Why?"

"Why? You ask me *why*? Why would we *stay*?"

"Jack, this is a chance to examine their culture, to — to see how we've influenced their artwork. Can you not see how important that is?"

"Not particularly."

Daniel rolled his eyes. "Mythology is one of the most important aspects of a culture, Jack. It allows you to see the world through someone else's eyes. It's why I spend hours trying to decipher artwork on the dead worlds we visit. Hell, it's one of the reasons archaeology exists in the first place. To understand a people, we have to know how they see themselves, how they relate to nature, how they explain..."

"Life, the universe, and everything."

"Exactly!"

Sam had moved closer to one of the windows. "I think we could do more harm than good by being here. There's already a crowd forming downstairs."

Jack grunted. "Hopefully there's a back door to this place."

The doors opened and Tychia swept inside. She gathered her dress in one hand as she used the other to close the door behind her. She smiled apologetically to the team as she walked to her desk.

"I hope you understand that I needed to take care of a few... details... in regard to your presence."

"Of course," Daniel said. "I'm sure it was quite a shock when you realized who we are."

Tychia nodded. "I've dispatched our phalanx to guard the Kyklos pavilion, and more security has been placed on the towers."

Daniel tilted his head. "Uh... why? You have nothing to fear from us, I assure you."

"From you, no," Tychia said. "But there can be no doubt that wherever the Tau'ri go, Goa'uld and Jaffa are certain to follow."

Sam said, "She kind of has a point, sir. Historically speaking."

"Especially the infamous SG-1." Tychia sat on the edge of her desk. "I suppose you're curious about what's going on. A few years ago, merchants and traders began telling stories about heroes who were standing up against Goa'uld oppression. It started with a tale about Ra's great palace in the sky being destroyed. It was said that these heroes caused him to flee in defeat before they killed him. As time passed, more stories began to be told. Soon, troupes of actors would learn the stories by heart and travel from world to world in order to spread the word through their performances. Through each *epikos*, seeds of hope are planted far and wide across the galaxy."

Jack said, "So... you're fans."

"Aficionados," Daniel clarified.

Tychia nodded enthusiastically. "Before the stories, it was difficult to believe there was any hope. People accepted the Goa'uld as a fact of life. The Tau'ri — you! — proved that they could be defeated. So it is an incredible honor to have you here, despite the risk your presence poses. I spoke with our arts society before I came back here and arranged a special performance this evening. I would like to invite you to be our honored guests."

Jack looked at Daniel. Daniel shrugged. "If there is a risk of the Goa'uld showing up because we visited, it might be best if we stuck around to deal with that threat."

"All right," Jack said, just barely managing to keep the irritation from his voice. "Tychia, we would be honored to be, uh... honored at your performance this evening."

Tychia grinned. "Splendid!" She clapped her hands together and stood up. She passed Jack to address Sam. "The society promised they would have something prepared by dark-two, which gives you time to relax. Dr. Jackson, if there's anything you would like to discuss, I know our historians would love the opportunity to speak with you."

"That — that would be amazing," Daniel said, barely able to contain his excitement. "Thank you."

"If you would like to refresh yourselves before the performance, we've set aside quarters for you here in the Hall. I can have one of the guards escort you."

Sam cleared her throat. "And... for the record, Colonel O'Neill is the team leader. Any official discussions you wish to have should probably happen with him."

"Actually," Jack said, "you ladies seem to already have a rapport. I don't see any reason to throw a wrench in things."

Tychia seemed relieved. "Thank you, Colonel O'Neill. And may I say, it's quite an honor to be in the presence of the man who defeated Ra."

Jack tried to act unmoved, but Daniel recognized the gleam in his eye. "Nice to meet someone who appreciates good work."

Tychia summoned the guards. "You have freedom to move about the city as you please, but I hope you consider having an escort. I don't know if you saw the crowd gathered outside, and I doubt any of them would intend to cause you harm, but as a safety measure—"

"We saw the crowds," Daniel said, "and we understand the need for escorts. We'd do the same thing at the SGC. Right, Jack?"

"Right," Jack said with a tinge of reluctance. "We'd be happy to have guides to your lovely city."

Tychia's eyes sparkled when she smiled. "An excellent attitude!" She extended her hand to Sam. "I look forward to speaking with you tonight, Major Carter. I'm certain you have any number of fantastic stories to share."

"Oh, a few," Sam said.

"Then I will be certain to sit next to you at dinner this evening." She took a deep breath and shook her head in disbelief. She laughed and spread her arms wide. "Allow me to officially welcome you to Catania."

Teal'c watched the Catanian guards without making them aware of his scrutiny. Their behavior was consistent with what Tychia said; they were serving as protectors, not as blockades. At one point Colonel O'Neill made a move toward an exterior door to gauge the response of their escorts. The guard quickly stepped ahead of him, peered out a window, and then allowed the colonel to continue on. O'Neill instead stopped by the window as if that had been his intent. He pretended to look out for a moment before he started walking again. The guard fell into step behind him.

When they reached their quarters, Teal'c glanced at the man who had been walking alongside him. He was closer to boyhood than maturity, his eyes wide with awe and perhaps a little fear.

"What is your name?"

The boy swallowed. "Zyli. They c-call me Zyli."

"Is there something you wish to ask me, Zyli?"

"Is... is that..." He tapped his own forehead with a trembling forefinger. "Is that real? Tychia said that you're really SG-1, so...?"

Teal'c said, "Indeed, it is real."

"Ouch."

He couldn't resist a smile. "An understatement."

The leader of the guard cleared his throat. "These rooms are yours for the duration of your stay. You're free to move about the building, but as Tychia said, it would be best if you were accompanied by guards beyond these inner corridors. Anything you require can be brought to you. She's asked us to attempt a lockdown, but we can make no promises. We hope you don't take offense."

"None taken," Daniel Jackson said. O'Neill shot him a look, to which he shrugged. "What? We don't. Like I said, it's nothing we wouldn't do if they showed up at the SGC."

O'Neill took a deep breath and let it out slowly, a signal Teal'c had learned to mean he was suppressing his initial, more aggressive response. "Thank you. We'll be sure to call for a chaperone before we go outside."

"Someone will return to escort you to the *epikos*, where your evening meal will be served. And we hope you enjoy the performance."

"I'm sure it will be something special," O'Neill said.

Their guardians departed, and O'Neill gestured for the team to join him in one of the rooms. He walked to the window again and peered out, then looked at Major Carter.

"What do you think?" he asked her.

She shrugged. "They seem sincere. Tychia strikes me as genuine. I could be wrong—"

"No..." He seemed almost irritated to admit it. "No, you're right. I was thinking the same thing. Those guards were more starstruck than anything else. Teal'c, what are the odds that us being here would bring the Goa'uld down on these fine folks?"

It was impossible to predict such a thing without knowing the planet's history and, though he had once been familiar with Hades, all of his information was now at least five years old. But of course O'Neill was aware of that. Teal'c had learned over the years, both from experience and from observing what the colonel expected from Major Carter, that his best guess would be enough.

"There are no indications that any Goa'uld have visited this world for quite some time. I do not believe our continued presence will be necessary."

Daniel Jackson said, "Or they're overdue for a visit. Let's face it, Tychia's reaction isn't exactly unfounded. Where we go, Jaffa tend to follow."

Teal'c inclined his head, accepting the point.

O'Neill said, "Okay, here's the plan. We stick around and kill time until our next scheduled check-in." He looked at his watch. "Which will be tomorrow, sometime in the mid-afternoon. We let these people do their little play, we let Daniel take a look at their arts and culture. If there aren't any red flags, we thank them for our hospitality and skip town before we bring anything bad down on Tychia and her people. Sound good?"

Carter said, "Seems reasonable to me, sir."

"To me as well," Teal'c said.

"And we know Daniel is happy, because he'll get to look at books and whatnot, so it's settled." He clapped a hand against his stomach and looked at Carter. "Do you think they're gonna serve moussaka?"

Not long after the sun went down, the team's escorts returned to lead them outside. A torch-lined flight of stone steps led down to what looked to Jack like a small soccer arena. Between the building where they were housed and the tall outer walls of the theater, Jack saw a small herd of deer grazing in a well-tended field. The creatures lifted their heads as the team passed, but showed no signs of fear of the humans.

Tychia was waiting for them at the entrance of the theater. She'd changed into a red chiton with gold fringe along the collar and the cuffs of each sleeve. A white corded belt was looped around her waist. Jack found himself wishing he'd brought his dress blues; the team was decidedly underdressed for the occasion.

"Welcome to the Odeon, SG-1. Allow me to show you to your seats."

"After you."

The theater was a flat half-circle with a raised wall at the back, which was draped with a painted sheet. A pair of curtains blocked the wings from view but Jack caught glimpses of the actors fussing with last-minute adjustments to their costumes. Tychia led the team to a row of thrones carved out of stone which were positioned between the orchestra pit and the three tiers of stadium seating. A few dozen citizens were already present and seated, and Jack tried not to notice everyone whispering and pointing at the team. More people were filing in through archways along the far wall, and every eye was drawn to the four newcomers.

"The meal will be served once the show has begun. If you'd like anything else, don't hesitate to ask your escorts."

Carter said, "You won't be sitting with us?"

"Oh... I would never presume to sit with the guests of honor."

Jack sat on his chair, placing his palms on each arm rest and slapping the stone. "Well, presume. Sit. You invited us to this thing, so it's only common courtesy to watch it with us."

Tychia hesitated again, but then shrugged. "If you insist. I would be happy to join you."

Carter sat between Jack and Tychia, with Daniel and Teal'c on Tychia's right. Jack squirmed on the stone seat and adjusted his shoulders so he was sitting up straighter.

"I like this. I have to talk to the local MegaPlex and see about getting some of these installed in their theaters. It might even make seeing the rest of those *Star Wars* prequels worthwhile."

Tychia smiled indulgently, obviously not understanding. Carter leaned closer to her and lowered her voice. "Even I don't understand half of what he says. I've learned smiling and nodding can go a long way."

Tychia laughed. "I shall take your advice, Major."

Jack said, "Carter... are you being insubordinate?"

"Never, sir."

"Good. Glad to hear it."

Over the next few minutes, the theater behind them filled with Catanian citizens. Soon, someone came onto the stage and signaled to Tychia. She nodded and stood, smoothing her hands over her tunic. "Everyone! If I may have your attention, please. I see we have a particularly large crowd tonight. That must mean that word of our special guests has spread. Please take a moment to give a warm welcome to Colonel Jack O'Neill, Major Samantha Carter, Doctor Daniel Jackson, and Teal'c!" She gestured for Jack to stand up.

Jack hesitated. He wondered if it was too late to lie and say Carter was really their leader. But he got to his feet and turned to look up at the crowd. Eager faces locked onto him, some people pointing as they whispered to their companions.

"Uh, hello. I'm Jack O'Neill... you may remember me from such classics as blowing up Ra over Abydos and, ah... the Ne'tu thing. Thanks for having us."

Tychia smiled and watched him for a moment, obviously expecting more, but quickly realized he was finished. "Wonderful! Thank you, Colonel O'Neill. Now I hope everyone enjoys tonight's performance: SG-1 Becomes Trapped In a Cavern, Under Attack by Horus' Jaffa'." She led the crowd in applause as she returned to her seat.

Jack leaned closer to Carter. "I'm not the best one to ask with these things. Does that sound familiar to you?"

She shook her head. "No, sir."

Two Catanian men appeared on stage wearing SG uniforms

that were obviously handmade and dyed green. The backdrop showed a cavern that stretched back into darkness. The men crept forward scanning for hostiles before motioning to some-one behind them. Two more actors approached, male and female. The man had a smear of yellow paint on his forehead. Jack noticed another woman on the edge of the stage dressed in a black tunic, one hand flat on her stomach with the other behind her back. She turned to address the audience.

"We join our heroes on a planet designated Ouranos, deep within the territory of the System Lord Horus. The Tau'ri known as SG-1 arrived on a simple mission of peace only to have the Kyklos activated not long after their arrival. They hid and watched in horror as their foes emerged from the shim-mering blue pool."

Three women and a man in shoddy Jaffa armor appeared from the opposite side of the stage. A chorus of hisses came from the audience.

Jack asked Carter, "You remember ever running into this Horus guy?"

Daniel leaned forward to give the answer. "It's Heru'ur. They're the same person."

"Couldn't decide on a name?"

"Well, it's a —"

Jack cut off a long-winded explanation with a wave of his hand. He knew Heru'ur, and he didn't need a history lesson at the moment. He wished he had access to their mission reports, because nothing about what he was seeing seemed familiar. They'd had their fair share of run-ins with Heru'ur — bald guy, goatee, actually went into battle alongside his Jaffa — but trapped in a cave? A quick glance at Carter and Teal'c revealed they were just as lost.

"Uh... Tychia? When exactly is this supposed to have hap-pened?"

Tychia said, "It's unclear. We trade back and forth, and some of the *epikos* are years old. This is one of the newer stories, however. Perhaps... a year ago?" She noticed the expression on Carter's face and looked over her shoulder to see Daniel and Teal'c also looked awkward. "Is something wrong?"

"Not wrong," Jack said. "It's just that if this really happened, it didn't happen to us."

"It's not an SG-1 *epikos*?" Even in the darkness, Jack could see the flush in her cheeks.

Jack said, "Look, it's an honest mistake. You folks were just —"

Tychia suddenly rose to her feet and faced the stage. "Stop! You must stop at once!"

"Oh. No, that's not necessary," Daniel said.

"No, it is. I wanted to welcome you with a performance of a proper *epikos*." She gestured to one of the actors onstage. He was tall and, even with the loose material of his tunic, it was clear he was nothing but a collection of thin, knobby limbs. He descended the steps and hurried to her side. She put a hand on his arm. "Steimous, you must begin a different story at once. This is not an SG-1 *epikos*."

Steimous' face paled. "But the man I traded with assured me that it was authentic!"

"It would appear you have been lied to. Do you have anything else prepared? A true SG-1 story?"

Steimous thought for a moment and then said, "I have nothing prepared for tonight. But I can guarantee something for the morning. By bright-three."

Jack said, "I'm sure the, uh, the cave thing is fine..."

Tychia shook her head. "I would much prefer showing you a proper story, if one can be found."

Daniel watched her for a moment and seemed to read more from her expression than Jack could see. "You want us to confirm how authentic it is."

She smiled almost bashfully. "The opportunity to show an *epikos* to the very people it has been based on is too rare to waste. I've always wondered how much truth there is in the stories we share, and how much has been altered through retellings. Please don't let this mistake affect your decision to stay. We'll have a special performance in the morning, before mid-day meal, so it won't interfere with your original plans."

Jack looked at Daniel, whose hopeful expression was almost as hard to resist as Tychia's. "If you insist... I mean, if you were a guest in my home and someone rented *Ghostbusters II* instead of the far superior original film..." She tilted her head in confusion so he gave up the metaphor. "We'll stick around."

Tychia breathed a sigh of relief. "Thank you for understanding, Colonel O'Neill. Steimous..."

The actor said, "I shall leave as soon as possible to search for more reputable markets in the circuit, Archontissa."

Obviously thinking that Tychia seemed particularly distraught, Daniel stepped forward. "It's really fine. We were planning to stick around until tomorrow anyway."

"You're very kind. Since you didn't get a chance to eat, I'll have your meals delivered to your rooms. If there's anything else you need, I beg you, don't hesitate to ask."

"Stop apologizing," Jack said. "So we have to wait until tomorrow. I always did prefer the matinee anyway."

Jack picked up one of the glasses off the table, peered inside, and plucked something from the surface of the water. He flicked away whatever speck he'd removed and took a sip. Daniel waited until the little ritual was over before he spoke. Teal'c and Sam were both in their rooms, but Jack had motioned for Daniel to follow him after the escorts were out of sight. He assumed it was to get his opinion on their hosts.

"They seem friendly enough."

"Friendly, hell." Jack gestured out the window and leaned against the sill. "They've got deer grazing on their front lawns. These people are straight out of Disney. And eager to please."

"Right. I don't think they have ulterior motives to keep us around. Tychia wants to test the accuracy of their myths, which isn't particularly diabolical. I'd probably do the same thing in her shoes. They truly just seem excited to have us here. They want to show us their play because they're proud of it. Like a parent who wants to show you the video of their kids' recital."

Jack grimaced. "Hopefully it'll be less torturous than that."

What they'd seen of the Heru'ur story didn't give Daniel much hope, but at least it would be fascinating. On Earth, Greece planted the seeds for what would grow into modern Western culture. The opportunity to see how the culture evolved on a different planet was exciting. Of course Jack probably wouldn't care about any of that, so he couldn't use it as an argument.

"The point is," he said, "we have a chance to learn more about this world by just sitting down and watching them perform for us."

"Like Teal'c and *Die Hard*."

"Exactly! Our movie nights are a way of introducing him to complex social elements without resorting to a bland lecture. He sees John McClane going through a divorce and how he interacts with people, he sees cooperation between McClane and... uh, the cop..."

"Al."

"Right. And Christmas. Although it's not technically a Christmas movie..."

"Hey!" Jack said.

Daniel held up his hands. He didn't want to have that argument again. "All I'm saying is that watching a play will do more than tell us a story. It will give us insights into how these people function. That will be useful in establishing diplomatic relations with them."

"Assuming they have something we want to trade for."

"They're Greeks," Daniel said. "Architecture, democracy, geometry..."

Jack's eyes were beginning to glaze over. "Okay, okay. We'll lay the groundwork for SG-9 to come back and see what these people need and what they want to give us in return for it."

Something glinted in the distance, drawing both men to turn and look. The Stargate was active, its event horizon reflecting off the pavilion in which it stood. It hadn't been apparent during the day but the entire structure was designed to make the light as visible as possible from great distances.

"Pretty," he said.

Jack said, "Nice defense. Always know when someone's coming in the middle of the night." He assumed it was the actor going off-world to seek out more *epikos* scripts, but he kept his eye on the pavilion until the Stargate disengaged just to be certain.

"Sure," Daniel said. "That, too."

Jack turned away from the window and walked to the bed. "All right. Go, eat, get some rest. We have a big day tomorrow."

Daniel moved to the door. "Whatever we get from this mission, it's nice that the only thing we have to face tomorrow is some amateur acting and bad writing."

Jack flinched and clapped a hand over his face. "Damn it. Why did you have to say that?"

"I'm sure I didn't jinx anyth —"

"Just go," Jack said, waving him out. "Go. Before you make it worse."

Daniel sighed and slipped out of the room, shutting the door behind him.

On the first night he spent on Abydos, after the uprising against Ra and the rest of the team had gone home, Daniel had questioned whether he would ever be able to sleep off-world. The stars were different, the smells were different, and there was so much to explore without worrying about grants or deadlines. How could he waste even a minute sleeping? When he joined SG-1, the same elements were there but with the added threat of potential Jaffa attacks coming at any moment.

But to be human was to adapt. Now he could sleep pretty much anywhere because he knew there might not always be an opportunity to lie down and get eight full hours. The benefit of being in a well-defended building with a huge featherbed to himself meant that he was asleep almost as soon as his head hit the pillow. He didn't wake until just after dawn when an alarm began sounding. He tried to dress as he moved toward the window, leaning against the wall to tie his boots as he squinted in the early light.

The courtyard directly below his window was full of people, most of whom seemed armed. Raised voices carried through the streets of the city and he could see rows of armored soldiers moving along the walls and taking position.

"Probably not a drill, then." He grabbed his glasses and left his room. Teal'c and Sam were already in the hallway, dressed for a fight.

"Colonel O'Neill went to find Tychia," Sam said.

"Do we have any idea what's going on?"

Jack answered him as he emerged from the stairs. "The snakeheads are coming, the snakeheads are coming." Tychia was right behind him. Her hair was down and she was dressed far more modestly than she'd been the night before. Daniel deduced that Jack had been the first one awake and ventured outside with her to find out what was going on.

Tychia said, "It would seem Colson's fears about your arrival were prescient."

"Seems the actor guy Tychia sent to find new stories went to a marketplace where this stuff is exchanged," Jack explained. "A Jaffa overheard him talking about SG-1, asked what his interest was, and the guy got cocky. He pretty much threw down the gauntlet. Said where we were and basically dared the Jaffa to come challenge us."

Tychia wrung her hands together. "You must understand, he was simply overexcited by having you here. Steimous immediately realized what he had done and raced back here as quickly as he could to warn us. We've been keeping the Kyklos vibrant from the moment Steimous returned so the Goa'uld cannot establish their own link."

Jack said, "That won't work forever."

"Teal'c and I can secure the gate," Sam said. "We'll contact the SGC and have them prepare reinforcements."

"Go."

Sam nodded to Tychia, who stepped aside so she and Teal'c could leave.

Daniel said, "What can we do to help?"

"Your help may not be required. We can hope that whatever Jaffa Steimous spoke to doesn't choose to act on the information."

Daniel looked at Jack, who seemed on the verge of going on a rant, and cut him off before it could begin. "I don't think we'll be that lucky. Even without knowing which Goa'uld he was loyal to, it's safe to assume that any of them would jump at the chance to come after us."

"The same way you folks jumped at the chance at having us as guests," Jack said. "But they take the idea of being a good host to a much different place."

Tychia looked pained, but seemed to concede the point. "I'll take you to the leader of the guard. He'll know where you would be most beneficial."

They followed her out of the building. Halfway across the courtyard, Jack slowed and tilted his head toward the sky. "We've got gliders. Everybody down!"

Daniel looked for a place to take cover. Tychia grabbed his arm and moved him a few paces backward so they could stand in an archway. Jack crouched behind the base of a statue and watched the eastern sky. By that point Daniel could hear the familiar whine of a Death Glider engine. Either they'd gotten spectacularly unlucky and the Jaffa was loyal to a Goa'uld who happened to be nearby, or the Goa'uld was willing to share the bounty with someone who was closer. Either way, it looked like they weren't going to have the nice, relaxed mission he'd been hoping for.

"Down!" Jack shouted again, waving to someone across the courtyard.

Daniel looked and saw several of the townspeople had stopped their retreat to gawk. "What are they doing? They have to hear the gliders."

Tychia's face was twisted with horror. "They're watching SG-1 in action." She leaned out and shouted their names. "Please, get yourselves to safety!"

The gliders passed overhead and released two shots, both of which hit tall marble columns and caused them to explode in a shower of dust and stone shards. Jack returned fire as the ships split away from each other and started a wide turn so they could make another pass. Daniel broke from cover and ran to the civilians who were still standing out in the open. One of them smiled and pointed at Daniel.

"Look! It's Dr. Jackson!"

"Get down!" He grabbed the man's arm and shuffled him backward toward the wall. Another blast took up a chunk of the tile courtyard, sending small shards of ceramic raining down on them. He heard the clatter of Jack's P90 as he fired at the retreating ships. Both ships unleashed volleys on the town below, destroying stone buildings in bursts of flame and smoke. He could hear people screaming now, though the people around him in the courtyard still seemed distracted by his presence.

The man Daniel was covering said, "I'm bleeding." A piece of shrapnel had hit his forehead. Thin lines of blood trailed down over his eyebrow and were now inching over his cheek. To Daniel's surprise, he smiled. "I'm a part of the *epikos*!"

Jack appeared by Daniel's side. "You're about to be part of a snuff *epikos* if you don't get your asses to safety. Inside! Now!"

Even strangers couldn't argue when Jack used that tone of voice. The civilians hurried away and Jack turned to scan the skies again. For the moment, the gliders seemed to have found other targets. He grabbed his radio and held down the button with his thumb.

"Carter, what's the situation at the Gate?"

"It's... evolving, sir."

Daniel could hear the sounds of a skirmish in the background. "Evolving...? What does that mean?"

"She and Teal'c can work it out. Right now we have to get these folks out of here."

Tychia had crossed the courtyard to stand with them. "We have to get my people to safety."

"We were just discussing that," Jack said. "Any ideas?"

"There are tunnels underground. They're meant to be storage, but they might withstand a blast from those ships."

"Can we seal it?"

"Yes."

"Then start leading people down there."

"What about you?"

Jack was still scanning for the gliders. "Now that those gliders have pinpointed our positon, they're going to land. Then we'll have a fun little group of Jaffa stomping all over the place. We'll hold them off as best we can. Once everyone is safe underground, we surrender."

"Surrender?" Tychia said.

Daniel was surprised as well, but it made sense. "We're the only reason they're here. If we leave, maybe they'll go and leave you alone."

Jack said, "So they take us prisoner. We've been prisoners of the Goa'uld before. It's not so bad. We'll just listen to a few obnoxious monologues, maybe get knocked around a little. Nothing we can't handle."

Tychia looked as if she wanted to argue, but the ground shook as the gliders took out another target. She cringed and gave him a reluctant nod as she scanned the area for more rubberneckers. A few townspeople were lingering nearby, so she rose and waved for them to follow her. As soon as they began moving, she ran to the entrance of the building and waited for them to pick up their pace.

Jack said, "Get inside or I'll start shooting at you myself! Go!"

The courtyard was finally clear of civilians by the time the gliders passed by again. They fired at something to the north and Daniel winced. He couldn't see architecture in this style without thinking it was something ancient and important. Hopefully whatever had just been destroyed was a tavern or something equally replaceable.

"Carter, do you read?" Jack waited a moment and winced when an answer didn't come. He was about to say something else when there was a double-burst of static over the line. "Okay... copied but can't respond. Carter, Daniel and I are going to surrender. You and Teal'c should do the same if the Jaffa give you the opportunity. Repeat, stand down if possible. We have to get the Goa'uld away from these folks."

Another double-burst of static.

"Okay," Jack said. "You ready?"

"Can you ever really be ready to surrender to a Goa'uld?"

"Good point. Just... try to look non-threatening."

"I'll give it a shot."

As Jack predicted, they soon heard the stomp of feet and the odd shuffle that armor plating made when the person wearing it was running. Two Jaffa appeared at the entrance to the courtyard with their staff weapons extended. Jack held both hands in the air.

"Yo!" Both staffs swung toward him and he flinched. "Whoa! Hey." He waved his empty hands. "Unarmed. See? Going peacefully. Uh... take us to your leader."

The Jaffa glanced at each other.

"Honest. No tricks. We're surrendering ourselves." He glanced at Daniel and kicked the side of his boot. "Stand up. Surrender yourself."

Daniel showed his hands and slowly straightened up from behind the pedestal. "Hi."

A third Jaffa approached, the gold glinting off his forehead identifying him as a First Prime. Daniel tried to make out the details of his tattoo, but he was still too far away when he stopped to make out who it signified. He smiled and raised an eyebrow.

"You are the famous SG-1."

"We're getting that a lot lately," Jack said. "And who might you be representing? Sorry." He gestured at his own forehead. "I don't have all the hood ornaments memorized."

"Amaterasu."

"Don't think we've run into him."

"Her," Daniel muttered.

Jack ignored him. "Always nice to meet new folks."

The First Prime narrowed his eyes. "We have been warned not to fall victim to Tau'ri trickery."

"No trickery. Honest. We'll leave our weapons here and go quietly. If you want to reward that with one of your comfier cells, I certainly wouldn't complain, but —"

"Silence!" He stepped forward the grabbed the P90 hanging from Jack's vest.

Jack said, "There's a clip... you have to unclip..."

The gun came free and the First Prime handed the weapon to one of the other Jaffa. "My Queen will be most pleased with this gift."

"Well, I'm happy for you. Maybe you'll get a big Christmas bonus this year."

He gestured for Jack and Daniel to walk, shoving Jack's shoulder for good measure. Jack glared at him. "Easy, pal. Just... take it easy."

Daniel lowered his voice. "So Sam and Teal'c...?"

"They'll stand down when we reach the gate," Jack said. "Tychia and her people will wait until the coast is clear and then they can get back to their lives."

Daniel looked at the destruction but kept quiet about how difficult they might find it to just go back to normal.

They were flanked by the Jaffa and marched out of town. Jack was calm about their situation, hands casually held out to his sides, but Daniel still couldn't make himself okay with the idea of being captured. He was a prisoner of people who wanted to kill him. He didn't know how someone could treat that as a minor inconvenience. When they reached the stairs leading up into the Stargate complex, the First Prime held up a hand to stop the other Jaffa. He paused and scanned the area but, as far as Daniel could see, nothing was amiss. The Stargate was active, but there was no activity within the pavilion.

"Kree!" the First Prime shouted, following by a string of Goa'uld that basically translated to 'hey, where are you guys?' He waited for a response and, when nothing came, approached Jack. "Where is the rest of your team?"

"Maybe they went home. They probably heard us surrendering and jumped through the gate. Hell, it's what I would've done in their place."

"You are lying."

Jack shrugged and looked around. "You see any green camo around here?"

"No. But I also see none of my men."

Daniel said, "Maybe they followed our friends through to Earth."

"That's probably it," Jack said. "I bet there's a big mess back at the SGC right now."

The First Prime drew his knife. "You will tell your men to stand down."

"First of all, one of them isn't a man. That's sexist. Secondly..."

He grabbed the Jaffa's wrist and twisted it, forcing the knife out of his hand. He threw his weight forward and used the First Prime as a battering ram against the other Jaffa. Daniel fumbled to get his revolver free as the remaining Jaffa moved toward him. He brought it up just as they were taken out of the fight by a volley of staff weapon fire that seemed to come from out of the sky. Those who spun around and attempted to return fire were quickly dispatched by quick bursts of P90 fire. Daniel covered his face and, when he looked again once everything quieted down, saw the Jaffa lying in a heap on the steps. At least one of them was still alive but was in no position to continue the fight. Jack had also dispatched the First Prime, leaving him alive but unarmed.

"Secondly," Jack said again, only a little out of breath, "you really ought to have tied us up." He looked up toward the top of the pavilion and gave Teal'c and Sam a quick salute. "Well done taking the high ground, Carter."

"Thank you, sir. We were able to take care of the Jaffa who came to reclaim the gate, so Teal'c suggested we call an audible on your surrender plan."

"Hey, whatever works. Daniel... this Amaterasu. Is she one of the reasonable ones?"

"Uh... relatively so, from what I've heard."

"Glad to hear it. So Primo... you only came here to take us prisoner and now you're going home empty-handed. By the time you get back here with reinforcements, we're going to be long gone. Your god already lost a couple of good men by attacking this world. She's not going to get much out of another assault. No matter what else happens here, it's going to be big loss. She's got nothing to gain by coming back and harassing these fine folks."

The First Prime grimaced. "She will not rest until she has taken vengeance for the lives lost on this ground."

"Then you're gonna convince her not to do that."

"Why would I help you?"

Daniel said, "Because right now, all she's lost are some foot soldiers. Losing a First Prime would be a much larger blow."

Jack said, "We leave. You leave. These people go on with their day like nothing happened. It's a win-win." He thought for a second. "Well, not for you or the guys you lost. But it's the best scenario you're getting. Clock is ticking on the offer."

"Very well," the First Prime muttered. "Will I be allowed to retrieve the bodies of my brothers and our gliders?"

"Sure," Jack said. "Why not? I'm feeling generous. Teal'c, why don't you come down here and supervise our friend's retreat?"

Teal'c bowed his head. "We will be down momentarily."

He turned and disappeared from view, followed by Sam. Jack watched them go and leaned toward Daniel to ask, "How do you suppose they got up there in the first place?"

Amaterasu's First Prime and the other surviving Jaffa gathered their dead in one location. They left in the gliders with a promise they would return only to collect the bodies. Teal'c remained behind to ensure they were true to their word. Jack led the rest of the team back to the city where he sounded the all-clear. Tychia released her people from the safety of their bunker, and it was clear that the novelty of being part of an *epikos* had worn off. Jack recognized the expression on their faces; these were people who had lost everything, who had seen dear friends hurt and bleeding in the aftermath of unexpected violence.

Daniel tried to convey apology and understanding, but no one was looking at SG-1. Not anymore. No one even seemed aware of their presence.

The team found Tychia near the building where they had spent the night. She smiled weakly and held her hand out to Sam. Sam took it and squeezed, and Tychia placed her free hand on top. "I am glad to see you are all well, SG-1."

"Did all of your people make it through?"

Tychia's expression wavered. "Yes, but there were injuries. A dozen people were in one of the buildings hit by the gliders. We have physicians tending to them now. Everyone will survive, but there may be permanent injuries. Amputations." She looked away and let her hand fall from Sam's grip. "I apologize for what Steimous did."

Daniel said, "Wait, I'm sorry, you're... apologizing to *us*?"

"It was his actions which brought the Goa'uld to our world for the first time in recent memory. You put yourselves at great risk to protect us."

"If we hadn't been here," Daniel said, "you wouldn't be rebuilding and tending to grievously wounded —"

"Daniel..." Jack warned.

Daniel glared at him. "So we're not even going to take responsibility?"

Jack returned Daniel's stare. "It wasn't our fault. It wasn't Steimous' fault, either. It was the Jaffa's fault. Amaterasu's fault. They've learned their lesson."

Daniel grimaced. "If there's anything we can do to help with the relief effort, the SGC would be glad to lend a hand."

"Thank you." She avoided his eyes. "But... there is some truth to Dr. Jackson's claims we will be spared from further attacks if you do not return. In fact, I'm certain it would be best if you depart as soon as possible."

Sam said, "We did make the deal with Amaterasu's First Prime. The longer we stay here, the more opportunity they have to call our bluff."

Teal'c joined them at that moment. "The Jaffa have been retrieved, and Amaterasu's First Prime is back aboard her vessel," he reported.

"Good," Jack said. "All right, campers. Let's pack it up."

Daniel wanted to protest, but he honestly couldn't see an argument. They made the promise to be gone in case Amaterasu came looking for revenge, and Tychia clearly didn't want them to stay. So instead of arguing, he moved closer to her and offered his hand.

"I'm sorry. I'm glad we got to meet one another."

She smiled sadly and took his hand, squeezing lightly. "Despite how things ended, I am grateful for that as well. Be safe, SG-1."

Daniel nodded and, with a final look at the destruction, turned away to follow his team out of the city.

Sam knew better than to get between Colonel O'Neill and Daniel after a mission like this. Both men fell silent as soon as Tychia left, so she dropped back to walk beside Teal'c. She caught him looking back and turned to see what had caught his eye. The statue of an SG team member — most likely Jack O'Neill, based on the exaggerated features — was still standing despite the aerial assaults. Teal'c caught her watching him and faced forward again.

"Something on your mind?" she asked.

"I do not understand their fervor. Why would they worship us?"

Sam said, "It's not exactly worship. Or maybe it is, but not the kind that the Goa'uld force on people. This, the *epikos* and sharing the stories, it's about possibility. It's about finding a glimmer of hope in the worst circumstances."

"And the false idol?"

"It's not an idol," Sam said. "It's a reason to look up."

Teal'c considered that for a moment and then finally nodded his understanding. Sam was glad she'd been able to explain it to him, but she was worried it was no longer true for Tychia and her people. After everything they'd suffered and the long recovery that was sure to follow, it seemed likely the *epikos* stage would go dark for a good long time. Eventually even the statue might be taken down.

She hoped the people of Catania would still find a reason to look up even after the statue was gone.

OUR AUTHORS

Jo Graham

Jo Graham worked in politics for fifteen years before leaving to write full time. She is the author of the Locus Award nominated *Black Ships*, the Spectrum Award nominated *Stealing Fire*, and the Rainbow Award winning *Cythera* as well as nine books of the top selling *Stargate Atlantis: Legacy* series. She is also the author of historical fantasies *Hand of Isis*, *The General's Mistress*, and *The Emperor's Agent*, as well as an additional Stargate Atlantis novel and an SG-1 novel. With Melissa Scott, she is the author of *The Order of the Air* series of historical fantasies set in the roaring twenties and the Great Depression. Jo Graham lives in North Carolina with her partner and their daughters.

Susannah Parker Sinard

Susannah Parker Sinard is a long-time Stargate fan. Her debut novel, STARGATE SG-1: *The Hall of the Two Truths*, was published in August 2016. A graduate of the University of Michigan, she holds a B.A. in English, as well as a master's degree and doctorate in the health care field. Many thanks to Mara Pheonix for her patience and insights and Claudia Henry for her technical expertise. This story is dedicated to Aimee, the littlest Tok'ra.

Melissa Scott

Melissa Scott was born and raised in Little Rock, Arkansas, and studied history at Harvard College. She earned her PhD from Brandeis University in the comparative history program with a dissertation titled "The Victory of the Ancients: Tactics, Technology, and the Use of Classical Precedent." She also sold her first novel, *The Game Beyond*, and quickly became a part time graduate student and an — almost — full-time writer. Over the next twenty-nine years, she published more than thirty novels and a handful of short stories, most with queer themes and characters. She won the John W. Campbell Award for Best New Writer in 1986, and won Lambda Literary Awards for *Trouble and Her Friends*, *Shadow Man*, *Point of Dreams* (written with her late partner and collaborator, Lisa A. Barnett), and for *Death By Silver*, written with Amy Griswold. She has also been shortlisted for the Tiptree Award. She won a Spectrum Award for *Shadow Man* and again in 2010 for the short story "The Rocky Side of the Sky". Her short story, "Finders," was been selected for Year's Best SF 2013. Her latest novels are *Oath Bound,* written with Jo Graham, the fourth volume of *The Order of the Air*, and *Fairs' Point*, the third full-length *Points* novel. Scott can be found on LiveJournal at mes-cott.livejournal.com and on Twitter as @blueterraplane. Her Stargate books are STARGATE SG-1: *Moebius Squared* (with Jo Graham), STARGATE SG-1: *Ouroboros*, and STARGATE ATLANTIS: *Wraith Queen*. She is co-author with Jo Graham and Amy Griswold of the STARGATE ATLANTIS Legacy series. Her next Stargate book, STARGATE ATLANTIS: *Pride of the Genii*, will be out in 2018.

Barbara Ellisor (competition winner)

Barbara Ellisor is a relative newcomer to the Stargate universe, having seen her first episode in the fall of 2015. She spent the next year reading and binge-watching everything related to Stargate she could find. Though she enjoys STARGATE UNIVERSE and STARGATE ATLANTIS (particularly Rodney McKay), STARGATE: SG1 is closest to her heart. She loves the team interaction and — of course — the humor.

Ron Francis (competition winner)

Ron Francis is the youngest of five siblings born to a New York City police officer and a stay-at-home mom. After receiving a bachelor of science in business from St. John's University and a Masters in religion from Liberty University, he spent several years working in Texas before returning to New York. Currently, Ron resides in sunny Orlando, Florida.

Keith R.A. DeCandido

Keith R.A. DeCandido is the author of the *SG-1* novel *Kali's Wrath*, as well as a previous Carter-and-Teal'c story in the anthology *Far Horizons*. He also did an overview of the *Stargate* franchise for Tor.com in 2015. He's written more than 50 novels and tons of short fiction and comic books in over two dozen licensed universes, as well as in his own worlds ranging from the fictional Super City and Cliff's End to the sort-of real New York City and Key West. Find him online at www.DeCandido.net.

Amy Griswold

Amy Griswold is the author of six STARGATE: SG-1 and STARGATE ATLANTIS tie-in novels, including *Murder at the SGC* and the STARGATE: *Legacy* series (with Melissa Scott and Jo Graham). She has also published two original novels (with Melissa Scott), *Death by Silver* and *A Death at the Dionysus Club*. Her most recent project (with Jo Graham), is the interactive novel *The Eagle's Heir*, a steampunk game of adventure and intrigue available now from Choice of Games.

Suzanne Wood

In the leafy greenness of the world's most livable city, Melbourne, Australia, Suzanne lives and works surrounded by books. Author of STARGATE SG-1: *The Barque of Heaven* and the first official short story crossover between STARGATE SG-1 and STARGATE ATLANTIS for the *Official Stargate Magazine*, she is currently undertaking a Diploma of Professional Writing and Editing while working on two new original novels. She has long-standing interests in Egyptology, ballet and watching Aussie pro cyclists, a new-found passion for family and Australian history, and occasionally rescues stray dogs. Her website is www.suzannewood.net.

Aaron Rosenberg

Aaron Rosenberg is the author of the best-selling DuckBob SF comedy series, the Dread Remora space-opera series, and, with David Niall Wilson, the O.C.L.T. occult thriller series. His tie-in work contains novels for Star Trek, Warhammer, World of WarCraft, STARGATE ATLANTIS, and Eureka. He has written children's books (including the award-winning *Bandslam: The Junior Novel* and the #1 best-selling *42: The Jackie Robinson Story*), educational books, and roleplaying games (including the Origins Award-winning *Gamemastering Secrets*). He is a founding member of Crazy 8 Press. You can follow him online at gryphonrose.com, on Facebook at facebook.com/ gryphonrose, and on Twitter @gryphonrose.

Geonn Cannon

Geonn Cannon is the award-winning author of over thirty novels, including *Riley Parra*, now a webseries from Tello Films. He's previously written STARGATE SG-1: *Two Roads*, and his next Stargate book, STARGATE SG-1: *Female of the Species* will be out in 2018. He lives in Oklahoma.

Stay in touch...
Follow us on Twitter
@StargateNovels

Find us on Facebook at
facebook.com/StargateNovels

Sign up for our newsletter
at StargateNovels.com

THANKS!

STARGÅTE SG·1. STARGATE ATLÅNTIS

Original novels based on the hit TV shows STARGATE SG-1 and STARGATE ATLANTIS

Available as e-books from leading online retailers including Amazon, Barnes & Noble and iBooks

Paperback editions available from StargateNovels.com and Amazon.com

If you liked this book, please tell your friends and leave a review on a bookstore website.